Murder
in the
New Forest

A Scottish detective tackles a very English crime

Carol Cole

THE
BOOK
FOLKS

Published by The Book Folks

London, 2024

ISBN 978-1-80462-279-7

www.thebookfolks.com

MURDER IN THE NEW FOREST is the first title in a series of standalone mysteries set in Hampshire featuring Detective Inspector Callum MacLean.

Chapter One

'You have reached your destination.'

Callum MacLean glanced at the satnav, rolled to a stop on the stone track, and cut the engine. Ahead, a locked wooden barrier barred further progress, and, beyond that, the right of way dwindled to a footpath winding between sapling birch and scrubby bushes. To his right, a row of oak trees edged a field where two grazing ponies lifted their heads briefly to watch him. The view to his left was partially obscured by a cluster of grey-barked gorse bushes crouching close to the earth as if they were trying to hide behind one another.

With a huff of irritation, he checked a text message to confirm that he had entered the correct postcode. He had. This was supposed to be Hale Purlieu, so where was this body?

He lowered the Camaro's window and aromas of damp peat and horse dung floated in. He couldn't hear any voices or police radios, just the ticking of his cooling engine and the twittering of small brown birds flitting in and out of the bushes. He raised his window and climbed out.

The rear seats were stacked with cases and boxes, and he lifted his jacket from the top of the heap. Threading his arms through the sleeves, he stood to his full height. The wind whipped his long hair across his face, and he tucked it behind his ears and scoured the land beyond the low bushes.

Yesterday he had driven from Glasgow to Hampshire, and he flexed his neck, left then right, feeling the pull on his shoulder muscles. Last night he had been pleased to slide between the sheets at his B&B, less pleased when his soon-to-be senior officer had phoned early, requesting that he immediately take up his post to cover the shortage of inspectors.

He focused on the seemingly endless folds of brown heath that rolled away, their colour fading to an indigo smudge on the distant horizon. Welcome to the New Forest.

The June sun was already high in the sky. In another week or two, it would be the longest day. He scanned the landscape and, in the middle distance, spotted two figures – uniformed officers, he thought – who were standing beside a saddled horse. He had found his body.

Callum strode through the heather, wiry stems dragging at the legs of his jeans and the breeze buffering white noise against his eardrums. Nearing the men, he saw that one of them held the reins of a large black horse that had its head down, pulling at tufts of grass. The other officer, a cigarette partially concealed in his cupped hand, watched Callum approach and then sauntered towards him.

'And where do you think you're going, fella?' he asked, before glancing over his shoulder at the other officer.

'And you are?' Callum was curt, his attention on the body he could now see behind the officer. It lay in a patch of deep heather and was obscured from view until you were almost on top of it.

'I'm asking the questions.'

Callum took out his warrant card. 'Detective Inspector Callum MacLean. Name, Constable?' He returned his wallet to his pocket and brushed past the man without waiting for his reply.

'PC Kent.' The constable's tone was defiant.

Callum stopped and turned back, locking eyes with Kent. Tension crept into his jaw as he waited for an appropriate response.

Kent lifted his chin but lowered his eyes as he curtly added, 'Sir.'

With her neck bent at such an acute angle, Callum could tell the victim was dead, but he knelt and felt for a pulse. The honeyed perfume of heather mingled with the ammonia of horse dung as his knee sank into something damp. There was no thread of life beneath his fingers, but her flesh was still warm and pliant. She had only been dead for a short time.

He stood and scrutinised the surroundings. Endless brown heath scattered with grey gorse bushes and the silvered trunks of a few birch trees. The only movement was the flicking tails of a herd of wild ponies, heads down, grazing beneath breeze-herded clouds. There was no other person in sight who might have witnessed her death. He blinked away a memory. It must be frightening to die alone.

'Has the doctor been informed?' he called to the constables.

'On the way, guv.'

Callum eased the damp fabric away from his knee. The woman was white, middle-aged, dressed in blue jodhpurs and a matching jacket with her navy skullcap beside her in the heather.

No bustling crowds here, no pavements or buildings, no racing engines or blaring horns. This was about as far removed from Glasgow as you could get. He glanced up at a lone buzzard piping on the wing, the call reminding him of childhood holidays at his grandparents' croft on Seil Island.

A shrill whinny sounded across the heather and the herd raised their heads, answered, and trotted away in single file. He had seen more horses than people so far this morning. He watched their retreat and the thought struck him that he had not properly considered his fear of them when making his decision to relocate to Hampshire. It was Grace who had loved the animals. He flicked a glance at the saddled horse. It seemed very large, and he hoped his decision wouldn't come back to bite him. But something about this scene was making him uneasy and, for once, it had nothing to do with his proximity to the animal.

'Guv? Dr Jones, medical…'

Callum raised his hand to halt the approach of PC Kent who was pointing to a large amorphous figure puffing towards them carrying a silver case. If this turned out to be a crime scene, the fewer boots trampling over it the better.

'Come on, guv'nor, this is an accidental. She just fell off her horse. I do know what I'm doing.' Kent's indignation bristled like static in the clear June air.

'Indeed? Then you know that we treat any death as a prospective crime while that possibility still exists. Now keep away.' Having missed breakfast, an argumentative constable was not improving the start of Callum's day.

Stiff-backed, Kent made a call on his mobile, his eyes resting on the senior officer.

Callum extended a hand to the incoming figure. 'Good morning. I'm DI MacLean.'

Her hearty handshake left him in no doubt of her physical strength. They built them well down here, he thought.

'Ahah. The new boy. I'm Martha Jones.' She grimaced as she struggled into a crime scene suit. 'These damn things get smaller and smaller.' Expelling a gust of air, she eased up the zipper. The breeze riffled her grey hair as she pulled up her hood and knelt beside the body.

'Right, then.' She addressed the interior of her case. 'What have we got here?'

Martha Jones was thorough and methodical. She murmured an accompanying monologue as her fingers traced the lines of bones with careful pressure and practised ease.

Callum moved around to the other side of her and saw the hoofprints that approached the body along a grass track. They were deep, in a straight line and he could picture the horse plodding along before throwing its rider. Beyond the body, when riderless, the animal had left shallow meandering indentations.

He unfastened his jacket. When they were finished here, he would get back to his original plan of finding himself temporary accommodation. The call from DCI Bertram Bellman would become a short-term inconvenience and one missed breakfast. The grumble of his stomach earned him a questioning look from Martha, which he ignored.

'You don't say much, do you?' she said.

'Not unless it needs saying.'

'I bet you've got older sisters.' She sat back on her heels, and he thought she was smiling behind her mask. It wasn't just Scottish women who were born nosy.

Martha's suit stretched like a sail in a strong wind as she paused, awaiting his reply.

'Fair enough,' she said when he didn't answer. A fruity chuckle rumbled in her chest, accompanying the mischievous glint in her grey eyes. 'As long as you don't feel intimidated by big women. We have a lot to offer, you know.'

A smile tugged at the corner of his mouth; she was certainly well qualified to present her opinion. He offered a supporting hand as she got back to her feet, and it was accepted without comment.

'Right,' she said. 'Initial observations, subject to confirmation. We have one middle-aged female, who appears to have fallen off her horse. Happens quite often around here, people falling off their horses. Cause of death is likely to be a broken neck – that doesn't happen so often.'

Callum glanced across to the straight line of hoofprints and the fastened chin strap on the riding hat in the cushioning heather.

'Time of death I would estimate to be in the last forty-five minutes at the extreme.' She pushed back her cuff to consult her watch. 'So, say between seven and eight this morning.'

'Very recently deceased.'

'Right. I don't usually get them this fresh.'

'Any anomalies?'

Her narrowed look held new awareness. 'As you ask, yes. There don't appear to be any other broken bones. You often pop a collarbone when you throw out your arm to break your fall, particularly when you hit the ground with enough force to break your neck. But not in this case, and there's no evident impact damage to her hands.'

'And her mouth?' Callum indicated the smear of blood glazing the corner of the dead woman's lips.

'Don't miss much, do you? Could be where she hit the ground; bit her lip perhaps. Let's wait until I get her on the table.'

Something was still gnawing at him. He looked more closely at the body, searching for clues. She was good-looking, verging on beautiful. A wide forehead, gently arched eyebrows, high cheekbones and a straight nose above a generous mouth. It was a well-balanced face, almost classical. The breeze teased her auburn curls, lifting the scent of her perfume.

'Nothing to identify her?'

'Not so far. But these might help.' Martha crouched down, moved the hair and the sun glinted on an earring. It was a solid gold profile of a woman's face with round brown stones representing curls. Their colour was an exact match for her hair.

'Bespoke,' Callum said. 'They should help.'

'Quality, if you like that sort of thing. Our dear departed is worth a great deal more than I am, and I'm not doing your job for you, Inspector, but it seems that the culprit–' she chuckled as she glanced across to the saddled horse '–wasn't motivated by greed.'

Callum absently rotated the single earring in his left lobe. It had been his one act of rebellion at university, and he'd kept it because Grace had liked it, and because he was stubborn. His mother called it his worry bead.

At the sound of galloping hooves, the black horse raised his head and whinnied. A girl riding a grey horse was heading directly towards them. With her blonde plaits and pink jacket, the child belonged at a pony club gymkhana, not a scene of death. Callum was about to shout to her to stay away when Martha raised an acknowledging hand. The horse slowed and walked up to Martha, the hoofprints forming a neat line next to those that Callum had studied.

'Sergeant Daisy Donaldson,' Martha informed him. 'Your number two.'

'Blootered puddocks,' he muttered beneath his breath. No one had mentioned babysitting when he accepted this post.

And then something caught his eye.

The sergeant dismounted and handed her reins to the constable who was holding the other animal. The horses touched noses before lowering their heads to snatch at the grass, tails flailing at the hovering cloud of flies.

'Good morning, sir. I'm Sergeant Daisy Donaldson. I heard you were in charge today.'

PC Kent's phone call must have been to her.

She removed her riding gloves, slipping them into her jacket pocket as she looked at the corpse. 'Poor Mary-Ellen.'

'You know her?' Callum asked.

Daisy unclipped the chin strap to remove her hat. 'Mary-Ellen Mitchell from Millers Farm along Hale Purlieu.' She refastened the strap and slipped it over her arm. 'She's married to Sir Michael Mitchell, and her horse is called Pirate. Is he okay?'

'He's eating.' Callum glanced at her. She seemed focused, despite her brain hopping about like a frog.

'Pirate's as safe as houses. I can't imagine how this happened.'

'She was an experienced rider?' he asked.

'Very accomplished. This doesn't make sense. How on earth did she come to fall off?'

Callum warily eyed the two horses. They were tall and solidly muscled, and he thought it would be easy to fall off, not that he ever intended to climb aboard in the first place. 'The horses are the same weight and build, Donaldson?'

'Pretty much. Same breeding. And Daisy is good for me.'

'Come and look at this then, Daisy.'

They studied the two lines of hoofprints. He pointed to one set and was aware of Martha kneeling beside the body, turning her head to follow his indication.

'Those are Mary-Ellen's,' Callum said. 'Why are they so much deeper than yours?'

'They should be about the same.' She studied the indentations. 'Both horses were walking in a controlled straight line. See how the back feet track up exactly in line with the front ones?'

He understood her explanation but wouldn't have spotted that himself.

'And see' – she pointed to the scattered shallow tracks – 'the hoofprints wander all over the place after she came off.'

'Okay.' He could discern the difference. Some of the latter prints were partial. They were unevenly spaced and weren't in any sort of line, straight or otherwise.

'And, if he was acting up then the hoofprints would be all over the place, so that wasn't the reason she came off.'

'So why did she come off? Why are her prints much deeper than yours?'

'You ask very good questions, sir.' She moved away to walk the tracks once more, her slight body inclined forward as she stared at the ground.

Callum waited. He believed he knew the answer, but he was looking at it logically because he didn't know much about horses. He didn't want to plant his thoughts in her head, conscious that he might be overthinking it.

'Right.' Daisy returned to stand beside him. 'She was controlling Pirate on the approach, and his prints are deep because there were two people on board. She was giving someone a bunk-up.' She tipped her head to one side to make eye contact. 'Yes?'

'Yes, there were two bodies on the horse. Good.' She had come to the same conclusion as him, but she wasn't quite there yet. 'What else do we know?'

'That she wasn't chucked off; no wiggly hoofprints, and she wouldn't have just fallen off because she was a good rider.'

He had given her long enough. 'Two riders, yes, but I think the other person was controlling the horse, not Mary-Ellen.' Now he realised what had been niggling him about the body. 'If she had been wearing her hat…'

'She always wore a hat. She was very safety-conscious.'

'…then it would have been on her head when she hit the ground, not fastened and beside her in that deep heather. Why did you refasten yours when you took it off?'

'Because Oliver is coming to collect Moses for me, and he will loop it over his arm… Oh, I see.'

'Good.'

She shook her head. 'You're saying she was already dead before she hit the deck.'

'I am, and I think the medical examination will confirm it.' The cut to her mouth was not caused by her biting her lip, he was sure of that. He had seen this pattern of injuries before. 'This is a secondary crime scene. She was killed somewhere else.'

Martha moved position and the wiry heather stems sprang up to obliterate any trace of her knee prints. They were unlikely to find any footprints from the second rider.

'Got it.' Daisy hurried towards the two uniformed officers, speaking into her phone, her pink jacket rippling with purpose.

Martha angled her head so that she could meet his eye without getting to her feet. 'You don't think this was an accident then?'

He shook his head. 'This is murder.'

Chapter Two

A pop-up circus of manpower, lights and a tent arrived, and a cordon was established around the scene. Daisy directed operations with speed and efficiency without once raising her voice. Callum's last sergeant, Rob McAllister, had been old school. A balding overweight bull mastiff whose loud voice, along with his bulk, had de-escalated many situations before they fully kicked off. This one was a chihuahua; small, unobtrusive and approachable. He hoped her bite was worse than her bark.

She came towards him accompanied by a tall black woman.

'This is DC Almadia Levens, sir. She's one of our team.' Daisy held up a finger. 'Sorry,' she said, turning away to answer her phone.

Levens was loose-limbed and moved with the ease and assurance of an athlete. Her orange trousers disappeared into thick socks and stout walking boots. She had the longest legs Callum had seen outside of an Olympic arena.

He looked up and saw that she was smiling. 'That's why they call me Legs, guv.'

He appreciated nicknames that made sense.

Daisy rejoined them. 'Legs is going to follow the hoofprints. Pirate has just been reshod with studs, so the sharp outlines will be easier to follow. They could lead us back to the kill point. If that's okay with you, sir. Sorry, I should have checked first.' She exchanged a look with Legs before adding, 'It's a while since we've had anyone to check with.'

Callum nodded. 'Work on the assumption that she was killed within the last hour. How fast does a horse walk, Daisy?'

'A horse like Pirate, max of four miles an hour with two up.'

'Then take that into account when you're considering distance, DC Levens.'

'Yes, guv. See you later, Deedee hun.' She set off across the heath, head angled downwards, and walked through the pink bell flowers that whispered in the breeze.

Callum watched her for a moment. Deedee hun? What happened to 'Yes, Sergeant'? What the hell had been going on at this station? His eyes followed the splash of orange into the middle distance. The list of things he was not happy about was expanding. He was impatient to escape the smell of horses and get to the station and into his comfort zone, to feel a solid floor beneath his feet.

A Land Rover and trailer rumbled towards them. He looked at Daisy for an explanation.

'They've come to collect Pirate so Forensics can give him a going-over.'

A young man in riding clothes walked towards Daisy.

'Hi, Oli. Thanks for coming so quickly.' She beckoned him forward.

'No worries. I was only having a coffee and chatting to Felix.'

'Sir, this is Oliver Phillips. He's come to ride Moses home for me. I don't usually turn up to incidents on horseback, but I was supposed to be off duty today.'

'Ditto,' Callum said.

The three of them moved across to her mount and waited while Daisy removed items from her saddle bag and zipped them into her jacket pockets. Oliver checked the tightness of the girth, before releasing a buckle under the skirt of the saddle.

'What are you doing?' Callum asked.

Oliver looked back over his shoulder. 'Lengthening the stirrup leathers. My legs are longer than Deedee's.'

He should have thought of that before. 'Can you check the length of the stirrups on Pirate?' It could help in eliminating people.

Oliver went over to the black horse. 'Just about perfect for me.'

'So that means the rider was your height?' Callum asked.

'They wouldn't be shorter, or their feet wouldn't reach the irons, but they could be taller and ride with a more bent leg, like a jockey.' He returned to Moses and lengthened the leathers by several holes.

If Pirate's rider was Oliver's height, someone else's boots had rested on Mary-Ellen's irons.

Oliver swung up into the saddle and slipped the strap of Daisy's hat over his left wrist. The smell of warm horses mingled with damp earth as Moses shuffled his hooves and stood square. Daisy's hat bounced against Oliver's thigh as he sat down in the saddle, closed his legs against the horse's ribs and Moses broke into a rocking horse canter. It looked effortless, perfectly harmonious; but the powerful muscles flexing in the horse's rump suggested to Callum that it would be easy to fall off.

A crowd had congregated on the access track. It wouldn't take long for the information to leak out, assuming the audience was locals rather than the tourists who flooded the Forest during the holiday season. Callum turned towards Daisy, noting a group of riders inching across a distant heath-covered hillside like black ants. In the middle of nowhere, there were suddenly a lot of people about.

'Daisy.' He nodded towards the watchers along the track. 'Get the names of the audience.' It wouldn't be the first time a murderer had returned to the scene of the crime to view the impact of their handiwork.

'Already onto that. PC Cooper is doing it as we speak.'

He couldn't fault her organisation – so far. He mulled over the facts as they moved back inside the cordon. They had identified the victim but had no confirmed cause of death, no scene of the initial crime and no suspects or motive. It was shaping up to be a long day.

'Who reported it, Daisy?'

'Mrs Ruby Deacon, a local pensioner. She was walking her dog Cleo when she spotted the saddled horse but couldn't see a rider. She didn't go closer in case Cleo frightened the horse, so she didn't see Mary-Ellen in the deep heather. She called it in as a loose horse when she got home.'

'Find out who else she saw on her walk. Names and addresses if she can' – his eyes moved to the spectators – 'and see if any of the names match up with that lot.'

'Already on to it. DCs Cooke and Hampton should be with her now. They'll let me know…'

Callum raised a questioning eyebrow.

'…let *us* know what they find out.'

She might look like a child, but she was confident in running the show. He hoped this stemmed from a lack of previous leadership rather than a confrontational disposition. Whatever the reason, he was happy to concede that wearing a pink jacket and looking as if she should still be in school had no bearing on her efficiency.

'Deedee.' A shout carried on the breeze across the open heath. The riders Callum had spotted in the distance were trotting towards them – two men leading the way, and a woman following, riding one horse and leading another. The younger man, perhaps in his thirties, seemed to be in charge.

'Stay there,' Callum shouted, irritation creeping into his voice.

The riders stopped and waited for the detectives to join them. The coarse heather stems snagged Callum's jeans and moisture seeped into his unsuitable shoes. He looked down at the robust boots brushing through the vegetation beside him. His boots were stashed somewhere in the back of his car amongst his lifetime of belongings. He hadn't expected to need them for at least another week.

Daisy spoke quietly at his elbow. 'I don't know the girl. Richard Devereux-Strauss is on the black and Jimmy Eastwood, our local agister, is on the bay gelding, Murphy.'

Did she intend to introduce him to every animal within a half-mile radius by name? Callum had never heard of an agister and made a note to google it.

'Locals?' he asked.

'Yes. Jimmy lives in the village at Half Moon Farm. Devereux-Strauss is a horse dealer from Devereux Manor, about three miles away by road. Less, across the purlieu.'

He noted the difference in the tone and manner of her address but a swift look at her face revealed nothing further.

The black horse was full of explosive energy, nervous as a ballerina before her first solo. Richard sat tall in the saddle, hands unmoving on the reins, legs pressed against the sweaty sides of his mount as he maintained control. Murphy stood quietly on a loose rein, resting a hind leg as Jimmy, who looked to be in his forties, leaned down to Daisy, anxious eyes searching her face.

'That's Pirate they're loading into the trailer. It's Mary-Ellen, isn't it?'

Daisy moved to the shoulder of the bay horse and patted the shiny coat before nodding at Jimmy.

'Is she badly hurt? Can I see her?' A muscle pulsed in his cheek.

"fraid not, Jimmy.' She introduced Callum to the riders, but Jimmy's attention was focused on her.

'Are you sure it's her? She was fine when I saw her yesterday.'

'Fuck's sake,' the other man shouted.

They turned to see a plastic bag floating towards them on the breeze like a malevolent ghost, an officer in swift pursuit. The black horse cavorted and twisted, before leaping into the air with a loud snort and trying to run away. The bag was captured, and Callum was unsure if the officer's red face stemmed from embarrassment or exertion. Richard brought his mount to a quivering halt in an area of churned turf. The girl with the two horses firmly kept control as they lunged away from the running officer. Then she stood apart, an interested expression on her face as she watched the activity at the crime scene. Callum thought it was probably the first time she had come this close to a body.

'Stupid bastard,' Richard called after the man.

'Mr Devereux-Strauss. When did you last see Mary-Ellen Mitchell?' Callum asked.

'What? No idea. I didn't know the woman. We didn't move in the same social circles.' Richard stared down his hooked nose at Callum. He controlled his still fractious horse with evident expertise.

'Mr Eastwood,' Callum said, turning to the other rider. 'Where did you see her yesterday?'

'Near Millersford Inclosure. A fence was down, so I rode Murphy over to mend it.' The horse flicked its ears sideways on hearing his name. 'Mary-Ellen waved to me when she cantered past on the firebreak.' His cough failed to disguise the catch in his voice.

'Stand,' Richard growled, as his horse pawed the ground and tossed its head, the metal bit clanking in its mouth.

'Come on, Richie.' The girl turned her horse to face the open forest.

'Have you finished with us, officer? Some of us have places we should be.' To emphasise his point, Richard glanced at an oversized watch on his left wrist.

His mount swung its rump towards Callum, who didn't back away, despite beads of sweat prickling his scalp. Richard glanced at the police cordon before riding off.

'She's dead, isn't she?' Jimmy asked.

Daisy nodded.

'I thought she had to be, with all this…' His voice tailed off.

'Keep this to yourselves for the moment, until we have notified the next of kin.' Callum addressed them all but it was Jimmy who replied.

'Then you'd better get on with informing her thoughtless excuse for a husband. News moves fast around here.'

'Thoughtless?' Daisy said, but Jimmy was already turning away and didn't answer.

Callum couldn't tell if it was just a trick of the light that made Jimmy's eyes glisten. He watched the retreating figures, Richard sitting tall and straight, while Jimmy slumped in his saddle, reins loose, letting Murphy make his own way home. The girl preceded them. She sat deep in her saddle and pushed her mount into a trot, clicking her tongue to the riderless horse, until it trotted up beside her. She was a strong rider, determined, and, Callum surmised, used to being in control.

'You don't recognise the girl?' he asked.

'No. Richard's groom probably. Riding and leading exercises, two for the price of one.' Daisy's critical gaze followed them. 'I wish my legs were as long as hers.'

Callum looked down at her.

'You get more contact with the horse's sides, better control,' she added.

He would take her word for it. 'Richard referred to Mary-Ellen in the past tense. Significant?'

'I didn't notice.' Daisy looked pensive.

'And Jimmy was upset?'

'That's what I was wondering about. He is usually so level-headed. What you see is what you get with Jimmy…' She hesitated and gave a shake of her head as they turned to walk back to the activity.

'But?' he prompted.

'But I was surprised by what I saw, and not sure what I got.'

'And Richard?'

'A class-A, arrogant dickhead, sir,' she replied without breaking stride.

Callum smiled to himself. His instinct was correct, there was history between the two, but the details would keep. For now.

Martha was supervising the removal of the body. She looked up at Callum and closed her case with a snap.

'Let me know when you want the low-down on your motley crew, and I'll meet you for a drink and introduce you to the local watering hole.'

She had caught him unawares and he couldn't bring a single well-rehearsed excuse to mind.

She barked a laugh. 'No strings, you're young enough to be my son… mind you, there's life in the old girl yet.'

Her hearty chuckle stayed with him when she walked towards a marked car, calling to the driver to give her a lift back to her vehicle. When Martha got into the passenger seat, the chassis groaned and dropped an inch. Callum wished that cause and effect were always so obvious.

* * *

The lights on Callum's Camaro flashed at their approach. 'Tell me about her husband, Michael Mitchell, before we break the bad news,' he said.

'Nice car, sir. He lives at Millers Farm with Mary-Ellen, and he's a painter.'

'And decorator?' He opened the boot and exchanged his wet shoes for a dry pair.

'More Van Gogh than a rag-roller. Paints portraits, I think.'

Sir Michael Mitchell? National Portrait Gallery and all that? If it was, then Callum had seen some of his work and admired it, with all the appreciation of the gifted amateur artist he was.

Daisy opened the nearside door and stopped when confronted by the steering wheel.

'I'll drive, Daisy.' He waited for her to move around the bonnet and open the offside door before sliding into his seat.

'I didn't realise your Chevvy is a left-hand drive.' She reached for her seat belt. 'Not had time to find a place to stay yet?' she asked, catching sight of the loaded back seat.

'I see why they made you detective.' He smiled at her.

Her chatter didn't annoy him and that was a surprise. At thirty-four, he knew he had gained a reputation as an intolerant misery and that suited him just fine. It stopped people from trying to get too close.

'They made me detective because I'm a good detective.' She took a cereal bar from her pocket and passed it to him. 'You missed breakfast.'

He hesitated, then took it from her. 'Thanks, Daisy.' He was not used to people looking out for him, but he was hungry.

The pulsing of the engine was accompanied by a burst of 'Hey Daisy darling' from the Karine Polwart CD that he had left playing. He silenced it, pulled away from the verge and Daisy's simmering laughter lasted until he had finished eating and tidied the wrapper into the door pocket.

'Tell me about the New Forest. Potted history,' he added when she took a deep breath. He liked to do his own homework, but Bellman asking him to start early had robbed him of that opportunity.

'Right. About two hundred-odd square miles, give or take, and it's a mix of open heath and lawns, ancient woodland and planted inclosures – that's with an *i*, not an *e*.' She glanced at Callum.

'Go on.' With that much open heath, he was lucky to have found the body at all.

'Mostly owned by the Crown, and the verderers look after it on their behalf. The Verderers' Hall in Lyndhurst is the court that deals with lawbreakers.'

'I thought the law was our job.'

'Not our law, the laws that just apply to the Forest.'

'Explain please.' Callum tapped his fingers against the steering wheel. He had already sensed that asking Daisy a simple question was no guarantee that he would get a simple answer.

'When William the Conqueror made it his personal hunting ground, he granted the families that already lived there five commoners' rights.' She counted them off on her fingers. 'One to graze stock. Two was pannage…'

Callum frowned. It was like learning another language.

'Putting pigs out in the autumn to eat the acorns.'

He had been mistaken in thinking this appointment would be much the same as his last.

'Then cutting peat, collecting wood and digging clay. I don't know anybody who still does the last three.'

'Thanks. Clear so far. And an agister?' He could tick that off his mental list.

'The verderers employ agisters, who are sort of Forest policemen, if you like. There are five, each responsible for a separate area. Jimmy, who you just met, is our agister, and he keeps an eye on stock, makes sure the owner feeds them in winter, that sort of thing.' Daisy paused for breath. She had provided a splendid example of multi-tasking by giving him hand directions while speaking, and now she signalled him to stop.

'Thanks. That'll do me for the moment.'

The New Forest was separated from Glasgow by more than miles.

Chapter Three

The white-on-black nameplate for Millers Farm was set into the high perimeter wall. Wild ponies cropped the grass at its base. It would take him a while to get used to animals running free all over the place. Open wrought-iron gates flanked a cattle grid sunk across the driveway, and the run-flats on the Camaro wallowed in every dip between the metal bars.

Clipped hornbeam hedges guided them along a gravel drive to a flagged courtyard overlooked by the house. A tumble of greenery hugged the brick façade as snugly as a buttoned cardigan with a spray of pink clematis on one shoulder. Shaded windows looked out across the trimmed lawns and geometric beds. The house sat comfortably in its surroundings with a staunch and dependable air. It breathed age, elegance and wealth.

A downstairs curtain fluttered back into position as Callum pulled on the handbrake.

'Bit smart, isn't it?' Daisy said. 'Looks like there's someone home.'

The studded oak door was swung open by a grey-haired woman in a navy dress that struggled to disguise her thickening waist. She stood on the threshold and waited for them.

'Ready?' Callum asked, looking at Daisy who was composed and calm.

'Yes, sir. Ready.'

Most people do not enjoy being cruel. Telling a person of the death of a loved one was bad enough, but having to tell them that the deceased was murdered was like delivering the unwelcome news twice over. This was the part of the job that most officers disliked, and Callum was no exception. For a second, his breath snagged in his throat as he remembered being told about Grace. He pushed the memory back into the dark, opened the nearside door and together they walked to the waiting woman.

Amelia Roberts was the housekeeper. Sir Michael had been away for the night and was not yet home, but she was expecting him imminently. With a whisper of tyres on the flagstones, a black Range Rover purred to a halt next to the Camaro. It settled, as sure of its place as a contented cat on a sunny windowsill. The driver had a full head of silver hair swept back from a high brow to ripple down over his collar like a sun-glazed stream. He stepped out of his car, lean and angular, and directed a frown of enquiry at the woman in the doorway.

'Mrs Roberts?'

'They're police, sir. They're asking for you.' She melted into the interior of the house leaving the door open.

He came towards them, hand outstretched, and Callum was surprised that Sir Michael was much older than he had expected considering the age of his deceased wife.

'I'm Detective Inspector Callum MacLean and this is Sergeant Daisy Donaldson.'

'What can I do for you?'

'We would like a word with you please, if we could step inside, sir.'

Sir Michael remained motionless. Perhaps he hesitated because his privacy was important to him. Or perhaps he had something to hide.

'It is very important,' Callum said.

'Very well. Come through to the library.'

They followed him into the house where the oak boards of the entrance hall creaked beneath their feet. The wood-panelled wall at the back of the room rose to a carved gallery, back-lit by leaded windows that shone mote-heavy beams of light at their feet.

Sir Michael dropped his keys into a dish on a polished table, ignoring the silver salver piled with what Callum assumed to be the morning post. The past was alive and kicking. Callum glanced around to see if Jeeves lurked in the shadows.

Single file, they entered a room where any wall not covered by bookcases was hung with paintings. The most arresting of these was a life-sized oil of a reclining nude. Callum recognised her. It was a breathtakingly beautiful Mary-Ellen Mitchell wearing just the gold earrings she was wearing that morning. Such perfection demanded an audience and Callum stood in front of it in silent admiration. He experienced a familiar prickling sensation across the back of his neck. His words were about to change this man's life forever.

'One of my better attempts,' Sir Michael said, looking at Callum. 'She was so beautiful.' His eyes returned to the portrait.

Callum and Daisy exchanged a surprised look.

'Was?' Callum asked.

'Well, she still is beautiful, Inspector. Just a little older now. I painted that on our honeymoon in Greece fifteen years ago. I knew the second I met her that I had to paint her. There's something captivating in her knowing innocence, that glimpse into inner beauty and the life lived.' He smiled at the picture. 'She is an exceptional woman. I am very lucky.'

Callum cleared his throat. 'When did you last see her?'

'Yesterday, Inspector. Why do you ask?' Suspicion captured his movement and interrupted his speech. His intense grey eyes punctured the distance between them, seeking out the information Callum was there to impart.

'I am sorry to be the bearer of bad news, Sir Michael. Earlier this morning, the body of a woman was found on

Hale Purlieu, and I have to inform you that it is Mary-Ellen. Her horse was nearby,' he finished gently.

Sir Michael raised a trembling hand to his mouth and moved his head from side to side.

'No,' he whispered and then again, with increased firmness, 'No. You must be mistaken. It can't be her. It can't be.'

The lines on his face deepened and he aged before their eyes. His legs buckled and he landed heavily on a red chair.

'I'm sorry, Sir Michael.'

'Can I get you a glass of water?' Daisy asked.

When she got no response, Callum's eyes directed her towards the door and he heard it close as she left them. Sir Michael rocked slowly backwards and forwards in his chair, his gaze distant, focused on something only he could see.

Callum lowered himself onto an adjacent chair. 'Do you know where Mary-Ellen was going this morning? Was she meeting anybody?'

'Going? I have no idea. I must see her. How did she die?'

'We're not sure of the cause of death just yet.'

'Are you sure it's her? I must see her. I need to see her.'

'We can arrange that.' Then, Callum asked the question that always seemed insensitive to the recently bereaved. 'Routine, sir, but where were you earlier this morning?'

The rocking stopped and the sudden hardness in Sir Michael's grey eyes was echoed in his voice.

'I was out. I stayed away last night, then I drove a friend to the airport first thing before returning home. You saw me arrive.' Sir Michael lowered his head.

'And was your wife at home last evening?'

'No. She took a client out to dinner. She runs her own business. As I was leaving, she came down the stairs.' His eyes lost focus as he remembered the scene. 'She was wearing a black sequinned dress. She paused on the bottom step with the light behind her. It shone through the ends of her hair like a corona around her head.' He expelled a slow breath, living in the memory. 'The quality of the light was breathtaking.' He stood. 'Do you know the picture of Beata Beatrix by Rossetti?'

'That hangs in the Tate? Yes, I do.'

'Very similar glowing backlight. Ethereal.'

Callum watched the other man's face. 'Didn't Rossetti paint that in his grief following the death of his wife—' he searched for a name '—Amy Siddal?'

Sir Michael tensed. 'It was Elizabeth Siddal,' he corrected, 'but you are right about the sentiment. I was drawing a parallel with the light.'

He sat down again, forearms resting on his thighs, and his head fell forward, sending the silver mane into disarray. A tremor skimmed his shoulders like the first warning of an imminent earthquake. Why had he referenced that particular masterpiece? Was there a connection, or was it just about the light?

Daisy came quietly into the room and placed a glass of water on a low table near Sir Michael. She glanced at Callum, who nodded for her to proceed.

'Did your wife have any enemies?' Daisy asked. 'Was there anyone who would want to harm her?'

'No, of course not.' His head snapped up to stare at Daisy. 'That's a ridiculous idea. Beyond credibility. Everybody loved her. Who would want to hurt her?'

'We're considering all avenues at this stage, sir.' Callum spoke carefully.

He saw the flash of understanding banished by disbelief. Sir Michael didn't want to contemplate the thought. The pallor beneath his tan made him a ghost of the man who had stepped down from his car a few minutes earlier. His shaking hand reached out for the water glass.

'Are you trying to tell me it wasn't an accident, Inspector?'

'We're keeping an open mind for the moment. Where was she dining last evening?'

'I wouldn't know. Check with her secretary, Nicole Watson.' He resumed rocking, his forgotten glass rhythmically slopping water onto the rug.

Daisy eased it from his damp fingers and replaced it on the table. 'We need to take a look at her bedroom, sir,' she said.

He waved them away on a choked intake of breath.

Callum looked at the bowed head and felt a surge of sympathy for the artist. He knew what it was like for your world to change forever.

* * *

They paused in the doorway to Mary-Ellen's bedroom, getting a feel for the space. It was a contemplation in cream and pink. The raw silk cover on the half-tester bed was so skilfully embroidered that at first glance Callum thought the surface was strewn with flowers. Toning fabric framed east-facing windows through which the morning sun lit the flower-sprigged wallpaper. The heat-teased smell of lavender polish was infused with a hint of the same perfume he had smelled earlier. The room looked… Callum struggled to grasp the thought… too neat, un-lived-in, like a picture from one of Grace's glossy magazines. Style but no identity. His eyes returned to the bed, neatly made. Had she slept there last night, or in someone else's bed while her husband was away?

In the adjoining bathroom, there were only her toiletries, no prescription drugs in the medicine cabinet, just an off-the-shelf painkiller, skin creams and a bottle of perfume. She appeared to live frugally for a wealthy woman, which surprised Callum. He was also surprised that there seemed to be nothing in the room that belonged to her husband. The laundry basket held her underwear, and he indicated to Daisy to put it in an evidence bag.

The clothes in the wardrobe were hers alone. The garments were colour-coordinated in sections, sweaters uniformly folded, and shoes lined up with military precision. It looked like a newly stocked shop display without the price tags, or perhaps the meticulous order of an obsessive–compulsive. He glanced around the room. He found the black sequinned dress Sir Michael had described, and Daisy bagged it for Forensics.

An evening bag was placed on the dressing table, precisely equidistant between a box of tissues and a vase of speckled lilies. Daisy opened it.

'Something here, sir.' She bent forward to examine it and her plaits swayed like ropes. 'Credit card receipt.'

The house creaked softly as the sun warmed it, like a ship on a slack tide, marking time. The scent of the flowers reminded Callum of funerals. Somewhere downstairs a clock chimed away the day.

'Payment to The Laughing Duck in Fordingbridge for last night.' She looked at Callum, eyes stretched wide. 'With prices like that, The Duck must be laughing all the way to the bank.'

Callum held out his hand and she passed the slip to him.

'Two starters, two mains and one dessert, so she had just one guest,' he said, 'but plenty of wine.' He dropped the paper into the clear bag that Daisy held open. 'Check the restaurant and local taxi firms.' He hoped neither had chosen to drive after drinking that much. 'Did she and her guest part on good terms? Where did they go after they left the restaurant? Check if they have CCTV or knew who was with her.'

'Perhaps they left together, went to his, things got out of hand…' She looked again at the receipt. 'No, seems not. This is timed at just after eleven and she arrived home by taxi at about eleven thirty and didn't go out again until she left to go riding at half past seven this morning.'

'How do you know this?'

'Mrs Roberts, the housekeeper. Told me when I was getting the glass of water.'

'In future, inform me of information as soon as you receive it, Sergeant.'

Daisy made an apologetic face. 'Sorry, sir. Out of practice.'

What had been going on under the previous DI? Had she been running everything on her own?

Mary-Ellen's wallet and credit card were in her bedside drawer along with a novel, progress marked with a bookmark from a children's charity – no despoiling dog-eared pages for her. There was no mobile phone or laptop. Callum swept his eyes around the room as they prepared to leave. No photos, no personal paraphernalia, nothing of the woman who hid behind order and exactness.

A memory of their bedroom in Glasgow barged into his mind; Grace's beads hanging down either side of the mirror, like coloured hair, her shoes tumbled together in the corner of the room and the musk of her perfume floating in the air. He saw Grace sprawled across their bed, laughing up at him, with her seductive smoky eyes and long-tangled locks. His chest hurt. He closed his eyes. He forced a slow breath and, behind his closed lids, summoned the image of a long straight road with a stand of leafy trees at the end. He took another virtual step towards them as he breathed out. Despite the many times he had completed this exercise, those trees were a long way into the future. One day, he hoped he would be able to stand in their shade.

'Sir?'

He opened his eyes. Daisy's head was tilted to one side, her blue eyes fixed on his face.

'Ask Sir Michael about her computer and next of kin when we go back downstairs,' he said, turning away from her.

* * *

In the hall, he motioned her towards the library while he flipped through the unopened post on the silver tray. A white envelope addressed to Sir Michael Mitchell was marked "Private and Confidential" and printed on the back was "Paul Jackson Solicitors, Southampton". What secrets were folded inside the heavy sheets of paper? Callum replaced the envelope and stepped into the library.

'No, neither of us has ever had children. My parents are gone.' Sir Michael was still seated where they had left him and now closed his eyes before adding, 'I have a brother, Gavin, but I haven't seen him since our wedding day.' He looked up at Daisy. 'Mary-Ellen has parents and a sister.'

Sir Michael spoke without emotion and there was nothing behind his eyes. Daisy wrote the details in her notebook before closing it and slipping it back into her pocket.

'Thank you, Sir Michael. Is there someone you would like us to call for you?'

'No. Leave me alone now, please.' He rose unsteadily to his feet in a gesture of dismissal, and both officers turned towards the door.

Callum heard Sir Michael sink into his chair and glanced back over his shoulder. Distress was crumpling the artist's face, softening his features like heat-melting wax, and his tears flowed into the fissures. His body rocked, keeping time with the ticking of the grandfather clock in the hall.

'We'll be in touch, sir. I'm sorry for your loss,' Callum said softly.

Amelia Roberts was waiting for them in the hall. Her back was stanchion straight and she had made a good job of disguising the tears on her pale cheeks. It was the rose rims of her eyes that gave her away.

'I'll look after him.' Her fingers grasped Daisy's hand for a moment, then she eased her grip. She lingered on the doorstep until they were seated in the Camaro. Then she stepped back into the gloom and shut out the sunshine.

Callum rattled back over the cattle grid, flipped down his sun visor and listened to Daisy.

'Amelia Roberts has worked for the Mitchells since they married fifteen years ago. Both individually well off, hard-workers, neither have been married before and they both do a lot for charity.'

Callum had come across some nasty villains who hid behind a veil of philanthropy. It was seldom that people portrayed the same image in public as they did in private. What they did behind closed doors was kept behind closed doors for a reason.

'They have separate bedrooms. Is that usual in marriage, do you think?' Daisy asked casually.

'Not in my experience,' he said and saw the corner of her mouth lift before she turned her head to look out of the window.

The overarching boughs of the tree-lined lane plunged them into shadow.

'And?' He realised she was digging and was annoyed with his unguarded response.

'Now this is interesting. She had discreet lovers, but they never came to the house. Amelia suggested we have a word with Jimmy Eastwood. She thinks he was the last one and that Mary-Ellen ended it.'

The tree tunnel gave way to leafy hedges and sunlight turned the tarmac into molten silver.

'Does she indeed,' he mused. 'Evidence?'

'Mary-Ellen got uncharacteristically annoyed when Jimmy rang the house one day–'

Daisy's phone buzzed, and she pressed it to her ear. Callum listened to her side of the conversation.

'Necrophilia is a criminal offence, Cookie, and she's old enough to be your mother,' she said calmly, then laughed at her caller's response. 'Get Bird to check The Laughing Duck. You do the taxi drivers.' She listened for a moment. 'I don't care if they do work nights. Get their home addresses and hammer on their doors until they open up.

Put Bird on.' She waited a moment before asking, 'What did you get from Ruby Deacon?' She nodded and wrote something in her notebook. 'Thanks, Bird.' She ended the call.

'Cookie, DC Thomas Cooke, is newly assigned and it's his first case out of uniform. DCI Bellman attached him to us to help out. He's his nephew.'

Why did they need help? he wondered, then switched his attention back to Daisy.

'He's clever and keen…' She tailed off with a dismissing hand gesture.

'But?' prompted Callum.

'But he's like a puppy, wants to be everywhere at once, full of waggy-tailed enthusiasm and in need of discipline.'

Callum snorted a burst of laughter and Daisy joined in before adding, 'Bird doesn't find it so funny. I put him in charge of puppy walking.'

'Bird?'

'DC Tony Hampton. Sorry. Should have said.'

'Okay. Did I hear you mention a black Range Rover? Because Sir Michael drives one, or was it something Bird said?' Callum slowed to steer around a refuse collection lorry emptying bins outside a row of cottages. A black bin liner sat on one lid, the neat knots poking upwards like interested cat's ears. It was rejected and tossed back onto the path. Callum's tyres bumped over the edge of the grass verge and the boxes on his rear seat shuffled position.

'No. Ruby Deacon, who phoned in the loose horse, lives with Colonel Deacon on the edge of the purlieu, close to where Mary-Ellen was found.'

He frowned. Purlieu was another new word to look up when he got a minute.

'Purlieu is just another name for the open heath.'

He added mind-reader to her list of talents. 'Thank you.'

'You're welcome. Ruby walks Cleo in the mornings and the colonel watched them leave this morning because

Ruby has a very watchable rear end, even though she's in her seventies.'

'I'll take his word for it.'

'It was just after half past seven and he saw three cars go by. Jimmy Eastwood's green pickup, another neighbour, and a black Range Rover.' She added a note in her book before continuing, 'Ruby named a couple of other dog walkers and a rider. Bird is going to check them out.'

Callum slowed and pulled over to let a car squeeze past in the narrow lane, his tyres once more bumping over a rutted verge.

'And Mary-Ellen doesn't keep a computer at home and takes her phone with her when she goes riding, according to Sir Michael.'

'Good work,' he said. 'Either the killer took it or Martha has it. Check back with her.' He slipped up a gear. 'Change of plan, Daisy. His name keeps cropping up. Let's go and have a word with Jimmy Eastwood.'

Chapter Four

Half Moon Farm was a smallholding, accessed from a lane behind the village green. Callum's fingers tightened on the steering wheel as the Camaro shuddered over the cattle grid onto a stone track where flattened green tufts snaked down the centre.

'Daisy, why does everyone have an infernal cattle grid? They're killing my tyres.'

Fenced paddocks on both sides were dotted with daisies and dandelions, heads raised to the sun.

'Wrong sort of tyres, sir. My Navara doesn't have any problem with grids.'

He heard the smile in her voice. She might be enjoying his vehicular inadequacies, but this could become an expensive day.

'And they stop the wild ponies getting into gardens,' she added. 'Quicker and easier than gates, and you can't leave them open by mistake.'

The grass brushed against his undercarriage when his wheels dipped into a rut. He sensed her glance at him then quickly look away. She was curious, puzzling to work him out. He hoped she wouldn't try too hard. He was fed up with people prying into his personal life.

The track ended in a dip where a cottage flanked by scattered outbuildings nestled like a mother hen surrounded by chicks. The dwelling was randomly constructed of brick, timber and large flints arranged in patches of red, brown and white. It reminded Callum of a patchwork quilt. A thin wisp of grey wriggled from the single chimney and vanished into the blue sky. He was surprised to find the disorderly construction curiously pleasing to his eye. His thumb touched the coiled spine of the sketchbook he always carried in his pocket.

In the adjoining orchard, a tall woman with wind-teased hair pegged washing onto a blue rope stretched between the apple trees. She paused, called over her shoulder to one of the wooden buildings, and as the car rolled to a stop, Jimmy appeared from the shadowed interior wiping his hands on a dirty cloth. Daisy got out of the offside car door and Jimmy raised a hand in recognition.

'New car, Deedee? Not what we're used to.'

'No. You met him earlier, new boss… and ditto.'

Callum suspected that Daisy rolled her eyes because Jimmy's face briefly relaxed before settling back into tight-mouthed dejection. He nodded to Callum who had been slower to get out and now leaned against the driver's door watching the agister. He put him in his forties, lean and fit. Jimmy's shoulders were rounded beneath the checked shirt and his fingers toyed with the cloth he held. There was no doubt that he was upset, he looked as if he had the weight of the world pressing down on him.

Possibilities chased through Callum's head. Had Amelia Roberts been wrong in thinking the affair had ended? Were they still lovers? Perhaps they had argued, and things got out of hand. He could have been on his way to kill Mary-Ellen when Colonel Deacon saw him in the lane. Callum looked across at the washing swaying as it was pegged along the line. Perhaps Mary-Ellen had threatened to tell his wife about the affair.

A black-and-white collie bitch, swollen with pups, came out of the shed and pushed her muzzle into Jimmy's hand. He caressed her head and glanced across to the woman in the orchard.

'Murphy looks well.' Daisy nodded at the bay horse grazing in the paddock.

Callum folded his arms. He would give her three minutes to get the niceties out of the way. If she didn't start asking questions by then, he would.

'He is,' Jimmy said. 'He's getting a bit long in the tooth now but he's a good old lad. Knows his job. I'm keeping an eye open for a second horse, ease his workload a bit. The drifts are getting a bit much for him now. If you hear of anything…'

Murphy wandered up to the fence when his name was mentioned, and Callum watched Daisy reach out to stroke the beast. He would ask her what a drift was later.

'I was thinking of getting one from Richie,' Jimmy continued. 'He's just bought in a load of new stock. I went over a day or two ago and that groom girl was driving back into the yard and showed me some of his horses in the boxes. You can't tell from just looking at them, so she suggested I ride out with Richie, see the horses working. But you saw what a hothead he was on this morning. Couldn't stand still to save its life. I need something reliable like Murphy.' He rubbed his flat hand across the brown face and the horse softly blew air through its nostrils.

'Where were you earlier this morning, Jimmy?' she asked.

'Over at Ben Martin's farm. He asked me to look at a bunch of yearlings.'

'How did you get there?'

'In my pickup. My tools are in the back, and he wanted me to check their feet. Not a bad bunch of colts. He's sending them down to Beaulieu Road pony sales now the market's picked up a bit. He won't get rich out of them, but he won't have to feed them through next winter either.'

'What time did you get back here?'

He thought for a moment. 'Eight or sometime after. Eight fifteen or twenty. I can't remember exactly. I put my keys in the kitchen, drank a coffee with Sue, then saddled up Murphy and headed over to meet Richie by Millersford Inclosure. He'll know the time. He always wears that big watch.'

Callum uncrossed his arms. If Jimmy was that late getting home from the farmer, then he had a window of opportunity to murder Mary-Ellen.

'Are you going to buy one of his horses?' Daisy asked with what sounded like genuine interest.

He shook his head. 'Too much money for too little horse. And I don't trust Richie not to sell me trouble. He'd sell his mother for a swift buck.'

'Did you see anyone else on your travels?'

He named a couple of neighbours on their way to work and the same dog walkers as Ruby Deacon.

'I wish I'd seen Mary-Ellen,' he murmured, his shining eyes magnetised by the gravel beneath his boots.

Daisy took the rag from his unresisting fingers. 'Come on. Let's walk down to the stream.'

Callum watched their receding backs. Did Daisy and Jimmy have a connection based on just their equestrian interests, or was there more to it? He was not alone in marking their departure. The woman in the orchard was staring after them. Then perhaps sensing his scrutiny, she looked at him and smiled. Hands in pockets, he strolled through the open gate as she resumed pegging children's clothes to the line.

She had rounded cheeks beneath heavy eyebrows that almost met above her nose, like kissing caterpillars. Her mouth was wide and generous, and her lips curved upwards as if a smile was never far away. The yellow peg she held between her teeth pecked a greeting to Callum.

'Susan Eastwood,' she volunteered, using the peg to secure a blue shirt and freeing a hand to shake his. 'You must be the new policeman.'

He introduced himself, singled out another garment from the basket and handed it to her. She took it, and it was soon dancing in the breeze on the makeshift line. She caught her lower lip between her teeth and held it there while she worked. Callum was comfortable with silence. Some people feel compelled to fill it with speech. Others could let it stretch and grow but Susan Eastwood wasn't one of them.

'Look,' she said, 'Mary-Ellen fell off her horse and died. That's tragic, but what's it got to do with my Jimmy?'

'It might not have been an accident.'

She took just a second to understand his meaning and her mouth opened then closed soundlessly. She looked again at her retreating husband then back to Callum and her brown eyes were soft with sadness.

'Wrong tree,' she said tenderly. 'Jimmy wouldn't… couldn't hurt anyone anymore.'

Callum remembered Morag. Five foot nothing and every weekend a victim of her husband's drunken temper. She never once fought back and refused to say a word against him, however hard they had tried to persuade her. Until the Friday he threatened their daughter. Then she had thrust a knife up under his ribs and into his heart. Everyone has a trigger point. What was Jimmy's?

'I understand they were…' He hesitated, choosing his words carefully. 'Friends.'

'Friends my arse. He had an affair with her. It's not the first, in case you were going to ask. That's just my Jimmy.'

She resumed her pegging and then laughed out loud at his surprised expression. It was a generous, engaging sound that creased the lines at the corners of her eyes, and he found himself smiling in response.

'I know my Jimmy,' she said, no trace of bitterness in her voice, 'every last inch of him, and he didn't kill her. Take my word for it.'

Callum stirred the grass with the toe of his shoe and admired her certainty. If he had a pound for every similar sentiment he had heard, then he wouldn't be standing in damp grass inhaling the pungent smell of a dung heap. Susan lifted the empty basket onto her hip and walked towards the house.

'It's wicked what killing does to a man, Inspector. It changes them. I think perhaps only a certain type of person can kill and not be affected by it. Jimmy's just not that type.' She sighed. 'Look, since the army sent him back to us, he won't even kill a wasp. He says even they deserve a chance at life, and we've got to learn to live with them.'

He silently commended both her honesty and her blind faith in her husband.

Susan put the laundry basket in the porch, pushed her hands into the front pockets of her jeans and watched a ginger cat with a tumble of kittens settle into the basket for a sleep.

'I've got to find homes for Marmalade's kittens before the kids get too attached to them,' she said, bending down to scratch the mother cat behind her ears. She turned back to Callum, her eyes searching his face.

He read her indecision. There was something she wanted to tell him but she was hesitating.

She walked over to the paddock gate, leaned her elbows on the top bar and waited until he joined her. She looked across the confetti of buttercups and daisies, past the grazing bay gelding until her eyes lost focus and Callum knew she had travelled further than the distant hedge.

'I was at school with Jimmy, and we shared a desk. He was the eldest of seven. His dad never went to school, and he didn't like them knowing stuff he didn't.' She brushed a fly away from her face with a lazy hand. 'He ruled them with his fists. Boys, girls and wife. Jimmy hated it and I hated that I couldn't do anything to help him.'

The gelding ambled across, swishing his tail to stop the flies crawling on him. Callum watched the play of muscles over the flat shoulder bones and caught the scent of sweet herbs disturbed by the brown hooves.

'As soon as he was old enough, Jimmy joined the army. He was the first one in his family to get some training, get a job and get a pay packet. I was so proud of him. We got married when he came home on leave, and it was the happiest day of my life.'

A warm smile skittered across her face and Callum thought that, for a moment, she looked quite beautiful.

'He was a good soldier, thrived on the life. We bought this place. The house had practically fallen down, but it was ours, and the bank's.' She smiled at the memory. 'We rebuilt it bit by bit with whatever materials were already here.'

Callum nodded. It explained the random construction.

She took a quick breath, a pulse fluttered in her throat. 'Then, just after our fourth baby was born, 3 Para was near Camp Bastion in Helmand protecting a group of women and children. One of the little boys took a fancy to Jimmy, like kids do. Called him "Dimmy" and followed him round mimicking his walk. Jimmy loved it. He missed our kids, and it was like a bit of home.' Her voice shrank to little more than a whisper and the skin around her eyes stretched tight.

'Jimmy was leading a patrol, and they were nearly back when they heard the screams. Insurgents butchered them. Women died trying to protect their kids. The little boy was still alive when Jimmy got to him, and he cradled him in his arms.' She paused and closed her eyes for a moment before continuing in a shaky voice. '"Dimmy, help," he said, before he died. Jimmy still shouts that in his nightmares.'

She cleared her throat. He didn't hurry her.

'When the other soldiers got to Jimmy, they said he was still kneeling clutching the boy, his hands wet with blood and his face with tears.'

Callum had learned not to be affected by what he saw or heard and breathed through the tightness in his throat. She turned her face towards him, her expression softening as her voice grew stronger.

'Jimmy had a complete breakdown, never served again.' She smiled at Callum. 'This is hard to explain, but Jimmy's will to fight died that day. It's been replaced by a burning need to help and protect, to make sure people get what they need.' She shooed another fly from her face.

'His nightmares aren't so bad now, and we've got better at coping with his black days when he beats himself up for failing to protect them.'

Murphy lipped at her hair until she gently pushed him away.

'You great soft lump of dog meat,' she said affectionately and the horse nickered softly through nostrils.

Callum tucked his hair behind his ears and watched the horse's long yellow teeth. He hoped he wasn't going to have to take Jimmy away from his family again.

'That's why he is taking Mary-Ellen's death so badly. It's the memories, you see. He thinks he failed and should've saved her. You do understand?'

Callum nodded. He didn't doubt her assertions about Jimmy but that didn't change the fact that the man was a trained killer, had possible motive and opportunity, and was still suffering from the effects of serving his country. He hoped for her sake that Jimmy's alibi checked out.

A warm smile transformed Susan's face as her husband and Daisy walked back into the yard. Jimmy's lashes were damp and spiky, and he dropped an arm around his wife's shoulders, resting his cheek briefly against her hair.

'Hi, Sue.' Daisy smiled. 'Say hello to the tribe for me. Sorry I missed them.'

'You won't be.' Susan slipped her arm around her husband's waist, and they melded, hip to hip. 'They've gone down to the horse pond with jam jars to catch newts. They never find any, but they come home with them full of stinky water. Smells worse than the dung heap.'

Callum joined in with their affable laughter, but this time he didn't believe her.

Chapter Five

The Fordingbridge police station was modern-looking and brick-built. As Callum turned into the entrance, Daisy told him it had been constructed on the site of a demolished mansion where murders had taken place, making it unsellable. He thought how convenient it was to be on the bypass rather than in the centre of the small narrow-streeted town.

The CID room was a babble of noise when Callum held open the door for Daisy to precede him. The murmur of voices stopped; heads swivelled to take a look at him but after swift scrutiny, everyone went back to work. More a nine-second wonder than a nine-day one.

The office was rectangular with all the windows down one side. Sunlight slanted through half-closed blinds throwing distorted shadows across the floor. Desks were paired back to back, some occupied, some not, and the rolled-up shirtsleeves and abandoned jackets evoked an air of industry. Stretching across the short-end wall was a half-glazed internal office, the grimy glass reminding Callum of a fishbowl filled with dirty water.

His attention was drawn to the long back wall of the office which displayed boards and a map. He presumed that was the area now under his jurisdiction. He was too far away to see any detail except a red pinhead near one edge, protruding like an angry pimple. An adjacent whiteboard displayed a picture of Mary-Ellen Mitchell, images of Sir Michael, Jimmy Eastwood and a third man that Callum didn't recognise. For no reason that he could fathom, someone had put up a headshot of the horse. Information was being updated by a man dressed in jeans, a navy sweater with the sleeves pushed up his inked forearms and a well-worn sleeveless waxed jacket. His short, grey hair grew in tufted patches resembling a rough-plucked chicken. He looked to be about fifty.

Callum moved closer to the board, chose a vacant desk and perched on the edge of it, crossing his straight legs at the ankle.

'Listen up, people. I'm DI Callum MacLean. Good to meet you all.' He paused at the murmur of responses as they gathered around. 'What have we got so far?'

'DC Tony Hampton, sir. Usually referred to as Bird,' said the waxed jacket, moving to one side to allow them sight of the board.

'The victim is Mary-Ellen Mitchell née Goddard, fifty-five years old, married to Sir Michael Mitchell, sixty-nine years of age,' he said, tapping the appropriate pictures with his pen.

'Time of death between seven thirty this morning when she left home, and just after eight, when first responders, PCs Cooper and Kent, discovered her body.'

Callum nodded to the two constables who leaned against the wall in the far corner. Cooper acknowledged him, but Kent folded his arms and looked away. An officer who didn't appreciate being reminded of the correct procedure, it seemed.

Bird continued. 'Probable cause of death was a broken neck – we're waiting on a heads-up on that from the doc – and it was made to look like an accident. We think she was killed elsewhere, and her horse was used to move her body, so we're looking for a rider.' He glanced at Daisy who nodded at him to continue.

'We can't narrow it down with footprints, because there aren't any. The heather is too thick where he dismounted. So, suspects are Sir Michael Mitchell, a very wealthy man, who doesn't ride but is rich enough to pay to get the job done. No alibi yet, and a confidential letter from his solicitor back at his house which may or may not be important. He drives a black Range Rover. There was one seen earlier in the area by Colonel Deacon, driver unknown.'

He pointed to the second picture. 'Jimmy Eastwood, local agister, ex-services so he knows how to kill, and had an affair with the victim, which we believe she ended. Rides well and knows the Forest like the back of his hand because of his job. Medically discharged from the army, PTSD. He's given us an alibi, two in fact, and they're currently being checked out. He has ability, motive and opportunity. My money's on him.' He stabbed his pen at Jimmy's picture and a couple of assenting murmurs confirmed that he was not the only one supporting that theory.

'Not in my book,' Daisy said. 'Who is the other guy?'

The door opened and Legs came into the room exuding energy and enthusiasm.

'Deedee hun, guv,' she said, addressing her superior officers before turning to the map and picking up coloured pins.

Callum frowned. Bird moved to one side to afford her access.

'Thanks, Bird,' Legs said. 'I followed the tracks but lost them close to Millersford Inclosure.' She marked the spot with a yellow pin. 'Unless they lived very close, they came in a car.'

'There's only that row of cottages along Forest Road, where the rubbish lorry was collecting, sir,' Daisy said. 'They're in walking distance. Uniform is checking.'

Legs tapped the map with her finger. 'There are two car parks close to Millersford Inclosure where I lost the hoofprints. I struck lucky when I chose this one first, Turf Hill car park.' She pushed a red pin into the map to mark a bulbous area of gravel at the end of a long track leading from a minor road.

'Locals park there to walk their dogs or go for a run,' Bird said.

'I picked up the hoofprints at the end furthest from the road. There's a patch where the horse was moving around on the same spot. That could be where she was killed. Time- and distance-wise it fits.' Her finger traced lines across the map. 'Her house to Turf Hill, meet someone, and then from there to Hale Purlieu. You could do it in the time, especially on a horse.'

'Good work,' Callum said, and she smiled.

She wrote the name of the car park site on the board in rounded script. 'Thanks, guv.' She switched her attention to Daisy. 'SOCOs are over there now,' she added. 'They'll let you know if they find anything.'

'We might be lucky. Keep me informed,' Callum said, 'and keep an officer over there when Forensics have finished. Someone using that car park this morning might have witnessed something. Same early tomorrow morning.'

'Onto it,' Daisy said.

'Who's the third suspect?' Callum reiterated the earlier unanswered question.

'Fletcher Edmunds,' Bird said, 'the client she took to The Laughing Duck. The manager confirmed that they dined together and drank a lot of wine. Or rather he did. Edmunds made a pass at Mary-Ellen which she rejected, so he drowned his sorrows at her expense. When she paid the bill, she got them to call a couple of cabs, and a waiter helped her pour Edmunds into one to deliver him to The White Horse Inn in Downton. When I got there this morning, he was still in bed snoring like a banshee. Still drunk as a skunk if you ask me. The staff said he stayed in the bar until about 0130 hours and then went to bed. Confirmed by the camera in the bar. He has a taxi booked for Southampton Airport and we've no reason to stop him leaving.'

'That's one suspect eliminated already,' Daisy said.

'Two-to-one shot on Jimmy now, Deedee,' Bird said. 'DC Thomas Cooke – Cookie there – was dealing with the taxi drivers.' Bird nodded at a gangly youth seated at the end desk speedily pressing buttons on a mobile phone.

Cookie raised his head and his black corkscrew curls jumped up and down as he grinned at Daisy. 'I did as you suggested and threatened to arrest the taxi drivers if they didn't answer the door and let me in,' he said.

Daisy frowned at him, and he lightly shrugged his shoulders before continuing. 'Mary-Ellen was dropped home alone at eleven thirty. By the time he'd turned round, she was indoors, and the outside light was off. That ties in with what the housekeeper said, hundo P.'

'Hundo P?' Bird queried.

'Yeah. Hundo P, Bird. Hundred per cent. And Edmunds was so drunk that his driver was concerned he was going to throw up in the back of his taxi.' He resumed pressing buttons on the mobile using both thumbs.

A flicker of something passed across Bird's face before he turned back to address the rest of the team. 'Cookie has got the victim's phone…'

'She has a name. Use it,' Callum interjected.

'Sorry, guv. Martha found Mary-Ellen's phone in the inside pocket of her jacket. The only prints are her own. Several from a gloved hand but she was wearing riding gloves. They released it to us, and Boy Wonder there' – he nodded at Cookie – 'is currently torturing information from it.'

Cookie didn't look up or interrupt his task when he spoke. 'Her last call was incoming at quarter to midnight last night from a Leon. Nothing since, except a voicemail this morning from a Nicole checking what time she would be in at work.' Cookie's brain worked more quickly than his tongue and his words tumbled out. 'I called the Leon number, but it's switched off now. I'm trying to trace it to see if it's Eastwood.' He snapped his head up as if to check that his audience was still there. 'In her contacts, her business numbers say who they are, what firm they're from and so on, but her personal contacts have code names, foreign ones, like Chu and Ean and Faol and Iasc, but for–'

Legs leaned across and ruffled his hair. 'You gotta remember to breathe, Cookie,' she said. 'We aren't all up to speed with our first aid.'

Cookie looked up and grinned at her. 'I've requested her phone records from her provider but that's going to take ages so I'm going through her calls and contacts to try and identify the personal ones.' Having finished his explanation, he dropped his head to pursue his mission.

'They sound like Gaelic words. *Iasc* is fish and I think *faol* is wolf,' Callum said, addressing the back of Cookie's head.

'Hunky-doodley, guv, checking as we speak.'

A muscle ticked in Callum's cheek.

Bird's eyes bored into the raven curls then he shook his head slowly. 'I sometimes think he's got a loose lead between the genius and common-sense departments,' he muttered.

Legs laughed. 'Not just you.'

Callum was getting his desired insight into the dynamics of his new team. For now, he was content to observe.

Bird went to his desk, checked his screen, and turned to Daisy. 'The doc's just given us the heads-up. Cause of death was a broken neck between…' He paused to consult the information. 'Between C2 and C3. The back of her head showed bruising from a left hand, fingertips, and palm' – he raised his hand and spread his fingers – 'and that tear at the corner of her mouth that you mentioned, guv, was down to the killer. They were wearing gloves, the surgical kind, and Martha found a small piece caught between her teeth, presumably where she bit the bastard.'

'That confirms that it was murder,' Callum said.

A sceptical glance passed from Kent to Cooper.

'I don't see any evidence. I still think it's an accident,' Kent said aside to Cooper, with sufficient volume to ensure his opinion was shared with the room in general.

Callum looked at the smirking PC. This questioning of his authority needed nipping in the bud. 'This is for your benefit alone, Kent, as you are the only one unable to interpret the facts, so pay attention.'

The collective eye turned on Kent whose cheeks reddened. Callum noted half-smiles of satisfaction on a couple of faces. He wasn't the only person to be irked by the constable's attitude.

'Bird,' Callum said, 'can you demonstrate how she got her injuries, please?'

Bird beckoned Daisy to him and turned her round to face away from him. He placed the flat of his left hand on the back of her skull and pushed her head gently forward. 'Obviously with a lot more force than that, and when you open your mouth to protest–' he paused '–I push a couple of fingers in it for leverage and wrench your head round and push it down. Snaps the spinal cord. Catch the body before it hits the deck.' He gave her a gentle push and she obligingly sagged at the knees before he caught her with his arm around her waist. 'Mission accomplished.'

'Then you lift her back on the horse, get up behind her, lengthen the stirrups,' Callum said, 'and away you go.'

'If anyone saw them, it would just look as if you had two up.' Daisy regained her feet and returned to stand next to Callum.

Bird nodded. 'That's about it. When they got to Hale Purlieu, they let go of her and she toppled to the ground, so it would look like she fell off her horse.'

'They would need to be pretty strong to get her back in the saddle,' Daisy said. 'And a good rider to control Pirate and stop her falling off.'

'And be taller than you to get her up there.' Legs smiled down at Daisy. 'And know their way round the Forest.'

'That doesn't narrow it down much,' Bird said. 'Nearly everybody is taller than the sarge.'

'Martha's report should be on your desk in the morning.' Bird nodded in the direction of Callum's office – the fishbowl at the end of the room.

'Follow up on those potential witnesses mentioned by Ruby Deacon and Jimmy Eastwood,' Callum said. 'I'm going to see what information we can glean from Mary-Ellen's fellow workers at her business, G-Smart Solutions. Daisy, you're with me.'

Chapter Six

Daisy dropped into the passenger seat of the Camaro.

'I thought we might need some lunch, so I got these from the canteen.' She peered into the first container as Callum stoked the engine.

He was unaware that it was lunchtime. Now he realised he was hungry.

'Cheese or…' She examined the others. 'Cheese?'

'Cheese, Daisy. Thanks.'

She took a hungry bite. Callum again drove to her hand signals, sandwich in hand, and they had both finished eating when he turned onto the tarmac driveway of G-Smart Solutions. He brushed crumbs from the front of his clothes and inspected the property through his insect-smeared windscreen.

The detached Victorian house, off Old Brickyard Road, Sandleheath, sat on raised ground amongst pine trees in a landscaped curtilage. It had been built to impress. The brick dentil line and carved stone lintels above the windows heralded extravagance and functionality in equal measures. Sculpted white fascia board dipped below the grey roof slates, like a starched lace petticoat.

Callum checked the cars parked in the "staff" spaces and concluded that Mary-Ellen must pay generous wages. Any motor dealer would be happy to get his hands on that lot. The sash windows gleamed and winked as they climbed the stone steps to the front door.

The reception area was decorated in restful greens. Leather chairs in shades of moss and malachite surrounded a low table covered in recent copies of expensive periodicals. He smelled the delicate perfume of lilies from an arrangement on a wooden stand. Mary-Ellen seemed to have had a penchant for the flowers, but they would always remind him of funerals. Their scent eased open the door that stored his memories.

The absinthe walls were hung with artwork, none by Sir Michael but they all looked like originals, as far as he could tell. He liked her taste of understated quality. Their feet made no sound crossing the carpet to the poised young woman behind the reception desk.

Following their introduction, the corners of her pink mouth curved downward, and her forehead ruckled with discontent.

'You need to speak to David Fellowes, Mrs Mitchell's business manager.' Her pink nail indicated a door emblazoned with his name in gold lettering. 'He was late this morning but he's in his office now.'

'Indeed. Why was he late?' Callum asked.

'No idea.' She folded her arms across her indignantly inflated chest. 'There was nothing in the diary, so you'd think he'd have the consideration to phone and keep me informed. Or at worst send me a text, but not a word.' Her petulance confirmed the perceived slight.

The phone on her desk purred. She lifted the receiver, tapped a button and the smile bounced back onto her face.

'G-Smart Solutions. Good afternoon. Karen speaking. How may I help you?'

Daisy gave a perfunctory knock, opened the door and preceded Callum into David's office. The sole occupant was leaning forward scrutinising papers spread out across his desktop. He looked up sharply, hustled the papers together and dropped them into a drawer as Callum made the introductions.

'Good morning, officers.' He briefly gained his feet in a nod to courtesy, before gravity sucked him back into his leather chair. His voice was breathy as if he had been running. 'How can I help you?'

Callum was reminded of a child's drawing of a face, small sharp eyes beneath lazy lids, a straight nose and shoelace lips. He put David in his forties, and decided he wasn't cheap to keep. Thinning grey hair was expertly styled to disguise imminent baldness, just as the handmade grey suit minimised his folds of belly flesh.

'I am already aware of the premature demise of my associate, Inspector, so I hope this isn't a wasted journey on your part.' He lifted a folded white handkerchief to his upper lip and dabbed at a bead of perspiration. 'What can I do for you?'

'How would you describe your relationship with Mrs Mitchell?' Daisy asked.

'Purely professional, if that is what you are hinting at, Sergeant. I am the backbone of her business.'

'A good working relationship, then?' Callum was interested that David described Mary-Ellen as his associate rather than his boss.

'None better, Inspector.'

'And where were you earlier this morning?' Daisy asked.

'At work.'

'And before that?'

'At home,' he said with the exaggerated patience of one answering persistent questions from an annoying child.

'And between the two?'

'Tra-vel-ling,' he said, segmenting the syllables slowly as if Daisy found comprehension challenging.

She made a note in her book. David sought eye contact with Callum over her bowed head, implying amusement at her expense.

Callum was against putting people in boxes until he had dug beneath the surface, but was getting a good idea of how he would label David's box.

'You were late for work this morning. Why was that?' Callum's tone was brusque.

The misogynist in David rankled.

'Guilty as charged.' A sheepish grin spread over the man's face, and he placed his hands, palm downwards, on the desk. The nails were manicured and buffed, reminding Callum of the pink-varnished talons of the receptionist.

'Haven't you ever been late for work, officer? So easy to be interested in a news item or have one more cup of coffee or just to oversleep.' He wheezed a laugh as if the matter was too trivial to warrant serious consideration, and several of his stomachs bounced about in mirth.

'And which of those excuses accounts for your lateness this morning?' Callum persisted. He was becoming annoyed with David's attempt at boys-own camaraderie.

'Bit of all three, I'd say.' His smile stretched his mouth wide, lips thinning like stretched elastic.

'Stop wasting my time.' Callum's voice was low and hard. 'I am trying to establish your whereabouts at the time Mary-Ellen Mitchell was mur-dered.' Callum glanced at Daisy, and the corner of her mouth twitched.

David gulped air. 'Murdered?' His Adam's apple bobbed like a buoy in a racing tide. 'If she was murdered, you can be sure I didn't do it.' His eyes skimmed over his desk phone as if he was willing it to ring.

'Look. I probably shouldn't say anything just yet, but we are expanding into London, and I am heading up the new office there. If I was to kill her, it would be like killing the goose who laid the golden egg.'

Unless the egg had already been laid, then killing the goose might not be a problem. It could even be a bonus.

'Will the expansion still go ahead?' Daisy asked.

'You're asking the wrong person, my dear. Mary-Ellen owned the company, lock, stock and contract-stuffed barrel. I have no financial investment in it. I am just a paid' – he straightened the knot of his tie – 'a very-well-paid employee. You'd better contact her beneficiaries.'

'And who might those be?' Callum said.

'God knows. Have a word with her secretary Nicole Watson. They're thick as thieves.' There was an edge to his voice. 'She has always had the ear of Mary-Ellen. Ask her.' David leaned back in his chair, hands linked across his body.

Callum thought he resembled a gloating toad, small eyes glimmering, watching for prey to show weakness so he could pick it off.

* * *

Nicole Watson invited them to sit and then crumpled back into her own chair. Pulling a tissue from the cuff of her cardigan, she dabbed at crimson-rimmed eyes with shaking fingers before verifying Mary-Ellen's dinner at The Laughing Duck with Fletcher Edmunds.

Callum gestured to Daisy to lead the questioning. Tearful women were outside his comfort zone, and he wondered fleetingly if he was as sexist as David in expecting Daisy to deal with the grieving secretary.

Daisy gave Nicole a confident smile. 'How long have you worked here?' she asked.

'Since Mary-Ellen started G-Smart Solutions when she left university. We just hit it off right from the start. Amanda Newman, our accountant, started at the beginning like me, and Rachel, our receptionist, joined us about ten years later.' She looked at Daisy; a smile fluttered like a butterfly across her lips before disappearing. 'She's on maternity leave, it should be any day now. I took a takeaway round to hers last night. She's on fine form but getting impatient now she's so near.'

That should be simple enough to confirm if they needed to. And being heavily pregnant ruled out the receptionist as a suspect. Nicole's distress was genuine. Callum didn't think she had anything to do with Mary-Ellen's death, and it seemed that Daisy was of a similar mind as she changed tack.

'How do you get on with David Fellowes?'

'Oh, he's all right… now.'

'Now?' Callum questioned.

'Initially, we were an all-girl team and there were a few issues when he first joined us. But he came round to our way of thinking.'

'What issues?' Daisy asked.

'David's a bit…' She searched for a word.

'Up himself?' Daisy supplied.

'You've met him then. It was the usual issue. Me man, you woman. Me boss, you slave.'

Daisy's soft laugh floated around the small room. 'Men can be so slow to learn,' she said, and Nicole's brief laugh joined hers, like harmonising parts of the same score. 'How was it resolved, out of interest?'

Callum knew that Daisy was establishing a rapport with Nicole, cultivating some common ground, putting him on the outside, but he was never comfortable with sexist generalisations. She kept surprising him. Was that really what Daisy thought? Not that it would bother him if it was, but he felt defensive at being the source of their humour.

He looked around the room, appearing to free up the airspace for Daisy while listening to every nuance in their words. The solid line of steel cabinets was overlaid with horizontal stripes of sunlight that had squeezed through the part-closed blinds. The grey walls and slate chairs were toned to harmonise the monochrome palette. The only injection of colour was a painting, a startling splash of gold, scarlet and purple abstraction trapped in a black frame. Another original? He studied it for a moment from his seat before realising that the conversation had stopped, and Nicole was watching him.

'Do you like it?'

Callum searched for a diplomatic reply and then settled on the truth. 'I'm not sure. I like the colours, the way they zing off each other, but I'm more of a traditionalist. I don't really understand abstract, I can never work out what they mean.'

'That's by a young artist that Sir Michael recommended. It's called *Rejection*. Mary-Ellen liked it. Sometimes she would just stand and look at it. She seemed to be able to see something in it that I can't.' Her voice cracked, and she fussed with her tissue.

Callum stood up and examined it at eye level as she regained control. Could the shards of gold be elbows pushing against the purple? A sudden flare of sunlight played across the canvas lighting the darks and it changed the balance of colour. Purple was king. He squinted at it, narrowing his focus. It still looked as if it was created by a chimp. If he had painted it, Grace would have asked if it was hung upside down. He turned his attention to the women, exchanging a quick look with Daisy and signalling her to continue. She repeated her question about resolving the teething problems.

'Very easily as it happened,' Nicole said. 'Mary-Ellen walked in when he was lecturing me on how to make his coffee and questioning my capabilities if I couldn't remember his simple instructions.'

'And?' Daisy prompted, easing forward in her chair.

'And in front of the entire staff, Mary-Ellen gave him a lecture on respect being earned and reminded him he was in his probationary period. Result. He went red and blustered a bit, but he never ordered me to make him coffee again. And to be fair, he's pretty good at the job.'

Daisy's splutter of laughter was echoed by Nicole. Callum's token contribution was reticent and short-lived.

'Were you moving to the London office or staying here?' he asked her.

'London office? I don't know what you're talking about.'

Callum explained, and Nicole shook her head.

'You've got that wrong. I deal with all her correspondence and appointments, so I'd be the first to know.'

He changed the direction of his questions.

'Nicole, are there any disgruntled clients, or staff to your knowledge?'

She considered, her eyes sliding over the filing cabinets as if searching for clues. Then she looked him in the eye and sat forward in her chair.

'I can honestly say that in the last thirty years, I can't think of a single client who was in any way dissatisfied or had any reason to complain. I really can't.'

'And staff?' he prompted.

'Three.' She answered without hesitation. 'We had an Australian student who stole from the petty cash. She was here in a gap year but got pregnant and didn't have enough money for her airfare home. Mary-Ellen didn't press charges, and, between you and me, I think she paid for her return ticket.'

Daisy made notes in her book.

'The next was a gardener. Mary-Ellen sacked him on the spot. No warning. I read in the local paper recently that he's in jail now for armed robbery.' Her mouth rimpled into a tight knot. 'And then there was Veronica.'

'Veronica?' Daisy asked, pen poised.

'Parsons, née Goddard. Her sister. It's probably six or so years since Mary-Ellen sacked her. Veronica was furious about it and made sure everyone knew it.'

'Why was she sacked?' Callum asked, his interest piqued.

'She didn't pull her weight. She would turn up late for work, forget to come back after lunch and then leave early. Not once or twice but several times a week.'

'What happened?' he asked.

'There was a showdown. Veronica barged into Mary-Ellen's office and screamed and swore. Then she shouted at Amanda that half the business should be hers, and she would take us to a tribunal so the truth would come out. Mary-Ellen would regret sacking her. It was embarrassing.'

'And did Mary-Ellen regret it? Was there any payout to Veronica?' Callum asked.

'Not as far as I know. We all knew Mary-Ellen made the right decision, apart from Veronica, that is. The business was far better off without her. Must have made Christmases a bit difficult though.'

Callum thought Christmas was difficult enough without any further complications. Especially now Grace wasn't there to tease his sisters, charm his parents and make them all laugh.

Nicole looked at the clock on her wall. 'Amanda should be in her office now. She'll be able to fill in any gaps on the financial side.'

'Thanks,' Daisy said, 'and you can't think of anyone else that would wish her harm? Her husband perhaps?'

'Absolutely not. She adored Michael and he worshipped her. They're a lovely couple, both very caring people. Do a massive amount for charities, you know. Both of them do… did.'

'Any particular charity?' Callum asked.

'Sir Michael supports art for children. Mary-Ellen said his knighthood had something to do with making art accessible to underprivileged children.' She looked at Daisy. 'Mary-Ellen supported women's charities and Barnardo's too. They're nice people.'

Nicole reached for her tissue. 'She was genuinely well-liked. She really was. Find out who did this. Please,' she implored.

'We fully intend to,' Callum said softly to her bowed head.

* * *

Daisy tapped on the accountant's door. Amanda Newman was sharp and direct. Decisiveness is often mistaken for efficiency but in her case, there was no mistake. She greeted them with a firm handshake and a scrutinising eye.

'Bad day. I spent this morning organising my mother's hopeless carer and now this.' Her tone was subdued, her voice under control, but her eyebrows spoke a language of their own. She was casually dressed, had gardener's fingernails, and the only jewellery she wore was a gold court wedding band.

Callum ran his thumb over the dent in his ring finger. It felt naked.

'We met at uni. Business and accountancy are happy bedfellows. Been working together ever since.'

'Friends though?' Daisy asked.

'Yes. Jenny is her best friend. They were at school together, she's local and they have lunch regularly. I've never met her myself, and can't recall a surname, sorry.'

'What was Mary-Ellen like?' Callum thought she would give him an honest assessment.

'Mary-Ellen tended to keep herself to herself. Not in a lack of confidence way, but more in keeping her life in separate compartments. And she was choosy about her friends. Selective.'

Callum understood. Mary-Ellen didn't court company just for the contact and wasn't afraid to spend time alone. He felt an unexpected connection to the dead woman.

'What can you tell me about Veronica Parsons?' he asked.

'Apart from the fact that they're chalk and cheese? You know they're sisters? Veronica is the elder of the two.' Amanda sat back in her chair and tapped each of her fingers in turn.

'Mary-Ellen has a strong work ethic, sense of fairness, loyalty and empathy' – she closed her hand into a fist – 'and Veronica, none of the above. Giving her a job was never going to work.'

'Why did Mary-Ellen employ her then?' Daisy asked.

'Sense of obligation and fair-mindedness, I always thought. You know the parents are still alive?'

'We do,' Callum said. 'Why did she feel obligated?'

'Mary-Ellen was very close to her grandparents and visited them in Ireland every summer. In our second year at uni, they died within a month of each other, and Mary-Ellen was devastated. She started her business right after we graduated, and Veronica was adamant that the start-up capital came from their grandparents and that she was entitled to some of it.'

That made some sense of the shouting when Veronica was dismissed.

'Family was important to Mary-Ellen. I think she felt sorry for her sister. Do you know Veronica was the only employee we've ever accepted without qualifications or references? She didn't have a very good work record.'

'Wasn't that a bit of a chancy decision?' Daisy asked.

'Mary-Ellen had it covered. One of the conditions of Veronica's employment was that she should do some training while on the job, and she signed her contract to that effect. Mary-Ellen arranged the training, but Veronica refused to attend. Thought she knew it all already. When she was sacked, she threatened to take us to a tribunal. She never did, of course, because she didn't have a leg to stand on.'

'And was the money left to her by her grandparents?'

Amanda brushed a stray curl back from her face. 'We never discussed where it came from, and it wasn't my business to ask. She never denied Veronica's assumption, so I suppose it could have been true. But it wasn't like Mary-Ellen to be unfair, so then again, maybe it wasn't.'

Amanda knew nothing of expansion plans, but they had never discussed projections, leases, or costings, and Callum acknowledged that those would have been the fundamentals of any preparation.

'I can tell you one thing, but it might have no relevance. I believe Mary-Ellen was preparing to dismiss David.'

'Did she tell you that?' Daisy asked.

'No, not in so many words, but there has been a bit of tension between the two recently. Last week I saw his contract on her desk, and she asked me to check the starting salary for someone in his position. But she didn't actually say he was leaving, and if he was, it could be his decision, I suppose.'

Callum felt a tick of annoyance. David had been economic with the truth.

'What do you think?' he asked.

'My instinct? Dismissal.'

* * *

A search of Mary-Ellen's office supplied nothing of relevance. There were no disgruntled or threatening letters, no suspicious diary entries, and no death threats. Nothing suggested any reason for her murder.

On his walk back to the entrance, Callum compiled a list of facts regarding David. He had not provided an alibi for the time of the murder; he had invented a convenient scenario that suggested he needed Mary-Ellen alive; he had failed to mention the recent tension between him and his boss. Callum deplored dishonesty and unfairness and the man's attitude got right up his nose.

'Check what car he drives, Daisy.' He slid behind the wheel of the Camaro.

'Onto it. I've requested bank and phone records, private and business for Mary-Ellen and Sir Michael. They promised them for tomorrow, with a bit of luck. Maybe.'

'Good.'

Daisy's timescale was optimistic, it was already late in the day. Callum rubbed his hand across the back of his neck and rotated his head through a hundred and eighty degrees to ease the tightness in his shoulder muscles. His neck clicked. This conjured an image of Mary-Ellen's body and his suspicions of how she had died. He dropped his hands onto the steering wheel where his fingers drummed lightly. They were well through day one of the investigation and so far, he had a wealthy, well-connected virtual saint who had been murdered by an unknown assailant devious enough to stage it as an accident. The suspects had either unconfirmed alibis or refused to supply one.

'Chase up Jimmy's alibi with the farmer. Let's see if we can at least eliminate him as a suspect,' he said.

Daisy's mobile buzzed and after answering, she relayed the incoming information to Callum. 'David drives a C-Class Mercedes, silver.'

He looked along the line of staff vehicles and spotted it parked between a red Audi and a green Renault. The cars looked like watercolour pans slotted into a paint box. Heat shimmered over the bodywork, blurring outlines and melding colours. There were no black cars, no Range Rover.

Daisy was still on the phone. 'Hang on, Bird.' She turned to Callum again. 'And Martha said the PM report will be on your desk in the morning. Do you want the nutshell version now?'

Callum nodded.

'Okay, Bird.' She listened for a moment before saying, 'Martha indicated that very early signs of lividity suggest she was sitting on the horse right after she died and there's post-mortem bruising to her lower ribcage and left thigh which confirms what we surmised, that they had put an arm around her waist from behind to hold her on the horse.'

Callum pictured Daisy's hat bouncing against Oliver's leg when he rode away on Moses. That would account for the post-mortem bruising to her thigh. So far, his theory was holding fast with no evidence to discredit it.

'Anything else, Bird?' Daisy put the conversation on speaker, so she could take notes. Bird's voice was clear and close as if he had materialised on the overstocked back seat.

'Bit of gravel in her boot tread, Deedee, spot of blood on her cuff and' – they heard the rustle of paper – 'a thread on the back of her jacket. There's about half a mattress of bloody horse hairs on her clothes but no prints on the tack except for the victim and' – more paper rustled – 'Louise Ashley, who is her groom.'

'Okay. Thanks, Bird. Anything from the car park?'

'SOCO is at Turf Hill now but nothing so far.'

'Thanks, Bird. Chase up Jimmy's alibi with both the farmer and Richard Devereux-Strauss and keep me posted. We're just going to visit Mary-Ellen's parents. They're only three minutes up the road in Station Close.'

'Wilco, and tell Glasgow Jock he's picked a bleedin' good case to start with.'

'Won't be necessary.' Daisy's smile was impish. 'You're on speaker so you just told him yourself.'

'Bollocks.' Bird disconnected the call.

Callum held his smile in check despite Daisy's amusement. He was beginning to appreciate the dynamics of these officers and get a feel for what glued them together as a unit. A flicker of anticipation caught him by surprise. These were people he could work with; he was looking forward to building them into a team.

Chapter Seven

'How long have you lived here?' Callum asked Daisy as he swept along the road.

'All my life. Except for when I went to university.'

That would be the reason that she seemed to know every man and his dog in the vicinity. A tractor towing a trailer came towards them and he slowed, pulling into a field gateway to let it squeeze past. The driver and his collie both looked down into his car and Daisy raised a hand to the driver.

'Steve Lawes. And Snip,' she said, confirming his earlier observation. 'When I came back after uni, my brother Dom was working all over the world and Mum and Dad moved to France for work. I stayed at the house with Felix, so it works really well.'

Callum thought that if Oliver was drinking coffee with Felix, then he must be Daisy's partner as she hadn't named him as family. He was considering asking, when she indicated for him to turn into a close.

'The Goddards are the second one along,' she said and released her seat belt as he drew to a halt outside the property.

The white bungalow was set back from the road behind a broad grass verge. Handles and grab rails sprouted from the walls like giant piercings and a gentle slope ran up to the front door. Meticulously maintained flower beds skirted the front of the building where red and orange blooms flickered up the walls. Callum raised the polished door knocker, and a black ribbon fluttered against his hand. He noted the lawn behind him, so thick and close-cropped that any green keeper's heart would have swelled with pride. A sharp snick and the door swung inwards.

Elizabeth Goddard was slight, but her upright stance gave her an air of brisk efficiency enhanced by the duster in her hand. Her jaw was a rigid line, the skin around her eyes tight. She absently rubbed the door catch with the yellow cloth before slipping it into her apron pocket. He understood that she was keeping herself busy, giving her life purpose, relying on the mundane to prove everything was normal. He knew that her life would never be normal again. No magic switches. No time-machine. No familiar smiling face.

He introduced himself and Daisy. 'I'm sorry for your loss and apologise for our intrusion at such a difficult time.'

There was a reserve about her, the wariness of a traveller arriving in an unknown place. She looked up at him but didn't speak.

'I wonder if you could help me by answering one or two questions? Questions about Mary-Ellen.'

'You're a Scot.' She studied his face with a hopeful expression as if she expected to recognise him. 'A Celt. Kinfolk.'

She extended her hand, and Callum held it for a moment, knobbly, like root ginger in his gentle grasp.

Her skin was pale to the point of translucency, her silver hair constrained in a low bun and in the slanting sunlight, he detected strands of faded copper when she moved her head. They followed her into the sitting room where Robert Goddard had just achieved the difficult exercise of rising to his feet from a low armchair. He was tall, raw-boned, and leaned to one side like a clifftop tree long bullied by weather. Distended maroon veins wormed along the back of his rough hands, but his grip was firm and assured.

Callum introduced them both for Robert's benefit and again offered condolences for their loss. The Goddards stood together with nods that expressed thanks, and eyes that registered pain. They were private people, self-contained, and he respected that.

Over cups of tea and slices of home-baked cake, they told him about Mary-Ellen. An academically able student, she had won a place at Oxford.

'She studied so hard for those exams and put such pressure on herself that I was relieved when she said she was taking a gap year.' The lilt of Elizabeth's Irish accent was just discernible. 'She changed in that last year; always had her head in a book, so serious and quiet. I suppose it was just our little girl growing up, but you worry, don't you? We never went through that with Veronica, our eldest daughter.'

'Did Veronica continue her studies like Mary-Ellen? How did they get along?' Daisy asked as Elizabeth poured tea into the cups.

'They weren't cut from the same cloth.' Robert sat down in his armchair. 'Veronica didn't enjoy school like Mary-Ellen, so she left and got herself a job.' He took the cup and saucer from his wife and placed it on the arm of his chair. 'And they got along just grand until Mary-Ellen came back from university and started G-Smart Solutions. After that, it was never the same.'

Elizabeth pointed to a silver-framed graduation photograph. 'She got a double first, you know. She deserved it, she studied hard and worked in a bar in the evenings. She never had time for boyfriends.'

'But there was a falling out with Veronica?' Callum prompted.

'More like an eruption,' Robert said gruffly. 'Veronica was always full of big ideas, but it was never more than talk. When Mary-Ellen said she was going to start her own business, I don't think Veronica believed she would do it.' His voice was warm with pride. 'But she did.'

'What caused the falling out?' Callum asked.

'My parents both died while Mary-Ellen was at the university,' Elizabeth answered. 'They lived in Kilshannig in Kerry on the west coast of Ireland. My mother died less than a month after my father. She couldn't live without him, you know. It was a difficult spring.' Her eyes drifted away over the grey Atlantic waters to the past. 'They barely left enough to cover their funerals, but Veronica got it into her head that they left money to Mary-Ellen.'

Robert cleared his throat.

'And now this,' Elizabeth said quietly.

Her husband reached across the gap between their chairs to cover her hand with his own and together they shared the memory.

'Veronica?' Daisy prompted after a moment.

'Veronica was convinced that Mary-Ellen had cheated her, and nothing we said would change her mind,' Robert said.

'Could the money have come from your parents, Mr Goddard?'

'The only father I ever knew was Dr Thomas Barnardo, although he was long dead by the time I went to Corris House. Happiest days of my childhood, they were.' He smiled as if he meant it.

'So where did the money come from?' Callum asked them.

'She saved it. She used to waitress at Devereux Manor at the weekends when she was at school, and lots of her friends did too. Then she worked in her gap year and had the bar job when she was away at the university.' Elizabeth's voice petered out and Callum allowed the silence to hover for a moment longer.

'Has their friendship been restored?' he asked after a few moments.

The couple looked at each other before Robert sighed. 'Veronica still has a chip on her shoulder.'

Elizabeth tutted at him but he ignored her.

'Mary-Ellen did her best to heal the rift by giving Veronica a job.' He paused to sip his tea and seemed to swirl his proposed words around his mouth with the liquid before deciding on the right selection. 'Veronica has always been immature, and that hasn't changed. When she worked for Mary-Ellen she didn't pull her weight. Mary-Ellen had to ask her to leave, and that was the wedge that drove them further apart.'

'That's unfortunate,' Daisy said, taking a bite of cake.

'Sergeant, my daughters both have the future they worked for.'

Once again, Elizabeth tutted at him.

'Do you disagree with your husband?' Callum asked.

'Do you have children?' she countered, a flash of fire in her eyes.

Callum shook his head. Without Grace, that possibility had slipped away, like dreams in the dawn light.

'You always want to think the absolute best of your children, Inspector, and sometimes that can be difficult. But to answer your question, no, I don't disagree with Robert. As always, he is being honest and truthful.'

Daisy ate her last mouthful of cake and Callum stood, preparing to end the meeting. He was already formulating questions for Veronica, who lived two streets away.

Then Elizabeth said, 'Of course, Mary-Ellen and Michael were so good to us after that problem with Edward Devereux-Strauss. Nasty man.'

Callum sat back down on his chair, weight forward, elbows resting on his knees. Was there a connection between Edward and the Richard they had met earlier riding with Jimmy Eastwood? 'Edward is what relation to Richard?' he asked.

'He's Richard's father. Mr Edward was old Mr Charles's only son.'

Elizabeth had joined the house staff at Devereux Manor, where she met and married Robert. They had risen through their respective ranks to housekeeper and head gardener, and their positions guaranteed them grace and favour accommodation for life – their reward for a lifetime of loyalty and low pay. They had been retained by Charles and his wife Lillian, but both had died, and Edward and his wife Penelope returned from overseas to run the estate.

'Different kettle of fish to his father, isn't he, Bob?' She glanced at her husband. 'Mr Charles would never have treated his staff like that.'

Robert nodded agreement, and when she continued, her Irish lilt was more pronounced.

'When we retired, Mr Edward had us leave our cottage, and said we had to go down to the old stables where the grooms used to live.' Her eyes sparked with indignation.

Robert's eyes rested on his wife for a moment, then he reached a meerschaum horse-head pipe from the mantelpiece and sucked air through the empty bowl.

'That terrace hadn't been lived in,' he said, 'since they got rid of the carriage horses. That was half a century ago. The track was overgrown, and I couldn't get the car down it. Lizzie and I aren't as sprightly as we used to be, and we need the car.'

Edward had refused to offer better accommodation, and Mary-Ellen and Michael had stepped in and bought them the white bungalow. Shortly after that, Devereux Manor submitted a planning application to demolish the old buildings to erect expensive executive homes. Mary-Ellen succeeded in getting the Georgian site listed status. This resulted in the refusal of planning permission, and an order to retain and upkeep the buildings in their original state.

'It was a lot of work she put in. It was the right result. A victory of manners over money, if you ask me,' Elizabeth declared with a satisfied nod as she opened her front door for them to leave.

* * *

Daisy stopped by the offside wing of the car. 'That must have cost him a shedload of money,' she said. 'Not getting the planning permission, I mean,' she added when Callum didn't immediately respond.

'I know what you mean, Daisy. And yes, architects' fees, consultants, solicitors...'

'Not to mention backhanders, palm-greasers and sweeteners.'

He snapped a glance at her face. Was she trying to warn him about something or was it just the cynicism that developed with the job? Her expression hadn't changed, and she looked him in the eye.

'His biggest loss was not getting planning. Do you know how much houses cost round here now it's a National Park?'

'Not yet.' His eyes skimmed the back seat of his car, and she laughed.

The incident had undoubtedly cost Devereux Manor financially, the most significant loss being the profit on the proposed development itself. He slid into the driver's seat. Could that be a motive for murder? The planning refusal had been a few years ago, so it seemed a bit late for reprisals. But he wouldn't dismiss the possibility. He had seen people killed on the streets of Glasgow for some perceived slight or a handful of change.

'I don't think her parents have quite come to terms with Michael telling them it was murder. They were adamant that nobody would want to hurt her,' Callum said.

'Elizabeth certainly hasn't, has she? "There's no person who didn't like our girl," she said, and she believes that.'

'Well, somebody didn't like her.' He fastened his seat belt.

'And they wouldn't hear a word against Sir Michael. Do you think loyalty, and their gratitude for the house, is blinkering them?'

'It's possible. Keep an open mind, Daisy.' His instinct said no, Sir Michael was not a murderer. But was it instinct, or wishful thinking born out of his respect and empathy for the recently widowed artist?

'I wonder what Veronica's like, sir.'

He pulled away from the verge. 'Five minutes and you'll know.'

Chapter Eight

Fordingbridge was like any other small town. It had rich parts and poor parts, mansions and terraces, private gardens and public playgrounds. All the dwellings in Long Close had manicured front lawns edged by colourful flower-filled borders, and new-looking cars parked outside their double garages. It suggested successful employment with handsome rewards and plentiful time off. Except for one.

Daisy checked her phone. 'That's definitely the correct address.'

This house looked as if it had been dropped onto the wrong street. The windows were opaque with dirt and the blinds drooped like sleep-starved eyelids. Leaks from the sagging gutters had stained the pallid walls with streaks of petrel grey. A pigeon amongst parrots.

The bell had a plaster stuck across it. Callum rapped his knuckles on the front door and watched the dislodged flakes of paint float down into the weeds around the step. Two doors down, a mother strapped her toddler into a BMW, both singing *Old MacDonald*. She smiled at the officers as she moved around to the boot to stow the buggy.

After his second knock, the door was tugged open by a woman. Smoke from her roll-up spiralled across Callum's face, he stepped back, and she exhaled a blast towards Daisy. The detectives exchanged a glance.

'Mrs Veronica Parsons?' Callum said.

'Who wants to know?' She patted her uncombed hair. 'Won the lottery, have I?' Her humourless grunt of laughter propelled a smell of beer towards Callum. Veronica was not what he had expected after conversations with her courteous parents or his glimpse into Mary-Ellen's ordered life. She shared facial characteristics with Mary-Ellen that marked them as siblings, but that was where the similarities ended. Veronica wore purple jeggings peppered grey with ash, crisp-edged holes dotting one knee, and her feet were bare if you discounted the black nail polish.

He introduced himself and Daisy, and Veronica's hand fell away from the door catch.

'I suppose you want to come in.'

The BMW drove past, and the girl gave a neighbourly wave. 'Arsehole,' Veronica muttered.

They followed her into the sitting room where she suffocated her cigarette in an already overflowing ashtray. Callum caught her sleight of foot as she nudged a beer can around the side of the chair and out of sight. She dropped onto the sofa and tucked her bare feet up underneath her. Wise, considering the state of the once-fawn carpet. She didn't ask them to sit, which saved Callum from having to refuse.

The bear-like man on the sofa pressed the remote, and the shouts from the TV reality show were replaced by the hum of an appliance and the steady plash-plash of a dripping tap, through the open kitchen door. The air smelt damp and mousey, reminding Callum of his grandfather's woodshed. It seemed housework wasn't their forte.

'If you're here about Miss Goody-Two-Shoes falling off her horse, Mum's already told me.' Veronica lounged back against the beige cushions, stretching her arms wide. 'Karma, isn't it? You get what you deserve in this life, I always say.'

Callum glanced around at the dust-covered surfaces, and the ironing board submerged beneath piles of crumpled clothes. The irony of her own comment seemed to be lost on Veronica.

'You think she deserved to die?' he asked.

'She was a tight-fisted cow. That's all I'm saying.'

Her mouth pinched into a knot as if to seal it and stop further words from escaping. Callum suspected it would be a short-term solution.

'We understand she did a lot for charity,' Daisy said.

'Charity should begin at home. Somebody needed to tell Mary-Ellen that.' Veronica folded her arms defensively.

'Indeed. And did you tell her?'

'People were talking. Her swanking around in all her finery and us…' She swept her arm around the cramped room, and the smell of cooked fat floated behind it.

'When did you last see your sister?' Callum cleared his throat, needing to ease the tension from his voice.

'Sunday. She goes round to the olds' every Sunday.' Veronica examined her nails. 'I usually pop in after school with Madison and Isabella, because Mum likes to give them pocket money.' She scrubbed a finger over her eyebrow exposing the wound of a past piercing, a pewter dot that matched those in her lip and nose.

'So, why on Sunday this week?' He watched her face.

Veronica glanced questioningly at the couch-dweller who shrugged.

'If you must know, Colin' – she flicked her head sideways – 'has lost his job. It's another unfair dismissal, obviously, and we'll be taking them to a tribunal and obviously we'll be getting compensation.'

Something was becoming obvious, and it had nothing to do with compensation or tribunals.

Veronica reached for a dented tin, flipped the lid and picked out an untidy roll-up. The plastic lighter flared to life, and she squinted to avoid the smoke. The tip glowed red as she filled her lungs, cooled to grey, then an acrid cloud billowed from the corner of her mouth. Callum was envious of the camel's ability to close its nostrils.

'And I asked her for some money, if you must know.'

Daisy's mouth tightened and he suspected her thoughts were similar to his own.

Veronica lifted her chin. 'She's got loads of it. And it's not for me, you understand? It's for Maddie and Izzy.'

He was beginning to understand very well.

'But can you believe it? She said no. She actually said no this time, didn't she, Col?' She hugged her arms around her raised knees, the glowing cigarette inches from the cushion. 'She's never said no before.' Indignation crept into her voice. 'And she owes me.'

'What does she owe you?' asked Callum.

'She stole my money to start her poncey business.'

'That's not what your parents say.'

She exhaled noisily, the smoky cloud hovering around her head. 'Course they don't. She was always their favourite. Mary-Ellen this, and Mary-Ellen that. Mary-Ellen with her double-bloody-first and matching halo.'

'And that was the last time you saw her?'

Veronica nodded. 'I told her I was never going to speak to her again after she said no.' Then her anger winnowed away, and her voice diminished to a whisper. 'Oh my God.' She looked across to Colin. 'What are we going to do now, Col?' She sniffed and wiped her nose across her forearm with a swift jerk.

Colin shrugged and rested joined hands across his roll of stomachs. Callum was reminded of Buddha, minus the benevolent smile. The corners of Veronica's mouth pulled down and Callum wondered if she was reflecting on karma.

'We'll see ourselves out,' he said.

The door slammed closed behind them, and Callum inhaled deeply. Daisy walked along the path, eyes focused on the ground, head moving slowly from side to side, as if she was searching for something among the volunteer weeds. He suspected that she shared his disbelief. Then the door crashed open again. They halted their retreat and Daisy looked at Callum when Veronica called urgently.

'Inspector. What does her will say? Do I get my money now?'

Neither of them replied. The pulse ticked in Callum's cheek and Daisy muttered something under her breath that it was probably best he didn't quite hear.

* * *

When the chatter in the office went suddenly quiet, Callum looked up to see a short dapper officer in full dress uniform standing in the doorway. Light flashed from the three pips on his silver-emblazoned jacket.

'Shit. It's Bell-end Bellman got up like a bleedin' Christmas tree,' Bird muttered and retreated to his desk.

'Can I help you, sir?' Callum tucked his long hair behind his left ear exposing his silver earring. He saw the moue of reproval.

'I expected you to have the courtesy to come and see me in my office on your first day, Detective Inspector MacLean.'

'Indeed, sir. In the early stages of a murder investigation, time is of the essence. We are preparing to round up today's findings.' He heard muted preparations, and knew they were all listening to the exchange. Callum ran his eye over the pressed uniform as DCI Bellman glanced at his watch. The man had 'urgency' written all over him and was anxious to be gone.

'Do you have time to join us, sir?'

'Sadly not, Inspector. I am on my way to a civic reception.' Bellman jounced on the balls of his feet. 'A strong constabulary presence is essential at these gatherings.' He raised his chin, and stuck his chest forward, like a cock grouse in the mating season. All that was missing was the crescendo of drumming from his tiny feet.

'That's a pity, sir.' Callum caught the brief eye contact between Daisy and Bird and heard someone in the office clear their throat.

'I expect results, MacLean. Results. Now I have a car waiting. Carry on.'

Bellman pivoted on the heel of his mirror-polished shoe, tugged down the rear hem of his jacket and marched through the doorway. His exit was followed by the draught of exhalation, many pairs of eyes, and the narrowed gaze of the Scotsman.

Callum's results were incontestable, but his methods had been considered questionable in some quarters, and he had a kaleidoscopic past with senior officers. Niceties and kowtowing were low-priority hindrances. His sole objective was to catch criminals. He turned towards the display board, reminding himself that he lacked both the mindset and inclination to crawl up people's arses. Time, patience, and diligence provided answers. He stared at the empty doorway.

The room bustled back to life and Legs went over to Daisy.

'Five minutes, Deedee hun.'

Bird had taken personal control of the marker pen and stood next to the board, ready to complete the update. He scored a line through Fletcher Edmunds. David Fellowes stared silently at them. A red question mark hovered over the head of Jimmy Eastwood.

'Ben Martin, the farmer with the colts, confirmed the time Jimmy left his place, 0720 hours, and he's sure because the postman had him sign for a parcel for his missus. I confirmed it with Royal Mail.' Bird put a tick against the text. 'And Legs spoke to Richard Devereux-Strauss on the phone. Jimmy got the times wrong. They met at ten to eight, at least fifteen minutes earlier than Jimmy thought. That means that if the victim—'

'Use her name.' Callum wanted the team to identify with her. Using her name helped them see her as a person.

'Sorry, guv. That means that Mary-Ellen left home at seven thirty, and twenty minutes later, Jimmy was riding with Richard, so he didn't have time to kill her. His bleedin' alibis are good.'

'Then why the question mark?' Callum asked.

'Don't know, but something's bugging me about him.' Bird scratched his spiky hair and then made to erase the question mark, but Callum stopped him.

'Leave it. If something doesn't feel right, then the chances are it isn't right, so let it stand for now.'

'You just want to hang it on an ex-squaddie,' Cookie said smirking at Bird.

'Bollocks,' Bird said, 'I want to hang it on the bastard who did it, and I think it's Jimmy.'

A verbal debate ensued which stopped as swiftly as it had started when the smell of food preceded Legs through the door.

'Pizza,' she announced to the room.

Moisture seeped into Callum's mouth, and he realised how hungry he was. Daisy thrust a serviette and a slice of pizza at him, and they all stood around the board chewing like cudding bovines. Cookie closed his eyes and made exaggerated 'mmm' noises.

'Last time I ring up for food for you, Wonder Boy, unless you shut up,' Legs threatened.

Cookie's eyes flew open. 'Oh, God. Sorry, Legs, I forgot. When you were out this morning, some old man called at the front desk for you, so I went down and asked if I could help, which I couldn't cos he wanted to see you. He said to tell you he would come back tomorrow.'

'Who was it?'

'A Reginald Holder from Forest Road, Hale.'

Daisy paused mid-bite. 'Did he have a cake with him?'

Cookie shook his head, his brow furrowed as he looked from Legs to Daisy.

'Never mind. Maybe next time,' Daisy said wiping a string of melted cheese from her chin and throwing her crumpled serviette into the empty box.

'Who's Reginald Holder?' Callum asked.

'Our Reg is a great admirer of Legs. She sorted something out for him, and since then he has adopted her as his private police force,' Daisy said.

'He's just a little old man, guv, who brings me information that could help in the fight against local crime,' Legs said, then added defensively, 'It's always good to have the public on our side.'

'Agreed,' Callum said.

'And have you solved any crimes yet?' Bird asked, brushing crumbs from the front of his shirt. 'Like money laundering perhaps?'

'Reg wasn't to know the machine was shredding paper not printing it.' Legs stood to her full height, arms folded, and faced a chuckling Bird eyeball to eyeball. 'One of these days he'll bring us something useful...'

'And then' – Bird chuckled, turning away – 'I'll eat my hat.'

Callum followed Bird into the fishbowl as he thought of his office, where Bird began emptying drawers and dropping the contents of DI Denton's reign into a bin liner.

After the second empty vodka bottle, Callum looked at Bird, and said, 'You don't seem surprised by the bottles.'

'I'd be more surprised if they had anything in them. He's supposed to be on medical leave, but we all know he won't be back.'

Callum began to appreciate that the tight cohesion he had witnessed, was their way of keeping a rudderless ship afloat, and heading in the right direction.

'Was DCI Bellman aware of this?'

'They belong to the same golf club.' And then a thought occurred to him. 'Do you play golf, sir?'

'No. I agree with Mark Twain, it spoils a good walk.'

Bird gave a puff of laughter. 'Nineteenth hole always sounds the best bit to me.' He emptied the final drawer of personal items and went back into the main office.

Callum looked at the white envelope on the edge of his desk with "DI Denton" written across the front in rounded black script. He picked it up and turned it over, but the back was blank. He saw a look pass between Legs and Daisy. Legs followed his actions as he tapped the envelope against his thumb before returning it to his desk. It could wait.

Early in his career, Callum had developed a habit of keeping personal notes of his cases for his own reference. The action of committing words to paper helped him clarify and order the information. Now, he made notes of his conversation with Sir Michael, the unopened solicitor's letter, the main points of his chat with Susan Eastwood, with the staff at G-Smart Solutions, and Mary-Ellen's parents and Veronica. Then he listed the issues he needed to address in the morning and slipped the paper into his desk drawer.

'Guv.' Bird returned to the fishbowl and cleared his throat. 'Sorry about that Glasgow Jock crack earlier.'

'What crack? I seem to be a little hard of hearing in my right ear today – difference in altitude, I expect, but it won't last long.' He levelled a look at Bird to emphasise his point.

'Don't you mean left ear, guv?' The smile in Bird's voice extended to his face, giving him a clown-like appearance with his short-tufted hair and large white teeth.

'Nah, Bird. He means the right ear. His car's a leftie.' Daisy was leaning against the door jamb, arms folded, seemingly enjoying the exchange.

'I always said Scots are a load of bleedin' foreigners,' Bird said in a stage whisper to Daisy. 'This proves it. They even drive on the wrong side of the road.' He chuckled as he brushed past Daisy and went back to the board.

Callum sat back in his chair and Daisy stood facing him. She placed her hands on the front of his desk and leaned towards him.

'Legs is a good officer.' Her voice was low and quiet. 'I would be very sorry to lose her from the team.'

He looked up at her in surprise and her eyes flicked to the white envelope and then back to him. The dynamics in this team were unusual and intrigued him. It was as if they had been abandoned on an uninhabited island and had evolved into a balanced, self-governing entity. They supported each other and deferred to Daisy for guidance, like a hive of bees with a queen. It was the first team he had worked with that didn't appear to have a sub-agenda, with back-stabbing knives honed and ready for use. He was also aware that he was an intruder. And he knew what a hive of bees could do to an intruder if they felt threatened.

He acknowledged her comment with the briefest dip of his head before moving out into the main office to address the team. The envelope remained on the desk, unopened.

'Right, people. It's late, so let's wind it up for today,' Callum said. 'In the morning, Cookie, get a list of local owners of black Range Rovers, and see if we can identify the drive-by. Chase up information from Turf Hill car park and get an update from the morning dog walkers. Someone must have seen something.'

'Hunky-doodley, guv.' Cookie gave Callum a salute.

'Legs and Bird, bring in David Fellowes for an interview. He's lied to us; he hasn't provided an alibi and I want to know where he was this morning. He's hiding something and wasting our time. Perhaps sitting in an interview room with you two leaning on him will focus his mind so we can eliminate him. Or not.'

'Wilco,' Bird said.

'Daisy and I will drop in on Sir Michael, have a word about his alibi, and the relevance, if any, of that letter from his solicitor. Thanks for staying to this hour, and sorry it is so late. Good work, people.'

Chapter Nine

They drove alongside Hale village green. The approach to Daisy's house was over yet another cattle grid, and Callum held his breath as he rattled across it. The single track ran between post and rail fences, down into a dip with a widened passing place, and back up the other slope. A thatched roof pushed up through the foliage to his left and he slowed, approaching the wicket gate.

Daisy flexed her fingers to indicate that he should drive on. 'That's where Oli and his mum live. His dad died last year.'

Light-sapping conifers plunged them into twilight, and the crackling of dry needles beneath his tyres echoed eerily in the pine-scented coolness. It was like passing into another world. A downward slope guided them into a clearing and there, backed by tall pines and fronted by lawns, was a timber house. The middle section was two storeys, with long single-storey extensions on both sides, beneath a shingle roof. The setting sun sparkled gold on the upstairs windows and transformed the whole building into a warm, cinnamon creature, arms thrown wide for a welcoming hug.

Callum rolled to a halt and waited for Daisy to climb out, but she showed no sign of moving.

'Is this it?' he asked.

'Yes, sir. Thanks for the lift. Have you organised anywhere to stay yet?'

Callum shook his head and looked at his watch as Daisy opened the car door but still didn't get out.

'You might have left it a bit late. There are four guest bedrooms in the west wing, and you're welcome to one of those until you have time to find somewhere else, unless you've got a tent in there?' she said, jerking her head towards the rear seats.

'The west wing?' he asked, stalling while he considered her offer.

Her laugh echoed around the car and out into the dew-heavy air, startling a pigeon that dived out of a fir tree and soared away into the darkness.

'My brother, Dominic, and I called them the east and west wings when we were little. I live in the middle bit with Felix and when my parents come home, they have the east wing. They live in France.'

There were no lights on in the house, so Felix was evidently not at home.

'And your brother?' he asked, acknowledging that his accommodation options were limited.

'Dom is my twin and at this moment he's in Alaska. When he's home, he stays in the middle bit with me and Felix.' She flicked a questioning look at him. 'I'll throw in pasta and salad for supper, and something for breakfast.'

Despite being loath to impose himself on people, and preferring his own company, he was bone-weary and didn't have a tent.

'That would be very welcome, Daisy, if it's not a trouble. Thank you.'

She got out of the car. 'Come and meet Felix, he keeps an eye on the place when I'm not here. Then I'll show you to your room.'

He got out and stretched his arms wide, inhaling the scent of sun-warmed soil and pine, and then blossom. Daisy called 'Felix' and a pony-sized dog bounded out of the back of a parked Navara and circled round behind Callum, stopping head down with a watchful eye. Not the Felix he had envisioned.

'Friend,' Daisy said.

Felix sat in front of Callum and raised one large white paw expecting to shake hands, and he obliged. She laughed and they followed the dog into the kitchen where he sat by his empty bowl.

The room was high-ceilinged with yellow walls and a stone floor. A central island doubled as a breakfast bar with stools along one edge and a bowl of fruit in the middle. The business end of the kitchen comprised soft-blue units and silver appliances that stretched across the back wall. The front wall was floor-to-ceiling glass, that was turned into a mirror by the enclosing darkness. It reflected the weariness of their movements after the long day.

'This way,' Daisy said, opening a door at the rear of the room.

A corridor ran along the back of the building, connecting all the segments. Framed black-and-white photographs of stark landscapes were spaced along one wall, while the other was punctuated by four doors. Opening one of these, Daisy preceded him into a bedroom and moved to one side to let him enter.

'Bathroom through there.' She pointed at an internal door. 'If there's anything you need, let me know. Supper in twenty.' She went back into the corridor, closing the door behind her.

Like the kitchen, the front wall of this room was glass, the sliding doors opening onto a shared veranda. This was dotted with tables and chairs positioned to enjoy the views across the garden and down the valley. Callum slid open the door and went out onto the decking. The far ground of her garden dropped sharply to a distant moon-silvered river fronted by treetops that formed an ocean of greens and shadowy greys. It was like being set adrift in a wooden barge on an eternal bosky abundance.

He remembered his grandfather shaking his head, and muttering in Gaelic, 'Away in yer *heid*, *ogha*, is it?' when as a ten-year-old Callum had journeyed into the world of his imagination. He smiled at the memory and was filled with warmth as he walked across the damp grass to fetch his overnight bag from his car. Felix materialised from the gloaming, escorted him back to his room, then sprawled on the veranda, chestnut head on his paws. Callum went to shower and the dog was still waiting when he returned.

Enveloped by the silence, Callum sat at the teak table and took the spiral-bound book from his jacket pocket. By the time he had opened it and found his pencil, he was fine-tuned to the clicking of the dog's toenails on the boards, the soft fluttering of birds settling in trees, and the rustle of night creatures in the bushes. There were no screaming sirens, swearing drunks, or pulsating bass beats blanketed beneath a perpetual drone of traffic. But it was not as quiet as he had first thought. This was a different kind of noise; different sorts of lives preparing for sleep and different hunters in the dark.

He turned to a new page in his sketchbook, wrote the date at the top, and soon, light pencil lines formed an image of the mixed textures of the Eastwoods' patchwork cottage. The orchard swept into life beside it, along with the wind-tugged washing, and the wisp of smoke that curled across the sky and then disappeared. As the graphite detail covered more of his paper, the years melted away until he was once more a wee boy, on his first summer break, alone with his grandparents on Seil Island on the west coast of Scotland.

He had been a shy lad who didn't say much but with three older, bossy sisters, he never really needed to. Grandpa didn't say much either, as his grandma spoke enough for all of them. On that first night, the old man had given him a small book and a pencil for him to do drawings of what he had seen during the day. A pictorial diary. It was far more inviting than struggling to spell words to write things down.

In the evenings, when his grandma was out at her neighbours', or singing as she bustled about in the kitchen, he and Grandpa would sit in companionable silence, on either side of the peat fire, and draw the things they remembered from their day. It was a habit that had stayed with him and, wherever he was, he always found a few minutes to add a picture to his book.

He studied his sketch, then worked in some darker marks below the gutter, windowsills and lintels, and added shading to the gable end of the cottage to show the light source. Felix sat up and rested his chin on Callum's knee.

He ran a gentle hand up the valley between the toffee eyes and over the top of his head, feeling the silky hair slide over the hard bone beneath. 'Is this what you're wanting?'

Felix made soft noises in his throat and thumped his tail against the decking. Callum sketched the dog into the foreground of his picture and then drew Jimmy Eastwood standing at his front door to give a sense of scale.

'That's good, sir.'

Daisy startled him with her stealthy approach. He flipped closed his book but not before she had spotted her dog in the drawing.

'Felix, you're an artist's model,' she said and stooped to pat him. 'Supper's ready.' She disappeared into the gloom with the dog padding along in her wake.

He pocketed the book and followed them, pausing only to watch some flittering bats dance through the air above his head with such aerodynamic agility that they never once collided with one another.

They didn't linger over supper. Daisy went to check on her horse, he finished his coffee and tidied the crockery into the dishwasher. The kitchen was a homely room. A horsey magazine on the island was open at an article on stallion bloodlines, and by the door, riding boots shed dried mud onto the floor.

A reminder to "buy dog wormer" was secured by a magnet to the fridge door, alongside a postcard featuring Alaskan sledge dogs, and a shopping list. It gave him a flavour of Daisy, her interests, and her day-to-day life. It was personal, unlike Mary-Ellen's cream bedroom. His mind drifted to the flat he had left behind in North Kelvinside. In the last three years, it had changed from an untidy, warm, Grace-filled sanctuary to a cold and tidy cell.

Swamped by tiredness, he walked back along the veranda to his room, calling a 'goodnight' to Daisy, who was walking back towards the house. The sky was immense, never-ending and the quietness was somehow liberating. The Glasgow sky had been a jigsaw of small starless fragments, snatches only visible between blocks of lighted buildings. Here, he might have been the last being on the planet as he walked along the boards, mulling over the events of the day. One thing jarred. Why did they call the open heathland of the New Forest a forest when there didn't seem to be many trees? At least not that he had seen so far. He smiled to himself, confident that Daisy would have a lengthy and tortuous justification if he was brave enough to ask.

He left the curtains open and settled his head on the pillow. 'Goodnight, Gracie,' he said, looking out into the dark. First, a pinprick of sparkle appeared, then beaded chains, and finally a shimmering tapestry of silver, woven intricately into the fabric of the night sky.

Chapter Ten

Daisy's Navara was better suited to the local terrain than his Camaro, and Callum had no objection to being a passenger. It allowed him to take in his alien surroundings, so very different from what he was used to. Her driving was confident and assertive, and she adhered to the speed limit. Despite her ongoing commentary, she kept her hands on the wheel, and her eyes focused on the ashy tarmac. Relaxing back against his seat, he relinquished his hold on the passenger grip and saw the corner of her mouth curve upwards. He turned away to look out of the window.

Hale was a fat, pear drop of grass, encircled by a narrow loop of road. One long side was bordered by agricultural hedging, but the remainder was dotted with thatched cottages, fronted by a grassy verge. Hale Primary School was one of these, an overgrown cottage with a bell canopy on the roof. It sat behind a chestnut paling fence that set it apart from its neighbours. Across the road, on the green, a bay mare grazed the short turf while her stick-legged colt suckled, head thrust up under her belly. Her tail flailed like a metronome at the swarming flies. It would take a while to adjust to ponies roaming free.

A splash of surprisingly lush turf in the centre of the green was surrounded by ancient metal railings.

'That's the cricket wicket,' Daisy said as they drove past.

It was mown tight, like his home ground at the Accies'. The hallowed turf was out of bounds, protected from ponies' hooves and infant feet by the removable fencing.

Opposite the school, a group of small girls wearing blue-and-white gingham dresses took turns to jump over a swinging rope twirled by two of their number. They chanted a rhyme, punctuated by the thump of the rope on the bruised grass, but Callum couldn't hear their words over the burr of the engine.

Daisy raised a hand to the woman outside the school gates watching the children.

'Mrs Redman, head teacher,' she said.

Daisy slowed to a gentle halt and lowered Callum's window. Eight pink fingers curled over the opening and the upper part of a child's face rose into view.

'Hello, Auntie Daisy.'

'Hello, Annie Eastwood. How are you today?'

Callum looked down at the wide forehead and peppered nose. This must be one of Jimmy's children. She climbed up onto the running board and the whole of her face appeared. The girl had her mother's eyes, brown and trusting, and they scrutinised Callum.

'I'm sad,' she said after a moment. 'And Daddy's sad. And I've got a wobbly tooth. Look.' She opened her mouth and wiggled a crinkly-edged lower incisor. 'It doesn't hurt though.'

'That's good. Why are you sad?' Daisy asked.

'Cos Mummy said we've got to find new homes for Marmalade's kittens, and I love them all.' Her bottom lip stuck out and showed the shiny flesh inside her mouth.

Callum pressed himself back against the seat and looked at Daisy. Tears would be her department. He turned back swiftly in response to Annie's exaggerated sigh.

'Life goes on I s'pose.' Annie fixed her eyes on Callum's face. 'Why have you got girls' hair?'

He looked at Daisy, who suppressed a laugh and the flesh at the sides of her eyes crinkled into folds. 'It's your hair, sir. Don't look at me,' she said.

Callum studied her for a moment before turning back to Annie, tucking his hair behind his ear and lowering his head conspiratorially.

'It keeps my ears warm in the winter, Annie.'

She flashed him her wobbly smile. 'I thought that. Same as me. Bye-se-bye.' And she jumped down onto the grass and skipped back to her friends.

Daisy chuckled as the Navara pulled smoothly away. 'Well handled, sir.'

Beyond the girls in the middle of the green, two boys in grey shorts played with a model aircraft. One stood, arm bent back like a bowler, and launched the craft into the breeze. It lifted and surged upwards, and they darted after it. Then, nose high, it stalled, spiralled into a dive, and crashed back to earth. Flotsam was strewn across the cricket wicket and the boys clambered over the railings to gather the shattered pieces.

'If you've finished socialising,' he said, 'perhaps we can get on with this visit to Sir Michael and find out where he was yesterday morning.'

'Onto it.' Daisy accelerated smoothly away.

He rested his arm along the sill and the breeze swirled in through the open window and plucked at his long hair. The blue sky was streaked with fine strands of high cirrus, promising another hot day. Dew pearls among the harebells turned into sparkling rainbows as their blue bonnets curtsied and bowed as they passed. Callum's assessment of the exact palette needed to replicate the flowers was interrupted by Daisy's phone. From the speaker, they heard the agitated voice of Amelia Roberts.

'I don't know what to do, Sergeant. Sir Michael has gone.'

'Hello, Amelia. When you say gone, what do you mean exactly?' Daisy's tone was low and reassuring.

Amelia's voice trembled like an anguished heroine in the opening bars of an aria. 'Gone. Disappeared.' Her words rose chromatically. 'When I came down this morning the front door was open, and his car's gone.' Her sob echoed like percussion in an empty auditorium. 'I'm so sorry. I said I'd look after him.'

'Don't worry. We're on our way to you now.' Daisy changed down a gear.

Callum tugged at his left earlobe. 'Don't touch anything, Mrs Roberts,' he added before Daisy ended the call.

'Daisy, put out a locate-and-stop for his vehicle. How close are we to Southampton and Bournemouth Airports?'

'Close enough. And there are docks at Southampton, and a ferry port at Poole.'

She ignored the speed limit and brushed through the narrow lanes and over the cattle grid to Millers Farm.

Amelia stood in the open doorway twisting her apron between her fingers.

'I went to his study to ask him what he wanted to eat but he wasn't there. I ran up to his bedroom, and then his studio, but he wasn't there either.'

'What time was this?' Callum asked.

'Just after eight. I couldn't find him anywhere. And then I realised the front door was not locked and his car was gone.'

'And you haven't touched anything?' Callum moved past her into the hall.

'No. But he didn't have any breakfast and when he goes out, he always leaves me a note.' She was grounding herself with the mundane because she was facing unexpected territory.

'Let's start with a look at his study, please, Mrs Roberts.'

They followed her across the hall to a closed oak door that Callum had noticed yesterday, partially concealed beneath the overhanging gallery. Amelia stood to one side to let them enter. It was a warm room in a palette of reds and browns, Van Dyke bookcases, a red leather chair, and worn sepia curtains. A patterned rug with an ochre border covered the centre of the oak floor. The room smelled of aged fabric with a touch of lavender polish lingering in the air.

Half a dozen hardback books formed an unsteady tower on the desk with a passport and wallet on top of them. A lead crystal glass beside the books had a splash of amber liquid in it. Callum leaned forward and sniffed the contents. Whisky. The passport and wallet belonged to Sir Michael, the latter containing cash, and a selection of credit cards. Callum searched for a note, examining the books for any loose piece of paper.

'What are you looking for?' Amelia asked from the doorway.

Callum didn't respond. Telling her he was looking for a handwritten suicide note would not have helped her rising level of agitation. Small mercies were sometimes easy to overlook.

'How was he yesterday, after we left?' he asked.

Sir Michael had refused the family liaison officer that they had offered, but that didn't guarantee that he was coping.

Amelia hesitated, transferred her weight from one foot to the other, and Callum knew she was weighing up the merits of being disloyal to her employer in favour of the truth.

'He was very upset. When I took him his cup of tea, I could tell he had been weeping, poor man. Afterwards, he went up to his studio and played Tchaikovsky, very loudly. It was still playing when I went to bed' – she resumed her apron-wringing – 'and I had to put in earplugs to get to sleep, so I don't know when it stopped, and I didn't hear him leave. I'm so sorry.'

'No need to apologise. It was the sensible thing to do.'

According to Amelia, nothing else in the office was out of place, it was just the way Sir Michael would have wanted it. There were no drawers left half open, nothing in the waste bin, no discarded papers, or folders. The last incoming call on the phone had been the morning before, which Callum thought unusual for the high-profile artist.

'That's his private line,' Amelia said. 'Anything general comes through the main house phone, which I answer for them. I tell him who has called, and he decides if he should call back. Neither he nor Mary-Ellen ever answer the house phone.'

That explained how she knew about Jimmy Eastwood. He had not thought she was the type to kneel and listen at keyholes.

'Do you know if he was contacted on his mobile?' Daisy asked.

'No, dear. But I can tell you that he never took his phone into the studio when he was painting. He said it destroyed his concentration.'

If he had received a call that resulted in his leaving, it would have been late, after Amelia had gone to bed and he had finished painting. What other reason could there be for him to leave so unexpectedly without taking his wallet with him, unless he was responsible for his wife's death?

Sir Michael's bedroom was next to Mary-Ellen's. The burgundy bed cover was smooth and undisturbed, except for the ruckled indentation where someone had sat to look in the bedside drawer. Callum leaned down and eased open the top drawer. It slid out easily and he reached inside to remove a white envelope. It was the one he had noted yesterday morning on the silver tray in the hall, and it had been opened. Folded inside was a single sheet of paper, informing Sir Michael that his recently amended will was now ready for his signature. It asked him to make an appointment at his solicitor's office in Southampton. Callum acquainted Amelia with the contents.

'Do you know,' she said, 'I have just realised how very little I know about them even though I've been here such a long time.'

'Go on,' he prompted. What she didn't know might have as much significance as what she did.

'Well, I don't know anything about their finances; their pasts before they married. I know it was a first marriage for both of them. Mary-Ellen runs her own company and Sir Michael paints portraits for people all over the world. I know where they go on holiday, but not much more than that. They are very private people. They like each other's company. Some evenings they would just sit together in the drawing room reading.'

'Did they do much entertaining?' Daisy asked.

'Not really. Practically never. It just wasn't them.'

Callum moved across the room to look out of the window down onto the forecourt. Just because they kept a quiet house didn't mean they never went to brash parties, or brothels, but he had to agree that it felt out of character from what he knew of them so far.

'We can only see what people intend us to see, Amelia.' Unless, he thought, you're a detective, constantly sifting through the detritus of people's lives, peering in dark corners and prising secrets from skeletons. You find out what people are really like from the things they don't want you to know.

Sir Michael's wardrobes were not as tidy as his wife's. His predominantly blue and grey clothes were in no specific order, and his shoes were in heaps, rather than pairs, on the wardrobe floor. Callum left the doors open and moved across to join Daisy. She was pulling open the half-moon handles of the desk drawers, and they rattled against the back plates as loudly as cymbals.

'Laptop and phone, sir.' She handed the mobile to Callum.

It wasn't locked and registered just one recent outgoing call, shortly after they had left him yesterday morning. The computer needed a password before it would relinquish any secrets. Someone at the station would sort that out.

In the bathroom, the shower cubicle was cold, the mirror steam-free and his toothbrush dry. Paint-stained clothes were heaped on top of the laundry basket and Callum could smell turps topped with a hint of something sweet and soapy. Coconut? He looked at the container in the shower. Coconut. There was a razor on the sink and toiletries crowded together on a shelf. Had he planned to leave taking nothing with him, or had he been forced to leave against his will?

'Inspector?' Amelia was still standing in the doorway but looking into the wardrobe. 'His leather overnight bag is still here.' She pointed to a brown Gladstone on the top shelf.

'Does he always take that bag when he goes away?'

'It's his favourite. Mary-Ellen gave it to him. He nearly always takes it.'

'Does he often go away on his own?' Daisy asked.

'Sometimes, if he goes to see a client or if Mary-Ellen has a charity function without him, then he might go away for the night.'

Callum exchanged a glance with Daisy. He worried the thought around his head and kept arriving at the same conclusion. Sir Michael would not be the first man to have a woman set up in a nice little flat somewhere, with no need to take personal items, because he had a second set already there. So where would they find her?

'Do you know where he goes?' Daisy asked.

Amelia slowly shook her head. 'Sorry, no, dear.'

She had a low sense of curiosity. Perhaps that was why she had got the job of housekeeper in the first place.

Daisy looked questioningly at Callum who shook his head, choosing to leave the matter there.

'Can we take a look at his studio now, please, Mrs Roberts?'

The studio was at the back of the house and had views of the garden. It was a long room with windows down one side and the walls, once white, were now flecked with rainbow splatter. Callum envied Sir Michael this dedicated space for expression without the need to curtail, confine or conceal. Racks of canvases were stacked on the floor across the width of the back wall in a haphazard manner. Some, perhaps those he was still working on, were mounted on easels, lit by the bright morning sun.

A workbench ran below the windows. Brushes were crammed into jugs dotted along the surface, bristles sprouting upwards like plants seeking the light. Containers of muddy liquid and open tubes of paint were surrounded by colour-stained rags and worm-covered palettes. Callum could taste notes of linseed, paint and turpentine on his tongue, bitter and acetous.

Nothing was out of place in the disorder except for two brushes that had been thrown to the floor with such force that a flare of yellow and a slash of red reached out across the peppered wood towards the windows.

He moved to view the canvas raised on the easel. It was the beginning of a head-and-shoulders portrait of Mary-Ellen. He recognised the colours, royal purple, crimson, and cadmium yellow. It was raw, her face vulnerable, eyes deep mines of emotion above hollowed cheeks. He shivered. It was stark and painful, and he felt as if he was trespassing on another man's soul. He took a step back to get a better perspective of the painting.

The brushstrokes were aggressive and angry, the image stripped back, naked, and brimming with emotion. It was a powerful statement. Was it some sort of confession or justification? Grief or guilt? Perhaps the absence of a note was voided by the painting itself. He took a photograph of the still-wet canvas.

'That's harsh,' Daisy murmured, coming to stand beside him. 'Hostile even. Her face reminds me of that screaming figure on the bridge. I thought you said he loved her.'

'Edvard Munch, *The Scream*. And Sir Michael loved Mary-Ellen so much that he is in deep pain, Daisy.'

She looked at it again, and he could tell that she didn't believe him. She went out onto the landing to join Amelia. Callum swept his gaze around the room one last time where it was arrested, once more, by the painting. He was touched by the depth, the emotion, the pain. He followed the women, closing the door softly behind him.

* * *

'Thoughts?' Callum asked as Daisy carefully steered her nearside wheels up onto the verge to pass two New Forest ponies standing side by side across the middle of the road. They faced in opposite directions, the swishing tail of one providing a fly swatter for the head of the other.

'I believe Amelia is telling us all she knows, and that she has no idea where he is. Sir Michael is either running away because he is guilty, or because he knows someone else is guilty of killing his wife and he might be next.' She raised a hand in thanks as a car towing a caravan slowed to let her pass. 'Holidaymakers. Or perhaps he's running towards something.' She paused to order her words. 'Perhaps he had her killed and now he's running towards a new life with a hidden mistress.'

She wasn't short on theories.

'Without his passport, or bank cards, or phone?'

'Perhaps he doesn't need them. He's already set up a new identity for himself. He can paint anywhere. Perhaps they have already left the country,' she said, warming to her theme. 'Perhaps he is setting up his easel in Montmartre as we speak. Paris is full of painters.'

'Perhaps you read too many books, Daisy.'

'Nah. You can never read too many books.' She grinned at him. 'Do you want my gut instinct?'

He nodded.

'Sir Michael is running away and hiding so he doesn't have to face the consequences of her death, like a little boy hiding after he's broken a plate because he can't put it back together again, and he's not sure what to do. My gut says he's running away from his fear of a life without Mary-Ellen,' she said quietly.

Callum closed his eyes, tilting his head to allow his hair to fall forward in a curtain between himself and his perceptive sergeant. That had been his exact response when Grace had died. But the problem did not disappear when you ran away. It was still there, waiting for you when you went back.

When Sir Michael came out of hiding, Mary-Ellen would still be dead. He would walk around his house and hear her tread on the stairs, catch a fleeting glimpse of her leaving a room, with the hint of her perfume lingering in the doorway, and hear her laughter echo in the calls of birds to be carried away on the wind. Callum knew all of this. His solution was to keep walking along that road towards the trees, not to be tempted back into the darkness. It is easy to get lost in the dark and never find your way out.

'I don't think he's doing himself any favours by running, do you?' she asked.

He knew she was looking at him by the directness of her voice. He tucked his hair back and turned his head towards her.

'Let's hold judgement until we have some facts. Give the man an opportunity to give us his side of the story.'

'Perhaps we'll get back and find Mr Supercilious Fellowes has confessed to bumping off his boss.'

'Perhaps. But don't hold your breath.'

She indicated and turned into the station. 'Wasn't going to, sir.'

Chapter Eleven

David Fellowes sat back in the chair, arms folded across his chest, his short legs extended under the table. Bird sat opposite, mimicking his position, and it was clear that David felt a connection with the male officer. He was not so comfortable with Legs. She stood beside the table, fists bunched on her hips, elbows sticking out like shark fins.

Callum watched with interest through the one-way glass window.

'So where were you yesterday morning, when you were supposed to be at work?' Legs' full lips framed her white teeth in what could, arguably, have been intended as a smile.

Her accent surprised Callum. It was significantly more pronounced than it had been yesterday.

'Did you kill your boss and dump her body for someone else to find?'

She leaned down, closing the gap between their faces, and David's smirk sloughed away. He pulled his feet towards his chair and pointed them towards the door.

'Because you gotta biiiig problem with women being in control,' Legs continued, 'making decisions for you, catching you out cos you no good at your job.'

'Now see here.' David's attempt to lean forward was curtailed by her hovering face. 'You have no idea what you are talking about.'

Callum hoped Legs was clear about undue pressure and intimidation. She held her position and a crimson tide crept up David's neck and along his jaw.

He looked at Bird. 'She doesn't know what she's talking about.'

Bird appeared disinterested.

David's colour deepened further, and he looked as if he might explode.

'So where was you?' she persisted.

David folded his arms and stared at his shoes.

Legs turned to Bird. 'You remember what happens when people don't answer my questions? I get cross and twitchy.' She rolled each shoulder in turn like a boxer limbering up for a fight.

David raised alarmed eyes to her face. Callum hoped Legs knew where she was taking this because he wasn't too sure that he did.

'Can't you make her sit down?' David whined to Bird who gave another disinterested shrug.

'Well?' Legs snapped.

David cleared his throat and his Adam's apple bobbed. 'All right. All right. If you must know, I was at a job interview. I was head-hunted by Prestige Profiles in Canary Wharf.' His gimlet eyes glittered.

'Why?' she asked. 'You said you were heading up a new London office.'

'Why? Because Mary-Ellen called me into her office and refused point blank to discuss expanding into London. Short-sighted and a waste of a good business opportunity because that's where all the action is. That's when I realised, I was undervalued. She did not appreciate my considerable skills so I'm going to London myself.' He raised his chin and his eyes challenged Legs.

'So that was all a load of bull?' Bird asked.

David shrugged. 'She was being a cow. It was my idea, and it was a good one. Her loss.'

Callum thought that Amanda was probably correct, and Mary-Ellen had intended to dismiss him. It was noticeable that David failed to share that piece of information. It was all set-dressing with him.

Legs turned to Bird. 'Do you believe him?' she asked. 'Looks to me like he just created a vacancy with a job for life without boss lady interfering.'

'Women in charge can be tricky–' Bird said shifting in his chair.

'Too true, they can,' David interrupted him. 'The thing is they have no killer instinct. She was all for asking the client what they wanted, pussyfooting around. Half of them don't even know. You just need to tell them, and then get on with it.'

Bird's grunt encouraged him to continue.

'She was too soft, that was her problem. And can you believe it? She was going to sack me. Me. I ask you.' He leaned forward, eager to confide his version of events.

Legs sat down at the table and began writing.

'What you need in this business is balls.' His smug glance skimmed over Legs and returned to the male officer.

Bird looked at Legs, a half-smile on his face.

She put down her pen. 'Yessir. Balls is what you need. But I don't sit on mine.' She pushed out her chest. 'My balls is bigger than your balls.' She stood. 'I'll just go and check you are giving me the full story, Mr Fellowes.'

Callum touched his earring as Legs strode from the room to check out the alibi. He listened as Bird gave David an in-depth lecture on wasting police time and interfering with a murder investigation. It lasted without David managing to utter a word until Legs returned.

She smiled. 'Alibi checks out fine, Mr Fellowes, so you can go now.' Her accent was back to normal.

David made a show of adjusting his cuffs until a narrow line of pink shirt peeked below the grey cloth. He flicked an invisible speck from his sleeve and walked to the door.

Legs waited until he had curled his fingers around the handle, then said, 'By the way, you didn't get the job. Bad luck.'

* * *

In the fishbowl, Legs sat on the chair opposite Callum's desk. Weight forward, knees pressed together, Callum thought she looked poised to make it out of the office before he could get to his feet. She glanced at the white envelope on the desk in front of him.

'Interesting interview,' Callum said. 'You got a result.'

'Thanks, guv. Bit of luck on my part.' Her fleeting smile didn't ease her frown.

'And the accent?'

She looked down at her hands before setting her shoulders back and meeting Callum's eyes. 'Sorry about that, guv.'

Callum was all for constructive initiative unless it strayed over the line and became destructive.

'When we went to get him, he was being a pompous little prat, ordering the girls around and acting as if he was doing us a big favour by coming to the station. He ignored me, only spoke to Bird. I realised he is used to nice accommodating girls, who do what he tells them, and I thought I could put him outside his comfort zone.'

She had certainly achieved her objective. 'And it worked,' he said. 'You got the information we needed and verified it.' He watched the tension leach from her body and knew she had been uncertain of his reaction to her theatrics. Perhaps she had been admonished in the past.

Callum picked up the envelope. He recognised the bold rounded script from her writing on the board and placed it on the desk in front of Legs. Her body tightened.

'This is addressed to my predecessor, not to me.' He watched her eyes. 'Do you think the sender would want it back now DI Denton's no longer here?'

Legs' long brown fingers moved towards the envelope and stalled just short of the target. She folded her hands together and placed them in her lap.

'Guv?'

He smiled at her to continue.

'Guv, it's my letter, and it requests a transfer.'

He nodded and got up to close the door. He sensed that this would be a conversation that deserved some privacy.

'And do you still want me to action it?' he asked, returning to his seat.

'No, guv.' Her voice was quiet but firm.

Callum sat back in his chair. 'Will you tell me why you wanted a transfer?'

She hesitated.

'It would help me,' Callum said softly.

'I'm black,' she began uncertainly.

He smiled and raised an eyebrow. 'That much I had worked out for myself.'

'Okay. I'm black and female, and gay.' She lifted her chin a notch and waited for his reaction.

'And?' Callum asked, certain there must be more to follow.

'And nothing,' she said, puzzled.

'Do those facts affect your ability to do your job?'

'Of course not, guv. Sometimes they make it easier.' The sun was coming out on her side of the desk.

'Then why did you request a transfer? I can't see the problem, DC Levens.'

'I think the problem has disappeared.' She sat back in the chair, stretched her legs and prepared to expand as requested.

'I married Gloria about six months ago, and they put a picture in the local paper. I think they only did it because we look ridiculous together.' She laughed. 'She's short and white and fair and I'm the opposite.'

A picture of tartan and white flashed into Callum's mind. Then Legs seemed to shrink into herself, and Callum knew he was getting to the crux of the matter.

'DI Denton saw it, and decided I needed a proper man. And he was just the boy.' She shuddered.

'Stupid man,' he breathed. 'So, you requested a transfer?'

She nodded. 'He wouldn't let up.'

'Did you not think to mention it to DCI Bellman?'

'I did, when DI Denton kept harassing me.'

'And?' he asked, disquieted that he might already suspect the answer.

'And DI Denton had already told him I was uncooperative. DCI Bellman said it was just a bit of fun, and I should man up and take it. Or perhaps find a different job better suited to my… disposition, guv.'

Callum believed her.

'But I love being a copper, so Gloria and I decided a transfer would be our best option. I put the envelope on his desk on what turned out to be his last morning. He didn't turn up for work, so he never saw it.'

'I'm sorry you had to put up with that.' Callum reached across the desk, took the envelope, and without opening it, tore it in half, then half again and dropped the pieces into his waste bin.

Legs smiled and rose to her feet, towering above Callum, who squinted up at her.

'I hope you will be very happy with Gloria, and I look forward to being introduced someday.' He shifted his position. 'Her height will be easier on my neck.'

Her bubble of laughter was carried out of the fishbowl and, standing to follow her, Callum briefly met the satisfied glance of his sergeant.

* * *

Possible murderers were slipping through their fingers at an alarming rate. Callum stood in front of the board. Bird's question mark still hovered above Jimmy Eastwood even though his alibis checked out. They had proved that David Fellowes was elsewhere, and Fletcher Edmunds had Bacchus as his alibi.

Which left them with Sir Michael. No alibi, and a possible motive if he knew about her affair with Jimmy. Changing his will was taking on a new significance. He was the closest they had to a suspect. And although it didn't feel right to Callum to consider him as such, Sir Michael hadn't helped his case by disappearing.

Daisy came and stood beside him. 'I reckon we should put the charming Veronica Parsons on the board.'

'Reasons?'

'She has a motive, aggrieved at the loss of the money she thinks she's entitled to, and Mary-Ellen sacked her, so sour grapes there. Veronica and Colin are both out of work and in debt, and Mary-Ellen has just refused to bail them out this time. Plenty of opportunities as neither of them has a job, and she obviously thinks she is featured in the will. The only problem I see, is that I don't think she's physically capable of murdering her sister, but Colin Parsons might be.'

'Check into his background for the record but I don't think they had anything to do with it. The murder was well planned and well executed, and that's out of the Parsons' league. I don't think they could organise a tassie in Campbeltown. But check with the neighbours, see if they went out that morning.'

Callum looked across the office and located Cookie, his head bent low over his keyboard.

'Cookie, anything from the car park surveillance? And did you get that list of four-by-four owners?'

'Nothing yet. We've got names and addresses from this morning, but it seems they don't all walk in the same place every day. Some of them were elsewhere yesterday. Apparently, dogs like a change of scenery. Nobody we spoke to this morning was any help. Do you want us there again tomorrow morning? See who else turns up?'

'How else will they know we need their help? We're there for as long as it takes. Now four-by-fours? Range Rovers?'

Cookie held up some printed papers and waved them at Callum. 'Lots of them, guv. I'll make a start on the Range Rovers after I've chased up the bank and phone records that I asked for yesterday.' He smiled broadly. 'And the outgoing call Sir Michael made yesterday morning was to Mary-Ellen's parents, Mr and Mrs Goddard. The first piece of the jigsaw in place.'

'Bloody shame no one left us the picture for the rest of it,' Bird muttered under his breath, before turning to face Callum. 'Guv, all right if I try and track down Sir Michael's estranged brother, see what he knows about anything?'

Callum nodded his approval. 'But first, get hold of Paul Jackson Solicitors. Find out what was in Sir Michael's original will, why he has changed it, and who is the new beneficiary.'

'Guv' – Cookie flapped his sheaf of papers – 'remember the night before her murder she took a call on her mobile from "Leon"? Well, it's the same number as that mobile you brought in this morning. Sir Michael is Leon.'

* * *

Martha was as good as her word and her report was Callum's desk. He had just begun reading it when his internal phone buzzed, and Bird's voice growled in his ear.

'Paul Jackson, guv. Request to speak to the organ-grinder. He won't give the bloody monkey the time of day.' He clicked the call through without waiting for any comment.

The solicitor was civil and professional, with a pleasant, well-modulated voice that informed Callum five minutes was all he could spare before his next appointment, so they dispensed with pleasantries.

'Do you know the whereabouts of Sir Michael Mitchell?' Callum asked.

'No, assuming he is not at home, that is. The last contact I had with him was a phone call requesting certain changes to his will, and these have now been implemented. The requisite letter has been sent to him and we are awaiting contact.'

The short silence following this statement was pregnant with unasked questions.

'Who is the beneficiary of his current will and the same for the new will?'

'Come, come, Inspector. Client confidentiality, as I'm sure you appreciate.'

The smile in his voice was reflected on Callum's face. It had been worth a try and Callum made a noise in his throat that could have been interpreted as either approval or annoyance.

'Inspector, I can give you one piece of information that may be of interest.'

'Which is?'

'Mary-Ellen was also my client, and recently she approached me about changing her own will, but never followed through with it. Neither, before you ask, did she disclose the identity of her intended new beneficiary.'

'How long ago?'

'A month or two from memory. If it's important, I'll instruct my secretary to contact you with that information, and details regarding her existing will.'

Callum asked him about the start-up capital for G-Smart Solutions but the only additional information the solicitor could share was that Mary-Ellen had wisely invested a windfall she had received before she went away to university. So, Veronica was wrong. The money had not been left to her by her deceased grandparents. She had it before they died. Where then, had an eighteen-year-old Mary-Ellen Goddard come by such a large sum of money?

Martha's report confirmed both the cause and manner of death as he had anticipated. Callum skimmed the internal information section, then stopped and reached for his phone. Martha's hearty tones punched a question in his ear.

'Problems?'

He thought he could detect a frown in her voice. 'Clarification,' he said diplomatically. 'Mary-Ellen Mitchell had a child?'

'Are you questioning my abilities, young man?' Her computer mouse clicked away in the background. 'Here we are. She had a full-term pregnancy historically. Now I say full-term, but I can't guarantee she had a live birth, and before you ask, I can't tell you how long ago it was, but it wasn't last week. Important?'

'That could be significant. The world and his wife have been telling us she never had any children.'

'Perhaps the world and his wife didn't know about it. She wouldn't be the only teenager to give birth without her parents knowing, believe me. Check it against her medical records when they arrive.'

She must have registered the silence that followed her advice.

'Sorry. Teaching my grandmother to suck eggs. Habit from dealing with students whose attention span survives about as long as it takes to cook a pizza and open the cider. Talking of which, don't forget that drink.' The call died in his hand.

'Whoop-whoop.' All heads turned to see the reason for Cookie's jubilation.

Callum looked up in time to see him spring to his feet, rush over to Bird and wave a sheet of paper in his face. Bird sat back in his chair, arms folded and waited for an explanation.

'Bird. I've found something.'

'Praise the Lord.' Bird turned his eyes up to the ceiling. 'I was worried you had a bad case of St Vitus' dance. What is it?'

'Her bank records have arrived and the outgoings on her private account are as regular as clockwork, same pattern, month after month.' He hopped from foot to foot. 'Same direct debits, donations to Barnardo's, other charities, mobile phone.'

'So?'

'So, eight weeks ago, she withdrew twenty thousand cash. Never done it before. Now that' – he performed a flourish like a magician – 'is unusual.' He looked expectantly at Bird like a puppy anticipating a treat.

'And what are you going to do about it?' Bird asked, unfolding his arms, and picking up his pen.

Cookie thought for a moment. 'Check with the bank to see if they know what she wanted it for. Check with her office accountant to see if it had something to do with her business, and…' He paused as Legs materialised at his shoulder. 'And look at her phone to see if there were any calls around that time, and try and find out who they're from? I'm still waiting for the proper records.'

'So why are you still standing there like a bleedin' choir boy who needs a pee? Get on with it,' Bird growled.

'Hang on,' Legs called to the retreating back, 'and check if she was alone when she collected the cash. See if the CCTV shows anyone outside waiting for her. She might have withdrawn it under duress.'

Callum saw Legs and Bird exchange a glance.

'Looks like the Boy Wonder is getting the hang of things,' Bird said quietly before turning away to answer his desk phone. He made notes as the call progressed.

When Legs placed a cup of coffee on his desk ten minutes later, he was still listening intently to the caller.

Chapter Twelve

Daisy tapped lightly on the open door of the fishbowl. Beckoned in, she slid a single sheet of paper across the desk towards Callum.

'CCTV picked up Sir Michael's vehicle at three thirty-five this morning travelling eastbound on the M27 near junction 3, which goes to the docks at Southampton. They're checking to see if they can find him further along the road. Junction 4 joins the M3 to London, and junction 5 is the turn-off to Southampton Airport.'

Callum picked up the printout and examined it closely. The index number was correct, but the driver's image was blurred. It looked to be male but Callum acknowledged that this was more surmise than fact.

'I know. Rubbish quality. I've asked them if they can enhance it, to get a better visual on the driver. It looks like Sir Michael. Sort of.' She raised her shoulders in a shallow shrug.

That was what they expected it to show, and Callum was aware that it was easy to manipulate the facts to support the desired theory. For all they knew, it was not Sir Michael in the driving seat, but an abductor, and Sir Michael was trussed up in the back behind the tinted windows. He handed the paper back to Daisy.

'Check any cameras along his route to that point, and see if you can get a better picture, please.'

'I wonder if he's headed for London. We've got his passport, so I doubt he's headed for the docks or the airport. Do we know if he belongs to a London club or anything like that?'

Callum shook his head. 'No, we don't and neither do we know if he has a boat moored along the coast. Ask Amelia about a club, and a yacht, then see if Cookie has managed to get into his computer yet. Check his emails, see if he contacted anyone and arranged to meet. Check his phone for texts. Does he hold a private pilot's licence? Or know someone who keeps a plane at Southampton Airport?'

'I think he knows where he's going,' Daisy said.

'And I think you are right. This is adrenaline-fueled. He's running to safety.' As the words left his mouth, he hoped he was correct.

* * *

Bird rose to his feet, papers in hand, and looked towards the fishbowl.

A 'whoop-whoop' from the other end of the office made him jump and drop his notes.

'Got you, my son!' Cookie bounced up from his chair, air-punched then sat down again.

'Cookie, you're a bleedin' pain.' Bird retrieved his papers and went to stand behind the jubilant detective.

'I got into his laptop and guess what?'

'His favourite takeaway is chicken madras.'

'Don't be ridiculous,' Cookie said, his fingers scurrying across the keys.

'That's not ridiculous, it's my favourite takeaway,' Bird said.

Bird tried to read the flashes of text that sped up Cookie's screen. Daisy and Legs joined him.

'Got it.' Cookie sat back in his chair and the others peered around him.

It was an email from Sir Michael to someone called 'Tipi', saying he would be over to stay the night before Mary-Ellen's murder. It was a sexual assignation, and the last paragraph made Cookie blush. Bird laughed at his embarrassment and ruffled the corkscrew curls.

'See, he is having an affair,' Cookie said, ducking away from Bird's hand, 'so he's got a mistress somewhere; all we have to do is find her.'

'Except I think it's a *him*, not a her,' Bird said, tapping his piece of paper. 'I've just spoken to Gavin, the estranged brother, and we can scrub him off the list of suspects.'

'How so?' Callum asked, joining them.

'He's a wheelchair user. Been in one since his father pushed him down the stairs when he was fifteen, poor little bugger. The mother left years before that, and it seems that Daddy was a bastard of the highest order. Fond of the bottle, had a temper and laid into both boys regularly.'

'Could be why the mother left,' Legs said.

'At the start of the conversation, Gavin said that when Michael decided to study art, the abuse went up a notch or two and Friday nights tended to end in casualty, for Michael, that is.'

'Weren't social services involved?' Legs asked.

'Informed, but not involved seems to cover it. Michael ran off to France to study, leaving Gavin at home with Dad.'

'Michael was just a kid himself,' Legs said.

'Five years later, he turned up out of the blue to find Gavin in a wheelchair, and Daddy dearest six feet under. Michael blamed himself but Gavin said if Michael hadn't left, the old man would have killed him.'

'What's this got to do with my mistress, Bird?' Cookie asked.

'Patience. Michael bought a property that the brothers shared, and they got on like a house on fire until one day

Michael came home and announced that he was marrying Mary-Ellen Goddard. That's when the shit hit the fan. They haven't spoken since the wedding.'

'Why?' Daisy asked.

'Now, this is where it gets interesting. Gavin only gave me half the story at the beginning. He thawed out a bit when we got chatting. The old man didn't just have a problem with Michael wanting to be an artist, homophobia was alive and kicking. He found out that Michael was gay and decided to beat it out of him.'

'Like that was going to work,' Legs said.

'After Michael ran, the old man watched Gavin like a hawk. One night he confronted Gavin who admitted that he was gay, too, and threw him down the stairs. But Gavin didn't let go of the old bugger, and they both went down. The old man snapped his neck, and Gavin broke his back and spent months in Stoke Mandeville Hospital.'

'Sir Michael can't be gay.' Cookie shook his head. 'He married Mary-Ellen.'

'Gavin knows him better than we do and said there is no chance he's bi-sexual. They are both out and out gay,' Bird said. 'Gavin saw the marriage as a betrayal of what they had suffered for. Michael pays a monthly sum into Gavin's bank account, but he's never spent a penny of it.'

'Explains the separate bedrooms at Millers Farm,' Daisy said. 'But why would Mary-Ellen settle for a–' she searched for an appropriate word '–platonic marriage? What did she get out of it?'

'Credibility, security, a friend?' Callum suggested.

'Explains her extramaritals,' Bird said, 'and why I think we're looking for a bloke with Michael.'

'Good work, people,' Callum said. 'Cookie, chase up the email address, and check for a land address or meeting place.'

'Get onto it, Wonder Boy.' Bird ruffled the curls with the flat of his hand before following Callum into the fishbowl.

'Guv, I thought I might get Traffic to check the nearest cameras to the last sighting and see if we can place him in a particular area. Okay?'

Callum nodded his agreement. 'Liaise with Daisy on that. Anything else from your call to Gavin?'

'Not really. He's a writer and had a couple of books published. He thinks Michael does all his charity stuff because he feels guilty about what happened when they were growing up. I think Gavin cares a lot about Michael and misses him. He's genuinely worried that he's gone AWOL. He asked me to let him know when we find him, and I said I would.'

'I'm considering a public appeal. We can't track his credit card use or mobile position because we have both here.'

'He could have bought a burner.'

'Without his wallet?'

Bird shrugged. 'I just hope he's not been knocked off as well. Gavin sounds as if he could do with a bit of good news, not bad.'

'I think everything points to Michael having gone into hiding,' Callum said. 'There's been no attempt to communicate with him at his house, no threats, nothing to suggest blackmail or extortion. Nothing to drive him away.'

Bird grunted. 'Why disappear then? Unless you've murdered your wife, that is?'

Callum sat back in his chair, elbows on the armrests, and laced his fingers together.

'Why do they call you Bird?' Callum asked. He bore no resemblance to any ornithological specimen he had ever seen.

Bird took solid steps back to Callum's desk. 'Not because I'm light and dainty like one.' He gave a deep bellow of laughter that drew a smile from Callum and caused heads to swivel. It seemed that Bird's laughter was a rare occurrence.

'When I came out of the army I met this woman, Helen, and we shacked up together. Still shacked up, as a matter of fact.' He seemed surprised by his own statement. 'We rescue injured birds – kestrels, buzzards, blackbirds, anything that's got feathers. Got a bloody goose someone found at the side of the road yesterday and delivered it to us in a wheelbarrow. It's the noisiest bird we've ever had.'

Callum laughed. 'My granny had a couple, and they gave Charlie-the-Post a run for his money. Used to frighten me to death when I was little. Good watchdogs though.'

'This one's more likely to become a good casserole if it doesn't pipe down. It's driving Helen round the bend.'

Callum watched Bird return to his desk. His often-fisted hands hung loose, and his shoulders were relaxed. Callum supposed that every fighter had to deal with the fallout from action and found their own way of coping. Jimmy Eastwood saw himself as the new superhero and Bird healed sick birds. That balanced out the ones who went around robbing banks and murdering old ladies.

Callum updated his notes. They had eliminated all the suspects except Sir Michael. That first burst of adrenaline was evaporating like a puddle in hot sunshine. Now the hard work would begin.

Where had Mary-Ellen's twenty thousand pounds gone? Amelia had told them that Sir Michael had surprised his wife with a red Mercedes convertible for her last birthday, and he was three months shy of his seventieth. Was she returning the compliment by organising a gift that she wanted to keep secret? He made a note in his neat script and drew his pen down to the next point.

He sketched an inkwell and quill in the margin. It was not unusual for people to change their wills. Perhaps they had jointly decided to update them, particularly considering Sir Michael's upcoming birthday, and Mary-Ellen was a little tardier in the implementation.

Or had Sir Michael redrafted his will because he had found out about his wife's affair? Did he expect fidelity and abstinence? Callum heard a phone ring and saw Cookie side-slide across the floor, cannon into Legs' chair, before answering his desk phone. The list of concerns he intended to raise with the team when this case was over was increasing.

Neither Mary-Ellen's parents nor her sister had mentioned the birth of a baby, so they had not known. Veronica would not miss an opportunity to tarnish her sister's reputation, to pull her down from the pedestal that the Goddards had placed her on.

He twisted his pen between his fingers like a baton-spinning major. In this close-knit rural community, everybody knew everybody else's business. How had Mary-Ellen carried a baby for nine months in secret? He was missing something. The pen flipped out of control and clattered onto his keyboard.

There had been times when one or more of his sisters were away from home, but these had always been planned absences. That was it, a planned absence. How could he have missed it? He retrieved his pen and wrote "gap year" in the margin.

Then he came to the point that puzzled him most. Why would an active heterosexual woman decide to marry a homosexual man fifteen years her senior? She was beautiful if Sir Michael's painting was anything to go by; in fact, she still was. He pencilled a quick calculation, then looked up when Daisy placed a mug on his desk.

'Coffee.' She hovered, and he saw that she was trying to read his list.

'She was thirty-nine when she got married, Daisy. Rather old, would you say?'

'Not by today's standards. Lots of couples cohabit. Marriage isn't the big thing it used to be…' She stopped mid-sentence.

What was it she had thought better of saying? Some comment about his marriage to Grace? His dark eyes held her blue ones for a second, and he read something there before she looked away. Had she been jilted, or had a long-term relationship gone sour? He hoped he hadn't brought back bad memories for her.

'But I like a good wedding, myself. Don't you?' she added brightly.

When she again met his eyes, he wasn't sure if he had imagined that earlier stab of pain. Perhaps it had just been his own, reflected back at him.

'Don't forget your coffee,' she said over her shoulder as she went into the outer office.

What had Mary-Ellen wanted from her marriage to the then-plain Michael Mitchell? Grace had wanted children, fun, and a partnership. She was a whirlwind of energy, enthusiasm, and sexiness. He remembered the chilly days walking on The Campsies, the balmy evenings boating on Banton Loch and the hot steamy nights in bed. Sir Michael and Mary-Ellen seemed to lead separate lives with no crossover of friends or interests, like birds on different flight paths returning to the same roost when darkness fell.

He cupped the mug in both hands and savoured the nutty smell before taking a sip. According to Gavin, Mary-Ellen knew Michael was gay, and yet she had still chosen to marry him. And if he believed what people said, it was a match made in heaven. He sketched the gold earrings she wore. She hadn't married for money. What had she needed from that marriage that Sir Michael had been able to provide?

Callum drained his mug and updated his list for the morning. If they had still not located Sir Michael, he would see Bellman about launching an appeal. He slipped all his papers into the top drawer and pushed back his chair. There had been some positives today. He knew more about Bird and Legs, which was pleasing. And more about

Bellman, and his predecessor Denton, which was not. The jury was still out on Cookie.

He closed the door of the fishbowl behind him and stood in front of the board, arms folded. He registered the sounds of his team closing drawers and preparing to leave for the day.

Daisy came over to him. 'Ready?' She jangled her vehicle keys.

'Hmm.' Just one man was remaining who did not have a cross through his photo. Callum responded to the 'goodnight' calls and followed Daisy towards the door. Some questions urgently required answers, and to get those answers, they needed to find Sir Michael Mitchell.

Chapter Thirteen

Felix greeted them as if they had been gone for a month, cavorting around the garden and making soft woofing noises.

'Idiot,' Daisy said to him as he picked up a garden trowel and presented it to her, tail wagging so vigorously that his body sawed from side to side. She patted him, chased him along the path and they disappeared through the door into the house.

Callum caught up with her in the kitchen where she was removing groceries from two bags on the kitchen island and sliding them into the fridge and cupboards.

'Mrs P, Oli's mum, was Mum's old housekeeper. She cleans for me and does my food shopping when I don't get time, like today.'

Her mother had a housekeeper? The North–South divide just widened.

Daisy switched on the radio and Ludovico Einaudi's *Brothers* filled the kitchen with the ripple of piano phrases.

He was taken aback, thinking her to be more pop than classical, or grunge or garage or whatever the youngsters went for these days.

'Helps me unwind,' Daisy said. 'I think I got hooked early on. Mum says when *Galloping Home* – you know, the theme to *Black Beauty* – came on the radio, I used to canter round and round the kitchen. What do you listen to, sir?'

'Callum's fine when we're not on duty.' He could imagine her as a petite fair-haired child pretending to ride a horse around in circles.

'Okay. Callum it is. Music?' she reminded.

'The same, and Scottish folk, I don't know. All sorts.' It was the pipe and fiddle that he first remembered hearing, and that still stirred his heartstrings.

'Can I help with that?' he asked as she placed a pepper, onion, ginger and garlic onto a chopping board. 'I am fully house-trained,' he added when she hesitated.

'Thanks, that would be a help. I want to check who that message is from.' She indicated the pulsing red light on the kitchen phone.

Callum rinsed his hands, eased a broad-bladed knife from the block and began stripping the onion.

'Hello, darling. It's me, your mother.'

Daisy rolled her eyes skyward, and Callum thought that supplying unnecessary information seemed to be a family trait. They listened to the message, punctuated by the beat of his blade on the board.

'I just wanted to let you know that Dom has won another photography award. Something to do with saving polar bears or Arctic whales. Isn't he clever? I'm so proud of you both.'

Daisy pulled a face, and they heard the chink of ice cubes dropping into a glass and a crackle as liquid was poured over them.

'I expect he'll give you all the details himself.'

Daisy took chicken breasts out of the fridge.

'Anyway, must dash, sweetie. Daddy and I have a tiresome embassy thingy this evening. You'd hate it. All high heels and polite conversation. Love you, darling. Stay safe. Kiss kiss.'

After a brief hiccoughing purr, the machine beeped once and switched off. Callum concentrated on reducing the slices of ginger to slivers but realised Daisy had caught his amused expression.

'Meet my mother' – she chuckled – 'and never, ever, mistakenly think she is as daffy as she sounds. Beneath the batty blonde act is a mind like steel, a photographic memory and interrogation skills to shame MI6.'

Callum smiled and wondered if such skills resulted from giving birth, as his mother was similarly afflicted. A sudden thread of homesickness tugged at his chest when he imagined his parents in their kitchen preparing supper together.

Daisy flash-fried the thin strips of chicken and added the results of Callum's effort to the spluttering wok. A sharp spicy smell billowed into the kitchen before being sucked into the extractor fan.

Oliver breezed in through the back door. 'Smells good, Deedee. I came to ask about Pirate. Louise is on holiday next week, and I said I would muck out and exercise him for her.'

'Aaawh. Lucky Louise. That's nice of you,' Daisy said with just sufficient innuendo to imply that he had an ulterior motive.

Oliver's healthy glow developed a pink undertone, and she laughed.

'We've finished with him, and Jimmy is going to look after him as Sir Michael is away.'

'Okay.' He reached across and filched a strip of chicken from the wok. 'Tastes good, Deedee.' He opened the door.

'It tastes better with all the ingredients in it.' She huffed a quick laugh as the door closed on the silhouette of Oliver stabbing his middle finger up towards the ceiling.

Callum enjoyed the supper, and Daisy provided an accompanying glass of wine.

'What's puzzling me,' Daisy said between forkfuls, 'is why she married him if she knew he was gay.'

'When we find him, we'll ask.'

'And it's odd that he has run away if he's innocent, don't you think?'

Callum felt the hot fizz of ginger on his tongue. 'You suggested he was hiding because his life is broken, and he doesn't know how to mend it.' Taking a sip of wine, the warm fruitiness tempering the heat in his mouth, he watched her over the rim of the glass.

'I know. But I've been thinking about it, and if something like that happened to…'

She hesitated, and he wondered if she was about to disclose the name of a boyfriend.

'To Dom, say, then I'd want to be here, making sure that people were trying their hardest to find out who did it. Wouldn't you, Callum, if someone you loved died?' Her head was tilted to one side, blue eyes wide with innocence.

She was fishing again. Her curiosity might make her a good detective, but he didn't appreciate being the subject of her enquiries. He took his time winding a noodle around his fork and smiled inwardly when, after a pause, she did the same.

'I think it's usual to want to get involved if you're in our line of work,' he said. 'But it's not the same for everyone. Some people just need a target to direct their anger at, some just want to apportion blame.' He chewed a piece of chicken.

'Maybe,' she said.

Callum recalled how helpless and angry he had felt when Grace died. Who could he blame for a heart attack in an otherwise healthy young woman? He was a detective, for God's sake. He should have noticed if something was wrong, it was his job. So, he had blamed himself. He speared the last piece of mushroom and wondered where

Sir Michael was just now, and if he was blaming himself for his wife's death.

Daisy clattered her fork into her empty bowl, straightened her back, and stretched her arms up towards the ceiling before holding out her hand for his empty dish. He handed it to her with a smile of thanks. He emptied the last of the shiraz into her glass as the lyrical snake-charmer notes of *Gabriel's Oboe* flowed from the radio. He was surprised that he was enjoying her company. It was a long time since he had felt this way. It was a part of the job he could get used to.

Callum selected a new page in his sketchbook, pencilled the date at the top and had made just two marks on the paper when his phone rang. Daisy paused in her loading of the dishwasher and motioned if she should leave while he answered it. He shook his head and muttered, 'Sister.' He trapped the phone between his left ear and shoulder and continued to wield the pencil. His side of the conversation consisted of a lot of 'uhh-hu' and 'is that right?' and 'well you know'. He noted that Daisy was pretending not to listen.

'You should tell Mother I'm fine. I'm staying with my sergeant just now as I've not had the time to find somewhere for myself. The bed is comfortable and I'm eating fine. Aye, tell her I'll ring her in a day or two. Love to all, Dolina. Bye now.'

He exhaled one long breath, and Daisy tilted her head to the side.

'So, Dolina is your sister?'

'Indeed. Along with Freya and Shona. They are emissaries of my mother and well-schooled in the ancient art of extracting information. Fair means or foul.'

'Hence the lack of information coming from you?'

'I don't want to spoil their finagling.'

'Finagling?'

She hovered, but when he didn't respond turned away to make coffee and sort through her stack of unopened letters. Asking about his sisters meant she wasn't asking about Grace.

She ripping the plastic skin from a newly delivered magazine and examined the horse head on the front cover. Sipping her coffee, she turned the pages, the downlighters illuminating a succession of glossy equines.

They all looked the same to Callum. He resumed the soft caress of graphite on paper until he had completed his drawing of a mare and colt, cropping the turf of the village green. The front legs of the foal were splayed wide, like a giraffe, as his lowered head stretched down to nibble at the grass, his short hedge-of-a-mane standing upright. Callum paused to assess his composition, then added a couple of horizontal lines in the background suggesting the cricket-pitch railings. He eyed it critically. It still needed something to balance it, all the interest was in the foreground. He remembered the two boys playing together that morning and sketched them in the middle ground with their bony knees and sharp elbows. They stood looking down at the debris of their crashed model plane.

Chapter Fourteen

Bellman's office was small and dreary. Grey walls, grey filing cabinets and a grey metal coat stand with the Christmas-tree jacket buttoned to attention on a wooden hanger.

'Inspector MacLean, have you arrested anyone yet?'

'Not yet, sir. We're pursuing several lines of inquiry—'

'I do not have a budget for endless lines of inquiry. I have a budget for arrests.'

Callum focused on the single window that looked out onto a bruised brick wall and digested this response. Bellman's face toned beautifully with assorted reds, and

Callum hoped someone was keeping an eye on the man's blood pressure.

Bellman rearranged a row of expensive-looking writing implements along the top edge of his white blotter, lining them up like drilled soldiers.

'Inspector, I have a spate of local burglaries, power-tool thefts every night and a gang of local youths putting out people's windows with ball bearings. I need an arrest and soon.'

'And I am confident that an arrest will follow our lines of inquiry.' Callum's tone was as hard and sharp as napped flint.

Bellman eyed him in silence, his small frame enveloped in a high-backed chair, elbows resting on the arms.

Suppressing a smile at the memory of himself as a skinny ten-year-old, sitting tall in his grandfather's fireside chair, Callum resisted the impulse to check if Bellman's feet were shy of the floor. Instead, he concentrated on the pot plant on the corner of the desk, its arched leaves spearing downward like a collection of Gaelic knives, *sgian-achlais*, sharp and deadly. Not unlike the man himself this morning, who seemed to be unsettled, distracted by something he was not sharing with his inspector. If confrontation was his natural disposition, small-man-spoiling-for-a-fight, then spending as little time as possible in his presence was looking like a good plan.

'Inspector MacLean, if you haven't come to inform me of an arrest, why are you here?'

'We are currently uncertain of the whereabouts of Sir Michael Mitchell, the victim's husband, and I would like to put out an appeal for information.'

'Is he a suspect? The husband?'

'Not at the moment, but he may have information pertinent to his wife's murder that could assist in apprehending her killer.'

Bellman pursed his lips and stared at Callum as if he was trying to see inside his head.

'Very well.' His eyes washed down Callum from his long hair and silver earring to the jeans and boat shoes. 'I will deal with it, MacLean.'

'Thank you, sir.'

'I expect an updated briefing later in the day. Now is there anything else?'

'Indeed not.' Callum turned in one fluid movement. He avoided the predatory plant and had reached the door when, in a noticeably smoother voice, Bellman asked, 'Inspector, how do you find Detective Constable Levens?'

Callum stood still.

'Your predecessor found her to be something of a troublemaker, I understand.'

'Really, sir?' He turned and held eye contact with Bellman. 'I find her to be a conscientious and knowledgeable officer, who is both keen and gifted in her approach.'

Bellman looked as if he had bitten into something he didn't like the taste of and wasn't sure what to do about it.

Callum pulled the door closed behind him. He had not liked any of his previous senior officers. But whilst liking them was not essential, forging an effective working relationship with them was. Bellman could prove as much of a challenge as getting the rest of the team in shape. He thrived on a challenge.

His job was fighting the bad guys, but he was happier when he was sure they were all on the other side of the fence. He eased back on his pace. Before making a judgment call, he wanted to have all the facts. He was unlikely to ever meet Denton. He believed what Legs had told him and his instincts were rarely wrong. Bellman had other things on his mind.

He pushed open the door of the office.

'We've got another one, sir.' Daisy's voice was muffled, and Callum couldn't immediately locate her.

The room pulsed with an energy that had been lacking when he had left to see Bellman. There was anticipation, and an urgency that was confirmed by Cookie speeding around as if he were on skates.

'Donaldson?'

'Here.' She rose to her feet with an untidy collection of papers in her hands that she seemed to have scooped up from the floor.

Cookie's closed fist made a circular motion against his chest but Callum didn't have time to ask him why he was using sign language.

'Legs and Bird are attending while I wait for you,' Daisy said.

'Where?'

'A stone's throw from where we found Mary-Ellen. We had a triple nine from a woman screaming down the phone about a rider with a broken neck who had come off her horse. That's all we've got just now. The caller wasn't making much sense, just kept repeating that "she's just lying there".'

She squared the papers, put them on her desk and lifted her jacket from the back of her chair. 'Looks like a possible second victim with the same MO. Martha's been informed.'

'Let's go then.'

Daisy's phone buzzed as she was getting into the Navara and she listened to the caller, one foot on the concrete and the other on the running board.

'Okay. Thanks, Legs, I'll tell him.' She turned to Callum who had paused at the passenger door. 'False alarm.' She locked her vehicle, and they retraced their steps.

'When Legs and Bird arrived at the scene, a woman was lying on the ground…'

'Alive?'

'Oh, very much so. She was just winded by the fall but got her breath back by the time they arrived on the scene and was swearing fit to burst. The other woman, the one who called it in, was threatening to break the neck of the man who sold the horse to her friend last week. It was supposed to be as safe as houses, but it spooked at something, and her friend sailed out of the side door.'

Callum considered the gullibility of horse riders. Why would they expect half a tonne of powerful equine with a flight mentality to stand still in the event of a threat? It wasn't an SUV, for God's sake.

'The friend was screaming at Sergeant Rodgers and demanding that he arrest the previous owner for selling a dangerous animal, which he declined to do, but I understand from Legs that he added a couple of new expletives to his vocabulary during the exchange.'

'And the horse?'

'Last seen heading back towards its previous owner. Richard Devereux-Strauss.'

'Hmm.' Callum held the door open for Daisy. Richard and his unruly horses were trampling through his investigation.

'Cookie.'

Cookie's head swivelled towards Callum, but his eyes remained firmly fixed on the monitor.

'Sir?'

'Turf Hill car park this morning?'

Cookie snatched up a couple of loose sheets of paper and scooted between the desks to join Callum in the fishbowl.

'Good info this morning, sir. Mrs–' he searched the paper '–Daphne Smart told PC Whitlock that she parked her car there on the morning of the murder to walk her dogs, Rufus and Paddy.' He bounced from one foot to the other.

Callum wanted to tell him to stand still but didn't.

'There was a vehicle there when she arrived, but nobody with it, so she thought they were walking their dog. When she returned after her walk–' he referenced the paper again '–just before eight o'clock, there was a chap in running gear just tying his laces before leaving in a black four-wheel-drive vehicle.'

'Make? Model? Index?'

''fraid not. But she's certain it was black, had back seats and a tailgate, so it wasn't a pickup. But she's not very up on car makes.'

'And the driver?'

'Better luck there. He was tall and slim and dressed totally in black. Baseball cap, long-sleeved top and what she described as ballet tights and trainers. She doesn't know if he was wearing gloves, and she isn't sure how old he was, as she only saw the back of him, but he had black hair. She thought he might be changing his shoes to drive home because she never drives in her wellies. She said to PC Whitlock, "As I am over eighty, young man, everyone looks young to me." So that's not much help.' Cookie fidgeted.

'Stand still. Anything else?'

'She didn't recognise him. She used to be the headmistress of the village school in Hale.'

Callum nodded. He had noticed the school yesterday when Daisy had stopped to speak to Annie Eastwood. 'Check with the other people who were parked there that morning,' he said. 'See if any of them saw that vehicle leaving, and if so, in which direction it went.' It was a slim chance, but a possible lead.

Cookie gathered himself for a fast exit.

'Wait.' Callum wasn't finished. 'When did this information come in?'

'About half an hour ago.'

'So why wasn't I informed? Why did I have to ask you for it?'

Cookie's curls stopped bouncing.

'Sorry. I was just going to bring it to you, but I was checking something on the web, and that led to something else and then I forgot.'

Callum let the silence stretch until Cookie's face was cayenne-hot to the tip of his ears.

'That is not good enough, DC Cooke.' Callum's voice was firm. 'If that had been information about a suspect carrying a weapon, that delay because you forgot to pass on the message, could have got an officer killed. Do your job. Is that clear?'

Cookie dropped his gaze to the floor. 'Sorry, sir.' His voice was a whisper. 'It won't happen again.'

Subdued, Cookie walked back to his desk, but his speed increased with every stride until a flamenco slide covered the last couple of yards. He sat for a moment, clawed hands poised above the keyboard, a raptor waiting to strike, and then the keys rattled into life. Contrition had a short lifespan.

In the fishbowl, Callum read through the information on the crumpled sheet of paper that Cookie had given him. His handwriting was small and spidery, difficult to decipher, and he let the note fall to the desktop in irritation.

Bird came to lean against the door jamb of the fishbowl. He glanced at Cookie before turning his attention to Callum.

'Guv? We've been chasing up camera sightings for Sir Michael, but that's the only one. His car doesn't trigger the next camera on any major road, so I reckon he's gone to ground somewhere in this area.'

He passed a map to Callum, with a black amoeba-shaped outline in the centre. It covered a section of Southampton, most of which was densely built-up, but with a few larger properties backing onto woodland.

'Needle in a haystack. We need to narrow it down, Bird.'

'Cookie checked his emails and phones, but no one has tried to contact him. He's working on that IP address location for the boyfriend as we speak.' Bird glanced over his shoulder at the flamboyant detective. 'My money's on someone hiding him, guv.'

'Agreed. When we get the responses from DCI Bellman's public appeal for information this evening, concentrate on any that indicate a sighting in your search area.'

'Oh great. Now we'll be chasing our tails investigating imaginary Sir Michaels from Southampton to bloody Stornoway.'

'What's this?' Daisy came to lean on the other door jamb.

'Bellman is doing a press call,' Bird said.

'Terrific.' Daisy rolled her eyes theatrically. 'Sir, Amelia doesn't think he has a London club membership or an anywhere-else membership. He doesn't play golf, belong to a gym or a country club, and he hasn't got a pilot's licence and doesn't own a yacht or go sailing,' she added.

Bird folded his arms. 'No help there, then.'

Callum's phone rang. 'MacLean,' he said. 'Thanks for ringing back.'

Bird and Daisy prepared to leave, but Callum signalled them to stay.

'Paul Jackson,' he said, replacing the receiver a short time later. 'He checked when Mary-Ellen spoke to him about changing the beneficiary of her will, and the date coincides with the withdrawal of the cash, which is interesting. Unfortunately, she didn't share the name of the intended new beneficiary, and, for reasons unknown, she never followed through.'

'Who's the current beneficiary?' Daisy asked.

'Her existing will leaves provision for her parents, and bequests to some charities, but the bulk of her estate, which is considerable, goes to Isabella and Madison Parsons, in trust. And the trustee is Paul Jackson Solicitors.'

Bird whistled through his teeth.

'Ouch,' Daisy said. 'Somebody's nose will be out of joint. Passed over in favour of her own kids and no chance of getting her fingers in the pie as a trustee either.'

'Wouldn't want to be in Paul Jackson's shoes when Veronica finds out,' Bird said.

'Grub up.' Legs placed an open, tartan-decorated tin on her desk.

Cookie was there as she finished speaking, and Callum realised that this was the way he negotiated life, at maximum speed, his agile brain, leaping past others.

'Wow, Legs, these look brilliant.' He reached an eager hand into the tin for a jam-and-cream-filled scone and bit into his prize.

Daisy and Bird ate at their desks, absorbed in their current tasks; Legs stood beside her chair, a piece of paper in one hand and a scone in the other. She scanned the note and dropped it onto her desk. Cookie seemed to be the only team member capable of switching his commitment on and off at will.

'What did Reg want?' Daisy nodded at the note Legs had dropped onto her desk.

'Third instalment in the vendetta of Reg and The Rubbish Man.'

Callum frowned. He had no idea what she was talking about.

'The story so far, guv. Reg lives in that row of cottages along Forest Road. In the local one night, he told Henners, the refuse collector, how to grow his runner beans. Henners has been gardening since the ark, so that didn't go down well.' She bit into her scone and Bird continued the tale.

'Any chance they get to piss each other off, they take it. It's usually Henners refusing to collect Reg's rubbish if the lids aren't closed properly, or the recycling is in the wrong bin. He doesn't need much of an excuse.' Bird thrust his thumbs behind imaginary braces. 'It's regulations, mate. Regulations,' he said, in a terrible cockney accent.

'This time,' Legs said, 'someone dumped a bag on top of Reg's bin and Henners wouldn't take it because rubbish must be inside the bin. He says his neighbours deny all knowledge, so I advised him to take a moral high, and put it in his bin ready for the next collection.'

'Will he?' Daisy asked.

Legs shrugged. 'Who knows? Mrs Holder sent us these scones, and very nice they were too.' She replaced the lid and put the empty tin next to her computer. 'Reg will be back tomorrow to collect this, so he might tell me then what he's going to do.'

'You know he's hoping you're going to have a go at his neighbours on his behalf,' Daisy said.

'Well, I'm not. It won't help us find out who killed Mary-Ellen, so Reg can sort that out for himself.'

'We wait with bated breath.' Bird flicked crumbs from his shirt front onto the papers on his desk. 'Perhaps you can get Reg to tell us who the bloody murderer is.' He shook the paper over his waste bin. 'And while you're at it, ask him where Sir Michael is.'

Chapter Fifteen

Turf Hill was one of about a hundred and twenty purpose-built parking areas in the New Forest. Callum found the spot on his map. It was a wobbly figure of eight surrounded by bunds of banked earth interspersed with a few fir trees.

The gravel for most of the sites came from the same quarry, and matched the stone in Mary-Ellen's boot tread, but all that confirmed was that she had dismounted from her horse, possibly on the morning of her death, in one of those car parks. It was just another piece in Cookie's jigsaw puzzle.

'Did you hear about Turf Hill?' Cookie asked and continued before anyone had time to answer him, 'PC Whitlock spotted a black pickup offloading power tools into a van with the help of its driver. He called for backup, put on his wellies and grabbed a loose strap from his vehicle. Get this, he hurried towards the van calling for "Bruno" and stopped to ask the men if they had seen his dog. Then our lot turned up and arrested them.'

Whitlock had received summoning whistles in the station corridors, and his colleagues gave him a toy dog with a "Bruno" tag dangling from its collar. Cookie laughed as he recounted the tale, and Callum hoped that Bellman would be similarly pleased to learn that his team had put a stop to the power tool thefts.

Bird called across the office to Cookie. 'Aren't you supposed to be at the bank finding out about that cash withdrawal?'

Cookie shot to his feet, grabbed his jacket, and whirled out of the door, leaving it open.

'Fuck's sake,' Bird muttered. He threw his pen onto his desk and lumbered across the office to close the door.

Daisy and Legs exchanged a look and Callum thought he read surprise on their faces.

* * *

Later, Cookie charged back into the office, slamming the door behind him.

'The bank clerk remembered Mary-Ellen collecting the money, partly because it was a large sum, and partly because she liked her jacket. It was just before lunchtime. They went through the money-counting rigmarole, and then she took Mary-Ellen's supermarket bag-for-life and put the cash in it. She went out into the public area and handed it to Mary-Ellen who was very cheerful but didn't say what the money was for.' He shrugged out of his jacket and hung it on the coat rack.

'I got the serial numbers. Then I looked at the CCTV.'

He glanced at Legs, but she was engrossed in something on her screen and didn't appear to be listening to him.

'No one was waiting for her outside, but…' He paused to waggle a finger at Bird. 'High Street CCTV shows her leaving the bank and then going into a coffee shop two doors down. She's inside for about twenty minutes and then comes out with another woman, and Mary-Ellen still has the bag. Presumably with the money still in it as the other woman only had a small handbag.'

'Do we know who she is?' Callum asked.

'Not yet. Similar age to Mary-Ellen, smart business suit, high heels, a good haircut and that's what she looks like.' He showed them a blurry picture. 'I gave the original to the techies to get it enhanced.'

Bird grasped the flapping paper and studied it. 'This is a crap picture. Her bleedin' mother wouldn't recognise her from this.' He thrust the paper back at Cookie.

'I went back into the bank, but no one there recognised her either.'

'I wonder why she wanted all that cash,' Daisy said.

'I checked and defo nothing to do with business. Hundo P,' Cookie said. 'I mean, hundred per cent,' he added quickly when Bird glared at him. 'And they said she was very strict about keeping business and personal separate.'

'So, we can assume it was a private matter. What do you spend 20 K in cash on?' Daisy asked.

'My mum used to put her cash in a running-away-from-home tin before Dad left,' Cookie said, his tone serious. 'But she never saved 20 K.'

'Paying off a lover, blackmail, contract for a killer, money laundering, illegal artworks, blood diamonds…' Legs counted the possibilities on her fingers.

'You should be with bleedin' Vice.' Bird turned his back on them and headed to his desk.

'Perhaps Sir Michael will turn up after the appeal and throw some light on it,' Legs suggested, ignoring Bird's comment.

'Shouldn't bloody count on it,' he muttered.

Bird sat, planted his elbows on his desk and dropped his head into his hands. After a few seconds, he rubbed his eyes, scrubbed both his hands over his tufted scalp and, with a soft grunt, turned his attention to his monitor. Something or somebody had rubbed Bird up the wrong way today. Callum glanced across to Cookie but sensed that, for a change, he was not responsible.

'I checked the birth records for 1983, Mary-Ellen's gap year, in the name of Goddard and I've got something, guv,' Legs said. 'Mary-Ellen gave birth to a baby boy in January, registered in Northern Ireland, father unknown and it was not in her medical records.'

'Cookin' on gaaaaas,' Cookie said, raising a fist to air-punch. The others ignored him.

'It was at a mother-and-baby home in Armagh, run by Sisters of Our Lady of Hope. Girls had their babies there and could have them adopted.'

'Still operating?' Daisy asked.

'Most of them closed down in the seventies and eighties, this one made it to the nineties, but they all got a pretty bad press at the time.'

'Why?'

'Adoption without consent and against the will of the mother. And money changing hands,' Legs said. 'Some women have come forward saying they never consented to adoption and their babies were stolen from them. There's an inquiry.'

'Sounds shady. Could be why it's not in her records,' Daisy said. 'What happened to the place?'

'Nothing. It's still a convent but under a new name. These nuns grow vegetables and keep bees.'

'Very eco-friendly,' Bird muttered.

'Records?' Callum said.

'There was a fire in the records office. Not many survived,' Legs said.

Eyebrows were raised.

'Most of the sisters from that time are dead but one, Sister Agnes, is still alive. She lives in Salisbury, in a home for retired clergy, and I am going to see her tomorrow.'

Mary-Ellen had a connection to Ireland through her grandparents who had lived in County Kerry. Callum was sure that Elizabeth Goddard had not mentioned the north, but she might have had relatives there. Was it stretching probability that an aunt or cousin had helped Mary-Ellen and then kept it secret from the Goddards? It was a possibility. But human nature being what it was, it was also a very long time to keep a secret, unless that secret had died with the grandparents.

Callum stood beside Daisy's desk and looked at the handwritten notes, trying unsuccessfully to read her shorthand scribbles.

'What have you found out about Edward Devereux-Strauss's planning application?'

She seemed amused that he couldn't decipher her writing. 'Do you reckon I missed my vocation as a medic?'

'Planning, Daisy.'

'Okay. The application was for eight executive houses in a gated development. They wanted to flatten the Georgian stables and carriage sheds and that row of old cottages where Edward expected the Goddards to live. It would have been worth millions if it had gained approval.'

Daisy pointed to the plans of the houses. 'I can see why Edward might be the teeniest bit annoyed.'

Callum had not grasped the size of the site. The proposed dwellings looked pretentious, and out of character with the village setting of small, thatched cottages. The local press had reported on it, and it briefly made the nationals following an ill-advised, unguarded comment from Edward after his unsuccessful appeal.

'"Her parents were menials for my father. She should keep her side of the kitchen sink and not meddle in matters that don't concern her,"' Daisy read the comment aloud. 'I'm getting to like Edward more and more.

Nothing like a sense of entitlement.' Her voice was laden with sarcasm, and Legs gave a derisive snort that carried across the office.

Edward was probably still wondering why the long arm of officialdom had swung decisively in favour of the daughter of his ex-servants, rather than the rich, and privileged. The local paper followed up on the refusal with an article about corruption and bribery in the planning system.

'I remember that,' Bird said, coming to stand next to Callum. 'There were rumours about the funny handshake brigade and an old boys' network. It got a bit heated for a while but in the end, it fizzled out.'

'No further investigations took place,' Daisy said, reading on. 'It died of natural causes.'

'One thing is certain,' Callum said, 'Mary-Ellen caused Edward time and trouble, and lost him a lot of money.'

Cookie came over and pointed at the screen. 'That's the sort of house I want to live in one day.'

The others looked at him with incredulity.

'Are you planning on making commissioner?' Daisy asked.

'Not for me,' Bird said, shaking his head, 'the neighbours would be complaining about my geese.'

'Geese? I thought it was goose,' Callum said.

'It was. But another one flew in to join the noisy bastard first thing this morning. At least the bloody thing's quietened down now it's got someone to talk to, and I might even get some sleep tonight.' He screwed his knuckles against his eyelids. 'Sodding bird.'

'What I came to say, is that he drives a black Range Rover,' Cookie said.

'Who bleedin' does?' Bird looked at Cookie.

'Actually, there's three registered to Devereux Manor. One belongs to Edward, one to Richard and another to Matthew who is Richard's older brother.'

'Is Matthew local?' Legs asked.

'He lives in London and works for Devereux Holdings.' Cookie read from a sheet of paper. 'It's a London-based financial company with branches in South Africa, South America and the Middle and Far East. Edward's name is pretty prominent.'

'There's a piece in the *Forest Journal* archive referring to Edward as an ex-international pentathlete,' Daisy added.

'Is there now.' Callum knew from personal experience that exercise was a habit hard to break once you got used to starting the day with a run. There were acres of open land right on the doorstep of Devereux Manor. Had Edward been out running the morning that Mary-Ellen died?

'Both Richard and Matthew were pentathletes at school,' Daisy said, 'and Matthew was a junior international.'

'Following in Daddy's footsteps.' Cookie laughed at his own joke, looked round at the others and when they didn't join in, referred once again to his paper. 'Fencing, swimming, riding, shooting and running. And he must be pretty good at all of them to be an international. Edward still competes in the old blokes' races.'

'Bloody knackering if you ask me,' Bird said.

'Riding and running,' Callum said to Daisy. 'Let's find out a bit more about Edward. Mrs Smart couldn't give us an age for the person lacing his trainers, but he was driving a black SUV. And ask the dog walkers who they see running there regularly.'

'And ask them if they've seen Sir Michael, while you're at it,' Bird muttered and returned to his desk.

* * *

When the outer door opened, Callum looked up to see Martha coming across the office towards the fishbowl. She tapped on the door before lowering herself carefully onto the chair opposite Callum. He raised an eyebrow by way of greeting.

'Yes, I've hurt my back. Yes, I fell off my horse yesterday, and no, it's not a bloody carthorse,' she said gruffly.

Callum's attempted look of surprise failed as this was exactly what he had been thinking.

Martha chuckled at his false solemnity. The twinkle was back in her eye. 'I asked him to turn left, and he thought I meant the other left. At least he waited for me and didn't shoot off home.'

'Nothing broken, I hope?'

'Good padding.' She patted her amply covered hips. 'Now, good news or bad news first?'

Callum thought that if she had elected to struggle along in person to deliver news, then it would be on the back of an apology, so he let her have her moment of glory first.

'Good, please.'

'Okay. The fibre on the back of Mary-Ellen's riding jacket is polybutylene terephthalate. PBT to you and me. Used in sportswear manufacture, running clothes, that sort of thing. They're working on tying it down to a specific brand or range, but nothing so far.'

'So, we're looking for someone wearing sports gear. And the bad news?'

'We missed something the first time around.'

Callum said nothing. It was not his policy to rant and rave. Nor was it his policy to forget.

'Do you ride?' she asked suddenly.

Callum shook his head.

'What do you know about stirrups?'

'Humour me.'

'Okay. Stirrups are parallel bars of metal. They can get a bit slippery in the wrong conditions, so for a bit of extra purchase, riders often put rubber treads on top of the metal.'

'Stops them falling off when their horse goes the wrong way?' he asked with a smile.

'Smart-arse. The treads on Mary-Ellen's are dimpled, like the underneath of an egg carton?'

Callum nodded.

'So,' she continued, 'we have a partial print on a dimpled surface. Not sufficient for an ID, but definitely not a riding boot, a trainer. Find the shoe though, and it might be a different story.'

Callum gave her a brief smile and absently rotated his silver earring. Even without Cookie's jigsaw picture, the pieces were slowly falling into place.

'Thank you, Martha.'

Her grey eyes were alert. 'Told you what you wanted to hear, did I?' She grimaced as she struggled to her feet. Once upright, she said, 'You don't want to buy a horse, do you?'

Callum's look of horror provoked her boom of laughter that had all heads turning towards the fishbowl.

'I'll take that as a no then.'

She left Callum deep in thought, which is how Daisy found him ten minutes later.

'Sir?' She tidied stray hairs back from her face.

'Daisy. What is it?' He beckoned her into the fishbowl.

'I've dug up a bit more on Edward, and guess what? He represented South Africa internationally, and Cookie was right, he still competes, but he does triathlon, not pentathlon now. He's still running. I don't think we should overlook him.'

He told her about the trainer print and PBT, and watched her narrow face widen into a smile.

'Interesting. Are we going visiting, sir?'

'Do the bawbags in Pollock get blootered on a Friday?'

134

Chapter Sixteen

The double gates to Devereux Manor stood open. Hinged onto tall railings, the intricate wrought iron was embellished with a gold coat of arms in the centre of each portal. Callum thought he could recognise a leopard and a hawk amongst spears and foliage, as they swept through.

'They're keep-out-the-riff-raff sort of gates. Do you think we should continue?' Daisy said, without lifting her foot from the accelerator.

Callum was getting used to her habit of couching observations as rhetorical questions.

The drive, striped by sharp shadows, ran bullet-straight through an avenue of mature lime trees. Their leafy canopies, like a guard of honour, directed his eye to a Palladian-style Georgian mansion dwarfed to a doll's house by the distance from the gates.

'I might run out of diesel before I get there,' Daisy said.

The air swirled with sticky debris, lime blossom glued itself to her windscreen and filled their nostrils with sweet perfume. It looked eerily like a snowstorm in the bright sunlight. The house was a daunting architectural specimen that reminded Callum of the Gallery of Modern Art in Glasgow, minus the equestrian statue of the Duke of Wellington with his iconic traffic cone hat.

Daisy squinted at the dark windows through her smeared windscreen.

'You wouldn't want the window cleaners' bill for this place, would you?' She pulled on the handbrake. 'Or the heating bill either.'

Double-armed steps climbed to a wide pillared portico shading the entrance door. Callum felt like a small child in a grown-up world as they ascended in stride, placing their feet in the hollows worn by generations of past visitors.

'Do you think we'll have to pay to get in?' She looked along the side of the building as they gained height and then up at Callum. 'Three black Range Rovers parked down there.'

'Noted,' he said, without averting his eyes from the over-tall front door. The sun was hot, and a bead of sweat prickled his scalp before they reached the canopied shade of the portico.

Security cameras mooned down at them, and they didn't find out if the bell-pull worked because the door swung open at their approach. They had obviously triggered a security beam and Callum glanced around but couldn't locate it. A grey-suited servant stood before them. His expression was of professional indifference, and his torso inclined forward, as if his hearing might be deficient. Behind him, the scent of lavender and the sonorous tick of a clock suggested a period drama, a cameo of polite society from a century ago. The illusion was quickly dispelled when a tall, thin man, wearing running clothes and a sweaty look, appeared beside the older man.

'That will be all, Briggs.' He stepped forward as Briggs reversed, like figures in a weather-house hygrometer.

'Edward Devereux-Strauss. Who are you?' He addressed the question to Callum who introduced both himself and Daisy.

Edward's eyes swept over Callum, but he didn't look at Daisy.

'What can I do for you?' His question was abrupt to the point of rudeness, but his brown eyes seemed friendly, his brow smooth, and Callum sensed that this was just his manner.

'We'd like to ask you some questions about Mary-Ellen Mitchell, sir.'

Edward stilled for a blink, lips parted, showing even white teeth.

'Is that the silly bint that fell off her horse on the purlieu and killed herself?'

'Yes. The lady did fall from a horse.'

'Well, I didn't know her so I can't help you.' Edward stepped back into the hall.

'It is the same Mary-Ellen Mitchell you commented on in the press after the refusal of your planning application,' Daisy said.

His cowled eyes skimmed over her, and the corners of his mouth pulled inwards.

He addressed Callum. 'In that case, my solicitor would be better acquainted with her than me. That's what I pay him for.'

'Would you remember her better as Mary-Ellen Goddard?' Callum asked smoothly. 'I understand her parents worked for you for many years.'

'For my father, perhaps. We employ many staff, in the UK, in South Africa and Argentina. I can't be expected to know every lackey on the payroll.'

'She lived here on this estate,' Callum persisted, keeping his tone conversational.

'I was away at Eton, and then university. I didn't live here permanently until my father passed.' He glanced down at his sports watch.

'But you saw her when you came home?'

Edward sighed. 'I cannot recall ever having met her.' He avoided eye contact.

Why lie to such a simple question when he had been truthful about everything else? Callum let it pass.

Edward said he had driven from London on the morning of the murder and arrived just after ten. He frowned when asked if anyone could verify that, but suggested they ask Richard.

'He had been out riding and was handing his horse over to that groom. That's two witnesses. Will that be sufficient for you?' He placed one hand on the door and the other on the jamb, a barrier between the detectives and his private world. Perhaps having his statements challenged was a new experience for him.

'I will check. Thank you, sir. I'm new to this area. Is the New Forest a good place to run?' Callum's tone was light as he nodded at the clothes Edward was wearing.

'It is. Both my boys and I run here regularly. A good place to exercise, clean air in your lungs.'

'Thank you for the advice, sir. And who do the Range Rovers belong to?'

'One is mine, one is my son Matthew's, and the other is Richard's.' He ran his hand over his cropped hair and there was a slight tremor in his fingers.

'And does Matthew live here?'

'No. In London. He's my finance director and, before you feel it necessary to ask, he has driven down this morning to deliver papers that I don't choose to entrust to a courier. Is that all?'

'Yes. Sorry to have interrupted your morning and thank you for your time.'

Callum followed Daisy out into the sunlight and down the steps. The sweet smell of newly mown grass drifted from a formal lawn where a gardener was producing perfect parallel stripes.

'Don't you love the smell of cut grass?' Daisy stepped down onto the gravel and vigorously flapped her arms as if preparing for take-off. She stared at her mimicking shadow. 'Thank goodness,' she said and walked on with her usual gait.

Callum chuckled. 'Worried you might be invisible, Daisy?'

'For the last five minutes I was, but it was a false alarm.'

They followed a high wall along the side of the house until a lorry-width gap gave them access to the stable yard. Coming out was a young man wearing a suit and polished shoes.

'Hello. Can I help?' He extended a hand towards Callum and smiled at both of them. 'I'm Matthew.'

Callum shook his hand. Matthew had the distinctive Devereux nose but seemed less guarded, and more approachable, than his father.

'We are looking for Richard,' Callum said, releasing Matthew's hand.

Matthew laughed good-humouredly. 'Good luck with that. I was hoping for a word before I drove back to London, but I couldn't find him. It will have to wait for another day.' He walked out of the yard and back towards the house.

Wooden loose boxes formed a U-shape that surrounded a central paved rectangle on which a couple of benches were placed. The left arm of the U had an upper storey with curtained windows, probably grooms' accommodation, but the remainder was single height.

The top doors of the boxes were fixed open, and several well-bred heads watched their approach. Callum could hear the rhythmic grinding of teeth on fodder, the rustling of hoof-disturbed straw and the snickering breaths of the horses. The breeze swirled sweet notes of hay, mingling them with warm horses and dung. One look at Daisy's rapt expression told him that she was in her element. Good job one of them was.

Behind the boxes on the right-hand side, and visible above the shingle roof, was an open-sided barn stacked with baled shavings, hay and straw. It was accessed by a wheelbarrow-width path that ran between the end box and the post and rail fence enclosing an all-weather manège. A bay gelding was tied to the outside rails and Daisy walked across to pat him on the neck. He snaked his head around in search of a treat.

'Not this time, fella.'

His saddle had recently been removed and his back steamed gently. Daisy idled along a row of boxes and looked over each door. She shrugged her shoulders at

Callum who had just joined her when they heard a girl's shriek of laughter from the barn, and Richard came round the corner into the yard, tucking his shirt into his breeches. Half a stride behind him was a moon-faced girl picking hay out of her black hair with one hand and carrying a bale of hay in the other.

The girl was looking up at Richard and giggling at something he had said. They both stopped abruptly, shoulder to shoulder, when they saw they had company. Callum recognised her as the girl riding with Richard and Jimmy Eastwood the morning of the murder.

Richard was good-looking in a more sculpted way than his father. He had the same hawknose and brow-line, but was clean-shaven and his hair, long on top, was undercut at the sides. He ran his fingers through it, then stopped abruptly when he spotted Daisy.

'Can't stay away from me then?'

'Police business.' Her answer was quick and sharp.

'Is there any other sort with you?' He ran his eyes up and down her body. 'One day…'

'Hell will freeze over. What time did your father arrive home the morning Mary-Ellen Mitchell was found dead?'

'Search me. Oh, you don't touch people, do you? I forgot.'

'We all have standards,' she snapped, her breathing quickening. 'Perhaps mine are higher than most.'

'Don't make it too difficult or you might find that shelf is so high you can't get down without a parachute.'

Callum was about to interrupt them when he noticed the girl. She put down the hay bale and stood with her arms tightly folded, mouth pursed, and her eyes, filled with green fire, scything from one to the other. He leaned back against a loose box door to unpick Richard's relationship with his groom and his exchange with Daisy. It was the first glimpse of a chink in her armour of good-natured affability. While it was not exactly a show of temper, emotion roiled beneath the surface of her sunny façade.

He had been right about some history between the two of them.

His interest in their conversation was consuming. It wasn't until he felt warm breath on the back of his head, and his hair being teased, that he realised the stable behind him was occupied. He sped sideways away from the door and out of the reach of the inquisitive horse. Daisy and the girl both burst out laughing.

'You daft sod.' The girl grinned at Callum as she brushed past him to get to the horse.

He looked closely at her generously applied make-up.

'He wouldn't hurt you, would you, Duke baby?' The muscles in her arms ridged as she rubbed her hand over the bony chestnut head before dipping forward to kiss his muzzle.

Callum stood at a safe distance and rubbed his hand over the back of his head. This was the closest he had been to a horse since a graceless skirmish with a police mount at a Glasgow Rangers match. The horse had triumphed that time, and he wasn't courting a repeat performance. The only signs of this encounter were horse dribble in his hair and an increased heart rate, both of which he would recover from.

The girls were still laughing. Daisy walked over to the stable door and whispered something to the groom who lowered her head to the shorter detective. The comment produced more mirth. Richard stood alone in the yard. He spun on his heel, and with stiff strides disappeared through an open steel-lined door. Emerging a few seconds later, he pitched a dandy brush at the girl with unnecessary vigour. Her reactions were quick, and her catch deft. She poked out her studded tongue at Richard, ran it along her bottom lip, and then blew him a kiss.

'Get on with the horse. Now.' Richard watched her athletic figure walk towards the tethered gelding.

Birds squabbled in the oak tree as she passed and a pigeon flew out, collided with the gable end of the boxes, and dropped to the ground. It lay on its front, wings fluttering weakly, and the girl stood over it for a moment.

'Poor thing.' She reached down and lifted the trembling grey mass.

With the brush held in her armpit, she put her hands around the bird's neck and gave a sharp twist. The head flopped lifelessly.

'It would have died anyway,' she said in response to Daisy's indrawn breath. She tossed the carcass into a wheelbarrow half-filled with straw and dung, before taking the dandy brush in her hand and moving towards the tethered horse.

The detectives exchanged a glance.

'What time did your father arrive here that morning?' Callum asked Richard, who shrugged.

'Ten, maybe later. I'd already worked two horses and we'd ridden out with Eastwood.'

'Do you usually ride with Jimmy?' Daisy asked.

'Not often, and it was a total waste of time. He said he was interested in buying a horse, then changed his mind.'

Not a waste of time for Jimmy, Callum thought. It gave him an alibi for the murder.

'Why did he change his mind?' Daisy asked.

'You tell me. Too much horse for him, I expect. He's no rider. Sits like a sack of spuds in the saddle. He'd be better off with a seaside donkey.'

Richard's attention was magnetised by the groom. She was stretching up to brush out the saddle mark on the bay horse. The long sweeping strokes pushed her breasts up against the thin material of her T-shirt. He followed her movements, his mouth half-open, a covetous look on his face. Daisy walked over to join the girl.

'What's her name?' Callum nodded towards the women, who were conversing in quiet voices. The groom had lifted the near foreleg of the horse and was supporting it on her knee as Daisy helped her do something to the raised hoof.

'I presume you don't mean Daisy keep-your-hands-off-me Donaldson?'

'You presume right.'

'Rose Brown,' he said, a half-smile on his lips. 'Sweet sixteen and eager to learn.' The defensiveness had left his voice and Callum wondered if this was because of his attraction to Rose, or because he was no longer conversing with Daisy.

'What were you doing that morning before you went riding with Eastwood?'

Richard smirked. 'I was "doing" Rose Brown, sweet sixteen and eager to learn.'

Callum thrust his bunched fists into his pockets.

Chapter Seventeen

Callum matched paces with Daisy as they walked back to her vehicle. She was uncharacteristically quiet; something was playing on her mind. He stayed silent and waited.

'Something's not right,' she said when they were seated in her Navara.

'Go on.' He had misgivings of his own and was pleased that she sensed something was awry.

'Something is off. How old is she? It's just a gut instinct. But I believe in going with your gut.'

So did he, but he was not about to encourage her to go flying off on tangents. These days, cosmetics and hair treatments blurred the lines; attitudes and dress codes changed, and he found it difficult to accurately assess the age of young women.

'Richard says she's sixteen.'

'He's thinking with the wrong part of his anatomy.' She pressed the ignition. 'Second, she might be being abused.'

'How so?'

'Because' – she steered slowly onto the drive – 'when we were looking at the horse's frog—'

'The what?'

'The pointy V-shaped bit under his hoof. Anyway, she pulled up her sleeve and there's a big bruise on her right forearm.'

'Circumstantial. She could have got that doing her job.' He remembered the force with which Richard had pitched the brush at her.

'Okay. But her left forearm's bruised, and so's her wrist. I bet it's Richard who put them there. Add that to the bruise on her eye, and the one on her cheek that she's trying to cover up with all that warpaint. He's got a temper, you know.'

Perhaps the animosity between her and Richard had something to do with this temper Daisy seemed to know so much about. Callum had also noticed the ochre and indigo discolouration under her make-up but hadn't drawn the same conclusion as Daisy.

'You don't think she just fell off a horse?' Callum said.

'It's possible, I suppose.' Gravel pinged beneath her tyres.

'Did you notice the way Richard looked at Rose?' Callum asked. 'And the way she looked from you to Richard?'

'No, but looking's not a crime,' Daisy said.

Fresh lime blossom swirled in through the open window and Daisy sneezed.

'Do you think she's a runaway?' she asked suddenly.

'Why do you say that?' What had he missed?

'Nothing concrete, just a niggle. She knows what she's doing with horses though.' She changed up a gear and closed the distance to the gate.

'Check missing persons, see if you can find a match, and Wales might be a good place to start. There's a touch of an accent, very slight but it's there. And her hair's not black. She's a natural blonde.'

Daisy looked at him sharply.

'Eyes on the road, Daisy.' His turn to take her by surprise. 'Helps to be tall. Her roots need touching up.'

With two-thirds of the driveway behind them, Callum touched Daisy's forearm.

'Slow down,' he said. 'What's going on here?'

A blue car had pulled onto the grass verge outside of the white railings. At first, Callum thought it was waiting for them to drive out but there was plenty of width to pass.

'Look, sir. Someone is walking through the trees on my right.'

A woman was taking careful paces across the grass towards the open gates. Her green tweed suit was a roomy fit and the skirt drooped at the back, brushing her calves. Callum tried to discern her age, but the knotted headscarf hid her hair and obscured her face.

The car driver stayed in the vehicle but seemed to be looking in their direction.

'Recognise either of them, Daisy?'

'Not yet.' She drove through the gate and pulled up on the opposite verge.

Callum opened his passenger door and approached the parked blue estate. It had seen better days, and he wondered if it was roadworthy beneath the dirt and dents.

The driver's door creaked open, and a young woman stepped out onto the grass.

'Can I help you?' she asked. Her voice was pleasant, educated, and she looked Callum in the eye.

He introduced himself and was surprised when her gaze didn't waver. People usually became overhelpful or had it away on their toes. The woman did neither. She leaned back against her car, one foot on the door sill, the other on the grass, and her elbow rested on the roof. He hoped the bodywork could take the pressure.

He asked her what she was doing there.

'I'm collecting my mother for a hospital appointment. And you?' She smiled. The skin around her eyes concertinaed into soft folds and he reassessed her age to mid-thirties.

He smiled back but didn't answer her question. 'And your name?'

'That's fair as I already know yours, Inspector MacLean. I'm Bryony Osbourne.'

She extended her hand to him. It was slim and manicured. The firmness of her handshake left him unprepared for the silky warmth of her palm against his, and he held the contact a little longer than he had intended.

'And your connection with Devereux Manor?' The scent of her perfume was light, and warm, like the taste of oranges in sunshine.

'I've already told you that I am collecting my mother, Penny Devereux-Strauss. Edward is my father.' There was an edge to her voice but just for a second.

Callum noted the different surnames and glanced at her ringless left hand before he could stop himself. She raised a questioning eyebrow, but he could bring no suitable comment to mind. Instead, he watched the gold St Christopher that nestled in the hollow of her throat, rising and falling with her pulse. It was the sort of necklace Grace would have chosen. Neither of them punctured the bubble of silence suspended between them until the scrunch of gravel behind him pulled their attention.

The woman that he and Daisy had seen walking towards the gate, now paused beside him, her hand resting on the white railings as she recovered her breath. Unfastening her headscarf revealed golden hair, lightly threaded with white. She looked younger than her slow progress had suggested.

'Hello, Mum. All right?'

'Yes, thank you, dear.' She folded the scarf and snapped it into her handbag.

Callum glanced from mother to daughter. Bryony was tall, strong-boned with a cascade of thick brown locks, in no way resembling the short, delicate woman, with pale skin and fine hair. Bryony had the stamp of her father about her.

He and Bryony turned their heads as a Range Rover sped up the driveway towards them. Callum placed a hand beneath Mrs Devereux-Strauss's elbow to steer her out of the way as Richard slid to a halt and opened his window.

'I'm late, Mother. Get out of my way.' He revved the engine as they moved to the verge then accelerated, tyres clawing at the loose surface and peppering Callum's shielding body with stones. They could still hear his engine long after he was out of sight.

The old woman's bones were thin beneath his fingers, and Callum asked if she was all right. She didn't reply. He looked at Bryony who tapped her ear, so Callum faced Penny and repeated his question.

'Absolutely fine, thank you. You are very kind. Bryony, I don't want to be late.'

Callum walked around the bonnet of the car and opened the passenger door. Penny nodded her thanks and dropped into the seat, placing her handbag on her lap. He pulled down the belt buckle, handed it to her, and closed the door as she secured it. Across the car roof he saw that Bryony was smiling.

'Why don't you collect her from the house?'

She hesitated then said, 'Ask my father.'

When her car disappeared around the bend in the lane, he realised that Daisy was watching him, her head tilted to one side.

* * *

Daisy and Callum stood in front of the board. She wrote "Edward Devereux-Strauss". The string of letters was so long that it curved up and over the question-marked Jimmy Eastwood.

'I think all suspects should have short names.' She scrubbed out his surname and replaced it with a tidier "D-S".

The clock on the wall said it was nearly four and Callum couldn't remember if they had eaten lunch, but he didn't think they had stopped at all. He knew he had pushed them hard, but no harder than he pushed himself. He took some notes from his wallet and passed them to Legs. 'Organise pizzas for us all, will you?' He picked a sheet of paper from his desk.

'And save me a slice. I'm off to update DCI Bellman before his press conference.'

* * *

Callum did not have time to fully close Bellman's office door before his superior spoke. 'Stop harassing Edward Devereux-Strauss.' Bellman wiped a hand across his brow.

Callum halted mid-stride. 'Sorry, sir. I don't understand. Sergeant Donaldson and I have just visited…'

'I am very well aware of that fact.' Bellman glanced at his desk phone.

Callum had not anticipated this sort of greeting. Speaking to Bryony Osbourne had only delayed them for minutes, but it was long enough for someone to have contacted a senior officer and complained. That complaint had dropped down the ladder to land on Bellman's shoulders and he didn't look happy about it.

'We are exploring a new lead. We have established a link between our victim and Edward Devereux-Strauss. It could help eliminate him from our inquiries.'

'MacLean. Listen to me.' Bellman's voice was low and deliberate. 'There is no link. Consider him eliminated.' He removed his glasses and pinched the bridge of his nose between finger and thumb. The sagging folds of skin beneath his eyes seemed heavier than before.

Callum felt a tick of annoyance and folded his arms. He had registered every quiet word Bellman had spoken. But he was more interested in what had not been said. He decided to dig a little deeper.

'He denies knowing her—'

Bellman surged to his feet. His glasses flew from his fingers onto the desk, scattering the neat row of pens lined up on the blotter.

'Enough. Leave it, MacLean.' He seemed startled by the aggression in his voice and sat back down. 'Look, I'm no happier about this than you are.' He loosened the knot of his tie, replaced his glasses, and realigned his pens.

Callum unfolded his arms and considered how to deal with the matter. He had once been warned off a line of investigation in an arson case. Ignoring the directive, he had followed his instincts and that time, he had been right. Was he right this time?

Bellman finished with his pens. They had both pledged an oath to represent all sections of the public without fear or favour. Callum's duty was to get justice for the victim. He had not sworn to massage egos higher up the food chain or become embroiled in internal politics. And he wasn't about to start now. Bellman had been as unhappy to deliver that warning as he had been to receive it. Where had it come from?

Callum decided that Richard was young, hot-headed, the impulsive type who would take action himself. Edward was a controller. Edward was calling the shots. Bellman's chair creaked but Callum didn't look at him. Instead, he focused on a spider. It was weaving a web and skilfully avoiding the razor edges of the dagger-leaf plant.

Bellman cleared his throat. 'Good. Good. Now, I understand you have cleared up the power tool thefts.'

'It would seem so, sir.'

'Good. Now, update me on your murder.'

'We have eliminated all the initial suspects, except for Sir Michael.'

'And you think that he murdered his wife?'

'No. We are looking further afield.' He resisted mentioning Edward again, but he wasn't going to forget about him.

'Have you eliminated Eastwood, then? Despite his background? He seems to fit the frame.'

'We considered him a possibility...' Callum hesitated. 'What do you think, sir?' He hoped his question sounded genuine, and that the answer would give some insight into what was going on behind the scenes to make sense of this strange turn of events.

'My advice would be to look at his history before you discount him. An ex-soldier, no stranger to death, PTSD and probably still traumatised by the death of that boy in Helmand. That's not something you get over in a hurry, is it?'

'Probably not.'

Callum felt a flutter in his stomach. This ground had been thoroughly covered. Didn't Bellman think him capable of doing his job?

'He has an alibi for the time of the murder.'

'Don't be naïve, MacLean. An alibi can be manufactured. Check it again.'

Callum sensed that he was being used as a pawn in someone else's game. And he didn't like that feeling one little bit.

'I'll bear that in mind. Will that be all?' He hoped it was. Trying to interfere in his investigation was one thing, questioning his ability to do his job was quite another.

'Are you married, MacLean?'

'I'm sorry, sir?'

'I enquired if you were married, Inspector.'

'Widowed. No children.' He wanted out of here.

'Siblings?'

'Three sisters.' He relaxed his hands, trying to think of a way to call time on the meeting.

Bellman looked him in the eye for the first time that day. 'They can be quite a responsibility, can't they? Mine is. It's difficult sometimes.'

'Indeed.' Callum had no idea what he was talking about. 'And the appeal for Sir Michael?'

'Will be broadcast this evening. I expect you to advise me that you have made an arrest.'

* * *

Callum closed Bellman's door quietly behind him. He stood in the corridor and looked down at the floor. If he had wanted a future in politics, he would have stood for the SNP. He looked up as footsteps approached. PCs Cooper and Kent gave him a curious glance but walked past trailing a whisper of cigarette smoke behind them.

Nearing the office, the smell of hot cheese seeped into the corridor. He quickened his pace and then halted abruptly two feet from the door. There was nothing written on the board about Jimmy Eastwood's reason for leaving the service, just "PTSD" below his question-marked name. How did Bellman know about the boy in Helmand?

When Callum pushed open the office door, his team were gathered around a table eating pizza. His eyes passed over each in turn. Legs stood shoulder to shoulder with Bird, like two sequoias, towering over his sergeant and Cookie.

Daisy nodded to a closed pizza box. 'We saved you some. It's in there.' She watched him, her head tilted to one side. She flashed a warning look at Cookie who, with melted cheese and a streak of tomato on his chin, was staring at the closed box.

Callum took the last two slices and motioned to Bird to join him in the fishbowl, conscious that Cookie's eyes followed the pizza.

'Bleedin' gannet, that one.' Bird closed the door behind him at Callum's directive, and frowned as he watched Callum inspect the desk drawers and a stack of folders. 'Problem?'

'Was anyone in here when I was out?'

'Don't think so, guv.' Bird's frown deepened as he thought back. 'I wasn't here all the time though. But Cookie was, or should have been,' he amended.

Callum nodded.

'Lost something?'

'No. When was the last time you had a one-to-one with Bellman?'

'What year was the plague?'

His tombstones shone but Callum remained silent and Bird's smile evaporated like dew in the morning sun.

'He's not exactly my cup of tea, guv. He's got a pretty low opinion of ex-squaddies and makes no bones about letting me know it.'

Callum felt a sudden empathy with the ex-soldier. Bellman didn't seem to be too keen on Scotsmen either.

'So, he hasn't asked you about the case?'

'No. Why?'

When Callum ignored his question, Bird continued, 'The others aren't chummy with him. Not even Deedee, but I don't suppose I should be talking about a senior officer like that. Am I in trouble or something?'

'Not with me. What about Cookie?'

'Not a lot of love lost. A bit Hamlet and Claudius.'

Callum had not suspected Bird of being a Shakespeare buff. The surprises with this new crew kept coming.

'What's the reason for the animosity between them?'

'No idea. But it's personal, not professional.' Bird thought for a second. 'Wonder Boy wanted plain clothes and thinks Bellman had him moved here so he could keep an eye on him.'

Callum's mouth tightened.

'Cookie's done nothing wrong, except for being a pain in the arse, so it has to be personal.'

'Fair enough. Thanks, Bird.'

Bird returned to his desk. Legs wouldn't be cosying up to Bellman after his lack of support with the Denton debacle, so that left Daisy. He caught her eye, and she came into the fishbowl.

'Anything on Rose Brown yet, Daisy?'

'No, and I bet that won't be her real name when we get a hit. Assuming she's been reported missing, that is. She might not be.'

'I'd like to think someone's missing her.'

'I hope so too. And the neighbours said that Veronica was definitely in that morning. The Parsons were having yet another loud, humdinger of a row about money. It's a regular occurrence.'

Callum gave her an edited version of his conversation with Bellman, and she confirmed that she had not spoken to him. She glanced at the board for confirmation that there was nothing written up about the boy in Helmand. Only one other option remained. Someone had read the personal notes that were in his desk drawer.

He hadn't told Bellman about Helmand because he didn't consider it relevant. But someone had told him. Someone with a personal agenda. And was that linked to the order to stop investigating Edward Devereux-Strauss?

Daisy watched in silence as Callum zipped today's notes into his laptop bag and balanced a thread on the lip of the drawer before closing it. She nodded her agreement when he asked her to keep the matter between themselves for now.

It boiled down to two questions, Callum thought as his eye played across the few remaining people in the office. Who would gain from compromising his investigation? And who would lose if he continued? Right now, they were questions he couldn't answer.

Chapter Eighteen

Daisy's kitchen smelled of the cottage pie bubbling in the oven. He was hungry despite the earlier slices of pizza.

Felix sprawled on the floor with a hopeful look in his soft toffee eyes.

Daisy laughed. 'No chance, Felix. We made a deal; I don't eat your food, and you don't eat mine.'

Felix made a noise in his throat and wagged his way over to Daisy who fussed him and kissed him on the snout. Then he padded over to appeal to Callum who stroked his head gently.

'I'm no kissing youse, you hairy monster. That's down to the woman in your life. She maybe likes a man with a beard.'

'Now that would be telling.' Daisy smiled. She picked up a handwritten note from the granite worktop, read it quickly then opened the fridge. On a shelf was a bowl of dessert that looked like a study of rock strata topped with custard and cream.

'Mrs P keeps a weather eye on things. I suspect she reports back to Mother who tells her to feed me, even though I am quite capable of feeding myself.' She closed the fridge door. 'But I am also quite prepared to put up with her mollycoddling as, boy can she cook.'

Callum wondered if there was a mother somewhere worrying if Rose Brown was eating properly.

Daisy tilted her head to one side. 'Bryony Osbourne seems nice, don't you think?'

'Indeed, she does.' He found plates and forks.

'Different surname from Edward. She must be married.' She opened the oven door.

'No wedding ring.'

The corner of her mouth twitched as she put the hot dish on a board.

'It's weird that she waits outside the gates for Penny. That's odd, isn't it? If it was my mother…' She paused when her phone rang to check the caller display. 'Speak of the devil.'

'Darling, just to let you know that Dom is flying down from Alaska to New York and he said he will be in touch. I'm hoping he might squeeze us in for a quick visit if he has time. Dad sends love. Got to dash.' The phone emitted a long screech before the dialling tone purred.

Daisy laughed. 'Bye, Mum,' she said to the empty airway then busied herself spooning out food. She passed him a steaming plate then forked food into her mouth, her eyes on his face. 'You know, I never noticed her lack of a wedding ring.'

Callum loaded his fork. 'You need to work on your observation skills then.'

They finished their supper in silence.

He made them coffee and watched Daisy eat every meticulously scraped trace of dessert from the inside of the glass bowl that Mrs P had put in the fridge. Sugar fix. He was sucked back to a rainy afternoon before his and Grace's last Christmas together. He had come home to find her sitting in the middle of the floor surrounded by torn wrapping paper and abandoned chocolate wrappers. 'False alarm,' she had sobbed. 'No baby, and I ate Dolina's present.' He had dropped to the floor, cocooned her in his arms, and they had rocked silently as the day died, his chin resting on top of her head. Her hair smelled of coconut.

After Grace, he had developed 'island syndrome'. He repelled people's interest in him and crushed any interest in others. He was startled that Daisy seemed to have slipped under his radar. He thought of Grace and his sisters and wondered if he was destined to spend his life surrounded by strong women.

Daisy glanced at the clock, took a remote control out of a drawer, and switched on the wall-mounted television.

Callum felt a tick of annoyance when Bellman's face filled the screen as it reminded him of their earlier meeting and now the man was invading his personal space. Bellman cut an authoritative figure in his pressed uniform, sitting against the backdrop of the constabulary emblem.

Daisy turned up the volume.

'I must stress that Sir Michael Mitchell is not a suspect, but we are concerned for his safety. If you have seen him, or have any information about his whereabouts, then please call the number now on the bottom of your screen.' Bellman leaned towards the camera. 'No piece of information is too small. It could save a life.' It was cleverly balanced, with sufficient urgency to imply concern without starting a witch-hunt.

'He does a good appeal, doesn't he, Callum?'

'We'll find out how successful it is in the morning,' he said. 'Your mum sounded pleased that Dom might be able to fit in a visit to Paris.'

Daisy started to speak, then paused as if a thought had just occurred to her. 'You do know that Mum's the military attaché at the British Embassy in Paris.'

His mouth fell open in surprise and he closed it rapidly. This was something he would never have guessed. Daisy's crack of laughter at his reaction had Felix on his feet, barking and wagging his tail.

'You thought my dad was the attaché, didn't you?' She wiped the back of her hand across her eyes and then patted her dog. 'Everyone thinks that.'

'I didn't know either of them was an attaché.'

'And you call yourself a detective.' There was sparkle in her blue eyes and colour in her cheeks.

He felt a warmth that he had not experienced for a long time and realised that inclusion was something he missed. He took his sketchbook from his pocket, opened it to a clean page and settled down to add to his pictorial diary.

Daisy opened the back door to let Felix out into the garden. She spoke to the dog, and he could tell from her tone that she was still amused by his ignorance. He could live with that. He wondered what else he didn't know about his sergeant.

* * *

The morning light splashed zebra patterns across the office furniture and dust motes churned in a sunlit kaleidoscope.

Cookie scrutinised pages as the printer spewed them out into his waiting hand. The click and swish synchronised with the tap of his toe. Daisy concentrated on her screen, her ponytail twitching as she moved her head, like a horse protecting itself from flies. They were committed to the task at hand.

The door to the fishbowl was closed. Callum detected a faint trace of cigarette smoke when he entered. The smell was stronger when he sat in his chair. Opening the drawer, he saw the cotton thread had dropped into the paper clips. Nothing else was disturbed. It was a professional hand at work.

Bird tapped on the open door. His sleeves were rolled up to the elbow showing the age-blurred edges of his tattoos. He sniffed the air.

'Cigarette smoke. Got a nose like a bloodhound since Helen made me quit.' He moved to the desk and sniffed again. 'Marlborough, I reckon.'

'Anyone here when you came in this morning?'

'Just the usual and none of us smoke. Filthy habit.' He barked a laugh. 'As an ex-smoker, I've turned into a sanctimonious git. Apparently.'

'Who still smokes?' Callum had not seen anyone so far, just smelled the aftermath on Cooper and Kent.

'One or two but nothing like the number we used to have.' He nodded towards the two PCs. 'They light up and old Johnny, the desk sergeant, but it would stink of garlic if it was him. Who's been in here then, guv?'

'Good question, Bird.' Callum filled him in on his meeting with Bellman and the DCI's surprising knowledge of Jimmy's past.

Bird glanced at the board just as Daisy had done.

'Right.' Callum nodded at the papers in Bird's hand. 'Anything yet?'

'Our Great British bleedin' public, guv.' Bird flapped his sheaf of papers at Callum sending an inky draught across the room. 'I said this would happen. He's been sighted everywhere from Falmouth to Fife, but we're concentrating on the close ones first. Probably leave the one in Corsica till after lunch.'

'Sound idea.'

'Couple of sightings in our target area and one of those is an off-duty traffic warden, or whatever they're called. She claims to have seen the car in Chilworth, Southampton at about 0400 hours. That's a posh area,' he added. 'We're following up on that one first.'

'Keep me informed.'

'Wilco.' Bird paused at the door and looked back over his shoulder. He tapped a finger against the side of his nose. 'I'll have a sniff around on that other little matter.'

His soft guffaw diminished as he moved away from Callum.

'Guv?' An uncharacteristically quiet Cookie stood in the doorway, his arms wrapped around a bundle of papers. Beckoned in, he perched on the edge of the chair.

'I've found something.' His usual confidence had deserted him. This was a side of the lad Callum hadn't seen before.

'What are those?' Callum asked.

'Phone record. From the vic– Mary-Ellen's mobile.'

'And?'

'You know all her personal contacts are coded, and all in a foreign language which you said was Gaelic? You were right about that, by the way.'

Callum wondered how long it was going to take Cookie to get around to the reason he had come to see him.

'Well, the call logs from her actual mobile and her records' – he shook the papers in his hand – 'don't match.'

'Explain.' The paper printout was a copy of the call register so it had to be the same.

'Remember the twenty-thousand-pound day and the murder day? Well, the night before both, Faol phoned her, and other times too, of course.'

Callum was sure that *faol* was Gaelic for wolf. Should they be looking for a stalker?

Cookie continued, 'But all traces were deleted from her handset, so we didn't know.' Cookie sat back on the chair. 'I made a mistake in not checking the deleted stuff. I only noticed when the two weren't the same. Sorry.'

'Anything else?'

'No. Faol is a pay-as-you-go, and it's off.' Cookie kept his eyes on Callum's face. 'I've asked to be advised if it's used again so we can triangulate the position.'

Callum nodded. 'And look at the other times they were in contact, time of day, who rang who. Look for a pattern.'

* * *

With Cookie immersed in his call records, it fell to Daisy to answer the phone. She spoke to the caller before going over to the fishbowl.

'Call for you, but your phone's engaged.'

They both looked at his receiver. Callum poked it with his finger, and it gently settled into its correct place.

'Who is it, Daisy?'

'Mary-Ellen's friend Jenny Walker. Remember Amanda Newman mentioned her? We left her a message to contact you, and she's just landed at Gatwick and turned on her mobile.'

'It's been switched off for the last three days?' Callum's question was shaded by disbelief. People were so addicted to social media that they couldn't survive a meal without checking their phones. An entire holiday should be in the record books.

'She's an estate agent and so she just switches off. She probably had other things on her mind, she was away with a, uh, friend. She did apologise for not getting back to you sooner.'

'Fair enough. Put her through, will you?'

'She's a bit shocked. She didn't know about Mary-Ellen.' Daisy returned to her desk.

Jenny's voice was husky, tight with tension and rhythmically interrupted by her sucking on a cigarette followed by her sharp exhale. Callum arranged that he and Daisy would meet her later that morning in Fordingbridge. He asked her about Sir Michael, but she had no idea where he could have gone. It looked as if Bird could be pinning his hopes on a traffic warden.

Callum summoned Cookie, Bird, and Daisy into the fishbowl, closed the door and nodded questioningly towards Legs' empty desk.

'Gone to meet Sister Agnes from the convent. She'll be back after lunch,' Daisy said.

'Okay, people.' Callum dropped into his chair. 'Someone was in here last night.'

'Any idea who?' Cookie asked.

'Nothing concrete. They're a smoker. Just be vigilant.'

Bird flashed his tombstones. 'I've got my nose to the ground on this one, guv,' he said, tapping his face.

Daisy rolled her eyes. Callum hoped they worked out who it was before Bird developed a sore.

'Daisy, you've been following up on Edward Devereux-Strauss. What do we know so far?'

'Pretty much what he wants us to know,' Daisy said. 'Rich man. He spent most of his early life in South Africa and Argentina doing good deeds and helping the growth of the local economy.'

'Lining his own bleedin' pocket,' Bird said. 'He owns a chunk of London, has a six-bed in Eaton Place, Belgravia, and Matthew and his wife have a flat round the corner also owned by Daddy. Not to mention the country pile and houses overseas.'

'He's got business interests in South Africa and Argentina, and it looks like he's making inroads into the Far East,' Daisy added.

'Following the money,' Cookie said.

'Lots of interests in mining,' Daisy said, 'and all his companies seem to be owned by other companies that he also owns. I got defeated trying to unravel the paper trail.'

'Standard business practice.' Cookie nodded.

'He's got a reputation as uncompromising, a hard bastard,' Bird said. 'And I bet his tax gurus save him more money a year than it takes to run this entire bloody department.'

'He's got connections,' Daisy said. 'I found some press shots of him with the Met commissioner, a few other "luminaries" and the PM, no less.'

'Money, prowess and power then,' Bird said. 'Anything else going for him?'

'Eton,' Daisy said looking at Bird, 'then Cambridge.'

'Fucking toffs,' Bird scowled, 'all privilege and no bleedin' brains. And they're running the country.'

Daisy glanced at Callum and smiled. She was the picture of innocence. Bird's top lip hitched in a sneer, and he looked up to find Callum watching him.

'Sorry, guv.' He grinned sheepishly. 'It's the army all over again. Getting off me soapbox right now.'

'The sports hall at Eton is called the Devereux-Strauss Complex,' Cookie said apropos of nothing.

'So?' Bird said.

'So, nothing. Just saying, Bird.'

'One thing is weird,' Daisy said. 'We know he married Penny, but she's never in any of the press photos. She might not exist for all I can find out about her after the marriage announcement. Except we know she does, because they've got three kids, and we saw her at the house.'

'Perhaps she wasn't a looker,' Bird said. 'Might have spoiled his public image.'

'The engagement picture,' Daisy said, handing a photo to Bird.

'That's my theory out of the window. No wonder the kids are all lookers.' He returned the photo to Daisy.

'The boys followed their father to Eton, didn't they?' Callum said.

'Yes,' Daisy said, watching him, 'but the girl went to the local comprehensive.'

'Really?' That was a surprise. 'Can't have been a financial decision. So why?'

'Perhaps he's not the father,' Bird said. 'Perhaps the missus played away, and he wouldn't pay to educate the kid. Might explain why we never see his wife in any of the press stuff. He must have a bloody good reason for hiding her away. Perhaps that's it.'

'No. She's his all right with that nose, Bird.' Daisy tilted her head to one side, her eyes on Callum. 'Looks better on the boys than on Bryony, don't you think, sir?'

Callum thought back to his meeting with Bryony Osbourne. 'Perhaps the school was her choice.' He nodded at his team. 'Let's keep this Edward stuff off the board for the moment, please, people.'

Bird directed a questioning look at Daisy as they left the fishbowl and Callum saw her shrug.

The noise level in the outer office dropped suddenly and Callum looked up to see DCI Bellman in the outer doorway. He looked around, eyes hopping from desk to desk, fingers tapping on the door handle.

Callum moved out of the fishbowl. 'Can I help you, sir?'

'Ah. MacLean.' His tone was conciliatory, and he looked weary. 'Has there been any response to my appeal?'

'Early days, but we've received some hopeful sightings. DC Hampton is following them up.'

Callum moved across to Daisy's desk. 'DS Donaldson and I are just leaving for a meeting with Mary-Ellen's best friend who has returned from holiday this morning. Will I come along to your office and update you when we get back?'

Daisy lifted her jacket from the back of her chair and she and Callum moved towards the outer door that was barred by their senior officer.

Bellman hesitated on the threshold. 'My office, MacLean. Later.' He retreated.

Callum had the feeling that he'd wanted to say something else.

Chapter Nineteen

The coffee shop in Fordingbridge High Street was warm and sunny. The mismatched furniture was painted yellow, green, or lilac and arranged in such random order, that it looked like early crocuses growing out of the floor. The hiss and burble of the machines drew Callum's attention, and his eyes lingered on the display of home-made cakes behind the glass counter. The coffee-and-walnut looked particularly enticing. As Daisy went to the counter, he pulled in his stomach muscles, stood a little straighter and located a woman sitting alone by the window.

Dressed in pink trousers and a cotton sweater with a scarf tied at her throat, she was tanned but not relaxed. She was stirring a spoon round and round in her cup, and the liquid breached the rim and slopped into the saucer. She looked up when Callum approached and dashed her auburn bob back from her face. When he introduced himself, she jerked to her feet, knocked the table and spilt her coffee.

'Oh, God. Sorry. I'm Jenny Walker.' She dabbed at the spilt liquid with a tissue.

'Thanks for meeting us on such short notice. Mrs Mitchell's death must have come as a shock.'

'Too right it did. She doesn't smoke. Doesn't drink. Takes exercise. Whereas me…' Her nicotine-heavy breath finished the sentence on her behalf. She dropped the sodden tissue onto the table and then reached into her bag for a pack of cigarettes and her lighter. Callum noted that they were a duty-free pack.

'Look. Two minutes, okay? I need a ciggie. Another one,' she said, heading for the door.

Daisy came to the table with coffee and cake. They watched through the window as the wraith-thin figure trod and re-trod the same four paving stones, sucking courage from her cigarette, and casting distorted shadows across the tabletop through the steamy glass. A procession of East Asian youths dressed in identical tops and wearing identical backpacks, split ranks and filed around her. They reminded Callum of turtles. Daisy replaced Jenny's spilt coffee with a fresh cup.

'Right, then.' Jenny slid back into her seat and put the cigarettes into her bag. 'I still can't grasp that she's dead.'

When told that Mary-Ellen had been murdered, Jenny's mouth formed a soft O.

'Are you sure? She's the least likely person in the world to make enemies. Ask anyone. Ask everyone.'

'We keep hearing that, but someone disagreed with you,' Callum said. 'How long have you known her?'

'Since we were twelve. We went to the grammar school together, same class. Friends since day one. Friends ever since.'

'You know her better than anyone else then?' Daisy said. 'Shared confidences, secrets. Is there anything you can tell us that might help us find out who did this? Anything at all, however insignificant it seems.'

Jenny shook her head and looked back towards her handbag.

'Tell me about school,' Callum said. If she kept nipping out for a cigarette this would take a long time.

Her eyes moved to Callum's face. 'Okay. She was a good student. She worked hard and got good grades but she was fun too. She had a nice sense of humour, not cruel like some girls, and she was always championing the underdog.' She took a sip of her fresh coffee and smiled her thanks to Daisy. 'She used to do a paper round before school, and in the holidays and at weekends she sometimes did a bit of waitressing at the manor. Devereux Manor, that is. You know her parents worked there? I worked there sometimes, too. A bit of extra cash never went amiss.'

Callum nodded. 'What about after school?'

'We planned a gap year travelling, just her and me. We were going camping in France and Italy and visiting the Louvre and La Scala and, well, you know, all the usual places. We saved up. And planned on getting casual work as we went.' She took another sip of coffee. 'She didn't have a boyfriend, but I started going out with Jack in our last term and he sort of upset things.' She drifted into a space they couldn't access, remembering.

'Did the gap year still happen?'

'Not for me. I fooled around with Jack and got pregnant. Dad had us marching up that aisle with both barrels in our backs, but six weeks later I lost the baby. Six weeks after that, I lost Jack to the barmaid at The Bat and Ball, and we divorced. Then I landed a job with the estate agents, and I'm still there. Never got married again. Gruesome mistake.' She chewed at the side of a green-painted fingernail.

'And Mary-Ellen?'

'Went without me. I can't say I blame her. I think she was brave. I wouldn't have wanted to go on my own. She went a bit earlier than we planned and just slipped off. Left me a note.'

'What did it say?'

'I can't remember exactly.'

'Did she contact you while she was away?'

'Just once, after Christmas – January, I think. She seemed a bit tearful. I thought she was homesick, and that made me feel guilty as hell. Bloody Jack!'

'Do you know where she went?'

She shook her head. 'Where she planned, I suppose.'

'Did you keep in touch afterwards?'

'Yes. Bit sketchy when she was at Oxford. But as soon as she came back and opened her business, we picked up where we left off. We've been meeting at least once a month since then. Lunch, or coffee. Sometimes the theatre, or a pub for a drink.'

'Where did she get the money to start her business?' Daisy asked.

'From her grandparents. They both died when she was away studying, and she was really cut up about it. She used to spend part of every summer holiday with them when we were at the grammar. I always thought she saw it as their legacy, using their money to start her company.'

When Daisy mentioned Michael, Jenny was quick to deny any problems in their relationship. Daisy snatched a glance at Callum, and Jenny looked from one to the other.

She placed her elbows on the table and leaned forward. 'You know that she had the odd fling, don't you?'

Daisy nodded.

'We never discussed it, and who am I to judge?' Jenny looked up at the ceiling for a moment, then continued. 'She's had a couple of short relationships over the years. Just sex, no commitment on either side, and Michael knew about them.'

'Any names?'

'Like I said, we didn't discuss it, but I know Jimmy Eastwood was the last one.' She eased back in her chair.

'And was it over?'

She looked at Callum. 'Yes. Mary-Ellen said Jimmy had started to get too serious and overprotective. She ended it earlier this year, or I thought she had. But a couple of months ago I saw them together at The Royal Oak, one lunchtime. I was with a–' she hesitated '–a friend. So, I couldn't speak to her, you understand?'

Callum nodded, translating 'friend' to 'someone else's husband'. 'And?' he asked.

'She was over the other side of the bar, facing me, but I only saw Jimmy from behind. The place was heaving. Jimmy was waving his arms about, and they seemed to be arguing, then he stormed out. I couldn't hear what they were saying. Jimmy rode away on a black horse. He shot off across the Forest as if he had a bee up his bum. Later I spotted Mary-Ellen at the bar paying, but I couldn't catch her eye. She looked a bit preoccupied.'

'And you're sure it was a black horse?' Daisy asked.

'Black as night.'

'Did she mention it when you next met for coffee?'

'We'd only just met a couple of days before that and she was happy as Larry, ultra-happy, I'd say. We had lunch just up the road from here.'

Callum thought of the grainy image that Cookie had lifted from the camera.

'She had a bag with her that day. Did you discuss the contents?'

Jenny huffed a laugh. 'We never discussed groceries. She calls me "the queen of the three-minute ping" because I don't do cooking.'

'And you didn't discuss The Royal Oak lunch the next time you met her?'

'Look, we didn't pry. Who am I to judge? She was a good friend, she never judged.' She blinked away tears. 'God, I'm going to miss her. So much.'

* * *

'Who do you think Mary-Ellen was with at The Royal Oak?' Daisy asked as she pulled into the station.

'We're sure it wasn't Jimmy?'

'Murphy's bay and a bright bay at that. Jenny said the horse was black and you couldn't confuse the two.'

He conceded the point.

'And,' she continued, 'Jimmy only has Murphy which is why he was thinking of getting a second horse from Richard, so it can't have been Jimmy.'

Callum held open the office door for her to precede him. 'He wouldn't have borrowed one?'

Daisy shook her head. 'The Royal Oak's a riders' pub,' she said over her shoulder. 'They've got a hitching rail and corral out the back. Anyone turning up on a horse was probably local. Long shot, but the staff might remember who she was with.'

Callum's phone rang. At the end of the brief call, he nodded to Bird and Daisy to join him.

'Where's Cookie?' he asked.

'Royal Oak,' Bird said. 'I sent him to try and ID the phantom horseman.'

Callum cleared his throat. 'Right, people. My phone call was good news. We've found Sir Michael Mitchell.'

'Where?' Daisy asked.

'Southampton?' Bird asked.

'Indeed. My call was from Timothy Pitman QC, who is in court in Geneva today. He lives in Chilworth, and it was after he left for Switzerland that Sir Michael turned up at his house on the night he went missing. That ties in with your traffic warden, Bird. When Pitman's housekeeper saw the appeal, she contacted her employer, who in turn phoned me.'

Daisy said thoughtfully, 'Nothing unusual in him turning up at Pitman's house if the housekeeper didn't report it until the appeal.'

'That's correct, Daisy.'

Her face screwed with concentration, then smoothed with comprehension.

'Timothy Pitman,' she said, stressing the first syllable of each word. 'Ti-pi. And he alibied Michael for the murder?'

'He did.'

Bird looked from one to the other, then realised what they had already worked out.

'He's the bleedin' love interest, guv.'

'Correct,' Callum confirmed. 'Pitman returns home tomorrow and will bring Sir Michael into the station for an interview after lunch. He is currently under the care of Pitman's doctor and Pitman has requested that we leave him alone until then, and I have agreed to this reasonable request. He's not coping too well with his wife's death.'

'It can't be an easy thing to deal with, sir.' Daisy's head was tilted.

'It isn't.' He felt her eyes on his face and when his hair swung forward, he took his time in tucking it back behind his ear. He heard Bird walk back to his desk.

The outer door crashed open, and Cookie tumbled into the room.

'Thought you were at The Royal Oak,' Bird challenged.

'I nearly was.' Cookie paused to unwind the scarf from his neck and drape it over the coat stand.

'In bleedin' June?' Bird nodded at the swinging snake.

'Style. You wouldn't understand.' Cookie grinned. 'Guess what?'

'Your uncle's Gok Bleedin' Wan.'

Cookie shook his head. 'Nope.' He drew breath to continue but Bird forestalled him.

'The Royal Oak. Why aren't you there?'

'I nearly was, then Darren called me – he's the barman I was going to see. The chap she was arguing with wasn't Jimmy Eastwood at all. It was Richard Devereux-Strauss.'

'He's sure?'

'Is the Pope a–'

'Cookie.' Callum's voice carried across the office.

'Sorry. Yes, he is sure. Jess, his sister works there too – Darren's, not the Pope's – and she fancies Richard something rotten.'

'God preserve me,' Bird muttered.

'When they drove home after their shift, she belted on about him and' – Cookie's voice rose an octave – '"Richard's eyes are wonderful when he's angry".'

'Did they hear what the argument was about?'

'No. It was manic that lunchtime.'

'Right, okay.' Bird's tone was brusque. 'How do you know this Darren?'

Callum registered the change in Bird's voice. Had he made them unnecessarily suspicious of each other with his convictions that the fishbowl had been searched?

'Chess club,' Cookie said. 'We both belong to the chess club.'

Callum studied Cookie's face and smiled to himself. Cookie must be a nightmare of an opponent.

'Sergeant Donaldson.' Daisy lifted her phone to her ear. She sat straighter in her chair and leaned forward over her desk. 'Slow down. Take a deep breath and start at the beginning. I'm listening.'

It seemed that the caller did as Daisy suggested, but Callum could glean nothing from her monosyllabic comments. He exchanged a glance with Bird, who gave an exaggerated shrug. Cookie was oblivious, body hunched over his desk, magnetised by the information on the screen.

When the call ended, Daisy came to the fishbowl.

'That was Rose Brown. She's in A&E in Salisbury with a broken arm, a split lip and a smashed phone, courtesy, she says, of Edward Devereux-Strauss. She wants to see me. On my own,' she added quickly as Callum pushed his chair backwards to stand up. 'She's feeling vulnerable. I think she's just realising that the young are mortal, and they don't rule the world.'

'Anything yet from Mispers?' asked Callum.

'No.' She shrugged into her jacket.

'I've to see DCI Bellman to update him on Sir Michael. When you're back, we'll go and see what Richard has got to say about not knowing the Mary-Ellen Mitchell he had lunch with.'

'Ooh, goody. I'm looking forward to that.'

Chapter Twenty

The strip lights in the corridor produced a shadowy escort to accompany Callum along to Bellman's office. One light emitted a chainsaw buzz and strobed dark and light. Five paces from his destination, the door swung open, and Bryony Osbourne stood there.

Her open-necked white blouse was tucked into belted navy trousers. Her head was turned away from Callum, her focus on figures whose voices seeped past her from inside. Bellman's was easy to identify, but Callum did not recognise the well-spoken female who was firmly making a point, and neither could he hear the dialogue.

Unwilling to interrupt, he waited. His eyes followed the ridge of Bryony's collarbone to the pulse at the hollow of her throat. He swallowed and studied the random pattern on the grey floor at his feet.

'Inspector.'

He looked up to find her smiling at him. 'Hello, there.'

The occupants of the office stepped into the corridor behind her, and Bryony was flanked on one side by a tall, angular woman with fag-ash hair and on the other by Bellman. Bryony stepped towards Callum, but Bellman cupped a restraining hand under her elbow.

'We mustn't keep the inspector, my dear.'

Bryony's jaw tightened and she lifted her elbow with a little jerk and moved forward to stand in front of Callum. The perfume she wore smelt like spring flowers. Bellman frowned disapprovingly but the other woman smiled, and the corners of her eyes crinkled.

She stepped towards him, her hand outstretched. 'As DCI Bellman's forgotten his manners, I had better introduce myself. Assistant Chief Constable Thelma Greyson. Off duty today, hence the mufti.'

She made no apology for her soil-streaked clothes or muddy shoes and her handshake was quick and firm.

'Thanks for your help today, my dear. Keep me up to date.' Greyson turned to Callum. 'Inspector, good to put a face to a name that has already been brought to my attention. We'll meet again.'

'Ma'am.' Callum met her eyes. They were frank and unblinking, but he was unable to determine anything from the connection before she broke the contact and turned to Bellman.

'Bertie' was all she said before ambling off down the corridor, hands thrust into her pockets and the slap-slap of her shoes leaving a trail of dried mud behind.

'Well, Inspector? What do you want?' Bellman looked at his wristwatch.

'You requested an update on the television appeal, sir.'

Bellman retreated into his room and Bryony said she would wait at the end of the corridor.

In the office, the perfume of spring flowers mingled with a whiff of cigarette smoke. Callum hadn't taken Bellman for a smoker, and there were no traces of nicotine on the fingers that plucked at the blotter. The men stood, one on each side of the desk, squared up like a couple of grouse cocks ahead of the mate. Callum smiled inwardly.

He was not going to find out the reason for Bellman's earlier confrontation by being confrontational himself. He adopted a more relaxed stance and told him about Sir Michael's whereabouts and the planned meeting.

'See what he has to say about Eastwood.'

'I intend to, sir.'

'And we are quite clear about not pursuing Edward Devereux-Strauss?' He lowered his eyelids but not quickly enough to hide the flash of panic that Callum saw there.

'Crystal. Message received and understood.' He was happy to confirm his understanding but had no intention of complying.

Bellman fussed with his pens, looked as if he wanted to add something, then changed his mind. 'Keep me informed, MacLean.' He turned his back to Callum. The meeting was over.

The flashing overhead light had died, and Callum stepped out of Bellman's office into the gloom. Bryony smiled at him from the end of the corridor.

'Walk me back to my car?' she asked when he joined her.

She was long in the leg, and they matched strides like drilled soldiers. He debated the best way to phrase his question, but she saved him the trouble.

'He is such an odious, sanctimonious little…' She paused as he held open the door at the end of the corridor. 'Mealy-mouthed, sycophantic…'

Callum's laugh ricocheted from the walls.

'Not on your Christmas card list then?'

She shook her head. 'He's on my father's, as he never fails to remind me. And I forgot proprietorial. He caught me on a bad day,' she said with a grin.

'I'm getting the picture.'

Bryony's car stood out like a retired pit pony in a stable of thoroughbreds. She opened the driver's door without needing to unlock it and he looked askance.

'I thought it would be safe in a police car park and look; I was right. No one has stolen it.'

Callum looked at the car, liveried in mud and dust. The bodywork was dimpled with shallow dents, and careless bumpers had gouged silver racing stripes along the sides. Perhaps no thief was that desperate. He rested his forearms along the top of the open door and Bryony leaned back against the door pillar.

'You haven't asked why I'm here, Inspector?'

'Why are you here, Miss Osbourne?'

'Bryony, please. I thought you'd never ask.'

He watched the St Christopher bob against her throat when she laughed. 'ACC Greyson has a bit of a pet project and I'm helping with it. I'm a solicitor.'

'Indeed?'

'Indeed.' She mimicked him, her voice low and stern.

Callum wondered if that is how he sounded to her, stern.

'I do a bit of pro bono for the Woman's Trust charity.'

He recognised the name as Mary-Ellen had donated to them. Had they known each other? Was this yet another connection with her family?

'Time and again in court I find an overpaid, smart-arse lawyer gets the perp off by producing a picture of my client having a good time on holiday, or just laughing with friends on social media. He gets off scot-free, and my victim gets a life sentence of anguish and self-doubt. Things have got to change.'

Callum was struck by the treacle-like flecks that flashed in her brown eyes. He wasn't sure what response she expected and was saved from answering as a car slewed into the space opposite them. A blur of red trousers and an orange top burst out of the vehicle like a firecracker ready to pop.

'Hello, guv.' Legs slid a curious glance at Bryony, who smiled at her. Legs strode to the door and Callum saw her swift check of the index number on the muddy car.

'My DC. Well, one of them. I have three.' He stood away from the car door and waited as Bryony slid into her driver's seat.

'You can never have too many DCs.' She smiled up at Callum who wasn't sure if she was making fun of him. She looked at her watch. 'Sorry, but I've got to go. I have to collect my mother from the hospital, she's unwell again.'

'I'm sorry to hear that.'

Callum closed the door as the engine purred into life on the first turn of the key. Surprise must have shown on his face because Bryony lowered her window.

'I never thought you'd be fooled by appearances.'

Callum opened his mouth to reply but she let out the clutch and whispered away towards the exit. He watched the twin points of red as she slowed before turning onto the road.

A half-smile hovered as he keyed in the door code and entered the building. He replayed his earlier meeting in the corridor outside Bellman's office. Why was the ACC already familiar with his name? What had Bellman been saying? She had said they would meet again. What she had not said was when, or why.

He opened the office door as Legs lowered her weight onto her chair and rolled towards her desk, long legs concertinaed like a grasshopper ready to spring. She was buoyant, excitement bubbled in her eyes.

She looked up at him as he walked past. 'Give me five minutes, guv.'

'Helpful meeting?' Callum asked and moved into the fishbowl.

'And surprising, guv.'

'When you're ready then.' Callum nodded to Bird and Cookie to join them.

'Should we wait for Deedee?' Legs scanned the office.

'Rose Brown was attacked this morning and Daisy is at the hospital. You can fill her in later.'

'Okay, guv.' She cleared her throat. 'We already know that Sister Agnes was a nun at the home in Armagh that was run by Sisters of Our Lady of Hope. Unmarried girls were taken in before the birth and some babies were given up for adoption.'

'Yeah, I get that,' Cookie said, perching a hip on the edge of Callum's desk, 'but if she made a mistake, why didn't she just have an abortion?'

'This is Catholic Ireland we're talking about here. Abortion was illegal, it wasn't an option. And' – she prodded Cookie's chest with her finger – 'why do you assume it was her mistake? Takes two.'

'Okay. Okay, Legs.' Cookie held up his hands in a gesture of surrender.

'Mary-Ellen Goddard, as she was then, had a baby boy in January of her gap year when everyone thought she was in Italy or wherever. Sister Agnes remembers her because she was English. Now some mothers have come forward saying their babies were taken without their permission and there's an HIA inquiry pending.'

'Is that what happened to Mary-Ellen?' Bird said.

'I don't know. Some babies were registered in Armagh, and then a couple of days later registered again, south of the border, with a new certificate showing the adoptive parents as the birth parents.'

'So, it looked as if the kiddywink was born to the adopted parents. Clever idea. Dodgy family trees, though,' Cookie said.

Legs frowned at him. 'Underhand. Everyone has a right to know where they came from.'

'What did Sister Agnes have to say about Mary-Ellen?' Callum asked.

'That she was quiet and polite, and intelligent. She didn't seem like the sort to get pregnant as she was so well-informed. Some of the other girls were young and scared and had been rejected by their families, and she was good at gaining their trust.'

'Regular bleedin' Florence Nightingale,' Bird muttered.

'Her parents said she didn't have a boyfriend,' Cookie said. 'Too committed to her studies.'

'One-night stand she didn't tell them about?' Legs said. 'Anyway, she had a healthy baby boy in January, and she left a few days later.'

'Without her baby?' Callum asked.

Legs nodded. 'And Sister Agnes remembers at least two other girls who were English.'

'Now that is interesting. Any names?'

'No. But Mary-Ellen was the first.'

'I reckon I could find their names,' Cookie said. 'Hundo P.' He looked out to his empty chair.

'When we're finished here,' Callum said. 'Did she comment on the birth certificate issue?'

'No, guv. But she knew about it, I'm sure.'

Callum had to agree. 'Okay. Cookie, trace the other girls and, Legs, check adoption records and deaths. That baby didn't just disappear. And make sure you update Daisy when she gets back.'

'Hunky-doodley, guv.' Before the others had cleared the fishbowl, Cookie was at his desk, fingers flitting over the keys, corkscrews bouncing.

Callum recalled situations where babies were raised by sisters, aunts and grandmothers as if they were their own. Often the truth never came to light until medical examinations or DNA tests forced the issue. Sometimes they lived their lives impervious to the heartache and compromise caused by their births, believing they were someone they weren't. Was that right? What did it do to a child to take away that anchor, to erase where they came from, and deceive them about who they were? Did they spend their years trying to fit in, a square peg? He thought of his father and grandfather. He had derived a sense of peace and security, a calmness in looking at them, and seeing the man he would become.

Chapter Twenty-One

When Daisy had still not returned from the hospital, Callum asked Legs to accompany him to Devereux Manor.

The lane from Woodgreen to Hale allowed him a close inspection of a steep-sided bank dotted with celandine and violets as Legs squeezed over for an oncoming tractor. He hadn't come across those giant machines in Glasgow and was surprised that they needed so much room. When the bank was behind them, spindly bushes rushed past like Olympic sprinters. They swept around zigzagged bends where spring water sluiced across the road and hissed beneath their tyres. Callum used the time to find out a little more about the constable.

'Made in Nigeria. Born in England, and so were my three sisters.' She laughed.

Callum wasn't sure if he should believe her, and his expression elicited a chuckle from her.

'Seriously. My dad came to my mum's village with a church group from England and they built a church and a school. Mum helped and when the church was finished, they were the first couple to get married in it. They came back to England, and I was born here. The rest is history.'

'Have you and your mum ever been back to Nigeria to see her family?'

'We all go back every September with donations for the school from my dad's congregation in Liverpool, and to see my mum's family.'

'Do you miss your sisters, living so far from Liverpool?' Callum asked.

'Yeah. And I miss my mum. My mum's lovely.' She sighed. 'And I've got Gloria, she fills the gap.'

Callum thought about Grace. Some gaps were bigger than others.

'What are your sisters called?' Legs asked.

The Daisy chain must be an information hotline. Perhaps he was set to be a nine-day wonder after all.

'Dolina is the eldest, then Freya, then Shona. Then me.'

She swerved sharply towards the verge as a black Range Rover swept towards them, horn blaring.

'My days. Someone's in a hurry.' Legs pulled back onto the tarmac.

'Edward Devereux-Strauss,' Callum said, checking the index number in the door mirror. At least, Bellman would be spared a further phone call.

* * *

Richard was in the stable yard. A black horse was tied to the manège rails, and its saddle had been removed and placed on the top rail of the fence. Richard's skullcap, stick and watch were discarded at the base of the fence post, next to a bucket of pink-tinged water. His polo shirt was short-sleeved and showed the play of tanned skin over muscled arms.

Richard cupped the fetlock joint of the near foreleg in one hand, just as Callum had seen Rose doing the other day, then swabbed the foot with a bloodied sponge. Head down, hair flopping over his face, he was examining the limb with such concentration that he was unaware of the officers until the horse swung its head towards them. Richard straightened up, released the leg, and pushed back his hair with damp fingers. A split in his lower lip was beginning to swell, and he had an angry-looking red cheek.

'Everything all right?' Callum asked.

'If it isn't the horse-loving detective.' Richard's smirk was distorted by his swollen mouth. 'I wouldn't come too close; he might breathe on you.' He touched his lower lip leaving a red streak on his finger. 'No irritating sidekick today?'

When Callum didn't answer, Richard shrugged and stretched out his left arm to pat the horse. There were marks on the back of his wrist that looked like a faded tattoo. A rough circle enclosed a spikey tree with mountain peaks behind it. It looked crude and amateurish; the flesh was discoloured like a sepia photograph. Callum's skin prickled when he realised the image was burned into Richard's skin like a brand. Some misguided youthful gang membership perhaps. Swiftly Richard reached for his large-faced watch and fastened it over the blemish.

Callum gestured to the bruised cheek and blood-beaded lip. 'Did you fall off?'

'I never fall off. I walked into a door.' He curled his right hand into a fist, cupping it in his left, but Callum had already spotted the bruised knuckles and wondered who had been on the receiving end of Richard's punch. He hoped it wasn't Rose.

'What happened to the horse's foot?' He stopped short of adding 'same door'; he needed this young man onside.

In Daisy's absence, Richard seemed more willing to engage with him, and Callum was pleased he had not waited for her.

Richard was wary and indecisive; his eyes avoiding Callum. Did he have something to tell them about Rose's injuries or this recent fight? Getting the information would require patience, and Callum had that in spades. He sensed a movement from Legs and hoped she wasn't about to jump in with a repeat of her interview technique.

Richard took the question at face value. 'He's young and unbalanced. He overreached.'

'What's overreached?' Callum asked.

Richard gave Callum an assessing look, the tension eased from his shoulders, and he looked boyishly enthusiastic.

'When horses move, they pick up the front foot before the back one goes down on more or less the same spot. If they get unbalanced, the back foot can land too soon and strike into the heel, causing injury.' He demonstrated by striking the heel of his left hand with his right fist.

Callum nodded. 'Like a clumsy toddler?'

'Exactly like that.' Richard was engaged and earnest. 'Because horses are so big, people forget they can still be young and green. They have to learn to listen to the rider.'

'It must be a skill getting something that size to listen to you.'

The horse pawed the ground, the grating of metal on stone ricocheting around the yard. Callum took a hasty step back and Richard laughed.

'Now why are you here, Inspector?' he asked.

'You told me you didn't know Mary-Ellen Mitchell.'

'I said, we didn't move in the same social circles.' There was a glint of humour in his eye.

'You had lunch with her at the beginning of April at The Royal Oak at Fritham.'

Richard patted the horse, ran his hand down the leg, then lifted the foot and examined it.

Callum began to think he wasn't going to answer.

'That was business.' Richard released the leg and stood up. 'She said she was interested in buying a horse but she was just wasting my time.'

'She didn't buy it?'

Richard shook his head. 'No. I don't think she ever intended to.'

'And you rode off in a hurry and left her there?'

'I was in a hurry. It was my birthday, and I had plans.'

Callum nodded, tucked his hair back and watched Richard's deft handling of the animal.

'No Rose Brown today?' Callum asked.

Richard lifted the saddle from the top rail and carried it into the tack room. The detectives exchanged a glance before following him into the shadowed overhang of the boxes. Heads appeared over doors; horses whickered as they passed, the sound mingling with music from the tack-room radio. A handful of sparrows flew up from a dust bath and fluffed and chirped in the gutter.

'She isn't here,' Richard said eventually.

Legs stayed in the yard, and Callum paused in the doorway until he became accustomed to the shadowed gloom. Two walls were studded with saddles on trees, brown cantles ridged outward like eyebrows. Girths rested across the seats, the buckles hanging down. Rows of bridles decorated the opposite wall, reins dangling from shiny bits.

'Look, I'm busy.' Richard stretched up to hoist his saddle onto an empty tree.

In the centre of the room, suspended from a rafter was a four-pronged hook. Richard hung his bridle next to the two sweat-grimed ones already there, waiting to be cleaned.

'Where is she?' Callum asked.

A chest of drawers was pushed against the wall beneath the steel-barred window. Cloths spewed onto the concrete floor from the partially open bottom drawer. Callum stooped to retrieve a sponge from the floor and caught the sweet smell of a bar of white-rimed amber soap on the surface. A splash of pink beneath the lower saddles snagged his eye. It was a mobile phone surrounded by glinting fragments of smashed screen.

'Yours?' Callum pointed at the phone.

Richard looked down at it. 'Not my colour. That's Rose's. Christ, look at the state of it.' He reached out a hand to pick it up.

'Stop.' Callum's voice was sharp. 'Let DC Levens do that.' He guided Richard out into the yard and nodded to Legs to go in and secure the item.

Richard's shoulders drooped. 'You know I took Rose to the hospital, don't you?'

Callum nodded. He did now.

'You might as well know the rest then.' Richard walked to the bench in the middle of the yard, and sat, his fingers worrying his watch face.

Callum followed him out into the sun.

'I didn't touch her.'

Callum sat next to Richard. 'Tell me what happened.' His voice was low, his tone conversational.

'When I rode into the yard, I heard her scream. I threw his reins over the post' – he nodded at the black horse – 'and ran inside the tack room. I thought she had cut herself or something, but she was curled up on the floor and he was standing over her.'

Legs moved out of the tack room, and the subtle shake of Callum's head halted her in the doorway.

'I shouted at him to leave her alone and he swung round.' Richard touched his fingers to his swollen cheek. 'He hit me first, just so you know.'

'Your father?' Callum asked.

Richard nodded. 'When we were kids…'

Bullies picked on the weak or vulnerable. Those they could intimidate and who wouldn't fight back. They sucked up power from every confrontation and their reputations grew with the trail of destruction left behind.

'And you hit him back?'

Richard flexed the fingers of his bruised hand.

'He was going to kick her. I gave him a right upper to his jaw. He wasn't expecting it. Rocked his head right back.' The cords in his neck bulged as he relived the blow.

'And then?' Callum asked, remembering the blaring horn of the speeding Range Rover.

'He was angry, said I broke one of his teeth. I chased him to the house, but he slammed the door in my face. When I got back here, Rose was leaning against the chest of drawers crying because her arm hurt, so I drove her to the hospital.'

'Why did he and Rose fight?'

Richard glanced at Legs, who was standing under the shaded eaves of the stables, and shrugged.

Callum decided on a gamble. 'Did he disapprove of your relationship with her?'

His probe found a nerve, and Richard's change of mood was mercurial. He surged to his feet. 'So, what if I was fucking her?'

Legs shifted her weight onto the balls of her feet.

'And Edward disapproved?'

'He still thinks he can dictate my life. Nothing I ever do is good enough for him.' Richard began to pace, punching his bruised fist into his left palm. 'When I was at Eton, I made the GB junior triathlon team. Pretty good, I thought, but do you know what he said?' He stopped pacing and faced Callum. 'He said it was a good job we had come back to England, because I wasn't good enough to make the South African team, like Matthew and him.'

He morphed into a small boy, confidence dented, unsure of himself.

'I tried so hard to make him proud of me, but nothing I did was ever good enough. It was always Matthew, Matthew, Matthew.'

Two sparrows squabbled over a strand of hay and a horse blew air through its nostrils.

'Well, it won't be for much longer. Rose and I are getting out of here.'

'You go nowhere without telling me first. Understand?' As the words left his lips, Callum wondered what Bellman would say about it. And in that same second, he knew he wasn't going to tell him.

Richard strode back to the horse tied to the rails and Legs came to stand beside Callum.

'Let's go,' Callum said.

* * *

'D'you reckon he's schizo, guv? I wouldn't trust him as far as I could throw him,' Legs said as they walked back to her car.

Callum certainly felt as if he had conversed with two different people. One was a hurt little boy who longed for his father's attention and approval, and the other – he searched his memory for Daisy's words – 'a class-A, arrogant, dickhead'. Her assessment was a good fit, right now.

The sun-baked car seats burned through the back of Callum's jeans. When Legs accelerated, he opened the window and welcomed the breeze moving through his hair, lifting it away from his neck.

He laid his forearm along the door frame, then snatched it away as the heat seared his flesh. That burn on Richard's wrist would have been very painful. Did Edward have something to do with it, or was it a stunt to gain his father's attention? Or a form of self-harm? Sweat prickled his scalp. He considered the dynamic between father and son and was thankful that he had never been made to feel like Richard.

Legs shifted gears and bumped over the cattle grid approaching Hale.

'He's one confused young man, isn't he?' she said. 'One minute he's all gooey over "Rosie", and the next he's angry and wants to kill Edward. Do you think he's a substance abuser?'

Callum thought of that sudden flare of temper when he had pitched the brush at Rose on their first visit; Richard's cruelty in teasing Daisy, and today his flick-flacking emotions. He had been near tears in his insistence that Edward had hit him first. And defensive about his intended escape plans.

'It's possible. What did you make of that burn scar on his wrist?'

'I didn't notice it, guv. But he's gonna have a hell of a black eye and a hand like a pitcher's mitt in the morning. What was the scar like?'

'I'll draw it for you when we get back. His watch usually covers it. That's why I hadn't noticed it before.'

Her eyes flitted to the smashed pink phone stowed in the centre console. 'I wonder what sort of shape Rose Brown's in.' She swung the car into the space next to Daisy's vehicle and Callum heard the Navara's engine tick as it cooled.

'We're just about to find out.'

Chapter Twenty-Two

Daisy was ending a phone call when Callum and Legs entered the office.

'Hey, Deedee hun, how's Rose?'

'Rhianwen Bowen' – she pronounced the name with an exaggerated Welsh lilt – 'is her real name and she will be fine.'

'Injuries sustained?' Callum asked.

'Black eye, split lip, sore jaw, bump on the head, and a broken arm. X-rays show a clean break to the ulna.'

'Who does she say is responsible for her injuries?' Callum asked.

'Edward. But she is very quick to defend Richard and tell me it had nothing to do with him. When she rang me, she was all set to press charges against Edward and hang him from the nearest tree. But by the time I got to A&E, she'd changed her mind. Which is completely understandable because I had a private word with the doc who said she did the damage herself when she fell.'

'You've located her with Mispers?'

'Yes. And you were right, she's Welsh. The nurse got her real name out of her, and she's seventeen, nearly eighteen years old.'

Callum thought that fitted with her tall, muscled physique.

'Richard lied, he said she was sixteen,' Daisy said.

'Perhaps he likes them young, so she lied to him.' Teenagers constantly lied about their age in his experience, but perhaps Daisy had never done so.

'Who reported her missing?' Callum asked.

'Eventually, her parents. She's been missing for three months but they waited two months before mentioning it to anyone.'

'Good God. Why?' Legs asked.

'The "Good God" is exactly why,' Daisy said looking at Legs. 'No offence, but her parents are part of a "happy-clappy" commune, and they told the police that they thought she had gone away to connect with God or something.'

'What were they thinking?' Legs said.

'That God looks after his own so she wouldn't come to any harm,' Daisy said, shaking her head.

Callum was about to ask if her parents ever read the papers or watched TV but maybe they didn't have access to either. Or they imbued God with more power than he did. His unsuccessful pleading and bargaining for Grace's life had left him angry, jaded, and disbelieving. And alone.

'Have her parents been informed, Daisy?'

'Dyfed-Powys Police are onto it. When I left Rose… Do we call her Rhianwen or Rose, now?'

'Rose,' Callum said. 'That's how we all know her.'

'Okay. Rose was sitting in the queue to be plastered. They're admitting her for observation for the next twenty-four hours because of the bump on the head. She said she would call me when she's free to leave.'

'At least we know where to find her when we need to talk to her. And we will be talking to her.' Callum went back into the fishbowl. He would also be talking to Edward again.

'Cruel. Go, baby, go.' Cookie dropped his phone onto his desk, stood up, twirled around once and sat back down.

'Cookie. Fuckin' grow up,' Bird growled and slammed his hand down onto his desk with a thump that turned heads in his direction.

Cookie walked over to Bird and stood beside his desk.

'Sorry, Bird.'

'What's all the bleedin' excitement about anyway?'

'Remember the contact that was Faol, who called Mary-Ellen before the money and the murder, but that was all deleted from her phone?'

Bird nodded. 'So?'

'It was a burner, off-network. Somebody used it this morning.' He fidgeted from one foot to the other.

'Location?'

'Salisbury Hospital.'

Callum was on his feet and out of the fishbowl. 'Daisy, Rose phoned you, but her phone was smashed on the tack-room floor.'

'She had a phone in the back pocket of her jeans. I thought she was just being over-dramatic about Edward damaging it.'

'Uh-uh, Deedee. I've just given hers to Forensics,' Legs said.

'Then where did she get that phone from?' Callum said. 'She was on her own in the tack room because Richard chased Edward to the house and got the door slammed in his face. Then Richard rushed back to Rose and drove her to the hospital.'

'She can't have been alone for more than a couple of minutes,' Daisy said. 'She had no time to go back up to the flat, so either she had a second phone on her…'

'That's unlikely,' Legs said.

'…or that phone was already in the tack room,' Callum said quietly.

'And it was put there by someone with access,' Bird said. 'That's either Rose, Richard…'

'Or Edward,' Daisy said.

'Okay, people. Moving on,' Callum said. 'Daisy, go back to the hospital. Find out where she got the phone from and then bring it in for Forensics to see if they can lift some prints from it. Legs, go with her please.'

Both women were quickly on their feet, and before the door closed behind them, Callum was standing at Cookie's desk.

'Cookie. Priority. Locate Edward. And speed up tracing the other two girls who had convent births.'

Callum beckoned Bird to follow him into the fishbowl. The smell of cigarette smoke was long gone but Bird lifted his chin and sniffed once or twice as he lowered his frame onto the chair.

'I've been keeping an eye on the smoking shed but I've only spotted a PC and the three men we know about.'

'Good.' Callum propped his elbows on the desk. 'Edward was driving down from London when Mary-Ellen was killed, and his alibi was Richard and Rose Brown. If they're victims of Edward's bullying, we can't rely on their accounts. Check when Edward left Belgravia. Confirm that he was where he said he was.'

'Anything else, guv?'

'Check the CCTV, make sure it was Edward driving. Speak to the staff.'

'He's probably got a bleedin' liveried footman who opens his door for him in the morning.'

Callum smiled inwardly at Bird's lowering expression. 'Then have a word with him as well.'

'Wilco.' Bird grinned and tapped the side of his nose. 'And I'm still working on that other little matter.'

When Bird left, Callum updated his notes and put them in his desk. He was balancing a thread of cotton on the lip of the drawer when he smelled violets. ACC Thelma Greyson was leaning in the open doorway to the fishbowl, arms folded, a frown on her face. The woman had the stealth of a wraith. How long had she been watching him? He shot a glance around the office. Cookie signed 'sorry', and Bird grimaced.

She jerked her head backwards. 'Don't blame them. They were trying to warn you. But they're more frightened of me than they are of you.'

Callum remembered his manners and shot to his feet. 'Ma'am.' He hovered above his chair uncertain if he should offer her a seat or just stand.

She scrutinised him for a few seconds that stretched into a lifetime for Callum, and then she grunted.

'For God's sake, sit down, man. You look as if you've shat yourself.'

Callum sank back into his chair, as she dropped into the one on her side of the desk.

'What can I do for you, ma'am?' This was unprecedented territory. Generally, it was he who, summoned by higher ranks, was assigned the chair on the wrong side of the desk. If he was asked to sit at all.

'I've been hearing things about you, but I like to see for myself.'

He had an uneasy sensation that she was looking right through his skin in search of his moral fibre. His insides fluttered as they had done sitting outside the headmaster's office in a past life.

'I don't suffer fools or sycophants. I say what I think, one of the privileges of rank, and I do what I say.' She emphasised her final five words.

'Yes, ma'am.'

'I hear you've got DCI Bellman in a bit of a flap.' She nodded towards the desk drawer. 'What's going on there?'

Callum tucked his hair back and cleared his throat, giving himself time to order his thoughts. If he gave her less than the full facts, she would find out and then he would be in the mire. But sharing his concerns would make working with Bellman difficult, if not impossible. Either way, he could be heading back to Scotland sooner than planned.

He met the grey eyes without blinking and told her about his snooper feeding information to Bellman, who had then ordered him to stop investigating Edward Devereux-Strauss and pursue Jimmy Eastwood instead.

'You're confident it's not your team tittle-tattling?'

'One hundred per cent, ma'am.'

'Tell me why you are investigating Edward Devereux-Strauss.'

She listened without interrupting.

'And this snooper? What are you planning to do about that?'

Callum told her. She was silent for a couple of moments before giving him a nod of approval.

'Fair enough. Don't tell any of your team about this note I'm telling you to write. Put it in your drawer and keep me informed. There are one or two things I'm going to check out for myself.' She rose to her feet and left the fishbowl in one fluid movement like an outgoing wave.

Callum watched Bird and Cookie become studiously interested in their screens as she passed them. He hoped he had made the right decision because one of the things she would be checking out was him.

Greyson disappeared into the corridor whistling her rendition of *The Ballad of Glencoe*. He'd been familiar with the tune since he was a bairn, but it was the first time he'd heard it in three different keys at the same time.

* * *

The outer door opened, Daisy and Legs came into the office and Daisy came into the fishbowl. She took a deep breath.

'Violets?' She sat down.

'Violets. How did you get on?'

'Okay. I'm not sure I believe her, but Rose said she saw the phone yesterday, for the first time, in the tack-room drawer when she was getting a sponge. Today, she was sending a text on her pink phone when Edward had a go at her for wasting time. She poked out her tongue, so he knocked the phone out of her hand, and it smashed against the wall.'

Callum could understand Edward's annoyance. Society was breeding a generation capable of only maintaining eye contact with a phone screen. He upbraided himself for sounding like a judgemental old man and tuned back into Daisy.

'She lunged to grab her phone but slipped, caught her face on that metal tack hook and ended up on the floor. She was down there screaming at Edward when the gallant Richard charged to her rescue. She was so angry when she saw her phone, that she took that one from the drawer while Richard was chasing Edward away.'

'Would she be thinking that clearly? Her broken arm would have been painful.'

'She was running on anger-fuelled adrenaline. The phone was dismantled, wrapped in cling film, but because the pain was kicking in, the nurse had to finish putting it back together so she could ring me.'

'And the argument was just about her using her phone?'

'So she says, but it could have been the straw that broke the camel's back. I think it has something to do with Richard. You should have seen what she was wearing, by the way. A low-cut tee over a bra two sizes too small and a pair of jodhpurs that are so tight you can nearly read the label on her G-string.' She wriggled in her chair.

Callum hid a grin, confident that if he had made those comments, Daisy would be treating him to a lecture on sexism.

'Richard's sleeping with her,' he said.

'I know, and she's got "yes please" running through her like a stick of rock. Pity about her age, I hoped he'd be for the high jump.'

'Who?' Legs asked from the doorway.

'Richard,' Daisy said. 'He is an arsehole, but he doesn't have a reputation for underage. Other men's wives are another matter.'

'She's legal,' Legs said, 'but I've seen sex workers with less on show.' She held up the bagged phone. 'A rash of Rose's prints and no one else's. Not even on the battery or SIM.'

Callum grunted. Whoever had used it to contact Mary-Ellen was careful and thorough, but it was still a disappointment. 'No more than we expected. The nurse was gloved-up, and the owner was careful. Give it to Cookie. Let's see what he can find.'

Rose was self-assured and confident. In his experience, that demeanour was a result of a privileged education or a criminal past. 'And see if she's got a record.'

Callum took a sheet of paper and drew the tattoo that Richard was so keen to keep hidden. He marked in the mountain peaks and spiky trees in the foreground and, as an afterthought, drew in a hand to show the orientation. On a clean sheet, he wrote a note and read it through. He worried his earring for a moment, then placed the paper in his drawer. He closed the door of the fishbowl behind him and looked around the office.

Daisy leaned back in her chair, clasped her hands above her head and stretched.

'You ready, sir?' She reached for her jacket.

'I am. Good work today, people. We've made progress. Sleep well.' He watched Bird and Legs turn off their machines and stand up.

'Legs, the burn on Richard's wrist looks like this.' He handed her the sheet of paper and Bird leaned across to get a look.

'That rings a sort of bell, guv. I've seen that before.' Bird rasped the back of his thumbnail against his stubbled chin. 'Can't remember where just this minute.' He took a photo of it with his phone.

'Sleep on it,' Daisy said from the door.

'Wilco. Right. I'm off. I've got birds to feed, then meself and then a cold beer.' He groaned as he eased himself into his moth-eaten jacket. 'I'm getting too bleedin' old for this.'

Bird was always protesting his age. Callum smiled to himself. He had never seen Bird move any faster than an amble, but he looked lean and muscled, his movements lithe. Perhaps we all need something to complain about.

'Home time, Cookie,' Callum said.

'Five more minutes, guv. I just want to finish this,' he said, and he laced his fingers, cracked the bones and launched another attack on his keyboard. They left him, his face a mask of concentration and his eyes bonded with the screen.

Chapter Twenty-Three

Felix greeted them by running in ever-widening circles until he ended up in a flower bed. The whirr of a startled pheasant was joined by the treble squeaks of bats flitting through the gloaming. The light had almost seeped away, but Callum could still discern the movement of the tree canopy, charcoal against the slate sky.

Daisy flicked switches and the kitchen jumped out of the darkness.

'I'm getting to like your Mrs P.' Callum peered through the glass oven door and inhaled a spicy aroma.

The downlighters threw sharp shadows on the floor, a study in light and shade. He experienced a sudden yearning to paint and wished that his acrylics and brushes were accessible, not buried in the back of his car.

Daisy laughed. 'There's a queue to join her appreciation society.' She leaned over to read a note on the island.

Felix picked up his empty food bowl with his teeth and waggled over to present it to Daisy.

'Nice try, Felix.' She took the bowl from the dog and patted his head. 'That note says Mrs P already fed you.' She tossed a dog biscuit into his basket and put the bowl back on the floor.

When Daisy opened the oven door, a cloud of spiced steam billowed out, and Callum's mouth filled with saliva. This was the first time since Grace that he had shared his living space with anyone else. He was surprised to find it so agreeable and wondered how much longer he could stay before Daisy tired of his intrusion.

They settled down to eat. His plate was nearly empty when his phone vibrated across the island, and he checked the display. In response to Daisy's questioning look, he pulled the face he had perfected as an adolescent, then put down his fork and picked up the phone.

'Mother.' He pushed open the kitchen door and went outside. 'How nice. I was going to ring Dolina in a day or so.' Before the door closed behind him, he glanced back at Daisy and knew she was trying to catch his conversation.

'I'm sorry Dad had to ask you to call because he's beside himself with worry.' He could picture his mother in their pink floral sitting room, curtains closed against the dark. 'Put him on for a wee word … Och, he's away to the darts?'

Felix came to the door behind him and barked. 'I'm still staying with Sergeant Donaldson. I've not had the time to find anywhere just now.'

Daisy pulled open the door and let Felix out.

'It's her dog wanting to be let out.' He screwed up his face and sighed, knowing their conversation was about to stamp across familiar ground.

'Did I not say my sergeant's female?' A bat swooped close to him, the draught disturbing his hair. His mother started along a path that was becoming irritatingly well-used.

'I know it's been three years.' A pulse bounced in his jaw.

Felix came and stood next to him, nuzzling his muzzle into Callum's hand. His mother paused for breath.

'Leave it, will you.' His voice was louder than he intended, his curtness fuelled by tiredness. He could almost taste the hurt in his mother's silence, sour, black olives on his tongue.

Seconds ticked by. Would his mother always have the power to make him feel like a seven-year-old, guilty of some misdemeanour?

A well-rehearsed scene played in his head; her sharp intake of breath, then wordless mawing below brimming eyes. He closed his own eyes to blank the image. Didn't she understand that when you picked at a wound, it took longer to heal?

The calm reassurance of his father's voice burred against his ear.

'Dad. Back from the darts? Hello … No, no problem, Mum rang me.' Callum strained to hear the brief, muted conversation between his parents.

'Aye. I know she worries.' Callum pushed open the kitchen door to let Felix inside and followed the dog. He ate the last of his supper then reached in his pocket for his sketchbook and mouthed 'yes' to Daisy who made a *C* symbol with her fingers and pointed to the cafetière.

'That's grand. What's his pup called?' He tried to slough off his mood, inject some cheeriness into his voice, when all he wanted to do was cry for Grace now the wound had been prised opened again.

'Meg. Nice,' he said.

Daisy poured the spitting water onto the coffee grounds. He breathed deeply.

'Aye. Tell them to keep "the Bridge over the Atlantic" open. I'll be up to see them on Seil, the first chance I get. Love to all.' He hesitated, undecided if he should apologise to his mother, but ended the call with his thoughts unvoiced.

Daisy filled his mug, and he knew that she was deciding which question to ask first. He recalled his grandma's reedy voice and saw her pickled mouth when she said, 'Prevention is better than cure, Callum lad.' He couldn't let Daisy ask about Grace. He wasn't ready for her to trespass on his privacy, so he offered a distraction.

'My grandad's got himself a new collie pup.'

'Called Meg?'

'Indeed, Detective.' He smiled, then changed the subject. 'What did you make of Rose Brown's parents when you spoke to them?'

She seemed content to accept his change of direction, and he pencilled the date on a new page in his book.

'If I had come across them in different circumstances, I might have liked them. They seemed level-headed and intelligent.'

'It's not intelligent to leave it so long before reporting your daughter missing.'

'I agree. I didn't want to upset Legs... you know her dad's a vicar?'

He nodded. 'Liverpool.'

'Well, they trotted out all this God crap. She was safe because God would protect her. It's like they had given up responsibility for her.'

'It's a fine line between devotion and extremism, Daisy.' He stroked pencil lines onto the paper, calmed by the rhythmic action.

'Yeah, but blaming God is a bit of a cop-out. We can't put him in court. And it's all about the money with Rose. She reckons on retiring by the time she's thirty, and she's barely old enough to work.' Her phone pinged and she read an incoming message.

'Felix,' she called the dog to her, 'Dom says to give you a hug and he'll come and see us after Paris.' She threw her arms around her dog, who made soft noises in his throat and wagged his body.

'Tell me' – Callum looked at her over the rim of his mug – 'why's he called Felix? That's a cat's name.'

Daisy took a deep breath.

He smiled inwardly and concentrated on his sketch.

'Mum and Dad always asked us what we wanted for birthdays and I always said a kitten. Then one birthday they came home with our presents.' She drained her coffee mug. 'I was so excited when I flipped open that pet carrier. I expected a little ginger kitten, but it was a puppy with comically big feet.' Daisy smiled at the memory and fussed Felix.

He glanced at the dog's feet. They still seemed disproportionately large for his frame. He pencilled in detail to the masonry of a humpbacked Clachan Bridge. The single arch spanned a sea loch, and when joined with its reflection, formed a full circle. He added a house to one bank beneath the protection of towering hills dotted with sheep.

'Is that where you lived?' she asked, looking at his sketch. Felix rested his head on Daisy's knee.

Callum shook his head and sketched the dog paddling along the shoreline, feet hidden beneath the water. He added a skein of geese flying towards the Atlantic, their reflections dispersed by the rippled surface of the loch.

When Daisy went out to see to her horse, he yawned and stretched as the door snicked closed behind her. He sharpened the stonework of the bridge before closing his book. Flexing his neck made it crunch and crack, and his mind jumped forward to the morning.

He had done the right thing with Thelma Greyson, but the situation bothered him. Bellman was an experienced officer who knew his patch and was insistent that Edward was not involved in the murder. He slotted his pencils into the correct places in their tin, soft to hard. Today Bellman had been on edge, evasive, but Callum sensed that was not the way the man usually operated. His eyes behind the owl-rimmed spectacles had looked at first frightened, and then almost apologetic. What had scared him? Callum wondered. And should he be afraid, too?

Chapter Twenty-Four

Callum pushed open the office door, paused, fingers on the handle, and listened. A rasping sound sawed the air, but the office looked empty. He waited, and the sound was repeated somewhere near his feet. Behind the door, Cookie was stretched out on his back, shoeless feet crossed at the ankle and his head resting on his jacket. He was emitting the stentorian snore of a drunk but without any smell of alcohol.

Callum nudged a toe against his ribs and Cookie opened his eyes. He turned his head towards Callum and scrambled to his feet, unbalanced as a newborn colt.

'What time is it?' He clawed at his cuff and then looked across to his desk where his watch worked unobserved.

'Early.' Callum took in the crumpled clothes and sleep-pressed features.

Cookie rubbed both hands up through his flattened curls and down to the nape of his neck. 'I thought I'd get an early start.' He avoided eye contact.

'Have you been here all night?'

'Not all of it.' Then excitement flooded into his voice as daylight eased away the slowness of sleep. 'I've found something.'

'Have you found the identity of the murderer? Are my officers in danger?'

'Nothing like that, guv. But I–'

'Good,' Callum interrupted him. 'Have breakfast and a shower then come and tell me what you've found.'

'But, guv…' He flailed an arm towards his desk.

'Thirty minutes, laddie. Now go.' Callum turned his back on Cookie.

Desk drawers plunked in and out like organ stops followed by the whispered click of the door closing.

The fishbowl harboured the thinnest trace of cigarette smoke that he could easily have missed. He inhaled slowly. Was it really there? Then he noticed his desk drawer was not fully closed. His visitor was getting careless, or had they been interrupted?

Feet slapped along the corridor and Daisy and Legs came through the door followed by Bird. He dropped his jacket onto his chair and settled his bulk. He looked across to Cookie's desk and sniffed loudly.

'Bleedin' burger crap. Stinks. Where the hell is he?' Bird looked around the office before peering into Cookie's waste bin. 'If he ate that crap for breakfast then he deserves to be in the shitter.'

A refreshed-looking Cookie skidded through the door and glided across the floor towards Bird, wet curls shedding droplets of water as if he were riding a surfboard. Callum missed the ensuing exchange because he answered his phone, but out of the corner of his eye, he saw Cookie and his wastepaper bin exit into the corridor.

He concentrated on the call, and the mellifluous tenor voice, the stretched vowels that became minims among consonantal crotchets. Timothy Pitman was polite, authoritative and to the point. He, and Sir Michael, would be at the station at noon to address Callum's concerns. Sir Michael would like to see Mary-Ellen's body if Callum would make the necessary arrangements and, as her next of kin, he would formally identify her.

'It's hit him very hard, Inspector, and he's bewildered by it. I hope that seeing her body will allow him to move on.'

'I hope so too, sir.'

Callum remembered the yellow curtain sliding away. Grace's wild hair was tamed as it had never been in life, the ends trapped beneath her. He had wanted to hammer on the glass and shout that she hated laying on her hair, she hated it being restricted, she hated being still. Instead, he had nodded once. The muscle pounding in his jaw threatened to break through his skin. His father's hand had guided him and kept him upright when he wanted to fall to his knees, sink into the floor and let the world walk on without him.

A knock on the door and Cookie stood in the doorway.

'Come in. Had yourself some breakfast?'

'Yes. Thanks.'

Cookie's wide-open eyes were like grey marbles.

'What did you want to tell me?'

'Two things. Well, three actually.'

Callum nodded for him to continue.

'I found the names of two other girls from the convent. They were after Mary-Ellen.'

'Did you locate them?'

'Harriet King is dead. Diane Smith, now Diane Adams is still alive, married with two boys and teaches at a school just outside Fordingbridge.'

'Good work, Cookie. Give the details to Daisy and ask her and Legs to call on her. Next?'

'I did more digging on Edward. Did you know he's a patron of loads of charitable trusts? And then I found this.' He proffered a sheet of paper.

Callum looked at the list of names, hesitating over the last. There was no reference. It could have been a lottery syndicate or a pub quiz team for all he knew.

'What do these relate to?' He failed to keep his exasperation out of his voice.

'They're the development company investors that backed the failed planning application. There's Edward' – he tapped the paper – 'and that one's a county councillor, he's a building inspector, and those are local business owners.' Cookie pointed at the final name. 'And him. That's DI Denton.'

Callum realised why he had recognised the name. Legs had written it on her envelope.

Cookie flapped his sheaf of papers. 'There were accusations about bribery and stuff, but nothing happened. I couldn't find out why.'

Callum could make an educated guess. Money had long arms and greasy palms. What he couldn't guess was why Denton's name was on the list.

'And I found this memo from Uncle Bertie, I mean DCI Bellman.'

It was the transcript of an email sent by him to Denton.

> You cannot serve two masters, Paul. In the interests of fairness following your long service, I am allowing you to address this situation before I make it official. Failure to act will ensure that this goes on your record.
> Your choice.
> Bertie

Callum looked at Cookie but was confronted by a dense mop of curls because Cookie's attention was focused on his shoes.

'Where did you get this?'

Cookie's innocent mask was at odds with his evasive eyes that slid past Callum.

'It fell into my lap, sort of.' He fidgeted.

Callum reread the message and changed tack.

'Cookie, how difficult is it to hack a computer?'

'Pretty easy if you have…' He faltered, and his cheeks glowed.

Callum's voice was sharp and precise. 'This is not the way we work. You know that evidence obtained by unlawful search is inadmissible.'

Cookie slid another sheet towards Callum. It suggested that Denton was being paid for information obtained courtesy of his position. Callum didn't ask how Cookie had come by that little gem. He sat back in his chair to think, leaving Cookie looking as if he wished himself invisible. He let Cookie sweat.

Callum had signed up to enforce the law, not bend it to fill his pockets, and he had zero respect for those that did. Perhaps Bellman was only guilty of trying to keep the lower ranks on the right path? Or was he in so deep that he would do whatever it took to derail Callum's investigation? What it did confirm was that he had been right to confide in Thelma Greyson.

'Is that related to our murder, do you think?' Cookie asked.

Callum had momentarily forgotten about Cookie, who was looking at him with a perplexed expression, his earnest grey eyes seeking reassurance.

'Early days. Anything else?'

Cookie shuffled his papers. 'Got some pics of a shoot on Edward's estate.'

It showed two rows of men in tweed, each with the barrel of a broken twelve-bore resting along their forearms. He recognised Edward centre front.

Cookie pointed out Denton in the back row. 'See Edward?' he said. 'That's more top brass on his left.'

Being warned off, following his questioning of Edward, made sense now. Just how many rungs of the ladder did the man have access to? Callum placed the papers in a neat pile and smoothed them flat. He knew the problem he was uncovering was unlikely to be ironed away as easily.

'Uncle Bertie's been a pain in the doodley lately,' Cookie added. 'He came round to ours the other night and had a garganch argument with Mum. I had to take my sister down to the chippie. She's deaf, but she's not blind.'

The mystery of why Cookie used sign language was solved. Callum looked again at the shooting party. If

Denton had the ear of the senior officers, then it could be that both he, and Bellman, would find themselves in an uncomfortable situation. This was an iceberg, the tip of a much bigger problem.

Cookie smiled, his first of the day, and he looked less like a startled poodle and more like himself.

'And what was the third thing?'

'Probably nothing, but I was getting a bit peckish about ten, and I nipped out for a burger and chips.' He flicked a look to the outer office. 'I think it's upset Bird though.'

'He'll get over it. Why is this relevant?'

'When I came back along the corridor, I saw PC Kent hurrying towards me as if he'd come out of our room. I wouldn't have thought very much about it if you hadn't said someone had been in your office.'

He would pass this all on to Thelma Greyson and let her worry about it.

Bellman's request that Callum go to his office for a case update raised the hairs on the back of his neck. He was leaving when Legs and Daisy appeared in the doorway of the fishbowl.

'We're off to meet Diane Adams in her morning break,' Daisy said. 'She told me I had the wrong person to start with, but when I mentioned Mary-Ellen, she agreed to see us.'

'And' – Legs gave him her beaming smile – 'Reg Holder is coming in tomorrow with cake.'

'Worth waiting for,' Daisy called over her shoulder.

* * *

Callum tapped the door and entered.

Bellman was seated behind his desk, face pale, body tight. 'Inspector?'

'We are making progress. Sir Michael is coming into the station at lunchtime, with Timothy Pitman.'

'Timothy Pitman the QC? Is Sir Michael a suspect?' Bellman sat forward in his chair.

'No. He was staying at Pitman's house after he disappeared.'

'I see.'

Callum doubted that.

'And you're going to arrest Eastwood? You've found a problem with his alibis?'

Callum lowered his eyelids. Grace had always told him that he was a terrible liar, and she had known him better than he knew himself. A soft fluttering behind his sternum made him catch his breath and he pressed his fingers against his chest.

'Inspector?' Bellman's lips parted.

'No. Both alibies are cast iron.'

Callum said nothing more. It was clear that Bellman was aware of the note that Greyson had told him to write.

Bellman frowned and slumped back in his seat; a series of emotions chased across his features.

Callum was surprised to experience a brief surge of concern and sympathy for the man. He would report back to the ACC as ordered and let her get to the bottom of it.

Silence stretched between them like a winter lake.

When he did speak, Bellman's face was ice-tight. 'MacLean, I may have dropped you into the mix a little too soon.' His voice was cold, his delivery crisp. 'You don't fully understand how things work down here. I will be recommending that you be removed from this investigation and a more locally aware officer be put in charge.' Bellman sat straighter in his chair and picked up his pen. 'In fact, I may take over this case myself.'

Callum held eye contact despite a muscle tugging at his cheek. His future was hanging in the balance, and it was no comfort that, for once, it wasn't his fault. He would have to prove Bellman wrong about his competency, by getting a result. Callum kept his mouth closed as he opened the door to leave. If he was going to find the murderer, he had better get on with it before he was taken off the case.

* * *

Ignoring the orders of a senior officer was not a good idea, but expecting him to ignore evidence was never going to happen. When Grace had died, he had wanted to walk away from the job. The perpetual cycle of punishment and recidivism had seemed futile. This was the first time since her death that it mattered to him to continue. When he hadn't been taking notice, the wind had changed, fanned a spark in the embers and it had smouldered unnoticed. Now it blazed into flames. He walked with a new lightness in his step. Grace would have said his timing was dreadful, that it was typical of him to only realise what he wanted when he was about to lose it.

In the office, he studied the board. He considered each picture in turn. Sir Michael Mitchell alibied. David Fellowes and Fletcher Edmunds alibied. Veronica Parsons alibied, and Jimmy Eastwood alibied by the farmer and Richard Devereux-Strauss. That left just Edward. Callum put up a photo of him and considered what they already knew about his connection to Mary-Ellen. Her parents had been employed at the manor, and she, along with half the girls from the village, had been casually employed there, but that was so long ago that he couldn't see any relevance. More recently, she had been responsible for the refusal of that lucrative planning application that lost him and his pals millions. Was that significant? Edward was a wealthy man, the type of man who didn't have problems. He just had solutions.

Bird came to stand beside him. 'Is Edward officially on the list of suspects then?'

Callum nodded. 'Yes. Any luck with his alibi?'

'Still waiting. I'll go and hassle the lazy buggers.' He turned away but Callum delayed him.

'I want you in on the interview with Sir Michael as you spoke to his brother,' he said.

'Wilco.' Bird hesitated then looked back at the board. 'Do you think Edward could have killed her?'

'Innocent until proven otherwise.'

'Fair enough. You don't want to put Matthew and Richard up there as well? They both drive black Range Rovers.'

Placating Bellman was a bit stable-door now. He wrote "Richard D-S" and "Matthew D-S", capped the pen and stepped back. 'And check out where Matthew was while you're at it.'

'Wilco.' Bird glanced across the room to the doorway, and Callum followed his eyeline. But there was no one there.

* * *

The sun threw sharp shards across the fishbowl that struck the wall behind Callum. He looked again at the photo of the men at the shoot. He read the caption beneath and saw that it was a fundraising clay pigeon shoot for terminally ill children. Was Edward a great philanthropist or just adept at generating smokescreens? Being a philanthropist didn't stop him from also being a misogynistic bully. Callum recalled the furtive backward glances from his wife Penny, the veiled comments by his daughter Bryony and his dismissive treatment of Daisy. In the photograph, he looked self-assured, at ease with the men around him, in control. What trigger was needed for control to develop into controlling?

He picked up his phone and called Thelma Greyson. The scent of violets might have evaporated from the fishbowl, but her quiet assertions stayed with him and the screw in his stomach twisted tighter with every new complexity.

'Greyson.'

She didn't interrupt him, and when she had heard him out, she huffed air through her nostrils. 'Don't pack your bags yet, MacLean.'

'I wasn't planning to, ma'am.'

'Good.'

The phone purred, confirmation that their conversation was over, for now. He listened to it for a moment before his thoughts turned to Sir Michael Mitchell. Under most other circumstances, he would have relished talking to the eminent artist. But now, they had too much in common. He closed his eyes and Grace was there, brown eyes flashing and her hair wild, like seaweed, tugged by an incoming tide. And he heard her laugh like a sound snatched by the wind, fleeting, fading. Her memory was beginning to afford him more comfort, and less distress. He opened his eyes when Bird tapped on the door to inform him that Sir Michael and Timothy Pitman were waiting for them.

Chapter Twenty-Five

The interview room was inhospitable. Sharp angles and hard surfaces were magnified by the shiny walls and artificial light. Sir Michael's cheeks were hollowed, with grey strokes of sleeplessness below his eyes, and stubble stippling his jaw. But he sat military-straight, shoulders squared, his hair captured in a knot at the nape of his neck.

Timothy was short, rotund and convivial. His bald pate was encircled by a fluffy cloud hovering just above his ears, his gold half-specs rested on the bridge of his nose. Cornflower-blue eyes sparkled with animation and a mesh of fine lines edged his eyes. It was a face designed for merriment. He sprang to his feet and extended a hand to Callum, who thought the men the epitome of comedy and tragedy.

Introductions were made; Sir Michael raised his eyes to Callum, who recognised a maelstrom of emotions. Timothy sat back in his chair and did not contribute to the interview.

Sir Michael was hesitant, his thoughts disjointed, but Callum let him tell his story and neither he nor Bird interrupted. When Michael had fled to Paris, a lonely, scared youth, he met Timothy, and they began a relationship. It had continued when they both returned to England. Neither wanted to make it public.

Years later when attending a charity dinner, Sir Michael had met Mary-Ellen Goddard. She had captivated him. At that first meeting, they had conversed like life-long friends. Soulmates.

'We married almost immediately. She was fully aware of my sexuality, and my commitment to Timothy and she embraced it. My relationship with her was not sexual, it was deeper, more spiritual. I thought it would last forever.'

Mary-Ellen had wanted him as a friend and confidant, a life partner. She valued the protection and respectability of marriage. Sir Michael knew about her discreet liaisons and confirmed that Jimmy Eastwood was her last.

'She ended it. He was showing too much concern, Inspector. She wasn't seeking commitment.' Sir Michael paused, and Timothy smiled his support.

'When did she end the relationship with Jimmy Eastwood?' Callum asked.

'January, definitely by February. He wasn't happy about her decision.' Sir Michael looked at Callum. 'I know it seems silly, but I keep wanting to ask her things or tell her something and then remember that I can't.' His next breath shuddered in his chest and Timothy gently placed his hand on Sir Michael's arm.

Callum unnecessarily consulted his papers for a moment. 'Sir Michael, about eight weeks ago, your wife made a twenty-thousand-pound cash withdrawal from her bank.'

He frowned. 'Why did she do that?'

Callum exchanged a glance with Bird. 'We hoped you could tell us.'

'I can't.' Neither was he aware that she had discussed changing her will, so he was unaware of a new beneficiary.

The QC leaned forward. 'Could the money have anything to do with Eastwood, Inspector? Did she pay him off?'

'The timing could work and the thought has occurred,' Callum said, though Cookie had found no trace of it in Jimmy's financial records. 'Could it have been for a charity, Sir Michael?'

'No. She was meticulous about paper trails and accountability. She never donates in cash.'

'Then it's safe to assume it was a personal expenditure.'

'I didn't think we had any secrets.' He sank lower in his chair.

When Bird mentioned his brother Gavin, Sir Michael seemed to contract like a slug touched by salt.

'How is Gavin?' Timothy asked.

'Missing you, sir,' Bird said, looking at Sir Michael. 'He asked after you.'

'Really? I find that hard to believe after what I did to him.'

'You took the sensible course of action at the time,' Timothy said. 'Removing yourself from the battlefield is a legitimate defence. It saved bloodshed.'

Sir Michael looked at Timothy. 'Perhaps I should go and see him. While there's still time.'

'I believe he would appreciate that, sir,' Bird said. 'He asked to be informed when we had located you.'

'Is he the reason you are changing your will?' Callum asked.

Sir Michael's breath whispered across his lips.

'No. I am setting up a foundation for underprivileged children to have access to art therapy. Art saved me all those years ago. I need to give something back. Something positive for the future.'

'And Mary-Ellen knew about this?'

'It was her idea. She knows what painting has done for me, Inspector. And she doesn't need my money.' He still referred to her in the present tense.

Callum paused until he was sure he had their attention. 'Did you know that she gave birth to a child?'

Sir Michael's head snapped up and both men looked at Callum.

'Are you sure? She was always adamant that she never wanted children.'

Callum nodded. 'It was nearly forty years ago. She had a boy, father unknown, birth registered in Northern Ireland. It seems probable that he was adopted, but the records are incomplete,' Callum said.

'She would have made a good mother.' Sir Michael's voice was quiet. The lines of his face softened, and his eyes filled with tears. He looked emotionally and physically exhausted.

Callum stood. 'I think we'll leave it there for today, gentlemen. Thank you for your time and cooperation.'

By mutual agreement, the identification of Mary-Ellen's body was postponed until the following morning. In an undertone to Callum, Timothy expressed the hope that Sir Michael would be rejuvenated by a night's sleep. Callum knew that one sleepless night would be followed by another.

He and Bird watched them walk away. Timothy strutting and clucking like a bantam, his cotton-wool halo vibrating, and Sir Michael two paces behind him.

'He didn't even ask if we'd caught her bleedin' murderer,' said Bird. 'Do you reckon he knows who did it?'

Callum shook his head. 'I don't believe he even knows what day of the week it is. He's still in denial.'

They watched the two men turn the corner, the tap and flap of footfalls echoing in their wake.

Bird folded his arms. 'If it was my Helen, that's the first thing I'd want to know. Which bastard did it – then I would go and make him wish he bloody hadn't.' Bird's breath rushed noisily through his nostrils.

'Our job is to catch them. Delivering justice is more effectively handled by the powers that be.' Callum didn't believe his own words, even as they came out of his mouth.

Bird snorted and ducked swiftly to one side, earning him a questioning look from Callum.

'Watch out, guv. Pork on the wing,' Bird said, opening the office door.

* * *

Callum had to admit that, despite his irritating manner, Cookie was very effective when it came to technology. But it seemed to be two steps forward then one back. He read the note Cookie had left on his desk, observing that it was both dated and timed. The handwriting was small and squashed as if the lad was concerned with conserving trees, and it took a moment to decipher.

It informed him that Rose Brown had discharged herself from the hospital and vanished. Staff had found her hospital gown in the toilet and her clothes and personal effects were gone. Cookie followed this information with a paragraph of speculation on where he thought she had gone. This was more novel than note, and another conversation with Cookie was looming.

With uncharacteristically good timing, Cookie tapped on the door. 'You got my note, guv?'

'A note is a precise and concise rendering of the facts. This is a blathering of fiction, Cookie.'

Callum tapped the page before dropping it onto his desk. He closed his eyes and saw Grace wagging a finger at him, so he opened them again. His Bellman encounter and being taken off the case was looping through his mind. He felt defensive and, as any cornered animal knows, attack is the best form of defence. But his career being in jeopardy was his problem, not Cookie's, or the others in his team.

'Next time, just the facts,' he said, indicating that Cookie should return to his desk.

Cookie ignored him. 'I went to the hospital, guv, after I left you the note.'

'Because?'

'I wanted to check the CCTV to see who collected her, and when she left.'

Cookie's brain was functioning more sharply than his handwritten note suggested.

Callum sensed Bird's interest from the outer office and saw him stand, arms folded across his chest, watching their exchange.

'And?'

'No one collected her. She walked out the front door just before ten and went off down the road.'

'Certain it was her?'

'Certain. Pink plaster cast and jodhpurs. So, I checked the bus timetables, and the 44 bus passes the hospital just after ten and goes through Downton to Woodfalls Cross, which is as good as Hale. She could have walked to Devereux Manor from there. Hundo P.'

'Leave a note for Daisy. That was good thinking, Cookie.'

Callum smiled when the detective sported a grin that must have made his cheeks ache.

The return of Daisy and Legs minutes later wiped the smile from Callum's face. Both women were quiet, and he detected a chill undercurrent that seemed to be binding the girls together. Daisy dropped her jacket over her chair and went to the board.

'Edward is up here now? That's funny.'

'Why so?' Callum moved to join her; he tried to gauge her mood and failed.

Her face was a tight mask of control.

Legs was more transparent, brows drawn down over fierce eyes, her movements less relaxed than usual. She wrapped her arms around her torso as if she was hugging her thoughts to herself.

'Not funny ha-ha. Funny peculiar,' Daisy said.

'Funny disturbing, more like,' Legs muttered.

'Let us in on the joke then.' Bird stretched back in his chair and linked his hands behind his head.

'Okay. Diane Adams, who was in the same convent the year after Mary-Ellen, is a teacher at Nelson's School in Downton. She used to live in Hale, went to the village school with Mary-Ellen and they went on to the grammar. Diane earned a bit of extra pocket money by waitressing at parties at Devereux Manor, the same as Mary-Ellen and Jenny did. There was stuff going on all the time when Edward was home.'

'And?' Bird said.

'She was waitressing there one July evening and the place was knee-deep in Edward's pals. "A parade of peacocks," she said. Bit of a contrast to the waitresses who had to wear black and white and tie their hair back. She described herself as "plain-looking and spotty", so preferred to wear her hair loose so she could hide behind it.' Daisy flicked a look at Callum, who realised she had noticed his ploy.

'At the end of the evening, Edward asked her to go round the gardens to collect empty glasses.'

'One or two of the waitresses always did that, so it wasn't unusual,' Legs said.

'A man in dark clothes came out of the shadows by the summer house, put a hand over her mouth and pulled her into the shrub border. He raped her.'

'Shit.' Bird lifted his hands from the back of his head and sat up. 'Did she report it?'

'No. And this is where it gets strange.' Daisy and Legs took a step closer to one another. 'It was over in a matter of seconds. He never uttered a word, just got to his feet and walked away.'

'He was prepared, then,' Bird said.

Legs stabbed a glance at him, but he continued speaking. 'He didn't prolong it as if he was enjoying it? No verbal abuse or deluded self-excuses like telling her it was her fault for wearing a short skirt? No threats of reprisals if she didn't keep her mouth shut?'

Daisy shook her head. 'Nothing.'

'Did he inflict any other injuries on her?' Callum asked.

'No. It was so quick she could barely believe it had happened.'

Callum felt a pulse of anger thump in his chest and realised that anger was what he had seen in Daisy.

'She was making her way back to the house, scared and upset, when she heard someone coming towards her. It was Edward. He asked if she was okay.'

'Bloody stupid question.' Bird's voice was gruff.

'She was so relieved to see a face that she recognised that she blurted out what had happened. He told her not to worry.'

'Typical man,' Legs muttered.

'She was only seventeen and it was her first time. Her dad was a sidesman at the local Methodist chapel, and she was frightened that her parents would find out and blame her. And she was worried about the social disgrace for her family if she got pregnant outside of marriage.'

'Some introduction to sex that was. Was she really more worried about the social consequences than the rape itself?' Bird asked.

'At that particular moment, yes. Edward said it was best not to tell anyone as probably nothing would come of it, and she could just forget about it.'

'As if,' Legs said quietly.

'Edward said, if she did turn out to be pregnant, he would sort it, and nobody would ever need to know.'

'And he said that because he didn't want any comeback on the estate, right?' Bird said.

Daisy shrugged. 'Then she found she was pregnant' – she tucked her hair behind her ear and looked at Callum – 'and she thought he would retract his offer of help, but he didn't. He was as good as his word.'

'Did he offer to arrange an abortion?' Callum asked.

'She didn't mention one, did she, Legs?'

Legs shook her head.

'Edward suggested a gap year,' Daisy said, 'sold the idea to her father, arranged the convent and took care of all the little details. Including, after the birth, a new bank account with a healthy balance. Enough to see her through university and beyond; and he swore her to secrecy. He said it was recompense for it happening on his family's property.'

'And,' Legs said, 'no one, not even her family, ever found out she was pregnant. They still don't know and, incidentally, neither does her husband. And she's still frightened of her father.'

'What happened to the bairn?' Callum asked.

'She doesn't know. Edward collected her after the birth, took the baby and gave her the savings book,' Daisy said.

'Did he?' Callum asked.

'Yes,' Legs said. 'Sister Agnes thought the English girls were all collected by a man in a big car, but she didn't know who he was. Do you think that could have been Edward too?'

'Better than evens, I reckon,' Bird said.

'Diane said she assumed Edward arranged an adoption of her daughter,' Legs continued.

'A few months later,' Daisy said, 'when she felt up to asking him, Edward and his family had returned to South Africa and only old Mr Charles was at the manor, so there was no one she could ask. She still beats herself up for selling her baby.'

'You'd think she'd forget after all this time,' Cookie said.

Legs shook her head. 'She'll never forget it. She still looks at girls as they pass in the street and wonders if they are her daughter.' Her eyes challenged Cookie.

'I've forgotten things in the past that I didn't like.' Cookie lifted his chin and jutted it at Legs.

'Such as?' she asked.

'Can't tell you. I've forgotten them, haven't I.' He drew circles on the floor with his toe.

Callum knew he was lying about having forgotten but turned his attention back to Daisy. 'And she has no idea who raped her?'

'She never saw his face. He smelled of drink and aftershave but so did most of the men. She thought he was taller and heavier than Edward because she couldn't move. That's all we've got.'

'Do you think Edward sold the kids?' Bird said. 'Nice bleedin' sideline that. Rich friends wanting kids without the bump.'

'What in God's name goes on inside your head, Bird?' Legs stood tall, eye to eye with Bird, and jabbed her finger at his chest. 'Women aren't playthings. They're not just a way for men to make a quick buck.'

Callum thought of the girls in Glasgow Green or shivering in pairs on Cadogan Street. They were owned by men: the pimps, the punters, or the peddlers. That didn't make it right. But it was a fact that some men used women to make money.

Bird looked at her stabbing finger and raised both his arms, palms towards her.

'Enough,' Callum barked. 'Save it for another time, people.'

Legs exhaled a long, slow breath and Bird turned away from her, thrusting his hands into his pockets.

Daisy looked from one to the other. 'Thank you, children,' she said in a Mary-Poppins voice.

A guffaw exploded from Bird and Legs smiled and shook her head. The moment of tension eased. Callum would not have relished getting between the two giants.

Daisy referred to her pocketbook. 'There is one thing that has always puzzled Diane about that night.'

'Which is?' Callum said, pleased to have them back on track.

'That there were plenty of attractive girls there waitressing, "pretty airheads" she called them. She doesn't know why he picked her out as a target.'

'Why indeed.' Callum rotated his earring and stared into the distance as a seed of an idea began to germinate. 'Why indeed,' he repeated quietly.

Daisy made eye contact with each of them in turn. 'This is important. Diane only agreed to talk to us on the condition that her name is not mentioned. She will never testify, supposing we were able to find the person responsible after all this time. She just wants to forget it. Even though she can't.' Daisy looked at the board. 'Pity we can't talk to the third woman,' she said.

Cookie bobbed up and stood beside her. 'I did a bit of research on her,' he said. 'Harriet King went to the grammar school, like the other two. She read psychology and sociology at uni and studied the high suicide rate of women prisoners in your neck of the woods, guv. Edinburgh, Greenock and Cornton Vale. Did you know that women only make up five per cent of the prison population but account for nearly fifty per cent of self-harm incidences, including suicides?' He looked around their faces.

'And?' Legs glowered at him.

'And she didn't marry or have any more kids.' Cookie flicked a look at Legs. 'She had a long-term female partner but committed suicide about twenty years after her baby was born. Painkillers and vodka. And she left a suicide note.'

'Poor girl.' Daisy's quiet comment echoed Callum's feelings. 'Do you think there's any connection between her death and Mary-Ellen's? Is Diane Adams in danger, do you think?'

Callum shook his head. 'No. The deaths are unrelated. They are a long time apart, in different locations, and Harriet King was a suicide. No connection.'

'There's no paper trail for her baby,' Cookie said. 'I tried following up other births, not just our three, and it's pretty much always the same. No further records. They were crap at keeping records at that place.'

'Or good at not keeping them,' Bird said before swivelling in his chair to answer his phone.

Callum looked across to the board and the picture of Edward staring down at them. 'Daisy, in the light of Cookie's knowledge of bus routes, let's go and check if Rose is at Devereux Manor.'

'She wouldn't be that stupid, would she?' Legs said.

'Richard is her knight in shining armour,' Daisy said. 'He protected her from the big, bad ogre, so I think she'll run straight back to him.'

'Agreed,' Callum said. 'She probably won't tell him she caused her own injuries. I have questions about her connection to the phone that she said she didn't know about. And she has nowhere else to go.' He picked up his jacket. 'I just want to make sure she's there. And I have a question or two for Edward Devereux-Strauss.'

Chapter Twenty-Six

Daisy parked beneath the lime trees at the end of the drive and she and Callum walked along the side of the house.

'Only Richard's vehicle here, sir. Edward must still be in London.'

They went through the archway into the stable yard. 'Pity. Get Cookie to check on his whereabouts.'

The stable yard looked normal. Horse heads appeared over box doors in response to their footsteps and they heard music from the tack-room radio. Callum noted that the windows of the groom's flat were closed, dark holes punched into the sun-warmed wood cladding.

Richard was schooling a chestnut mare in the manège and didn't notice their quiet arrival. They stood at the gate and watched him at work.

'That's two twenty-metre circles in collected trot,' Daisy said. 'See how relaxed the mare is, she's flexing at the poll, and her ears are flicking forwards and sideways. That shows she's listening to her rider.'

Callum watched the mare's feet and tried to see if her back hooves tracked up over the print left by the front ones but failed.

Richard circled large, trotting around the outside of the school. The second he saw them, his body tightened, and his eyes flicked to the flat above the loose boxes.

He halted in front of them on the other side of the gate. The horse smelled sweat-hot, and lather flecked its chest. It mouthed the bit, blew air through distended nostrils, and drooled white foam onto the bark surface of the manège.

'What the fuck do you want?' Pimples of sweat glistened on Richard's forehead below the peak of his hat, and his bruised eye was colouring up nicely.

'Good morning to you, too.' Daisy's voice was sugar-sweet, and she leaned on the top bar of the gate.

'Brought a bodyguard with you?'

'Do I need one?'

'Depends on what you want.'

'I want to know when you last saw Rhianwen Bowen.'

'I don't know an anyone Bowen.'

'You know her as Rose Brown.'

The mare quivered as he tensed in the saddle. 'I already told your horse-shy boss there that I took her to A&E yesterday.'

'And that's where we found out her real name, Rhianwen Bowen.'

Richard's sneering mouth puckered into an O before stretching into a tight line. Just in time, he stopped himself from again looking up at the flat and instead studied a lone magpie sitting on the gable end of the stables. It cawed once, took wing and flew towards the village.

'I wonder what her father would have to say about her living here…' Daisy said.

'Her father is dead,' he snapped. 'As usual, you blunder in without all the facts.'

Daisy held his eyes for a moment before lowering her lids and turning her head away. Callum was confused by her body language, but Richard clearly found it liberating. Encouraged by her momentary silence, he swept to the moral high ground.

'You never got the full facts last time, Daisy. You had no right to ride roughshod through the village, spreading rumours and lying about me. I had every right to kill those dogs. They were worrying my horses.' The mare fidgeted beneath him, and he firmed his grip on the reins. 'You would have done the same.'

'No, I wouldn't. There was no need to kill them.'

'I was protecting my stock.'

'They belonged to a six-year-old girl, and your horses weren't harmed. Then you dumped them on my doorstep. I just told the family the facts.' Daisy's voice was calm, almost matter-of-fact, but two spots of colour sat high on her cheeks.

'Things like that come back and bite you. Just remember, Miss High-and-Mighty, there's always a pay-off.' The mare struck at the ground with a hoof, and Richard tightened his legs against her flanks. 'You should be more responsible and have a duty of care.'

'Oh, I care,' Daisy said. 'I care about girls being beaten and abused.'

'I never touched her, that was Father. He's the bully, not me. I never laid a finger on her.'

'Yes, you did, Richard. You told DI MacLean that you slept with her.'

Richard leaned down from the saddle until his face hovered above Daisy's. 'Jealous? She begged for it.' He ran his tongue across his bruised lip.

'Enough.' Callum's gritty response shot Richard backwards in the saddle.

The mare shuffled sideways in surprise and Richard stared at Callum as if he had forgotten he was there. Dismounting, Richard pulled the reins over the horse's head and loosened the girth a couple of holes. The mare took a deep lungful of air and exhaled noisily, blowing mucus onto Richard's jodhpurs. He unlatched the gate, swung it open and towed his horse out into the yard. There was plenty of room to avoid Daisy, but he deliberately passed closer than was necessary.

'Keep out of my way,' Richard said sharply.

The dangling stirrup irons bounced against the horse's sides with every stride and one clipped Daisy on the shoulder.

'Why don't you run the irons up the leathers like normal people?' Daisy asked, her fingers massaging the point of contact.

'I'm not normal people.' The sneer returned. 'I'm warning you, keep out of my way.'

He walked the horse into a loose box and pulled the half-door closed behind him.

Callum shot a questioning glance at Daisy who responded with a shallow shrug of her shoulders before they followed Richard. Straw rustled inside the stable, the saddle thumped onto the top of the door then the bridle was hitched over the cantle. Richard came outside, lifted the tack, and flicked the bolts closed, a muscle bouncing in his jaw.

Daisy followed him to the tack room, but Callum leaned back against the wall in the shadow of the overhang. He heard the horse inside the box greedily sucking water and the chirp-chup of sparrows. He looked up at the darkened windows of the flat. A curtain swung back into place. He could just discern the outline of a pink plaster cast before it melted back into the shadows.

He pushed away from the wall and joined Daisy in the tack-room doorway.

'So, if she asked you to hurt her, that makes it okay, does it?' Daisy demanded.

'Of course not. Don't be fucking ridiculous. I'd never hurt her. I love her.'

'That makes everything all right then, does it?'

Richard's Adam's apple bobbed up and down. He clenched and unclenched his fists and looked as if he was contemplating a physical response to her needling.

Callum touched Daisy lightly on the arm and addressed Richard. 'Thanks for your time. We had to eliminate this as a possible location before we pursued other avenues. Our intelligence suggests that she is probably heading for London, but if you should hear from her, please let us know.'

Callum turned away and walked towards the entrance. It was a moment before he heard Daisy's footfalls behind, and then beside him.

She looked up at him, about to speak, but he gave a slight shake of his head, and she remained silent until they had climbed back into the cab.

'Intelligence? London? Why didn't you ask to look in the flat? He might be lying.'

'He is lying. She's in the flat.'

'Why didn't you tell him we wanted to look inside then?'

'Because he'd have been lawyered up within fifteen seconds and demanding a search warrant. By the time we got one, she'd be gone and I want answers about who used that phone. If he thinks we don't know she's there, they'll feel safe and stay put.'

'For her own safety, we should go back and get her.'

'My call and my responsibility, Sergeant. We play it my way.'

'But…'

'But nothing. She's in no danger from Richard.'

Daisy started the engine and pulled onto the gravel drive. Her shoulders were hunched and tight. She had got used to running the show, making the decisions for the team, so he cut her a little slack.

'I saw her plastered arm behind the curtain when she was watching you and Richard.'

'You might have said.' She changed up a gear.

'You could have worked it out for yourself. He didn't speculate on her whereabouts, or show any concern that the apparent love of his life was missing?'

'Now that you mention it. I suppose that's as good as confirming he knows where she is.' She pulled out onto the lane.

'We'll get a search warrant and go back tomorrow.'

'You're quite sneaky, aren't you?' She grinned, and her fingers relaxed on the steering wheel.

'Not an original observation, Daisy.' He was pleased that her usual good humour seemed restored. 'And it'll give him time to cool off. You made him a bit hot under the collar.'

'I might have accidently needled him, a bit.'

Callum looked at her sharply as the village green flashed past outside her open window. Her satisfied smile had him wondering just how accidental the needling had been.

'I thought for a moment there that you might have to intervene and protect me.'

The same thought had occurred to Callum.

* * *

Bird went over to the fishbowl.

'They've just sent me Edward's CCTV footage. He was definitely in London when he said he was. He comes down the stairs carrying a briefcase and nods to the bloke in tinsel, who opens the door for him. Then the camera out the front picks him up. Some chap drives his Range Rover to the door and gets out as Edward puts his case in the back. Matey hands over the keys and closes the door when Edward's in the driving seat. Times on both cameras coincide and it was 0800 hours. Just like he said.'

'Ruling him out as a suspect,' Callum said.

'Dunno. Too many things don't add up for my liking. He put his hand in his pocket when she had a baby, and he doesn't seem the charitable sort to me. Then she made a fool of him in the press with that planning thing and cost him a fortune – well, a fortune in my eyes, just a few million quid in his. Do you reckon he paid someone to do it? Made sure he had an alibi?'

'The planning was a while ago. Why now, Bird? What happened recently that changed the status quo?'

'Can't put a finger on anything, guv. There's a link with the phone you found at the stables, which means he was contacting her. But if contacting her was all legit, then why use a burner? He's filthy rich, he's got to have paid someone else to do his dirty work, don't you think?' Bird said.

'It's possible. But why now, what changed that caused someone to kill her? We need to find the trigger.'

'You got me there. There's nothing in her work diary, no fishy correspondence, and Sir Michael said she seemed especially content recently.'

'Jenny Walker said Mary-Ellen seemed "ultra-happy" the last couple of times they met up.' Callum rotated his earring. 'I wonder what makes a woman like Mary-Ellen ultra-happy.'

'No bleedin' idea, guv. Helen would be happy with a squashed box of chocolates.' This was said with such certainty that Callum suspected she had been the recipient of such a gift.

He thought of Grace, who had embraced life and always saw a silver lining. People fell into two categories, he thought, those who were dour until someone else cheered them, and those, like Grace, who were naturally happy until something made them unhappy.

'Mary-Ellen was a happy soul.'

'So not money, she had bleedin' tons of it. She'd just ditched Jimmy and her friend said she was taking a break from the extramaritals, so it wasn't a bloke.' Bird looked at Callum. 'What else is there apart from love and money?'

'Good question, Bird,' Callum said as the detective went back to his desk.

* * *

Shadows made moving mats on the floor and the afternoon sun was withdrawing her warmth from the day. Callum looked at the team and thought about what made them happy. Bird wanted peace and quiet. Legs wanted love and acceptance. Daisy wanted her family and animals. And Cookie? Who knew what Cookie wanted? Cookie probably didn't know the answer to that question.

Callum looked up at the ceiling. What did he want? In the five years of their marriage, he had wanted a family with Grace. That could never happen now. Beyond that, he didn't know. And Mary-Ellen? If they were to believe what they were told, then she wanted for nothing. She had a happy marriage with her soulmate where she felt secure and protected. She had a successful business, financial security and loving and supportive parents. What was she missing?

Callum answered his phone.

'Inspector. Brief heads-up. Goes no further. Understood?' Thelma Greyson waited for his reply.

'Yes, ma'am.'

'Bellman has allowed himself to be blackmailed by Denton. Right bloody balls-up. Pictures of DC Cooke's sister. Compromising.'

Callum remembered Cookie telling Legs there were things he chose to forget.

'Ma'am—'

'Shut up, MacLean. Denton was your snooper. Bertie made a clean breast, devil and the deep, family first. It's sorted. Cut him some slack.'

Callum stared at the purring receiver for a moment before putting it back on his desk. Thelma Greyson had just risen in his estimation. She had acted with both speed and common sense, which was a welcome change. He didn't have any right to that information and was aware that she was extending a courtesy. She was fostering a smooth future working relationship between him and Bellman, so she was expecting him to stay. He had been right to trust her. But she was swift and deadly, and he wouldn't want her for an enemy.

'Okay, people. We'll have a search warrant for the stables in the morning,' Callum said, walking out into the office.

'Just the stables? Not the Manor as well?' Daisy asked.

'Correct. Insufficient cause at this juncture.' Callum ignored Bird's disapproving grunt. 'Bird and Cookie, dig a little deeper into the Devereux-Strauss past. Not just Edward, the offspring as well.'

'Including Bryony Osbourne?' Daisy asked, head tilted. Her eyes were round and innocent, the suggestion of a smile being held in check.

'Including Bryony Osbourne, Sergeant. Business and personal life. Bank accounts, phone records. Everything. Cookie, go over Mary-Ellen's phone records again, calls and texts. We've missed something.'

'Yee-hah.' Cookie twirled an imaginary lariat around his head before launching it in Bird's direction. Bird shook his head to Daisy who grinned at him.

Daisy's phone buzzed. 'Hi, Oli. What's the problem?' As she listened, the colour leached from her face and her legs buckled. She sat; her face creased with concentration.

'Are you sure, Oliver?'

Callum detected echoes of Mrs Donaldson in her tone. The others fell silent.

'Stay with him, please. I'll be there in ten.' Daisy was on her feet and reaching for her jacket as she ended the call.

'I've got to go. Felix has been killed.'

'What? Go,' Callum said as she hurried to the door. 'And keep me informed.'

'Deedee hun, anything I can do?' asked Legs.

Daisy glanced over her shoulder. 'No, thanks. Bird, give the DI a lift to mine. You go home that way.' And without waiting for a response, she was gone.

They stood motionless for ten seconds then settled down at their desks. The clatter of the keyboards and scraping of chair legs seemed muted, the smell of coffee diluted, and busyness exaggerated. Occasionally, someone would look at the open doorway as if hoping Daisy would reappear and the status quo be resumed. As if they were scared to tempt fate, no one mentioned Felix.

The ringing of Callum's phone made him start.

'DI MacLean.' There was a pause, and soft breaths fluttered against his ear, but nobody spoke, so he focused on the background noise. He heard hushed voices, footsteps, the punctuation of beeping machines, and then a controlled exhalation of breath from his caller.

'Callum, I need to come and see you in the morning. I have some information for you.' Bryony's voice was low, taut with tension.

'Hello, Miss Osbourne, Bryony. If it's urgent, I can be free now.'

'I can't. I'm at the hospital. My mother's dying.' The last word was truncated, snatched away by a sob.

He hesitated before replying, 'I'm sorry to hear that, Bryony.' He sketched a magpie on the paper he had been writing on and waited for her to continue. He could hear her struggling for control, and then someone called to her.

'I have to go, Callum.'

'Tomorrow,' he said. But she had already gone.

His stomach contracted on a surge of adrenaline. Had Penny fallen and injured herself? Was Edward responsible? He speculated on what Bryony wanted to share with him. Did it concern Bellman, Edward, or the murder of Mary-Ellen? He searched for connections and patterns, but he found nothing tenable.

Bird interrupted his reverie.

'Guv, more info on the Devereux-Strausses.'

Callum indicated to Bird to sit, and the chair creaked under his solid weight.

'Matthew is a bleeding genius. Eton, Cambridge, a mathematical whizz-kid. He's the financial director of the whole kit and caboodle. Apart from some student nonsense, he's squeaky clean and bloody good at what he does. Not such a ruthless bastard as Edward. Recently married, she's a looker with one kid down the spout and one on the way.'

'Any connection with Mary-Ellen?'

'Not so far, guv. Bryony Osbourne went to a local school, then university. She studied law. Works for a Southampton firm and her name keeps popping up, pro bono for women's justice and all that malarkey. Again, squeaky clean, not even a speeding to her name.'

'Is there a husband?' He avoided Bird's eye.

'No. Osbourne is her mother's maiden name. She's been using that ever since she started work.'

'I see. And Richard?'

'I've just been talking to Richard's old housemaster from Eton. He's got a rock the size of Gibraltar stuck in his gob, but he was full of info. Remember the sports arena was named Devereux-Strauss Complex? Well, it's not in recognition of an old Etonian's achievements, which is what I thought. It's because Edward paid for a whole new bloody complex after Richard burnt the old one to the ground.'

'Why did he do that?'

'Just getting to that,' Bird said. 'Edward was a bloody good athlete and scholar, and Matthew was the same, Oppidians, the academic elite.' He huffed a breath through his nose. 'Richard wasn't quite such a brainbox, but he was a brilliant athlete and desperate to impress the old man. Thompson, the housemaster, said Richard was obsessed with what his father would think of his performance and achievements. And, to quote–' he referred briefly to his notes and effected a plummy voice '–"his approach to winning could be ungentlemanly in the extreme."'

'Much like his father where business is concerned, if we are to believe all that is written,' Callum said.

'Yeah, the apple didn't fall far from the tree. Richard was a bit of a loner, popular but no close friends except

Chet, a foreign student who was a loner himself, so they gelled.'

'The fire?' Callum said.

'The school has a final-year run-and-swim competition. Edward's name is on the trophy, and Matthew's, and when it was Richard's turn, he won by a country mile and was cock-a-hoop. He went charging up to Edward with his trophy, and all his old man said was, "Matthew's time was better than yours."'

'And Richard was not happy?'

'Understatement,' Bird said. 'He went off on one and the sports hall was torched; it was never proved who did it. Edward paid for a new one with a full orchestra of whistles and bells and they were so stunned by his generosity that they named it after him. No further action.'

No problems, just solutions, Callum thought again.

'What happened to Richard?'

'Nothing. He left. Disappeared. Fell off the face of the earth and then turned up again three years later as if nothing had bleedin' happened. Money and privilege,' he grunted.

'And in those three years?' Callum asked.

'Boy Wonder's onto it.'

They both looked across at the raven curls bobbing in time to some imagined beat.

'We'll call it a day now. All right for that lift, Bird?'

'Yeah. I hope Deedee's okay. She loved that dog. See you in the car park.'

Callum stopped by Cookie's desk on the way out. Lines of spider droppings covered a sheet of paper, and having failed to decipher them, Callum realised they were a sort of personal shorthand.

Cookie looked up at Callum with a smile that crinkled his nose.

'Don't stay too late, Cookie.'

'Okay. I won't. Nighty-night.' His eyes dropped back to the screen before Callum could summon an adequate reply.

Chapter Twenty-Seven

Bird was waiting by the wing of a mud-speckled black Barbarian, checking messages on his phone. He looked up and unlocked the vehicle when Callum came into the car park. A whiff of wet dog and something herby perfumed the cab; hay, Callum decided, looking at the floor beneath his feet as Bird guided the vehicle out onto the road. Callum reached up to grasp the hanging strap and Bird gave a guttural guffaw.

'I'm too old to drive like a silly little tosser with a death wish. Not only that, Helen'll kill me if I crash her car. She's only let me drive it because mine's in for service today.'

Callum tucked back his hair and failed to imagine Grace driving something that size. He had yet to meet Helen and wondered what she was like.

'What do you drive, Bird?'

'Same. Only older and cleaner.' He lowered the driver's window. 'Hers is a bleedin' pigsty. Stinks in here.'

Bird had an easily offended nose for a copper.

The houses eased away behind them, replaced by open heath. The carpet of brown heather was patterned with dots of pink bell blossoms and textured by patches of acid-green fern fronds. Fold after fold, distance washing out the pigment until all that remained was a haze of timeless blue-grey where the land merged into the sky. Unchanged for centuries.

Past generations had trampled that heath, and it had provided them with warmth and shelter and fed their children. Callum watched the repeated images flash past like a giant slideshow. It was primal. You don't own land like this, he thought, the land owns you. He was startled to

231

find himself wondering how it must feel to ride across it on horseback.

'Do you ride, Bird?'

Bird flicked a look at Callum. 'Yep. You should try it sometime.'

'Hmm.' Daisy's observations about his prowess with equines had made it back to the office.

Callum felt the pulse of engine vibration beneath his feet and the cab tilted to one side as Bird changed down a gear and mounted the verge to ease past ponies that stood in the road.

'I might have to look into replacing Lassa with something like this.'

'Lassa?'

'My Camaro. Grace, my late wife, named it Lassa. Stands for Low-Slung Arse.'

Bird's gruff burst of laughter eased the punch of pain in Callum's chest.

'Might be a sound idea. This is summer. You wait till we get a bit of winter rain, not to mention the bleedin' mud. You'll need water wings.'

Two girls played ball with their dog on the green and Callum heard their shrieks of laughter through his open window. The truck glided over Daisy's cattle grid and whispered down her track. They both raised a hand to Oliver who was walking towards the house, a soil-gammed spade over his shoulder. He gave a tight nod of acknowledgement.

Bird pulled up next to Daisy's Navaro and pointed to her standing on the lawn. They joined her without speaking. She was looking down at the body of Felix. The sun was slipping below the treetops and the three of them cast long shadows across the body. A tall one each side and a short one in the centre, a child's drawing of a happy family.

'The vet came out,' Daisy said. 'Felix has a broken neck.'

'What happened? Did he have an accident?' Bird asked.

'Not unless he managed to carry himself to the doorstep and lay along it after he was dead.' Her voice was flat with no trace of emotion.

Oliver joined them. 'Ready, Deedee.' His shadow overlaid theirs at a right angle and made three crosses that rested over the body of the dog.

She refused their offers of help and struggled across the garden with Felix in her arms. Oliver trailed in her wake.

'Bastard,' Bird said with gravel in his voice. 'Felix was an innocent pet. Bastard.' He hurried back to the Barbarian and drove away.

The crunch of tyres diminished to a whisper and Callum stood in silence. The bats swooped and danced, the soft umbrella flap of their wings teasing his hair.

Eventually heading into the kitchen, he switched on the lights and filled the kettle. A 'Mrs P offering' bubbled gently in the oven and he put plates and cutlery on the island. Daisy was taking a long time.

When it was too dark to do anything other than imagine an outside world, she returned and kicked off her muddy boots. She held her grimy hands up in front of her.

'I need a shower.' She nodded at the plates. 'Ten minutes, okay?' And she was gone.

Callum thought he heard water running somewhere above his head and settled down with a cup of tea and his sketchbook.

Scrubbed pink, with damp hair, Daisy returned and spooned food onto their plates. She ate with a mechanical rhythm, forking food into her mouth, chewing, and then swallowing. She didn't seem to want to talk, and he didn't know what to say to her. That supper was the quietest meal they had shared, and he missed the soft click of the dog's claws on the stone floor.

'Did anything happen after I left the station?'

Her voice was calm, matter-of-fact, but didn't deceive Callum for one second when he saw the bleakness in her eyes. He updated her on Bird's findings.

She tipped her head to one side, eyes over-bright. 'Law degree, eh? If Bryony represents her family, she should have plenty of work lined up.'

'You could be right, CPS willing, of course.'

'Won't it make things difficult, you bringing a case against them?'

He found Bryony an attractive personality, but Daisy was reading from books that had yet to be written.

'In what way, difficult?' he asked, holding eye contact.

She shrugged, cleared the plates, and turned her back on him to splosh water into the sink.

He concentrated on his sketch, pencilling in a graphite outline of open heath punctuated by spikey clumps of gorse bushes and the occasional exclamation mark of a silver birch trunk. He added a plantation of conifers in the middle distance directing the focus onto the foreground. Satisfied, he began adding detail to the furled fern fronds. He became aware that the only sound was the graze of his pencil against the paper and looked up.

Daisy was standing silently by the sink, back towards him, her shoulders jerking rhythmically, her knuckles chalk-white where they grasped the edge of the granite.

He got up and stood behind her, his humming-bird hands hovering above her shoulders. Acts of tenderness had been buried with Grace. He didn't know what to do and experienced a sudden spike of fear. Then he sighed, lowered his hands gently onto her shaking shoulders and felt the warmth of her body beneath his palms.

'Daisy.'

His voice snagged on memories that choked his breath and burned his chest. She turned and threw herself against him, sobbing silently. He tensed for a heartbeat; eyes closed against the stab of tears. Then he folded her in his arms and dipped his chin to rest it on top of her head. He held her until her sobs subsided into snuffling hiccups, then he cleared his throat and eased her away from him.

Sniffing, she wiped her nose along her cuff. She took a slow shaky breath to speak, and he raised a finger to stall her. She had nothing to apologise for. It was a natural response to loss and, he now acknowledged, a necessary part of the recovery process.

His epiphany had been a long time coming. He had raised barriers that grew higher and blacker until he was consumed by anger and despair. He pushed away the people who cared about him. He rejected the concerns of friends, and offers of help from colleagues, preferring to take solitary walks on the Campsies, along the paths they had shared. He knew that Grace was dead, yet one afternoon he heard a bubble of her laughter float across the fell and chased after it. The stinging wind had whipped the moisture from his eyes, and it ran down his face. Sprinting, chest on fire, he had lost his footing and collapsed into a hollow on the hillside and accepted that he had lost her. He sobbed like a bairn until he was exhausted. Then he had slipped into his first sound sleep in months. He was woken by the whispered conversation of two boys who were about to go through his pockets. Their excitement at finding a dead body had dissipated when he opened his eyes and sat up.

Those eyes now rested on Daisy, who seemed dishevelled but calm.

'Your turn to make the coffee, Daisy.' He turned his back on her, settled on his seat, and picked up his pencil. His heart thumped in his chest, and it surprised him that holding another person had any effect on him after three years of abstinence.

'It's always my turn.'

Her grumble was good-natured. He heard her fill the kettle and put mugs on the granite. She tore off a sheet of kitchen paper and blew her nose before snapping closed the rubbish bin. He looked up briefly when a spoon clattered to the floor, but she had knocked it off stretching to reach a tin from the cupboard shelf. The smell of coffee filled his nostrils when she placed a mug in front of him.

'Cake?' She lifted the lid from the tin on an uncut Victoria sandwich.

'Not for me, thanks.'

Daisy cut herself a large wedge and bit into it. Jam oozed and dripped down her chin. She caught it with a finger before taking a second bite.

'Mrs P?' He indicated the tin with a bob of his head.

Daisy nodded, finished her first slice, and cut another, then another. Like a chain-smoker – a cake chain. She was comfort-eating. Grace used to do that, and then blame him for not stopping her. He smiled at the memory.

'Sure you don't want any, Callum?' Her hand hovered over the skinny slice left in the bottom of the tin.

He shook his head. 'No, thanks.'

He returned his attention to the comforting skirl of graphite on toothed paper, to the new world hatching in front of him on the page. He sketched a fern, a multi-limbed creature, arms spread wide to soak up the sun, and dark shadows beneath.

Daisy took a sip from her mug and looked at him over the rim. 'I think I know who killed Felix.'

He laid his pencil across his drawing and faced her. 'Who?'

'Richard Dick-head Strauss.' The whites of her eyes were still threaded with red, and her hair stuck out around her head like a halo. It was refreshing to meet someone so confident in themselves that they were not bothered by their appearance.

'Why? Explain, please.'

'Remember he killed those two dogs for supposedly chasing stock on his land?'

He nodded. She hadn't told him how they had died, and he'd assumed they had been shot. That's what landowners usually did. Now he addressed his assumption and felt a jolt as loose wires made a connection.

'He broke their necks, did he?' Floating strands of information began to form a pattern.

'He did. Both. Clean break just like Felix.' She said his name without reaction and Callum thought that although she might shed a few more tears for her pet, they wouldn't catch her by surprise like this evening.

'Motive for killing him?' he asked.

'I pissed him off when we went looking for Rose this afternoon. He threatened me for interfering. Said, "Things like that come back and bite you. There's always a pay-off." I didn't think much about it at the time. He's always blowing off steam. I should have taken him seriously.'

Callum picked up his pencil and drew a bird probing the foreground turf with a sharp beak. Richard was childish and volatile. He didn't conceal his emotions or seem worried about consequences. Would he harm Felix in retaliation? If he had to narrow it down to a yes or no, then it was a yes.

'Tomorrow we'll see what he has to say for himself.'

* * *

That night, Callum lay in bed, the curtains across the tall glass doors open to the velvet darkness. He wondered what Grace would have made of this place, of Daisy and the Devereux-Strausses, of Thelma Greyson and Cookie. He thought she would have liked Bryony and Bird but not the wide-open spaces.

Eclipsed by clouds, the slow strobe of the moon flashed across the ground like a morse light sending messages to Earth. Callum looked across the garden noting the soft tonal variations caused by the shape and texture of the plants. The memory of street lights was fading.

Then he was startled into wakefulness. A sudden patch of moonlight silhouetted a figure on the lawn. Callum slid out of bed, body concealed behind the curtain, head craned around the drapes to focus on the spot where the man had stood. The clouds shuffled, but the man had gone. Then Callum's heart hammered in his throat as the figure sprang forward out of the darkness and tapped on the glass door. His heart slid back to its proper place when the moon spotlit Bird. Callum eased out a long breath and opened the French window.

'Sorry, guv. Didn't mean to give you a bleedin' heart attack.' He stepped into the bedroom, tombstones gleaming, and Callum closed the door behind him.

'Do you usually prowl around in the middle of the night dressed like that?' His eyes floated over the black combat gear and what Callum assumed to be night-vision glasses hanging around Bird's neck. Once a soldier... he thought.

'I prefer me bed these nights. Getting old. But I got to thinking about Felix and it being some sort of vendetta against Deedee, else why put his body on her doorstep instead of hiding it? I thought I'd have a bit of a prowl and see if there was anyone about.' He lowered himself into the wicker chair that Callum indicated and it squealed as he settled his weight and eased off his gloves.

Callum sat on his bed. 'Daisy tells me that Richard broke the necks of those two dogs that strayed onto his land.'

'He did. I only remembered that when I was chatting to Helen over supper. Daisy read him the Riot Act afterwards but there wasn't anything we could do about it. They were dead and there was no proof of what they had done. End of. But Richard's taken every opportunity since then to needle her because she told the kid's parents and that made him a bit unpopular in the village.'

'Richard threatened her today when we were at the stables. Told her there was always a payback,' Callum said.

'He's got a temper, bit of a knee-jerk jockey.'

Callum had seen for himself the mercurial change of mood in Richard when things didn't go his way, the cruelty beneath a veneer of civility. 'He was angry and struggling to control his temper when we left there this afternoon.'

'He's just a bully. We had kids like him in the army. They make efficient killers. With no thought for the victim, but when they are on the receiving end, it can be a different story. I would never trust them.' He squared his shoulders and drifted off to some place in his past.

'The army doesn't have the monopoly on bullies, Bird.'

'Probably not.'

Callum studied Bird. He was still muscled and carried his body with an authority that stemmed from confidence in his abilities. Perhaps there was a little extra flesh around his ribs and jaw since his army days, but he assessed him to be a man you could rely on in a tight corner, a team player.

'Is there anyone about?' Callum looked out into the darkness.

'After you two finished in the kitchen…' Bird paused and Callum knew he had watched the Daisy episode. 'And the lights went out, I expected anyone interested to appear. No one did. I was over in the trees on the other side of the garden and all I saw was a badger, a fox and two deer.'

'Deer?' Callum would like to have seen the deer, painted them perhaps.

'Roe and calf. They leave the baby hidden in the day and go back at dusk, suckle it and then they go for a wander. Cute as you like. Real Walt Disney.' He grinned. 'Tastes all right too, when it gets a bit older.'

'That they do. You can't beat a good venison stew.' Callum wondered if Forest venison tasted the same as the Highland beasts he was familiar with.

'I wouldn't say that in front of Daisy if I were you. I'm going to walk back through the fir trees and then sign off.' Bird eased himself out of the chair and pulled on his gloves.

'Fair enough.' Callum slid open the door.

Bird paused on the threshold and turned back. 'Is Deedee really all right, guv? She loved that daft mutt.'

'She's in better shape than my shirt front.' He pointed to the crumpled garment on top of the chest of drawers. 'But she's coping, I think.'

Bird grunted a soft laugh. 'That's our Deedee. I was thinking about that warrant in the morning...' He hesitated. 'I'm not telling you how to do your job...'

'But you're about to.' Callum kept the smile out of his voice. He liked the fact that they looked out for each other but found it disappointing that Bird thought he wouldn't be doing the same. His predecessor had been a poor example of a senior officer, and it was going to take his team time to adjust.

'She's had a bit of a tough week.'

'Daisy will be going nowhere on her own.' He smiled at Bird.

'That's good. I was just saying, that's all. No offence meant.'

'Nor taken,' Callum replied. The support they gave each other was something to be nurtured, not trampled underfoot. And he liked the ex-soldier, which was why, with a straight face, he added, 'Are you getting soft, Bird?'

'Bollocks to that.' And with a flash of white teeth, Bird melted into the darkness.

Callum lingered in the open doorway, arms folded, and looked out at the stealthy figure melding with the shadows. A gunmetal cloud shot a splatter of raindrops across the decking that puffed dust up into the air. He closed the door against the unexpected chill.

Chapter Twenty-Eight

The atmosphere in the office was subdued. Legs squeezed Daisy's shoulder as she passed by and received an easy smile in response. Bird was in mother-hen mode, more watchful than usual, casting covert glances at Daisy when he thought no one was looking. Only Cookie's world seemed untouched by the death of Felix. Perhaps he had never suffered a problem that contracted your insides with such force and pain that you wanted to curl up and hide.

When Daisy's phone buzzed, she checked the caller and then listened in silence. The soft curve of her lips flattened to a straight line and Callum knew that something else was wrong.

'On my way.' Daisy replaced the receiver and hurried into the fishbowl. 'Jimmy Eastwood has been attacked,' she said. 'That was Sue on the phone. He's in hospital with a head wound.'

'Circumstances?'

'When she got home from taking the tribe to school, Jimmy was lying unconscious on the path and the cottage was on fire.'

'Paramedics? Fire service?'

'On scene. She doesn't know what happened.'

Callum felt the screw in his gut tighten and a tingle race up his spine. He had a bad feeling about this.

'Get along to the hospital, Daisy,' he said. 'Take a uniform with you and post them outside his door.'

There was a connection between Mary-Ellen and Jimmy, and he had to consider that Jimmy was a possible second victim. 'Have a word with Sue, find out what he was doing this morning and keep me informed of his condition. Go,' he added.

Daisy snatched up her jacket, gestured to a PC and they hurried out into the corridor.

Callum went into the outer office, shrugging into his jacket as he walked. 'Cookie. Find out where Edward Devereux-Strauss is and let me know the second you locate him. Same for Richard, but don't alert either of them. We don't want a disappearing act before we execute that warrant.'

'Yes, sireee.' Cookie's eyes were filled with excitement.

'Legs, check on the warrant and hurry it up. Bird, with me. Let's go and have a word with the fire officer.'

* * *

241

Bird's unmarked Barbarian pulled up at the Eastwoods' cottage where the grass in front of the house was littered with debris and fire vehicles. Thin tendrils of grey smoke seeped from beneath the eaves and a ground-floor window was open, scorched black, the frame warped. A steady flow of water was being directed through the opening by a fireman whilst another doused the roof and the closest buildings. The site was a mess. Water dripped and pooled on the path in front of the door. Ash motes hovered in the air, before floating down to settle like black confetti. The acrid smell was rough on the throat.

A burly man who was directing operations peeled away from the action, stepped over the bloated water hoses and went to Bird's open window.

'Simmonds. Green watch. And you are?'

After the introductions, the three men stood together by the wing of the truck.

Simmonds removed his white helmet to run his fingers through his hair. 'CID presence? The damage isn't as bad as it looks. You're here for another reason, aren't you?'

'Which is?' asked Bird.

'That it was started deliberately. Early days, but I'd bet my pension on it,' Simmonds said.

'Shit. That's attempted murder then, guv. No accident.'

Simmonds' focus switched from Bird to Callum. 'We found no casualties; the house was empty. What do you know that I don't?'

'At present, nothing for certain,' Callum said.

'An ambo left as we arrived, and I haven't had an update. Our priority was to search for victims and extinguish the fire. Thankfully none.'

Callum looked at the trampled grass. Footprints from any crime had been puddled in the mud, obliterated by the corrugated soles of fire boots. Any vehicle tracks would probably have suffered the same fate. He scanned the debris strewn between the fat hoses; a ride-on tractor, a pink bicycle, an upturned wheelbarrow, a football. Not much left of the original crime scene, if a crime had been committed.

'It's pretty much out now. It hadn't managed to get a hold. Stone floors. The worst damage is in the kitchen, just inside this window and it's consistent with an accelerant being used. We're just damping down,' Simmonds said, putting his helmet back on his head.

'Can we take a look around?' asked Callum.

'As long as you stay outside and don't get in the way of my men.'

Close to the front wall of the building, where the grass was less trampled, there was a strong smell of smoke and burned fabric. A blackened curtain that might once have been blue gingham flapped from the open window.

'Bleedin' stinks. Gets in your throat.' Bird wrinkled his nose and coughed.

A shrub, speckled with ash, was moated by run-off water. Callum nudged the leaves aside with his foot to reveal a bald tennis ball and an abandoned toy truck. And a glimpse of something else. He bent down and parted the leaves. A green plastic petrol can lay on its side, the unscrewed cap at the end of the umbilical chain. He motioned to Bird and then caught a flash of light from the other side of the bush. Moving closer, he saw it was a hand axe.

'Nasty weapon,' Bird said.

The cutting edge was sharp, cleanly reflecting the light. The poll was dark and wet. Callum dabbed a gloved finger at the stain and examined the red mark it left behind. Blood. Why had the attacker discarded it where it could so easily be found? Perhaps they assumed it would be destroyed by the fire. Or they panicked.

'Here you go.' Bird held open an evidence bag and Callum dropped the axe inside it. 'And I'll take that petrol can for Forensics. We might get lucky with some prints.'

Simmonds joined them and ran an eye over the petrol can. He pulled off his gloves.

'The damage is at this end of the cottage,' he said. 'It's minimal and, as I said, no casualties.' He glanced down at the crimson smear along the inside of the bag containing the axe. 'Well, not from the fire, anyway.'

Bird stowed the evidence in his vehicle and walked back to Callum.

'Let's take a look in the outbuildings, Bird. Check nobody stayed around to take in the floor show.'

The galvanised roof corrugations channelled water into gutters unable to cope with the volume. Drips overran, slapped onto the soil at the base of the timber walls, and the smells of wet earth and damp wood permeated the pervading stench of smoke.

Callum paused in the open doorway of the woodshed. Chopped logs, grained ends outwards covered the far wall in a chest-high mosaic. Light winked from the shiny-tipped teeth of a circular saw set in the bench beneath the window. In the centre of the earth floor, a bill-hook was sunk into the scarred edge of a block next to a heap of lighting wood. The sweet scent of sawdust was a relief after the acrid smoke.

'No guard on that blade' – Bird nodded at the saw – 'and the buttons for the motor are only knee-high. Nice kiddy-friendly place this is, guv.'

A growled warning from beneath the back of the saw bench had Bird squatting in the sawdust to peer beneath it. He murmured nonsense in a sing-song voice and extended the back of his hand. The growl smoothed to a whine and Jimmy's black-and-white collie bitch limped over to Bird. He fondled her ears but when he ran his hand down her body, she flinched and pulled back.

'It's her shoulder, I think. I bet she ran out to protect Jimmy and got kicked.' The dog crept back to Bird, her distended belly difficult to miss. 'She's pretty close to having those pups. Hope she's okay.' Bird placed his hand gently on her head.

'Give the vet a call. Get him to come. She'll be happier staying here for now,' Callum said.

'There you go, girlie. You cuddle down and we'll get Corgi to come and give you the once-over.' Bird rose to his feet.

'Bedside manner courtesy of the army or the police, Bird?' Callum swiftly moved outside to hide his smile.

The workshop next door was well lit by a large window, protected on the inside by a sheet of rusted weldmesh. Shelves covered one wall and were littered with tools, rolls of wire, tubs of nails, and a chainsaw next to a row of fuel cans. A litter of kittens, well-grown and inquisitive, had climbed onto the shelves and peered down at the men. Little ginger faces with tip-tilted noses and Christmas tree tails peeked out between cans of paint and dusty boxes. The mother cat, a marmalade ribbon, threaded herself around their legs and purred.

'Looks like Jimmy was sharpening tools.' Callum pointed to the whetstone clamped into a vice with a jumble of hand tools behind it.

Bird went to the bench. 'Perhaps he was just starting on the axe when' – he swung round to face the door – 'he heard the dog bark, and with the axe still in his hand went to see what the commotion was.' Bird went outside.

Callum ran his hand along the spine of the cat and up her tail before following Bird, who was walking towards the cottage.

'He clocks the intruder about here, shouts at him and then runs with the axe still in his hand.' Bird loped forward. 'About here, he raises the axe and swings it at the intruder...' Bird raised his hand above his head and brought it down on an imaginary foe before looking back at Callum.

Callum caught up with him. 'But the assailant takes the weapon from Jimmy, hits him with it, then tosses it away as he runs back to the window and leaves Jimmy unconscious on the path.' He bent down to examine a dark patch on the stone path.

'That's it, guv. Someone was throwing petrol in the house, Jimmy didn't hear them, but the dog did. He comes out and shouts at the chap, who comes over and belts Jimmy with the axe. Then tosses it away and goes back to setting the fire.'

Callum stepped over the fire hoses. 'That fits. Then he finished pouring petrol through the window, threw the empty can behind him, and dropped a match.'

'I reckon that's spot on for the where and how. And we already know the when – just before 0900 hours. We just need the who and why.'

Simmonds joined them, having silently watched their reconstruction. 'It's safe for your team to move in now. I'm afraid my boys have probably trampled over any evidence. Sorry.'

'It can't be helped. They did a good job.' Callum looked down into the good-natured face. You couldn't levy criticism at someone for doing an efficient job, even if they had destroyed his crime scene in the process. 'Can you forward me the fire investigation report as soon as, please?'

Simmons nodded. 'Will do. Dave Meadows will be the FIO for this one. He's a good bloke.'

Callum looked around the scene once more, then they walked back to their vehicle.

'Drop me at the hospital, Bird, and get those to Forensics. Let's hope we get some prints from them. And get SOCO out here.'

'Okay, guv. No chance Jimmy fired it himself to conceal evidence that he killed Mary-Ellen?'

'The scenario we walked through seems a tighter fit. And I don't think he'd set fire to the house they built themselves and deliberately make them all homeless, do you?'

Bird started the engine. 'Me neither. And he's not the sort to risk putting his animals in danger either. He's soft on them.'

Callum rotated his earring.

'I agree,' he said as Bird pulled out onto the road. 'And he didn't hit himself over the back of the head with that wood axe, either.'

Chapter Twenty-Nine

Callum stepped down onto the hospital forecourt and heard Bird pull away behind him. The automatic doors swished open to reveal Bryony Osbourne walking towards him. Her hair had escaped from its tie and a swathe hung down onto one shoulder. Tendrils rested on her forehead and through them, he saw lines of tension creasing her brow. Dark smudges hollowed her eyes, making them appear unnaturally large in her pale face.

'Good morning, Bryony.' His eyes asked her a question.

'My mother died, Callum.' Her shoulders sagged. She looked exhausted.

Callum nodded towards the café just inside the foyer. 'Can I get you a coffee?'

'Yes, please.'

When they were seated, she stirred the froth around her cup, disintegrating the leaf design.

'I was going to call you. I was getting things straight in my mind first.'

'I'm sorry for your loss,' he said.

She looked up and gave him a tight smile. 'Thank you.'

'How did you know that she was going to die?'

'Meningococcal sepsis. There was nothing more they could do for her.' She took a sip of coffee. 'She had Alport syndrome, and her kidneys failed some years ago and, as you know, it also affected her hearing.'

Callum nodded, remembering their meeting at the gate.

'She came here for regular dialysis. The fistula that connects her to the machine got infected. She thought she had flu. They pumped her full of antibiotics, but it was too late. Her body was being attacked on so many different levels.' She looked away and blinked. 'I think she gave up. She just couldn't fight anymore.' Her voice was reed thin.

He reached across the table to place his hand over hers for a moment. He felt it tremble like a butterfly beneath his palm.

'She's not my birth mother, you know.' Bryony's hazel eyes met his. 'When her kidneys were failing, I tried to donate one of mine, but I wasn't compatible. That's when I found out.'

'That must have been a shock. Did you ask her about it?'

'Not then. I thought that I was the result of Edward having an affair.'

'But you did ask her about it later?'

'She mentioned it to me. I've always thought of her as my mother. She brought me up, encouraged me, mopped up the teenage tears, and put up with the tantrums. She was a mother to me.'

Callum nodded in agreement. He had seen his fair share of mothers who had done nothing for their offspring except exploit and abuse them. There was a lot more to being a mother than giving birth.

'She gave up driving when her health deteriorated so I took her to her appointments.' There was an edge to her voice. 'No one else would find the time to do it. One day, she leaned across the car and put her hand on my arm. "You should know, you are not my daughter, Bryony." That's when I told her I already knew.'

'And she told you who your birth mother was?'

'She didn't need to.'

'Did your father tell you?'

'Edward wouldn't tell me the time if he was standing next to a clock. I'm a girl, and girls don't count.' There was no bitterness in her voice. She had long ago accepted her father's attitude.

'Is that why your brothers went to Eton and you to a local school?'

She smiled. 'Have you been checking up on me, Inspector?'

'In the line of duty,' he said levelly, but smiled back at her, bunching the laughter lines around his eyes.

'I know who gave birth to me because after a row with Edward when I still lived at home, I searched his office. I don't know what I was looking for, but I found our birth certificates; two for each of us. The second certificates show Penny and Edward as our parents, which is not true. Those were dated a couple of days after the first one showing our real mothers, and "father unknown".'

'Being the only girl, it was obvious who my mother is. Her name is, or was, Diane Smith. At the time I tried to trace her, a bit half-heartedly and mostly to annoy Edward, but do you know how many Diane Smiths there are? And I have no idea what I would have done if I had found her. Probably nothing.'

'Will you try again now your mother has died?' Callum knew that her birth mother didn't want to be found. Sometimes it seemed wrong to keep information from people if you felt they had a right to know. But it wasn't his place to tell her.

'I might. I don't know. She might not want to know me. I don't think she's ever tried to find out what happened to me, and there will be a good reason for that. I think it is important to make the best of the hand you've been dealt.'

'Indeed. I believe you're right.' It could have been Grace speaking.

'I recognised Mary-Ellen Goddard's name on one of the certificates, and now she's dead. When we came home to England so Mattie could go to Eton, Mrs G was our housekeeper.'

He noted that she regarded England as home. 'Did you miss Africa?'

'Not really. The boys were treated like lords. Mother was not.'

'Why did she put up with it?'

'Because she loved him. Simple as. Edward is a powerful man, charismatic when he tries, and my mother adored him.' She took a sip of coffee. 'She told me that soon after they got married, she miscarried a baby and they diagnosed Alport's. It's hereditary and Edward would never risk her giving him imperfect children. He thought her family had cheated him into marrying her.'

'Why not just divorce her?'

'She came with a very advantageous settlement, Callum. The Osbournes own streets in Dublin and acres of land on both sides of the border.'

He liked the way she pronounced his name, with a long first vowel as if she was savouring it in her mouth. He drank his remaining coffee, confident he had found the link between Edward and Ireland.

'Edward sees illness as weakness.' Her eyes glistened.

'Is he here with you?' His voice was gentle, his annoyance with Edward held in check.

She shook her head. 'Only the strong deserve his patronage. He'll drop you in a second if you don't measure up to his standards. I failed at the first hurdle by being a girl. I left him a voicemail, but he hasn't come.'

Edward's upbringing in South Africa had protected him from the peculiarly British affliction of championing the underdog.

'Did your mother know who your birth parents are?'

She shook her head. 'She assumed my father had affairs to punish her and we were the results. He brought home the babies, and she dutifully raised them just like a normal family.'

There was very little that was normal about her family.

'Did anyone else, apart from Edward, know about the birth certificates?'

'Not initially, but Richie was championing Edward, so I told him about it.'

'When was this?'

'About three months ago. But he didn't believe me.'

It was the first time since they had met that Callum had cause to disagree with her.

* * *

Callum took the stairs two at a time to level 4 in search of Daisy and Susan Eastwood. He followed the wall-mounted signs along a corridor that displayed paintings by a local art group. He snatched glances at them between checking his messages and dodging other walkers.

The two women stood in the corridor, their heads close together. Sue's arms were folded, and Daisy placed a hand on her friend's forearm. For a snatch of a second, Callum thought Jimmy was dead. The smiles on their faces when they turned to greet him assured him that he was wrong.

'Hello, sir.'

'Daisy. Mrs Eastwood. How's your husband?'

'Sue, please. He's just regained consciousness. They shooed us out so they could poke him and prod him.' Her cheeks were flushed, her eyes bright but an anxious frown crept across her brow. 'The doctor's been in there for ages. I hope everything's all right.'

On cue, the door opened.

'Mrs Eastwood?' The doctor came towards them, dangly elephant earrings swaying as her Dr Martens squeaked on the composite floor.

'How is he, Doctor?'

'He's surprisingly unscathed.' She raised her eyebrows to show how surprised she was. 'Mild concussion but otherwise fine. I was a little concerned when he started asking about a panda...' She paused at Sue's splutter of laughter and grinned. 'I now understand that Panda is his dog who is having puppies. There are no problems with his vision, but he has a couple of stitches and a headache.'

Relief relaxed Sue's features.

'We're going to keep him in for observation but he's a very lucky man.'

'Thank you so much,' Sue said.

The doctor glanced down at a text, raised a hand in farewell and hurried away down the corridor.

'That's my Jimmy,' Sue said. 'Tough nut.'

Callum held open the room door for the two women to precede him, then stood at the foot of the hospital bed. 'How are you feeling, Mr Eastwood?'

'Pretty good, thanks; except for a headache from hell.' Jimmy winced when he tilted his head to make eye contact, so Callum sat on the bedside chair.

'Can you remember what happened to you?'

'Yes, I think so.' Jimmy nodded his head then stopped abruptly. 'Whoa. That's a bad idea. It feels like loose bits inside my head are banging against each other.' He grimaced.

Sue slipped her hand into his and sat on the opposite side of the bed.

'Take your time. Tell me what you remember.' Callum heard Daisy flip open her notebook.

'Okay. Sue took the kids to school, and I sat at the kitchen table and started on my list of phone calls. I got hold of Ben Martin and told him one of his mares is lame. Then a farmer to discuss buying winter fodder. Is that what you want to know?'

'Yes. Go on.'

'Then I went out to check on Panda; she's close to whelping, but she was fine. I made a coffee and took it to the table to call Richie.'

'Richard Devereux-Strauss, why?'

'Because he muddled up the time of my alibi. I was going to double-check with him before I called Daisy.'

'Sue's already told me–' Daisy began but Callum interrupted her.

'Let Jimmy tell it, Daisy.'

'On last night's local news, they did an update on an earlier piece about badgers and TB. I watched the original the other morning because we've got a sett in the top meadow.'

'The thing is,' Sue said, 'the initial report was after the eight o'clock news, so Jimmy was still at home then.'

'Richie saying I met him at quarter to eight, was wrong.'

Perhaps Bird had been right to leave that question mark over the agister. Callum glanced at Daisy. Jimmy was back on the list of suspects.

'And you got hold of Richard?'

'Yes. First, he said I was wrong until I explained about the badgers, and he went quiet for so long that I thought my mobile had dropped out. Then he suggested we meet straight away.'

'And did you?'

'To be honest, Richie has been a bit of a moody bastard for the last couple of months, and I was busy. So, I said no. He said he would sort it out.'

'Sort what out?' Callum asked.

'The alibi cock-up, I thought. I made a couple more calls, got bored and went out to the workshop to sharpen some tools.'

'Good. What happened next?'

'I had just started on my wood axe when I heard Panda yelp. I ran out of the workshop, and she was running back towards me from the house. A man was leaning in our kitchen window. I thought he was looking for me, so I shouted "Hello", and he turned round. It was Richie.'

Jimmy rubbed his hand over his face before gently touching the patch of shaved scalp and the stitched wound. 'He had something in his hand and looked surprised to see me. At first, I didn't work it out, then I realised he was tipping petrol into our kitchen, so I started running.'

'Why?' Sue raised a hand to her mouth. 'Why would he do that?'

'I didn't get a chance to ask. Richie charged at me...' Jimmy faltered, searching for more images, eyes flicking from side to side before they widened in panic. 'I can't remember anything after that. The nurse said I was hit on the head.'

'You were,' Callum said. 'And it's quite usual not to have total recall at this stage. It's nothing to worry about.'

Jimmy's breathing returned to normal.

Memory didn't always surge back as a complete picture. It could take hours, days, weeks even, and in some cases, victims never remembered. The mind was good at self-protection.

'That's very helpful, Mr Eastwood. You are certain it was Richard Devereux-Strauss?'

'For God's sake, call me Jimmy. I keep looking round for my old man.' He tried another experimental turn of his head, before carefully looking back at Callum. 'I'm positive it was Richie, the bastard. How's Panda? How's the house?'

Jimmy's order of priority was warming, in a skewed and greedy world.

'Panda seemed fine, but Bird asked the vet to check her out as a precaution.'

'Thanks for that. And the house?'

The fire service got it under control very quickly, but the kitchen suffered most. The rest of the house is smoke and water damage.'

'Worse things happen at sea.' Jimmy squeezed his wife's fingers. 'We'll manage, girl.'

'No question about it.' Sue smiled down at him.

Callum swallowed the lump in his throat and looked towards the door.

'If you remember anything else, either of you, please let us know. And I'm sorry about your house.'

Sue shook her head, a smile on her face. 'It doesn't matter. The kids are okay and so is Jimmy. We built it once, so we can do it again. But this time' – she winked at Callum and Daisy – 'this time I want an island in the kitchen, a window seat would be nice, and a proper larder.'

Daisy laughed aloud as she closed her notebook.

Jimmy groaned, but his smile was broad. 'See what I have to put up with, Inspector?'

Sue smiled at her husband. 'You'll survive.'

Callum's heart was a stone in his chest. Daisy looked at him, her head tilted so obliquely that her frown ran uphill.

Once outside the door, Callum saw that the constable had strayed along the corridor and was laughing with a nurse.

'Constable,' Callum shouted, rather louder than he had intended.

The officer spun round to face him, but Callum turned to Daisy. 'Daisy, get him back on this door immediately. Tell him, no visitors for Jimmy without clearance from me. Get a car to Devereux Manor and stop anyone from leaving. Well, go on, make it snappy. I need a quick word with Sue.'

Callum slipped back into the room, returning as she finished admonishing the constable who was back in position.

He turned to Daisy as they set off along the corridor. 'Daisy, Penny Devereux-Strauss died this morning.'

'She didn't look very old. Was it an accident?'

'She was ill. Long term. She died in this hospital.'

Daisy jogged a stride or two to keep up. 'At least we know where to find Edward then. I don't get why Richard attacked Jimmy if it put Jimmy back in the frame with no alibi.'

'Because Jimmy was Richard's alibi. If Jimmy got to speak to us, then Richard would become a suspect. There's his motive for attacking Jimmy.' Callum's phone buzzed and he read the incoming message. 'Edward's not here. He's at the manor and so is Richard.'

'Odd man, don't you think?'

He didn't know who she was referring to, but the comment applied equally well to both Devereux-Strausses.

Callum heard his name called and looked up to see Timothy Pitman and Sir Michael approaching. Sir Michael looked slighter than Callum remembered, his face tinged grey, heavy eyelids hooding bloodshot eyes.

'Officers.' Timothy was less jovial than he had been at their first meeting.

Sir Michael extended a hand, and Callum felt the chill of the fingers in his grasp.

'Good morning, gentlemen,' he said. 'How are you this morning, Sir Michael?' The hand trembled against his palm and fell away. 'Thank you for coming to identify Mary-Ellen. I know this isn't easy for you.'

'Would you come with us please, Inspector?' Sir Michael's eyes were fixed on Callum's face. Beside him, Timothy rocked on the balls of his feet, hurrying life along.

'Of course.' Callum felt a muscle tug at his jaw and Daisy glanced at her watch. 'Ten minutes will make no great difference to our day, Sergeant Donaldson,' he said.

They walked quietly, Sir Michael with bowed head, hands clasped in front of him and Timothy bouncing along at his side. The temperature dropped and the corridor lighting seemed to dim as they neared their destination, but it was not clear if this was by design or accident.

Callum opened the door, and the two men preceded the officers into the room. Yellow curtains. He was sucked back into the past. Cool air and the antiseptic smell prised open the lid securing his memories. He forced himself back to the now. The body lay on the other side of a glass divide. He watched the reactions of both men and heard Sir Michael's sharp intake of breath. Mary-Ellen looked beautiful, a classic marble sculpture, flawless. The sheet was pulled up to her chin. She could have been sleeping.

Often, like Timothy, relatives snatched one glance and then looked away. Just sufficient to satisfy themselves that it was the right body, that no mistake had been made and they could climb out of limbo and onto the grief train. He started to turn away but paused when his companion remained immobile.

Sir Michael's initial glance was tentative, then he moved closer to the glass and placed his palms against it. He studied his wife's face, her fine arched brows, high cheekbones, slender nose above well-defined lips. He scrutinised every inch of visible flesh, her pale arms on top of the covering, strong hands devoid of jewellery and then the outline of her slender body shaping the sheet. His face was intense as he captured a memory that would last for eternity.

Timothy glanced at Callum, a question in his eyes.

'He's committing her to memory.' Callum's voice was low and burred as Grace breached the closed doors to his past. He thought those barriers didn't open as readily as they once had; that he could think about her without suffering that breath-robbing stab of pain. He slipped his hands into his pockets, dropped his chin to his chest and stood motionless.

Daisy fidgeted beside him, and he hoped she would stay silent and allow Sir Michael those last precious moments with his wife. Then Sir Michael's eyes slid closed.

Timothy glanced at Callum then moved forward to rest a hand on Sir Michael's shoulder.

They gave the men a few moments before Callum asked, 'Are you all right, Sir Michael?'

Sir Michael cleared his throat. 'Yes, thank you, Inspector. Timothy's staff have established that Matthew Devereux-Strauss is Mary-Ellen's son. It was the birth date. I intend to meet him.' The tread of his loafers as he joined them at the door was more positive than when he had arrived.

'Michael has already made an initial approach,' Timothy said. 'And we are meeting him next week. We are very much looking forward to it.'

'I have already met him, and he seems to be a very nice young man,' Callum said. Men with wealth and power created their own timetables.

'Now, I hope I didn't inconvenience you, Inspector.' A faint spark glimmered in the misty depths of Sir Michael's eyes.

'Not at all. I was already here, because Mr Eastwood was admitted this morning following an assault.' Callum watched for a reaction, and it was not the one he had expected.

'Is he all right? I hope he isn't badly injured.' Sir Michael's concern seemed genuine.

Timothy stood still, eyes sharp, any trace of joviality eradicated. 'Michael has been with me all morning, Inspector.' Perhaps lawyers, like detectives were never off duty.

'I would like to visit Mr Eastwood,' Sir Michael said.

Timothy spun around to look at him open-mouthed.

'That would be in order,' Callum said carefully. 'If you are sure?'

Sir Michael nodded. 'I am. There is a matter that needs resolving. It's been on my mind, and now is as good a time as any.'

There was a new calmness, a sense of purpose about him as he walked away. Timothy, less enthusiastic, his gait shackled by uncertainty, trailed in his wake.

'Daisy, get hold of the constable. Make sure he lets them in to see Jimmy.'

'Shouldn't we have gone with them?' There was censure in her tone.

'Why, Sergeant?'

'Because Jimmy had an affair with his wife.' She trotted after Callum as he strode away from her.

'Sanctioned by Sir Michael. No secret about it between the people who needed to know.'

'But Jimmy has just been attacked…'

'Not by Sir Michael. They're big boys and they'll play nicely. Trust me.'

'Okay then.' She laughed. 'And if they don't, then Sue can referee.'

He looked down into her animated face. 'And how are you this morning, Daisy?'

'Fine, thanks, Callum. All under control.'

Her jaw was a little tighter than usual, he thought, as the automatic doors swished open, and they blinked into the colour-sapping sunlight.

'Good. Office, search warrant, then Devereux Manor.'

Chapter Thirty

Callum and Daisy were barely through the office door before Bird summoned them.

'Guv, you need to see this.'

They stood behind his chair and looked over his shoulder at his monitor.

'I couldn't remember where I had seen Richard's tat, the one he hides under his watch, so I emailed it to a mate. I can't tell you what he does or I'll 'ave to kill you.' His guffaw rippled through him, and Daisy rolled her eyes.

'And?' Callum glanced at the clock on the wall.

'And it's a sub-sect of the LRA.'

'Who?' Daisy frowned.

'Lord's Resistance Army. Joseph Kony. Africa?'

Daisy nodded and Legs got up from her desk and joined them.

'They used children in the war,' Legs said.

'That's right.' Bird gave her a quizzical look. 'In hostilities, abduction, child sex-slavery.'

'I thought they were a religious guerrilla group,' Daisy said.

Legs wrinkled her nostrils. 'No God condones the things they did. They're nothing better than terrorists hiding behind the cloth.'

'We came up against them in…' Bird paused and a vein did acrobatics along his neck. 'In somewhere. Not a nice bunch of Boy Scouts. That's why I remembered that tat.'

Physical removal from the action didn't stop the mind from storing images, smells, and sounds; triggers that lifted the lid on the past. Callum knew all about that. He dropped his hand briefly onto Bird's shoulder. 'Good work.'

Cookie swivelled around in his chair to face them. 'And, guv, remember that Chet chappie Richard was friendly with at Eton? I found him. He was killed in a hostage ransom switch that went wrong. There's a clip online somewhere, I'm trying to find it. The timeline fits with Tricky Dickie coming back here. Do you think they were there together?'

'You might have just filled in the missing three years,' Callum said. On its own, a clip of Chet wasn't going to be much help with this case, but it might lead them somewhere relevant. 'And see if there's any connection to Edward.'

'You fancy him for it, guv?'

'I'd like to be sure that he's not involved.'

'Yes, siree.'

'Search warrant?' Callum looked at Legs.

'Ready, guv.' She flapped a sheet of paper in the air.

'When we get there, Bird and I will go to the house to ask Edward about those three girls and Rose Brown's broken arm. Daisy, you and Legs execute that warrant and take Rose into custody. Kent and Cooper will also be attending.'

The two uniformed officers sauntered towards the door.

'And given this morning's developments,' Callum continued, 'I will arrest Richard for the attempted murder of Jimmy Eastwood, but we'll save that little surprise until we have Rose secured. Understood?'

The team murmured assent.

'Cookie.' Callum waited until the detective lifted his head to look at him. 'You stay here and chase up Forensics on the axe and petrol can. Follow up on a record for Rose. And find that video footage.'

'Hunky-doodley.'

Legs held the door open, waiting for Callum to catch up with them. 'What about Richard and Felix?'

'Let's get him back to the station. We can ask him about that once we have him in custody. Come on, people, let's go.'

* * *

Their convoy of vehicles created an unnatural bow wave in a sea of normality. Soon Callum would see his team tested in action, although he didn't anticipate more than Edward retreating behind his solicitor and Rose being reluctant to leave her boyfriend. He just hoped that Daisy would keep things in perspective when confronted by Richard.

Two Range Rovers were parked at the side of the manor, and the team positioned their vehicles to prohibit an escape. Callum signalled the uniforms to remain with the vehicles, and the team prepared to split up. Then, above the noise of rooks and a distant tractor, raised voices were carried to them on the breeze.

'Plan B,' Callum said.

The detectives followed the sound to the stable yard, halted behind the encircling wall, and Callum peered around the stone pillar. He recognised the two men standing close together by the gate to the manège.

Both were red-faced and oblivious to the arrival of the officers. Edward stabbed a finger at Richard's chest and his son pushed forward and swung a fist at his father's head. Anger had robbed him of control and Edward effortlessly blocked him.

'You wouldn't be doing this if it was Matthew,' Richard was screaming, eyes wild.

'I wouldn't have to do it if this was Matthew. He has morals.'

'Who the fuck are you to talk about morals?' Richard rushed Edward again, a windmill of fists and expletives.

Callum sensed Daisy move beside him and held up a stilling finger. 'Not yet.'

Edward slapped Richard hard across the face. The sound reverberated around the yard like the crack of a rifle. 'You're unstable. Control yourself.'

Heads appeared over box doors and a horse gave a nervous whinny.

'Fuck off, you pervert. Rose and I are leaving.'

'You won't last five minutes. What are you going to use for money?'

'Bit of good luck, your whore dying.' Richard sneered at Edward. 'She changed her will for me, so I don't need your filthy money.'

'Say that again.' Edward's voice was tight with menace, and he stepped towards Richard, who retreated into the stable yard.

'Now,' Callum said, and the team surged through the entrance, feet slapping on the flagstones.

Edward halted, turning to watch their approach, but Richard withdrew to the tack-room doorway.

'Fuck off,' Richard shouted waving an arm at them. 'Fuck off and leave me alone.' He spotted Daisy. 'Found any dead dogs, Miss High-and-Mighty?' His crackling laugh raised the hairs on Callum's neck and tightened the screw in his gut. Jigsaw pieces were snapping neatly into place. Richard had the motive, the opportunity, and the ability to kill Mary-Ellen Mitchell.

Callum signalled to the team to halt. Daisy appeared not to see and ran further into the yard with Legs at her shoulder.

'Boy,' Edward shouted, his flare of anger replaced by tight control.

'Stop calling me boy, you bastard.'

'Richard' – Edward lowered his voice – 'I'm trying to help you. A bad decision will ruin your whole life.'

Callum stood next to Edward and his phone pinged with an incoming text from Cookie headed "Eureka". Cookie's timing was impeccable. He viewed the short video as Richard continued cursing Daisy.

'This might interest you,' he said to Edward and pressed play.

Edward glanced at him, then focused on the screen. The footage showed two young men in combat fatigues on a scrub-dotted hillside, sharp shadows highlighting a drop behind them. One had an automatic weapon, and the other's arm encircled the neck of a man wearing a charity T-shirt. The camera focused first on the face of the hostage, rigid with fear, then individually on the two hostage takers.

Edward grasped Callum's arm to tilt the screen towards him when he saw the man restraining the hostage. 'That man holding the hostage is Richard's friend Chet.' He breathed the next words so quietly that Callum barely caught them. 'And that's Richard.' He looked across the yard at his son, who was baiting Daisy.

On the screen, a holdall, thrown from out of shot, landed at Richard's feet. Unzipped, it revealed cash. Richard closed the bag, shouldered it, his gun trained on someone out of shot, and he and Chet turned to leave.

Edward relaxed his grip on Callum's arm only for it to snap closed again with the strength of eagle talons. With one sharp wrench, Chet snapped the neck of the hostage. A last feeble jerk and the body was motionless in his grasp. Chet fell as bullets punched holes in his jacket from a gunman they couldn't see. Richard grabbed the holdall and disappeared over the lip of the drop into the ravine.

Edward released Callum's arm. 'I had no idea that's what he was doing.' His voice was dulled by disgust and disappointment. Edward stared at Richard, the distance between father and son far exceeding the length of the stable yard.

Edward cleared his throat.

'Leave it.' Callum's voice was firm. 'This is my call.'

Richard's red face roiled with emotion as Daisy stepped towards him. She stopped a few feet from him with Legs a stride to her left. Callum noted her repositioning and hoped she was just narrowing possible escape routes.

'Richard Devereux-Strauss,' she said.

Callum realised she was going to ignore his orders and issue a caution. 'I am arresting you on suspicion—'

A banshee scream and a flash of colour exploded from the tack room as Rose charged at Daisy. Light glinted on a knife blade that arced down towards her target.

Legs lunged, shoulder down, tackling Rose hard from the side and they both slammed onto the paving stones. The knife jolted free, skittering safely out of the girl's reach.

'Let her go,' Richard shouted.

Rose hit Legs in the face with her plastered arm then howled with frustration as Legs cuffed her behind her body and hauled her to her feet.

A movement to his right caught Callum's attention. Richard had picked up the knife and was running at Daisy, eyes wild, his arm plunging towards her head.

'Bird,' Callum shouted and raced forward, heart pounding.

'Shit, fuck and bugger it.' Bird launched himself into a sprint behind Callum, sucking in noisy lungsful of air.

Both detectives were still strides short of Richard when his scream gutted the air, and he launched himself at Daisy. She raised both her hands above her head, stepped forward under the arc of his attack and grasped his descending arm at the wrist. The momentum threw her backwards onto the stones, pulling Richard down with her. To stop Richard's body crashing onto hers, she brought her knees up to her chest, the soles of her boots braced against his descending torso, and then she straightened her legs. Richard was propelled through the air. His right arm was anchored by Daisy's grip on his wrist just above the knife. He landed on his back with a thud and lay silent.

A horse coughed in one of the boxes. Daisy rotated on her hip without releasing control of his arm and jabbed her boot hard against the side of Richard's neck. It all happened in a flicker of time as Callum closed the gap between them.

'…of the attempted murder of Jimmy Eastwood. You do not have to say…'

Richard cursed over her words and struggled.

She twisted his wrist with shoulder-dislocating pressure. '…something you later rely on in court.'

He stopped struggling and screamed.

She raised her voice. 'Anything you do say may be given in evidence.'

Callum and Bird halted on either side of her. Daisy huffed a breath upwards to float away tendrils of hair that had escaped from her ponytail.

'Are you okay?' Callum said.

She was breathing hard, and Richard's unsecured left hand clawed towards her face.

'Never felt better.' She ground the heel of her boot harder against the cords of Richard's neck.

Callum stood on Richard's flailing left arm, knocked the knife from his right hand and tossed it out of reach.

'Bag that,' he called to the constables who were only now joining them. 'Let's turn him over, Bird.'

Daisy released her grip on Richard. Callum grasped a fistful of clothing and, together with Bird, manhandled the blasphemer onto his front and cuffed him behind. Richard kicked out and contacted PC Kent's shin. Both men swore loudly.

'Shut the fuck up, fella,' Bird growled and sat on the thrashing body. 'Get some restraints, Cooper,' he said. 'Before I draw me bleedin' pension,' he added when the constable was slow to respond.

Daisy expelled a noisy breath and rolled over. 'Just like buses,' she said, looking up at Callum. 'Never there when you want one, then four come along at once.'

He bent down, his face close to hers, and said quietly, 'I told you to wait.'

'I did, until I saw Rose with the knife,' she replied softly, not ducking away from his intense eyes.

'You interfering, fucking bitch. Couldn't keep…' Richard hissed.

Bird adjusted his weight and the abuse ended with a scream.

'Shut up, you imbecile.' Edward joined them, a muscle tugging at his cheek as he looked down at Richard. 'You boys had everything. Everything…'

Daisy turned onto her knees and Callum offered his hand to assist her back to her feet. She stood beside him, and flexed her right shoulder, her exploring fingers discovering a rip in her shirt.

'I'm getting new bruises quicker than most girls get new shoes.'

'Stand still.' Callum put his hand on her shoulder and examined her wound.

'You'll live.' Her skin was warm beneath the ball of his thumb, and he withdrew his hand. 'It's just a graze, but get it looked at when we get back.'

Kent and Cooper worked up a sweat strapping Richard's legs, then Bird removed his weight, and the three officers hauled him to his feet. Daisy watched, her face impassive.

'Fuck you,' Richard said and spat at her.

'Do that again, fella, and you'll find yourself in a hood,' Bird growled, tightening his grip on the cuffs.

'No chance. I've got standards.' Daisy turned her back on him.

'You tell him, Deedee hun.' Legs held the arm of a defiant Rose.

Inky rivers ran down the girl's cheeks and her kohled eyes were smudged charcoal like a carelessly made-up Pierrot. 'Why did you do it, Richie?' she shouted with increasing distress, as he was carried towards the police vehicle.

Edward quietly watched the pantomime, his face deadpan. His apparent calm acceptance of the proceedings was a surprise to Callum. He had expected protests, threats of lawyers, and mention of senior officers. Perhaps Edward was reviewing past happenings, seeing them in a new light after today's revelations.

'I assume you have evidence to support your actions, Inspector, and this is not just a fishing trip?'

'Your assumption is correct, sir. And we have a search warrant.' Callum took the paper from his jacket pocket. He offered it to Edward who waved it away.

'You won't need your warrant. Search where you like. I've done him no favours. It's time he took responsibility.' He looked across to the police van. 'I thought he was sowing wild oats in those years after he left Eton. I had no idea. But I won't condone this.'

Callum thought that Edward would have understood wild oats and would have defended and championed his son. That video had shaken him to the core.

Edward and Callum stood side by side and watched the police van turn from the gravel driveway out onto the lane.

'You were never curious about where he was?'

Edward shook his head. 'He is intelligent. He is strong and the strong survive. I knew he would come home when hardship overcame his hedonism, so I stopped giving him money. He came home.'

Callum recalled Bryony's comment that Edward would drop you in a second if you didn't come up to his standards. At the time, he had thought she was justifying some incident in her past. Perhaps he had been incorrect.

Daisy and Legs assisted Rose into the back of a police car. She had stopped calling for Richard and was quiet.

Edward watched; cold eyes flecked with steel. 'Everything was fine until that girl appeared on the scene.'

'Rose said you broke her phone,' Callum said.

'I don't deny that I broke her phone. She's a gold digger and a troublemaker. Richard can't see it, but I can. He's always been susceptible where women are concerned, but I never saw him as a killer. Now, if there's nothing else, Inspector, I need to phone my solicitor.' He walked towards the house and Callum fell into step beside him.

'I had thought to find you at the hospital, sir.'

'It wouldn't have stopped her dying.'

'I'm sorry for your loss.'

Edward made a non-committal noise in his throat. 'The loss was years ago.'

Bird caught up with them. He had barely broken into a sweat.

'Just one final question,' Callum said. 'What relationship did you have in common with Mary-Ellen Goddard, Diane Smith and Harriet King?'

Edward halted and looked across his land to the tree-dotted horizon. 'I think you already know, Inspector.'

'I'd like to hear it from you.'

'Then you'll be aware that my association with them was purely philanthropic. They all worked at the manor, all got pregnant, and to save them from embarrassing their parents, I arranged for them to have their babies in the safety of an Irish convent on my wife's land, and not to let it spoil their lives. They all had prospects of an excellent future. They were all exceptionally intelligent girls.'

Callum's heart hurried a beat. There was the key. The girls had been selected for their intelligence. It rankled that they would never be able to prove that Edward had raped them. DNA could confirm him as the father, but he would argue consensual sex, and there was no one alive who was prepared to dispute that. Callum had plaited the strands into a rope, but he knew it would never be strong enough to hang anyone.

* * *

Briggs, the silent employee that Callum and Daisy had encountered on their initial visit, directed them to Richard's bedroom. Floor-to-ceiling drapes still covered the three windows despite the hour, and the once-black fabric had faded to grey in places.

Callum pulled back the curtains and light burst into the room providing the dust motes a pathway to dance along. Scuffed floorboards were carpeted with discarded clothes and the bed was unmade. There was a head dent in the pillow, covers thrown back, a phone charger plugged into the wall and an empty glass on the bedside table.

The floor creaked as they walked. The *shhsplip-shhsplip* of a tap dripping in the bathroom syncopated with a loud ticking of a novelty wall clock.

Bird nodded towards it. 'Tasteful,' he muttered, watching the well-developed female nude swing her arms around to indicate the time. He flicked an eye to Callum and grinned. 'Could 'ave been worse, could 'ave been her legs.'

They were in a teenage time warp.

The bathroom was clammy, with wet towels tossed into the shower, uncapped toothpaste on the sink, high notes of a citrus deodorant clinging to the thick air. Callum pointed to the laundry basket and Bird lifted the lid and sniffed.

'Smoke, petrol, dirty socks and bleedin' horse shit.' He wrinkled his nose and bagged the items, one by one, for Forensics. A wide grin chased away his frown when he lifted out a pair of navy gloves. He raised them to his nose.

'Petrol. Got you, you little bastard.'

The wardrobe smelled of horses and mothballs. Pushed to the back was a holdall with a yellow emoji on the side.

This seemed to wink at Callum when he lifted it out into the light as if it knew something they didn't. It gave up its secret with a growl of protest from the zipper.

The supermarket bag inside was stuffed with bundles of cash, each held with a band bearing the logo of Mary-Ellen's bank.

'Look at this.' Callum held up some notes.

'Cash.'

'Twenty thousand, would you say?'

Bird peered inside the bag and nodded. 'But I don't get it. If that was the twenty grand she took out, what's Tricky Dickie doing with it?'

Callum dropped the cash back into the bag.

'Good question, Bird.' He slid the zipper closed. 'Think birth certificates.'

Bird rubbed his hand over his scalp. 'Sorry. You got me there, guv.'

'We know Bryony told Richard about the birth certificates, and I think he found them. Edward told him to end his relationship with Rose, but his lifestyle is financed by his father and Edward has withdrawn his financial support before, so Richard knew he would do it again. Then he thought of a way to get some easy money.'

'Keep going.'

'He recognised Mary-Ellen Goddard's name because her parents worked here, and he told her that he was her son.'

'Right. I get that. And he asked her for money, and she withdrew the cash for him,' Bird said.

Callum placed the bag next to the other items on the bed. 'She thought she'd found her son.'

'That was the trigger you were on about. I couldn't think what would make her ultra-happy.'

'Richard thought she'd changed her will in his favour — she may have told him she had — and that's what he was shouting about to Edward in the yard earlier.' He indicated for Bird to search a chest of drawers. Finding the clothes

Richard wore when he killed her would make their case against him watertight. 'Sooner or later, she was going to find out he was lying, so he had to get rid of her before she realised.'

Bird pulled open the drawers and examined the contents. 'Nothing else here…' He looked round to Callum. 'How would Mary-Ellen have found out Richard was lying? Did Edward have something to do with it?' Bird crossed to the bed and with a grunt dropped to his knees to look underneath it.

'They had lunch at The Royal Oak in April. Richard left in a hurry because it was his birthday.'

'I remember.' Bird sat back on his heels, a pair of underpants in one gloved hand and some coins in the other. 'So?'

'So, we found the birth record. Mary-Ellen had her son in January.'

'I remember. Not something she was going to get confused about, so she knew he wasn't her son. That he'd tried to cheat her. Bummer.'

'And that's why she didn't change her will,' Callum said. 'Matthew is her son, not Richard.'

Bird lumbered to his feet as Callum signalled to a constable to start removing the bagged items. 'As you said, Bird, it's all about love and money.'

'That's the last pair of trainers.' Bird dropped them into a bag. 'That's eight pairs. He's only got two feet,' he grumbled as he scribbled on the paper. 'I hope Martha can match at least one of them to the print on that stirrup. I was hoping to find a bag full of the running stuff he wore when he killed her.'

'Never give up hope, Bird.'

Callum would also be much happier if they could find a bag of clothes to prove without a doubt who murdered Mary-Ellen. The murderer was strong, a good rider and someone who knew the Forest. Richard met the criteria. And he had motive, expecting to gain an inheritance once Mary-Ellen was dead. Callum fiddled with his earring. His alibi with Jimmy was dead in the water and Rose would swear black was white if he asked her to so he also had opportunity.

Legs and Daisy came into the room and started to gather the bags of evidence. Callum motioned Legs to come and join him. Bird picked up an armful and followed Daisy down the stairs.

'Yes, guv?' Legs asked.

'Remember Reg and the uncollected bag of rubbish that he says is not his?'

She nodded.

'Go and see if he's still got it.' He told her about the refuse collectors throwing a bin liner back on the path as he and Daisy had driven past on the morning of the murder. 'It might be nothing, but at least we can eliminate it, and turn our attention elsewhere.'

'Okay, guv.' She turned her head at Bird's heavy tread on the stairs.

'I didn't have this much crap when I moved in with Helen,' Bird said, scooping up the last of bags to put in his vehicle.

'That doesn't surprise me.' Daisy sounded buoyant despite flexing her shoulder before following him onto the stairs. She caught Legs' eye. 'Have you ever seen him in anything other than what he's got on?'

Legs shook her head. 'Perhaps he hasn't got any other stuff.' There was a glint in her eye.

Callum suppressed a smile.

'Course I bleedin' have.' Bird sniffed loudly and walked to the opened back door of his vehicle. 'I just keep them for special occasions.'

Daisy laughed. 'They must be so old they'll look like fancy dress.'

'Let's organise a nineties theme party, Deedee hun. Then he can give them an airing.' Devilment danced in

Legs' eyes, but Daisy cut short their teasing to answer her phone.

Bird looked from one to the other, then turned to Callum. 'Help, guv.'

'You started it.' Callum turned back towards the house so they couldn't see his smile.

Chapter Thirty-One

When Bird had gone back to the station and Legs was off searching for bin liners, Daisy and Callum climbed the outside stairs to Rose's flat. Daisy pushed open the door and he followed her straight into a sitting room. It had a kitchen at one end and the two open doors confirmed the location of the bedroom and bathroom. It was surprisingly tidy. Callum glanced out of the window down into the yard. This was where Rose had been standing when he caught the movement of the plaster cast as she hid behind the curtain.

'That was Cookie on the phone.' Daisy interrupted his memory. 'Rose has got a juvenile record, and she's now wanted for skipping bail.'

Callum knew they were keen to keep juveniles out of court unless it was a serious offence. She would have probably received a caution for shoplifting or another minor misdemeanour.

'What was the juvenile offence?'

Daisy was on the same wavelength. 'She had a caution for theft and fraud, but it escalated, so they prosecuted.'

'And what was she on trial for when she violated bail?' He searched the top kitchen cupboards, leaving the lower ones for Daisy.

'She attacked and attempted to strangle a family member earlier this year. Her father unwisely posted her bail and now he'll be out of pocket because she skipped. Nothing here,' she said, moving to another area of the room.

Callum looked at the neatly folded stack of running clothes on the counter above the washing machine. They were identical to those they had just removed from Richard's bedroom, and he wondered if Rose did his washing for him. Or being as tall as Richard, she might borrow his clothes.

He recalled the garments strewn across Richard's floor and acknowledged that he was the untidy one. Rose was the tidy one, the organiser.

Callum stood by the bed and his suspicions grew. How had he missed it? Rose was no stranger to violence; she had broken the pigeon's neck with no display of emotion. Rose was strong, she had carried a bale of hay with one hand. She was strong enough to get Mary-Ellen back onto Pirate, and rode well enough to move the body to Hale Purlieu. She had given Richard a false alibi and in so doing had provided one for herself. He remembered her saying she wanted to retire early. She was the one with a motive. She was the one he had overlooked.

'Bag any running gear you find, Daisy.' He shared his theory with her, and he heard her opening and searching drawers as he looked in the bathroom. The towels hung neatly on the heated rail and the top was on the toothpaste. Very much Rose's domain.

Daisy found her birth certificate in her underwear drawer along with pink fluffy handcuffs and a riding crop.

'She's a dark horse. And how she can ride in that beggar's belief.' Daisy winced for effect as she held up a spaghetti-thin G-string. She lifted out a pink sparkly book and passed it to Callum. 'There's something for you to read. Her diary.'

He left Daisy to finish her search, took the diary out into the sitting room and sat in an armchair. Callum flicked through the pages. They contained a meticulous and detailed record of her relationship with Richard and their plans for the future. Some of her comments about their sex life would make Cookie blush.

It was clear that Richard had indulged in pillow talk. Rose knew about the cash payment and Mary-Ellen's intention to change her will in favour of Richard. She also knew that Richard lied about being her son.

> Richie's birthday is in April, but if she's dumb enough to believe that he's her son, that's her funeral.

What Rose did not understand was why Richard was prepared to wait until Mary-Ellen died of old age when they could hurry her along.

The last few pages detailed her plan to murder Mary-Ellen Mitchell. Richard kept a phone hidden in the stables, that he used to contact Mary-Ellen, and Rose had used it to ask Mary-Ellen to meet her at Turf Hill. That much Callum had surmised, although he had thought that Richard had sent the text. She had taken spare clothes with her, and after she had killed Mary-Ellen and left her body and Pirate on Hale Purlieu, she had run back to Richard's car and changed. She put her used clothes in a bin liner, drove back along Forest Road and put them on top of the refuse bins waiting to be emptied.

Daphne Smart had seen someone lacing their trainers in a black SUV and he himself had witnessed the refuse collector tossing a bag from the top of the bins back onto Reg's path. Could it be that simple? He hoped Legs was successful with her search.

Had Richard told her how to break a neck or had she searched the internet for information? Perhaps she already knew. Cookie could check the search history on her phone. Richard had told her things that he would have been wiser to keep to himself but, as Daisy had observed, he was thinking with the wrong part of his anatomy. At the bottom of the last page were two hearts with arrows piercing them. The first had "Richie and me" written along the arrow, and the second had "me and Rosie" written in a different hand.

Daisy came to stand beside him, leaned in to read the diary and he looked up.

'Bag her computer. We've already got her phone.' He disliked people crowding him to read over his shoulder.

'Okay. And I found this.' She handed him a photograph. It was of a fair-haired Rose standing next to a smaller version of herself. Side by side, arms around each other's waists, the younger girl was looking up into Rose's face and laughing. Callum turned it over.

Rhianwen and Olwenna.

Someone would be missing her.

* * *

Daisy pulled out onto Hale Lane and then glanced at the dashboard display when her phone rang.

'Sue Eastwood.' She made an anxious face at Callum before answering it on speaker.

'Sue, Jimmy okay?' Daisy's tone was upbeat, a smile in her voice.

'Great, thanks. He's persuaded them to let him come home if he promises to behave. I'm just leaving now. I've got things to sort out, like where we are sleeping tonight.'

'Got a tent you can borrow if it helps.'

Sue laughed. 'I might take you up on that. I suggested moving in with my dad for a bit while we clean the place up, but Jimmy won't hear of it. He won't leave the animals on their own.'

'Neither would I.'

'I just wanted to tell you that Sir Michael Mitchell came to see Jimmy after you had gone.' She hesitated. 'Isn't he old!'

Daisy laughed. 'What did he want?'

'He was nice though. I quite warmed to him, poor man. He wanted to know if Jimmy would like to keep Pirate. He doesn't ride and said Mary-Ellen would have wanted her horse to go to someone kind, who would look after him. It was really nice of him.'

'That sounds like a great idea. Jimmy said he was looking for a second horse. Ideal.'

'That's what Jimmy said. I think he was touched by the gesture. I rather liked Sir Michael,' she said. 'He's sort of…' She searched for a word. 'Stately. I like long hair on a man. Might get Jimmy to grow his while he's still got some.'

Daisy laughed with her, and Callum stopped himself from tucking back his long hair as they turned into the station car park.

The team were there before them and marched across the station car park like a laden colony of ants on the move. Callum was bringing up the rear when a car door swung open beside him.

'You're not one of these incomprehensible people who doesn't drink, are you, MacLean?'

He grinned and turned to face Martha who popped out of her car to stand beside him. The bodywork lifted a centimetre or two with a groan.

'Glad to see your back's better.'

'So am I, thanks. Thelma tells me you're not just a pretty face.'

Callum quelled his surprise and narrowed his eyes. 'Indeed.'

'Oh, very indeed. I hear you've made an arrest, amongst other things.'

'Sergeant Donaldson made the arrest. She has a bit of an injury that could do with the once-over, if you've a minute.'

Martha frowned. 'Tell Daisy I'll be up. You've not asked me how I know the ACC.'

'No need. I can see you're itching to tell me.'

277

'Smart-arse. Her horse is stabled at the same yard as mine.' A bubble of merriment rose in her throat at his wary expression and she threw back her head and laughed.

He was beginning to realise that horses were the glue holding this community together. Everything seemed to have some connection to horse flesh.

'You didn't answer my question, I notice.' She looked towards the building. 'I think you're needed. I'll nip along and take a look at Daisy.'

Thelma Greyson was standing in the stairwell window, her eyes focused on Callum. She beckoned him with her forefinger. Possible reasons for the summons sped through his mind as he climbed the stairs.

'I'm getting complaints about you, MacLean,' she said when he stood before her. 'The custody sergeant's got writer's cramp and earache from your suspect. Lost property is full of power tools, and Forensics is muttering about overtime. Do you create this much work wherever you go?'

'I try my best, ma'am.'

'I believe you do. Good work, MacLean.'

'Thank you, ma'am.' He was warmed by her commendation.

A tuneless whistling of *Mull of Kintyre* followed her along the corridor with the diminishing fragrance of violets.

* * *

Daisy was reading an incoming text just as Callum came through the door.

'Is Legs back yet?' he asked.

'That was her. She's on the way.'

Callum looked around the office at the rest of the team. Cookie was jigging in his chair and mouthing the words to a song as he studied his screen, stabbing at his keyboard as if it were a piano. Daisy was looking out of the window and flexing her neck from side to side. Bird crashed his fist down on his desk, making the loose pens bounce into the air. Everyone looked around in surprise. Cookie scooted his chair across the floor to bump knees with Bird.

'Problem, oh wise one?' He looked at Bird's screen. 'There's nothing there.'

Bird sat back in his chair and scrubbed both hands over his sparse hair before turning to Cookie.

'I know there's nothing there. It's eaten my bleedin' report. Fucking machine.'

'Okey dokey tiddley tokey.' Cookie spun Bird's chair out of the way, sending him freewheeling across the floor. His fingers flashed across the keyboard and the document reappeared.

Bird stood up and pushed his chair back to his desk as Cookie scooted out of the way.

'Where was it?' Bird rasped the back of his thumb across his chin.

'Where you put it.' Cookie grinned. 'In the trash. And you might want to run it through the spellcheck before anyone who speaks English sees it.' He laughed and ducked as a paper clip skimmed through the air and landed in his curls.

'I'm getting too old for paperwork,' Bird said to no one in particular and settled back in his chair.

They were in such high spirits that Callum didn't want to dampen their levity. He was sure they had enough evidence to charge Richard with arson and attempted murder, but most of the evidence against Rose was circumstantial. She could argue that her plan for the murder was hypothetical, and they had no forensics to back up their case. Her lack of an alibi would not secure a conviction. They needed something concrete and irrefutable.

'Ta-da.' Legs stood in the doorway with a spotty tin in her right hand and a black bin liner in her left. She dropped the bag to the floor next to her desk and placed the polka-dot tin on the table.

'I've just been to see Reg, as you asked, guv, and the lovely Mrs Reg gave me a cake, but I will generously share it with you all.'

With a whoop, Cookie was beside her. Legs got a knife out of her desk. Daisy found a kitchen roll to use as serviettes. They surveyed the treat – layers of yellow sponge laced with lines of jam; the whole topped with pink swirled icing dotted with rainbow speckles.

'That looks like a "pretty please" cake to me.' Daisy looked across to the knotted black bag as Legs sliced the sponge.

'Spot on, Deedee hun. The guv sent me to see if the bag was still there and Reg handed me the cake with one hand and the rubbish bag with the other. I couldn't take one without the other. God, this cake is good.'

Mumbles of agreement came from the others. Cookie was already wiping stray crumbs from his chin and eyeing the uneaten remainder.

Daisy lifted the black bag onto an empty table, and Callum motioned her to open it. Butterflies did circuits and bumps in his abdomen. She teased open the double knot and looked inside. Bird peered over her shoulder.

'Holy shit.' He looked across to Callum. 'You've got to see this, guv.'

Daisy pulled on gloves and removed the contents. When the bag was empty, they had a complete set of running clothes from trainers to baseball cap. They studied the items.

'The running gear looks exactly the same as that stuff in Richard's room. Different brand of trainers though from the ones we bagged at the manor, they're a smaller size,' Bird said, 'and there's peat in the treads. Do you reckon that can be matched to the print on the stirrup?'

'And look at that,' Daisy said. 'Horsehair on the lower leg of the trousers. Same colour as Pirate.'

Callum lifted a surgical glove from the table and examined it. A small piece was missing from the tip of one finger. If Rose's DNA was inside the gloves, and Mary-Ellen's on the outside, it was irrefutable proof of murder. Thank you, Locard, he thought as he replaced the evidence.

'Icing on the cake, guv. Good old Reg.' Legs looked round in surprise as Bird started opening, then slamming his desk drawers. 'What've you lost?'

'My hat. I said I'd eat it if Reg ever brought us anything useful.'

Bird's tombstones flashed at his audience, and there was a twinkle in his eye as laughter rippled around the room. Callum joined in and Daisy smiled at him, her head tilted. It was a long time since he'd felt so included; since he'd allowed himself to feel included.

'Get that bag along to Forensics for processing,' Callum said and watched Cookie sling it over his shoulder, scoot out of the office and disappear along the corridor.

Bellman appeared in the open doorway, hesitated, but didn't come in. Callum met his grey eyes for a second, before turning his head to watch Daisy sweep cake crumbs from her desk into the bin. The next time he looked, the doorway was empty.

'We're all meeting for supper, at The Woodfalls Inn,' Daisy said.

Cookie skidded back through the door. 'Count me in, Deedee.'

'Helen and me have got something for you, seeing as how you're short of a watchdog,' Bird said, his voice gruff.

'Aww. Thanks, Bird. What is it?' she asked.

'My bleedin' geese. They've got hearing like bats and are as territorial as badgers. Better warn the postie though.'

'Thanks, Bird.' She looked up at Callum. 'You will join us tonight, won't you, sir?'

'First round is on me,' he said.

Cookie whooped his appreciation.

'Let's wrap it up for today, people. Very well done. See you all later.' Callum was surprised to find himself looking forward to the pub meal.

He glanced down at an incoming text. It was from Bryony, asking if he would like to meet her in the morning for a coffee. For once, Daisy hadn't noticed because she and Legs were teasing Bird about what he would be wearing that evening.

Callum slipped his phone into his pocket. This was one piece of information that he had no intention of sharing with his team.

Character List

Jenny Walker – Best friend of Mary-Ellen

Mary-Ellen Mitchell – Businesswoman married to Sir Michael Mitchell

Sir Michael Mitchell – A portrait painter married to Mary-Ellen

Nicole Watson – Secretary to Mary-Ellen

Oliver Phillips – Looks after Daisy's animals

Paul Denton – Detective Inspector replaced by Callum

Penelope Devereux-Strauss – Wife of Edward Devereux-Strauss

Paul Jackson – Solicitor to the Mitchells

Rose Brown – Groom for Richard Devereux-Strauss

Richard Devereux-Strauss – Youngest son of Edward Devereux-Strauss, a horse dealer

Robert Goddard – Father of Mary-Ellen

Reg Holder – Local, helpful citizen

Susan Eastwood – Wife of Jimmy, mother of their four children

Timothy Pitman QC – Friend of Sir Michael Mitchell

Acknowledgements

I want to thank two groups of people who have provided critique and encouragement in equal measures. Firstly, Lisa, Sandra, Valerie, Penny and Jan, and secondly, Louise, Emma, Sam, Zab, Veronica, Tracy and Caroline. They are all writers, and I am privileged to have their support. Thanks also to beta reader Helen, to Hugh Bond for all things medical and Inspector Martin Nutbeam (retired) for police-related information. This would have been a very different book without their input, and I cannot overestimate the importance of all the above to the finished novel.

My gratitude goes to the team at The Book Folks who have been all-round amazing and a pleasure to work with, and especially Arianna for her extreme patience.

My special thanks go to my husband for his endless enthusiasm, unstinting support and his belief in me.

I hope you enjoyed this crime novel and that reading about the New Forest will encourage you to come and visit us. Explore the open heaths, grassy lawns, planted inclosures, herds of wild ponies and history that dates back to William the Conqueror.

If you enjoyed this book, please let others know by leaving a quick review on Amazon. Also, if you spot anything untoward in the paperback, get in touch. We strive for the best quality and appreciate reader feedback.

editor@thebookfolks.com

www.thebookfolks.com

Other titles of interest

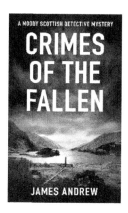

CRIMES OF THE FALLEN
by James Andrew

When DI John Belivat is called to the scene of a murdered woman, left naked on the seafront of a Scottish town, it brings back all his fears about the fate of his own missing daughter. He focuses on the victim, trying to establish her identity. But only after another body is found will the detective be able to piece together a motive and find a killer.

FREE with Kindle Unlimited and available in paperback!

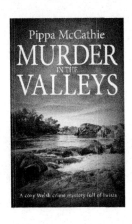

MURDER IN THE VALLEYS
by Pippa McCathie

Having left the police following a corruption investigation, ex-superintendent Fabia Havard is struggling with civilian life. When a girl is murdered in her town, she can't help trying to find the killer. Will her former colleague Matt Lambert stop her, or realize the value of his former boss to the floundering inquiry?

FREE with Kindle Unlimited and available in paperback!

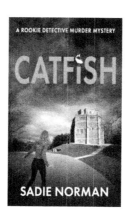

CATFISH
by Sadie Norman

It is not without some malice that rookie detective Anna McArthur is called "crazy" by her colleagues. She certainly tends to act first and think later. But when Anna discovers the body of a murdered woman who has "catfish" carved into her chest, she feels a personal duty to do everything she can to up her game and find the killer.

FREE with Kindle Unlimited and available in paperback!

Printed in Great Britain
by Amazon

55601971R00169